CRAWLSPACE

The young man with the strange, almost religious, look in his eyes had returned. Living in the crawlspace under the house, surrounded by a nest of dried bones and the half-eaten bodies of small animals, Richard Atlee had come to inject the venom of his hate and anger into the quiet retirement life of Alice and Albert Graves.

Why did he wish to terrorize the charming, childless couple?

Books by Herbert Lieberman

Brilliant Kids
City of the Dead
Crawlspace
The Eighth Square

Published by POCKET BOOKS

CRAWLSPACE

—

HERBERT LIEBERMAN

PUBLISHED BY POCKET BOOKS NEW YORK

POCKET BOOKS, a Simon & Schuster division of
GULF & WESTERN CORPORATION
1230 Avenue of the Americas, New York, N.Y. 10020

Copyright © 1971 by Herbert Lieberman

Published by arrangement with David McKay Company, Inc.
Library of Congress Catalog Card Number: 78-155255

ISBN: 0-671-43068-8

First Pocket Books printing June, 1972

20   19   18   17   16   15   14   13   12   11

POCKET and colophon are trademarks of Simon & Schuster.

Printed in the U.S.A.

FOR JUDY

And if a stranger sojourn with thee in your land, ye shall not vex him. But the stranger that dwelleth with you shall be unto you as one born among you, and thou shalt love him as thyself; for ye were strangers in the land of Egypt.

LEVITICUS 19:33

I watched her puttering for a while, waiting for her
to speak.

"What is it, Alice?" I said, finally. "What's bothering
you?"

CRAWLSPACE

Chapter One

I LIVE on a rural road in a northern suburb. My nearest neighbor lives in a farmhouse two miles south of me. My name is Graves. If I speak in haste, it's out of a desire to say what has to be said as quickly as possible, then having said it never to mention it again. For to restate things is to relive them and to relive them is to suffer anew. All I hope for now is to purge old demons and in doing so to reach a tiny island of quiet within myself where I can spend whatever time remains me untroubled by memories and inaccessible to prying people. In nearly sixty years of living, what a pitiable thing it is to say that all I've learned is that we are all mostly men of good will and no resolve. But forgive me if I've sounded cryptic; I've seen what I've seen and I know what I know. Give me fifteen minutes of your time and I shall make you loathe me.

I came here two years ago at the suggestion of my doctor, a certain cardiologist by the name of Palermo with a vast number of letters beside his name. I'd suffered my second heart attack and so the firm for which I'd worked some twenty-odd years decided in their infinite charity to award me a small but adequate pension and send me away. Dr. Palermo's sole prescription to me was to live quietly for the rest of my days. Presumably, I'd reached a state, in his august opinion, where instructions as to medication and daily diet seemed scarcely germane.

Being by instinct and temperament an urbane creature, I made the transition to rural life with surprisingly little difficulty. My life here up until the time of which I now speak has been pleasant. I rented a house—the old Quigley place—out on the Bog Road. It's a good house, as houses go. What real estate ladies like to call "Your typical Georgian Colonial"—white stone, black shutters and trim. Nothing remarkable.

1

The house dates back to 1782; it sits on a tidy parcel of land surrounded by crumbling stone walls which used to define the metes and bounds of the first homesteads in this part of the country. The pastures and meadows of the old farms of centuries ago are now forest—full of deer, fox, and partridge. When you read the deeds to these old places—full of names like Mosher, Bullock, Starbuck, and Macy—all vanished folk, you get an eerie feeling. I'm even told our house has a ghost. If so, a not particularly amiable one. I've not seen hide nor hair of him since we arrived here.

There's grass all around the house, and a good many trees. All along the border of the front lawn is a line of ancient oaks with their rough, deeply lined trunks like the worn, wrinkled faces of benign old men. To one side of the front door stands a holly, to the other a dogwood. The lawn winds round the house and sweeps out the back —a rolling, rock-spattered thing—and in its irregularity, very pleasing to the eye.

Additional trees are scattered here and there about the place—a huge tulip tree, several copper beeches, a shag-bark hickory, an ash and maple joined at the hip and seeming to spring from the same root, a scattering of apple trees, an enfeebled birch, some evergreens and a dying catalpa.

The lawn reaches back a hundred yards or so to where the forest begins. To the right of the house is a clover meadow. Behind the house is a copse. Here sleek, black crows rise heavily out of the branches and go squawking off through the trees. At night, with the window open, you can hear the wind singing like a lyre through those trees.

Beyond the copse is a bog. The only way to reach it is directly through the copse. I've been back there several times. It's a forlorn and dismal place. All the trees are dead. The ground is always wet. It's an area of heavy drainage, and over the years the earth has become a black, tarlike ooze that sucks and gurgles at your feet. I've always entertained the private and amusing notion that beneath the bog lies a graveyard full of the bones of prehistoric monsters who trod the earth millions of years ago. But the only signs of life back there today are the sleepy dragonflies dreaming on the stalks of cattails and the bullfrogs intoning all night long.

My wife Alice's single passion is her garden. It's a genuine pleasure to see her in those seasons when the garden is in full cry, bent to the soil, a great, floppy sunbonnet on her head, inching her way through a blaze of blooms—the Dutch irises, the sweet peas, the dwarf carnations, the violas, the Gloriosa daisies, the Madcap hollyhocks, the blood-red deCaen poppies, and the dazzling array of hybrid dahlias.

When Alice handles a bulb or a corm, it's the way some women handle an infant—with infinite tenderness and a kind of pity. As if she saw in their vulnerability and the brevity of their lives a mission for herself.

She has, too, a vegetable garden that yields for us each summer a bounty of Prize Head lettuce and Red Cherry tomatoes. In late summer the tomatoes look like clusters of rubies on the bush. After the rain the heady breath of basil, dill, sage, sweet marjoram, and thyme comes wafting up on the evening breeze, enters our windows and screen doors, and fills our house.

Our life here is simple. It all has a kind of deadly regularity. And yet, it's not unpleasant. The last thing a man in my condition needs is surprises. We have no children. Our wants are few. Each Sunday we go unfailingly to church. In the day we walk in the forest outside the door and pick blackberries and apples. We enjoy identifying wild birds from our Peterson and wild flowers that we stumble on in the woods. It's oddly pathetic to think what a triumph one feels in spotting a bit of henbane or pauper's grass, or in being able to identify a titmouse or some such foolish thing.

Our only visitors to the house are the possums and skunks who come at night to bump around the trashcans and in the day the innumerable wild birds who flock to our feeders. During the cold weather we spread seeds and crumbs and hang suet balls. We have a special affection for the sparrows, the slate juncos, and the blackcap chickadees who live out in the icy blasts all winter. We have no feelings at all for the birds who fly south.

At night we take comfort in our fire, the logs sizzling and crackling on the grate, and enjoy the sense of security one feels around a bright warm spot while in the middle of an encroaching darkness.

One day several weeks ago the oil man came to us. He was an amiable young man. He wore a suit with a shirt and tie and drove an automobile with the name of the fuel company painted on it in a bright red shield in the shape of a heart. It was his job to come and read the fuel gauge, to instruct us in the proper use of the furnace, and to keep us as clients, cozy and content. His name, he said, was Richard Atlee.

We rarely ever had visitors out there, and so I fear we made a bit of a fuss over him. When you're alone as long as we'd been and normally used to a rather busy social life, even the appearance of an oil man can touch off a flurry of excitement.

It was unusually warm that day and as he puttered over the pipes and gauges down below in the basement, I offered him something cold to drink.

"Would you like a glass of lemonade?" I called down the steps. "It's freshly made."

He came smiling to the foot of the stair, a gash of grease struck down the center of his forehead. "That'd be nice." His voice was very soft.

He tinkered long in the basement, and when he finished and reappeared upstairs, it was late dusk and near the supper hour. My wife had set the table. When the oil man came up from the basement he appeared tired. He gazed wistfully at the plates and silver, the small napkins in their rings. To my surprise, my wife asked him if he would join us. "It's a long time since I've cooked for anyone," she said.

He smiled a shy, twisted little smile and glanced back and forth, as if he were taking the measure of each of us, one by one. It was a "Now let's see about you two" sort of glance.

"Would it be all right?" he asked in his soft, shy voice. It had a poignant quality about it.

Alice had made a small roast, surely enough for two or three—even four in a pinch. Whenever she offered the oil man an additional serving he accepted it, each time holding his plate up to her and staring straight ahead. He accepted up until the point where she and I through swift glances and a tacit understanding took no extra portion for ourselves so that we might be spared the embarrassment of not having enough meat to feed the oil man.

As he ate I had an opportunity to study his face. It had an almost primitive look about it—the hair clipped short, the forehead broad, the nose somewhat flat, the lips quite full, and the eyes penetrating and very blue. I suppose you might say it was a brutal face, and yet it had an oddly beautiful quality—rather religious, in some indefinable way—like an Eastern Saint.

When he finished his supper he lingered long at the table, talking little and listening to my wife and me chat aimlessly. He appeared to be studying us intently. Several times we attempted to engage him in conversation, but with very little success. I poured him three or four glasses of wine and hoped that he would go.

When indeed he actually made ready to go, I led him out through the library. He stopped there and looked at the books, his eyes roaming up and down the length of the shelves. There was an expression of wonder in his face.

"You read 'em all, Mistuh?"

"Most of them," I said.

"When?"

"At one time or another."

"How long it take to read 'em all?"

I laughed. His wonder flattered me. "Quite some time."

"You know all the stuff in 'em?"

"Hardly," I said, laughing, and in a curious way I found myself wanting to boast.

I watched his hand reach tentatively for the shelves and creep upwards to one of the volumes, his bony, nervous index finger lingering caressingly over its spine. His voice dropped to a whisper. "What's this one?" It was as if he'd entered a holy place.

"That's an early edition of the poems of a man by the name of Blake." I took it down and handed it to him so that he might examine it.

"What's it about?" he asked.

"About a lot of things. Love, Fear, Death. God."

There was a keen excitement in his face. "Kin I take it?"

In his shy, oblique way, he was amazingly direct.

The book he'd asked for was a very old edition and quite rare. It had been given to me by my father on the occasion of my graduation from college. Naturally, I didn't want to let it out of the house. Moreover, I've always considered it an impertinence for a person to ask to borrow anything as intimate as a book.

Still I didn't say no. It wasn't that he'd flattered me. He had, but I'm not a foolish man. Nor am I a timid man. I wasn't afraid to say no. Nevertheless, to my surprise, I heard my voice, as if at a very great distance, say, "You promise to bring it back?"

Alice's astonished glance flashed at me from across the room.

He nodded, holding the book between two fingers of large, rough hands, as if he feared to contaminate it by his touch. "Sure." We all laughed a little nervously. Then he was gone.

Later that night as we undressed for bed, Alice said, "Why did you give it to him?"

"I don't know. I'm sure he'll never bring it back." I started to laugh rather foolishly.

We didn't see the oil man for several weeks. When he came again we didn't even hear him drive up. I'm not entirely sure he did drive. It's possible that the second time he came on foot, although when you think of the distance he'd have to cover to get out there from town, it seems a bit improbable. Still, as I recall now, we saw no car.

We were outdoors separating the irises and covering

them, for we'd had a frost the night before. It was my wife who saw him first. She looked up and there he was standing at the bottom of the garden. No sound preceded him.

I didn't see him at all. At least, not at first. What I saw instead was Alice's movements come abruptly to a halt. I didn't actually see that, either; I felt it, or sensed it. When I looked up she was leaning motionless against her rake—staring at something across the garden. Still I didn't see him. Instead I followed the line of her gaze a hundred yards or so, the way you find a kite by following the string—until I saw, at last, a small yet distinct shape standing just beside the dying catalpa at the bottom of the garden.

My legs wobbled, and even before my mind grasped the identity of that shape, I could feel the thump of my heart accelerate in my chest. The next moment I was smiling and waving to Richard Atlee, signaling him to join us.

Coming toward us shyly like a wary animal, he said he'd come again to look at the gauges. There was something he wanted to check, he said, and there was that wry, secretive smile on his face as if something only he had just seen had amused him. It never occurred to me to ask why he had come from such an unexpected direction—that of the bog.

Once again he descended into the basement and remained there for the rest of the afternoon. It seemed odd, his remaining down there so long. Several times during the afternoon we heard the faint, light tinkle of his wrench and hammers striking against the pipes. I played with the idea of going down there. Surprising him at his work. Not for a moment did I believe that he was doing anything. He was just playing at doing something, and stalling for time. But still I didn't go down.

When he finally emerged from the basement, it was once again the supper hour. This time we were not anxious to invite him. But he sat in the parlor and then lingered so long in the library that it became awkward. My wife and I exchanged glances.

He stared fixedly at the table as if he were admiring the plates and glasses, the neat, tasteful symmetry of crockery, silver, and white linen. It was an oddly childish sort of thing—so naked and undisguised. In the next moment, to my amazement Alice once again invited him to stay.

"By all means," I said. He had looked to me to see if it was all right. "It would please us." My voice was wavery and a bit too high.

He went directly to the table and sat down. It was as if he knew he was to be invited; as if the thing had been decreed elsewhere, independent of us, and all he awaited was some small signal or gesture that was guaranteed to come.

I stood there stunned while he sat quietly at the table, hands folded in lap, eyes lowered, waiting for us to join him.

As soon as a plate was set before him, he fell ravenously on the food. All the while he ate, we watched him with the food untouched on our own plates, and I kept thinking about my Blake and mourning its irretrievable loss.

There was no conversation, and Alice—to fill in the gaps—kept thrusting bowls and plates of food at me, a look of desperation on her face and I suppose one of perplexity on mine. At the end of the meal I was still mourning my Blake, and not a little edgy. Finally I spoke, "How've you been getting on with the book?"

"What book?"

"The one you borrowed several weeks back."

He looked at me as if I'd spoken in a foreign tongue. Then his face brightened. "Oh, that."

"Yes. The Blake. Have you finished it yet?" I looked at him with a vague hope that he might ask me questions.

"Haven't started it." He spoke with a full mouth and as he did so his fork reached across the table and speared another chunk of lamb. I felt anger rising in me. "Well, if you're not going to read it, I'd appreciate it back."

"Sure." He smiled, not looking at me. He was busy replenishing his plate.

When he left again, it was well on to midnight. He took several additional books with him.

For a while my wife and I didn't speak. We were too confused and flustered. Instead we busied ourselves with the task of carrying soiled dishes from the table to the sink. The place where the oil man had sat was in a ruin. It was as if a large animal had pastured there. A good deal of food that had been on his plate was now on the table as well as under it. From an overturned wine goblet leaked a languid trickle of burgundy, creeping its way across the table and blooming suddenly into a large purple blossom.

I looked at Alice peering dreamily into a sinkful of dishes. "Why did you invite him again?" I asked.

She turned the taps on and watched the water rise in the basin and the soap bubbling into suds. "I don't know. He seemed so alone. So hungry."

"He works. I'm sure he doesn't go hungry."

"He seems half starved." She tied the ribbons of her apron behind her. "I'm sure he's all alone and doesn't look after himself. Did you see his clothes?"

"Yes," I said, recalling it was the same suit of clothes he wore when he first came to the house.

"Filthy." Her voice was a mixture of indignation and pity.

"But he tries to keep them presentable—doesn't he?" I said.

I went back out to the dining room and gathered up the corners of the table cloth with its crumbs and morsels and soiled napkins.

"I don't believe he's a day over eighteen," Alice said the moment I got back to the kitchen. "Nineteen at the most. Seems helpless."

"What?" I said, startled out of some dreamy preoccupation.

"I said he seems helpless."

"Oh— Yes."

"Must be awful—being alone like that."

"Yes—I s'pose."

"Why did you give him more books? He hasn't returned the other."

"Yes. I know."

"Well—why did you give them to him?"

"I don't know," I said, staring down at the suds. And that was the truth.

We washed the dishes and set them in the drainer to dry overnight. When we finished we turned out all the lights and went up to bed. Somewhere on the stairway she turned to me and said, "He frightens me."

"We won't have him here again," I said.

We didn't see Richard Atlee for several weeks. Then one chilly morning we discovered we had no heat in our radiators and no hot water in our taps. I went down into the basement to look at the fuel gauge. In the past I'd spent very little time in the basement. I'd go down there for a tool or a piece of gardening equipment. That was the extent of it.

The oil gauge was at the rear of the basement in a somewhat inaccessible area. I had to thread my way through a clutter of cartons and boxes. When at last I reached the gauge and read it, I discovered that our tank was empty.

I turned to go up and just as I did, I passed a cupboard in which my wife keeps Mason jars of relish and preserves. The door of it had been left slightly ajar. When I reached to close it, my eye caught something gleaming on the shelf within. I opened the door and there on the shelf I found several objects I immediately recognized—a small milk-glass angel, a scrimshaw raven, and a jade paperweight I'd purchased in Singapore. The angel and raven came from the curio cabinet in our parlor; the paperweight sat on my desk in the library. There was in addition a piece I didn't recognize. It was in a small black jewel case. When I opened it I found a Prussian Iron Cross; it lay on a cushion of purple felt—the sort of thing you find in cheap novelty shops. On the shelf below and to the right I found my Blake along with the other books Richard Atlee had borrowed.

There's a door in our cellar that leads out to the garden in the back. It's a small door with an uncommonly shallow lintel. Even a man of slightly below-average stature would have to stoop in order to pass through it.

The cellar itself is what is called a three-quarter cellar, which means that three-fourths of the cellar is a solid, full stone foundation; the remaining quarter of the cellar is a crawlspace, some three or four feet in height, which runs out beneath the kitchen. It's not part of the original foundation, but an extension added on at a later date. It's a dank, gloomy space smelling of mold and rodents. The Quigleys, who had the house before us, kept cats in the crawl, presumably to keep down the rodents. As a result, in wet weather the stench of rutting cats hovers oppressively over the place.

The entrance to the crawlspace is directly opposite the small garden door with a distance of some twenty-five or thirty feet between them. It's no more than a black, shadowy square carved into the white limestone foundation about halfway up the wall.

I can't say what made me cross the short distance to the crawl but I did, in three or four wobbly strides, and then stood directly before the square peering into the dark shade.

At first I could see nothing. I stood there squinting into the darkness trying to adjust my eyes. In the next moment I stood on tiptoes and poked my head through the square. It was something like the clammy sensation you get when you press your face against a cold pane of glass.

I looked around, but still I could see nothing. We kept a flashlight in the basement for emergency use; I found it quickly and went back to the crawl and flicked it on.

Motes of dust swam up and down in the beam of light. Beyond that hung rusty pipes festooned in cobwebs. Sprawled on the ground was an ancient and decrepit extension ladder. In addition, there were some planks of lumber and a random carton here and there. Nothing remarkable.

I was about to turn away when my eye caught a squat, hump-like shape pushed off into a far corner. It turned out to be a mound of dry straw heaped on the ground about twenty-five feet from the entrance, set just below an overhead tangle of pipes and joists.

What struck me so curious about it or why it even caught my attention at all I can't say. Perhaps it was simply the incongruity of seeing it there. Such an unlikely place for a mound of straw; also, I'd been in that crawl several times before. You had to go in there to turn on the water to the outside taps in the garden, and I was certain I'd never seen such a mound of straw there before.

Suddenly I had the distinct impression that I ought to leave. Turn my back on the place. Get out as fast as I could. It's curious the way you sense things like that. As if some awful disclosure is about to be made to you, and the mind reasons that if you can just avoid having that disclosure made, then the dangers implicit in it will never come to pass. Like avoiding the doctor when you have alarming symptoms.

But I didn't leave. Some grisly fascination drew me on. In the next moment I'd dragged a small stool over to the crawl and begun to climb in.

The ground over which I walked was cold and hard. It seemed to be made of a coarse sand that had been congealed by dampness and frigid weather. I had to stoop as I groped my way toward the humped shadowy shape. I recall being a little breathless. In the next instant I felt the tip of my shoe brush against straw and I turned my light full on it.

What I saw at my feet was assuredly a straw pallet, the kind of thing you imagine beggars might sleep on. It was not the pallet, however, that troubled me; it was what I saw around it—the bones. Almost a charnel house of them strewn about here and there; clumps of animal fur and feathers; bits of paw and that sort of thing. It looked like the lair of a weasel with the carcasses of all its hapless victims strewn about.

I moved deeper into the crawl, stooping as I went, one

trembling hand holding the light, the other clapped over my mouth—coughing into my fist from the dust and dampness.

Before I'd gone another half-dozen paces my foot kicked something else, which went rattling loudly over the hard earth. I swung my light over the ground in the direction of the noise. There at my feet, half in and half out of an old coffee tin, were toilet articles. Some of them had scattered across the ground when I kicked the can. There was a razor, a beaver brush, and a pair of fine old isinglass cufflinks which I recognized as my own.

I must have remained there only a few moments more. Then I quickly gathered up all those strewn articles, replaced them in the coffee tin, and put the whole thing back beside the pallet.

For some inexplicable reason I left the books and all the stolen items exactly where I'd found them and in the next instant I was clattering up the stairs, a twinge of pain at my chest, thinking about getting the police, dialing the number in my head and muttering the story aloud and a little breathlessly to myself. I was planning how I'd present the thing to the sheriff over the phone in a plausible way.

I got upstairs, happy to discover Alice out; down in the garden somewhere, out of earshot. My hands trembled at the directory pages while I made a sickish effort to fight down the panic. For a moment I caught a glimpse of a greenish reflection of myself in the mirror about the phone. POLICE wasn't listed under P as I'd thought. Then what was it listed under? S for Sheriff? C for Courthouse? Finally I recalled that the police are generally listed under government departments, and so I went on tearing through the tissuey pages until somehow or other I found it.

I started to dial and had even gone through the first three digits when suddenly and quite unaccountably I put the receiver down. The wave of panic subsided, and in the next instant I sighed and sank wearily back into a chair by the phone. "Why the police?" I suddenly thought. What was he that I had to have the police for? A boy of eighteen or twenty. A poor creature who simply wanted to come in out of the cold. And pleasant enough at that, too.

But all the same, I didn't know the first thing about him. And living out that far you hear some pretty hair-raising tales about vagrants and itinerants and the like. Oh, apocryphal or exaggerated, most of them. I'm sure—— But all the same——

Still, though, this was not the same sort of thing. I knew the boy. Had talked with him. Even sat down with him twice to dinner. He didn't seem the type to— Still, it was obvious he couldn't be permitted to remain down there in the crawl. But the police seemed a drastic step. And even if they came, all they'd do would be to put him out. That struck me as an even greater danger. What if he were a spiteful or vindictive sort and I'd had him driven out of the county by the police? What then could prevent him from coming back here some dark night looking for revenge.

So I didn't call the police. Instead I called the fuel company. It was a small rural business, and I spoke to the owner himself.

"Is Richard Atlee there?"

"Who?"

"Richard Atlee. Your representative."

"Oh, him. He quit."

"Quit?"

"Up and left about two weeks ago."

"Two weeks," I muttered. There was a pause in which I could hear myself breathing into the receiver.

"Who is this?" said the voice on the other end of the phone.

"Mr. Graves. Albert Graves."

"Oh. Out on the Bog Road?"

"That's right. The Quigley place."

"I know you. We seen you at church. Been meanin' to introduce ourselves. Atlee your man out there?"

"That's right. He was supposed to look after our fuel. Now I discover our tank's empty."

"That's too bad," said the voice on the other end. "I'll try and get someone up there this afternoon. Can't promise a thing, though. All the trucks are out."

"I see."

"Sometimes one comes in early, though. And if it does—"

"Please do. It was below freezing last night, and I'm not very well."

"What?"

"Never mind," I said. I didn't want to go into all that.

"Atlee," said the voice again, and it made a clucking sound. "Queer duck he was. Just lit out without a word of notice. Left us all up in the air. Didn't even bother collecting his pay."

"You know who he is?"

"What?"

"Do you know anything about him?" I said.

"Nope. Drifter. Kept to himself. Pleasant enough, though. Amiable. Seen plenty of that type. Blow into town from nowhere. Work for a while. Get a little coin stashed, then—light out. Common enough."

"I see," I said, my voice huskier than usual.

"Yop. Just up and lit out. Not a word of notice or parting. You'd think the law was on his tail. Queer duck."

He was silent, waiting for me to respond. When I didn't, he simply rattled on. "I'll try and get a man up there to you this afternoon. Can't promise a thing. Got a fireplace?"

"Yes."

"Burn it. Burn logs. If I don't get up there today, I'll get up before the week's out, anyway."

"I see," I said, suddenly feeling terribly alone.

"Sorry about any inconvenience. Happens, though. Oh —by the way. My name's Beamish."

Just as I hung up, Alice came in, her cheeks glowing from the pinch of late October air. In her arms were bundles of marigolds and dahlias. She bustled cheerfully across the kitchen to the sink. "Thought I'd better get these in before the frost gets them completely. Aren't the dahlias grand?"

I looked at them blankly.

She filled a vase with water and started to arrange a bouquet. "That you on the phone just now?"

"Yes," I said distantly, all the while thinking of the grim place just beneath our feet. I'd decided not to say a word to her until I knew what I wanted to do. And at that moment I hadn't the slightest notion of what I wanted to do.

"Who were you talking to?"

"The fuel people."

"They sending someone out to fix the furnace?"

"The furnace is fine."

She turned from the sink, the water still running behind her.

"The tank's empty. That's all."

"Oh—Did you tell what's his name?"

"Atlee."

"Yes. Atlee. Did you tell him?"

"He's gone."

"Gone?"

"Gone. Quit his job about two weeks ago. Just disappeared into thin air."

Her mouth fell open, her arms crossed, and her chin came to rest in the palm of her hand. "Just like that?"

"Just like that."

"Where do you s'pose he's gone?"

"I don't know," I said vacantly, looking at the floor and feeling my bowels turn within me.

"Well, I hope they're going to get some oil up here. We can't live like this. The place was cold as a tomb last night."

"They say they'll try and be out this afternoon."

She set a copper kettle on the stove. "I'm disappointed in that boy. Letting us down like that. And we treated him so well. Like some tea, dear?"

"Where do you keep the key to the cellar door?" I asked. She turned around and looked at me oddly.

"You know very well. Right up above the stove. Where

it always—" Her hand reached up to a small shelf above the stove and groped about. "Now isn't that funny?"

"It's gone," I said. "Isn't it?"

The fuel company didn't come that afternoon. That night a thick fog and biting frost settled in around us. Gray, swirling mist licked at the window panes, and we built the fire high and sat at the supper table in thick wool sweaters.

When bedtime came we banked the fire, put out the lights, and went upstairs. I lay there for a time in the dark listening to the slow regular breathing of my wife beside me. Outside, the high, keening sound of the wind moaned over the bogs like the sound of someone mourning on a distant hill. I kept thinking of the grim place below the kitchen, wondering if he was down there now, imagining him as he looked crouching in the darkness, surrounded by his pitiful little mementos and the animal bones.

Suddenly I heard something—a faint, light tinkle, like that of a metal wrench being struck against a pipe. In the next moment I could hear the distinct sound of metallic tapping ringing up from below through the radiators. The sound was unmistakable. Richard Atlee was in the house.

Chapter Two

I SAID nothing to Alice about the noises I heard coming from the cellar that night or, indeed, what they meant. The fuel truck came the following afternoon driven by a big, jovial red-faced man. His size was reassuring, and I snatched at the opportunity of following him down to the basement. I had no idea what I'd find there.

He puttered, tinkered, and fiddled with pipes, whistling all the while he went about his work.

"When's the last time you had this smoke pipe cleaned?" he said, hustling round the furnace adjusting nozzles and gauges. "You gotta keep the flue open," he went right on, not waiting for my answer. "Clean. Know what I mean?"

He brushed past me, the beam of his light swiveling round the cellar, poking into corners. All the while he chattered, my eyes ransacked the place for signs of Richard Atlee. I checked the cupboard and found the books and other mementos exactly where I'd left them.

I wanted to get back into the crawlspace while I had the security of the driver down there with me. I was certain Richard wasn't there now, but there was always a possibility that I might be wrong. From observing the pattern of his routine I guessed that it was his habit to desert the cellar for the entire day, emerging from his lair in the cool gray hours of the dawn, then returning late at night after we'd gone to sleep, all the while letting himself in and out through the small garden door, thus avoiding any chance of running head-on into us.

What he did in the daytime I couldn't imagine. But I reasoned that he spent these hours in the bog or back deep in the forest hunting birds and small animals, then returned each night to eat his kill.

"I don't seem to be getting any heat up through the kitchen radiator," I said to the driver. That wasn't true. I lied in order to get him to go into the crawl.

"Where's your kitchen?" he snapped. Before I could answer, his eyes swiveled round the cellar and came to rest at the crawl. "Out that way?"

"Yes. Right above the crawl."

He was there in a moment, peering through the square, throwing his light around. "Helluva place to get into." He wiped his forehead with the sleeve of his shirt. "Wanna hold that a minute?"

He handed me the flashlight and I held it while he scrambled up into the square. Then he reached back and took the light. I followed him.

Once in there, he moved swiftly, ducking here and there under the maze of joists and sweating pipes.

"Smell sewerage?'" he asked. The beam of his light swept right past the mound of straw and he moved on without having noticed it. "Your sewer lines go out this way?"

"No. Out there. Over the other side."

While he busied himself examining pipes, I peered back in the direction of the straw pallet. The squat ugly hump of it stood out clearly in the shadows, and when I drew closer I could see the signs of bones and animal debris. But there was no sign of Richard.

"Can't see no reason why you're not gettin' heat up there," said the driver. "Might be the radiator valves." He was tapping pipes and coughing a great deal. "When's the last time you flushed 'em?"

By the time we climbed out of the crawl, his face was quite red. "I'll send someone up here to clean that flue. Cost a few bucks, but you'll make it right back in efficiency. Lower your oil consumption. Know what I mean?"

I told him I did and nodded dumbly. All the while he spoke, my eyes were riveted on the small gray square leading into the crawl.

Later when I walked out to the truck with him I was in a state of agitation.

"You got about three weeks of oil in the tank now," the driver said. He tore a bill off his pad and handed it to me. "I'll get someone up here about that flue. Make all the difference in the world."

He climbed into his truck while the name Richard Atlee stuck in my throat and refused to come out.

The truck lurched down the gravel driveway, then gasped as it shifted gears at the bottom of the hill, turned left, and started up the steep hill that runs alongside the orchard in front of our house. I clung to the fleeting sight of it until it vanished over the hill. As it did so, a great hush fell over the earth.

Once more we were alone.

That afternoon we walked in the forest and picked apples and wild raspberries. When we got back we went into the garden and picked several ripe pumpkins. That night we baked pies. When, at last, we turned out the lights and went up to bed, the house was warm from the oven and full of the smell of molasses and cinnamon.

Sometime early in the morning, perhaps 2 A.M., Alice woke me.

"What is it?" I asked, foggy with sleep.

"The pipes are banging."

"It's nothing. Just the radiators. Go back to sleep."

"It doesn't sound like the radiators."

I sat up in bed shaking my head while the banging grew louder.

"That's no radiator, Albert. Go down and check."

I had no intention of going down to the cellar. But I couldn't stay there cowering under the covers and let on to what I knew. In the next moment, I climbed out of bed and put on a robe.

Outside at the landing, I flicked on the stairway light and started down to the kitchen. I paused at almost every step and listened with frozen horror to the banging. It took me several minutes to get down the entire flight.

Once down in the kitchen, I was standing directly over the crawl gazing transfixed at my feet while the pipes in the radiator gonged up from below. Several times Alice called down from above.

"Albert?"

"Yes."

"Are you all right?"

"I'm fine."

"Is there anything there?"

"Nothing I can see."

Then she was silent, but the banging in the pipes grew louder and more insistent. After a while I could feel each stroke in my stomach. At one point when it reached a peak of unruliness I panicked. Lying near at hand was a large kitchen knife. I grabbed it and started banging frantically back on the pipes.

Instantly the noise ceased and silence roared in upon me. All I could hear was the thudding of my heart. The next moment there was a scraping, shuffling movement just below my feet, the kind of noise you associate with small animals rummaging in a confined area. Then I heard nothing.

"Albert."

"Yes."

"What is it?"

"Nothing. Go back to bed. I'm on my way up."

Before I went up I locked the door leading from the library to the cellar. When I got back to the room, she was sitting up in bed, her eyes wide and staring. "What in God's name was it?"

"Only the pipes. I made an adjustment."

She must have seen something in my face, because she looked at me oddly. "Go back to bed, Alice."

"Albert?"

"Go back to bed." This time my voice was harsh. It wasn't a voice she was accustomed to hearing. She stared at me for a moment, then without another word, slipped obediently under the covers and turned her back on me.

I sat on the edge of the bed gazing at the frost-fogged windows and listened to a naked branch scratching at the eaves. When my hands stopped trembling, I reached back and touched her head ever so gently. "I'm sorry, Alice. I'll tell you all about it in the morning."

It rained the rest of the night and on into the next day. A cold, steady drizzle mixed with sleet rattled down on the rooftops.

Alice was standing at the breakfast counter in a wrap-around shawl, beating eggs. For the most part she was silent, waiting for me to speak. I, for my part, was attempting to arrange in my mind the exact words with which to describe the sequence of events that led up to what had occurred the night before.

The copper kettle on the stove began to hiss. Just as Alice was reaching for a canister of tea, her gaze fell on the shelf above her.

"What on earth—"

When I looked up at her, a spoon of blueberries slipped from my hand and clattered loudly on the table.

She watched berries rolling off the table onto the floor in a dozen directions. "For God's sake, Albert. If you wanted a slice of pie, you could've simply—"

By that time I was across the room, past where she stood, and gaping at the pies. They gave the appearance of having been pawed by an animal. Fully three-quarters of all three of them had been devoured. What remained had been smashed and ground into the Pyrex plates with such force that the fruity innards had splashed over onto the shelf.

"Dear God, Albert—what is it?"

Standing there, gaping at smashed pies, I imagine the expression on my face must have been horrible. Not only did Richard Atlee have the key to the garden door, he also had the key to the library-cellar door.

Alice looked at me oddly and our eyes met. "You didn't do it, did you?"

By that time she knew something was quite wrong.

Isn't it curious how long you can live with a person, feeling certain you can predict his or her behavior in any given circumstance, then discover that you've been *wrong*. But not merely wrong; wildly and incalculably wrong.

Thus it was with Alice (with whom I've lived for nearly a quarter of a century) when on that morning I sat her down and attempted to explain our situation. That explanation, I realize now, must have sounded strange to her: I did it slowly and laboriously, my voice a curious mixture of measured calm and barely repressed hysteria. I was like a man carrying a hot soup bowl, seeking desperately a place to set it down.

All the while I spoke, a high, nervous laugh kept erupting from somewhere deep within me. It was a strange laugh—one I'd never heard before. It was like hearing a stranger laughing somewhere near you in the dark. I can't say I cared very much for the sound of it.

It was all acutely embarrassing to me. And it must have been tedious for her, because as incoherent as I'd been, she'd grasped the whole thing in an instant.

I suppose what I was waiting for was an immediate upheaval, a sudden outpouring of fear and outrage, wringing of the hands, and demands for immediate police intervention. What I got instead was a kind of hushed pity. Even now I recall her sitting there looking at me as I spoke, seeming unnaturally small and doll-like, her hands folded in her lap, her head shaking slowly from side to side, her soft, gray eyes wide and unblinking, oddly magnified in her glasses.

I kept talking and waiting for the explosion so that I could pacify her the way I'd planned. But nothing like that happened, and it left me up in the air with no place to go. You see, I was prepared for hysteria, not queenly serenity. When I'd finally got the whole thing out—after I'd said it all—she was still sitting there quietly with her hands folded in her lap and shaking her head.

"Well," I said, almost furious, "aren't you going to say anything?"

"Perhaps he could stay with us a while." She said it just like that, dreamily and looking through and past me as if I weren't there.

I was certain I'd heard her wrong.

"Just till he gets on his feet," she added.

"You're not serious?"

"Yes, I am."

I looked at her, thunderstruck, tying to catch the glimmer of a smile or a snicker across her face.

"You mean you'd really invite him to stay?"

"Yes."

"Just like that?"

"Yes."

"Knowing what you do about him?"

"What do I know about him? Really very little. He seems like a nice enough boy."

I was flabbergasted. "You know that he's come into your house and stolen things."

"Oh come, Albert. He hasn't stolen a thing. He's merely moved a few pieces from one part of the house to another."

By that time I had the distinct impression I was being ridiculed. "I really think you must be mad."

"Why?"

"Why?" I snapped. "It's not everyone who'd take a perfect stranger in off the streets."

"Oh, Albert—"

"That's not a very clever thing to do."

"Well, you asked me, and I made a suggestion. So he's living in your cellar. What do you intend to do about it?"

She'd put it directly, and I had to answer in like fashion.

"Well, of course, he has to go."

"Then you're going to ask him to go?"

"Well—not directly."

The trace of a smile flickered across her mouth.

"Well—" I said, "what if he were to refuse and get nasty?"

"Oh, Albert—"

"Well, what do I know about this boy—his motives—"

"If you're so worried about his motives, call the police."

"I've thought about that, but before I get involved with them and start pressing charges—"

"You're frightened of him."

"I'm not frightened of him at all." I felt a rush of heat to the back of my neck. "And what if I were? Would that be so terrible? It wouldn't. It would be wise and prudent. Didn't you say he frightens you?"

"He did at first, but not any more."

"That's a hasty change of heart." I looked at her skeptically. "And not at all prudent."

"Prudent?"

"Yes," I said, and started out in disgust.

"Well, you're not going to let him stay down there in all that filth," she cried after me.

"I never said I would."

"What are you going to do, then?"

I paused for breath. "Well, for one thing—change all the locks. We'll see where that gets us."

She made a face as if she pitied me. "You mean just lock him out?"

"Yes. He's out now. When he gets back tonight, he'll find all the doors barred to him. Easy enough."

"I suppose you know what you're doing." She rose quickly and started to go.

"You're not really serious about all this?" I called after her.

"Why not?" She stared at me unflinchingly. "Just a helping hand until he gets himself another job."

"A helping hand—" I was a little breathless. "Do you know what that entails?"

"Of course I do."

"This isn't some flower in your garden, Alice. This is a person we're talking about. Not a flower you transplant from one place to the next and water daily, then forget about."

The point failed to impress her. "Well?"

"Well," I said, "you just don't move any old stranger into your house."

She looked at me a long moment.

"I don't understand you, Alice." My voice was softer.

"It's really not that mysterious," she said. "It does get lonely out here from time to time." She turned again and walked slowly out through the door, murmuring as she went, "Poor boy. Poor, poor boy."

I'm afraid all this makes me sound unduly harsh. Perhaps I should explain I've always maintained that it's enough of a job for a man to get himself through this world in one piece. I married Alice quite late in life and then only after a lengthy, on-again, off-again courtship, in which I was awed by the sense of enormous responsibility I was undertaking. I'm not one to take responsibilities lightly. Once I assume them, they're mine, and I don't disassume them if the burden should become onerous.

Perhaps I get this from my father, an unduly stringent man who was a missionary in China, where I was brought as a boy and remained until I was sent back to this country to attend the University.

Life in China is very cheap—as it is all throughout

the Orient. If you're not a wealthy aristocrat in China, you learn at an early age to look after yourself. You learn to fight for a bit of space to live in and for every scrap you eat. It's a precarious business, and one learns very quickly not to undertake unnecessary responsibilities, even if they are attractive.

I know this sounds narrow and selfish, but I don't believe in altruism as such. I don't believe there's such a thing as a purely altruistic act. Even my father, a selfless and saintlike man, who died at an early age trying to ease the suffering of the poor in the wretched slums of Hong Kong and Nanking—even he never acted out of pure altruism. What he was actually seeking in those appalling places was no more than his own salvation—since, like most saints, he had a crippling sense of his own sins.

Accordingly, that afternoon we drove into town. I went to the small hardware store and purchased three of the heaviest locks I could find. When we drove back later, it was still raining, but the rain had changed to a kind of icy drizzle that hailed down with a pitiless persistence. I turned on the heater of the car and we drove in silence listening to the wipers wooshing back and forth, carving, as they went, a wide arc across the slushy panes.

Alice gazed out the window on a desolate landscape. There was no green left in the land. The distant, slumbering hills looked like the heads of men that have gone gray overnight. I could somehow only recall them as green. Now they looked like total strangers to me. The trees had a stark and tortured aspect.

"When are you going to put the locks on?" she asked suddenly.

"Now."

We drove a bit, listening to the wipers wooshing back and forth.

"It'll be bitter cold tonight," she said.

"Yes," I said, knowing precisely what she was thinking. The car felt its way along warily over the iced and rutty road.

As soon as we got back, I went to work on the locks.

Alice went instantly to the kitchen, making herself busy, as if she couldn't bear to see what I was doing. From time to time, she'd come out, wiping her hands in her apron, and look at me. There was nothing reproachful or accusatory in those glances. If anything, it was rather a quiet dismay—as if at that point she wasn't certain if it was actually me she was looking at—was it really her husband there on his knees fumbling with the tumblers in a frantic race against the coming dark?

By dusk I had changed the locks on every door leading into the house from the outside. I padlocked our shed and garage. I had also changed the lock on the door leading from the cellar up to the library. Before I went up to supper, I locked all the doors, then went down to the basement and searched the crawl to make certain it was empty. Several times I picked up the phone just to hear the comforting buzz of the signal. In spite of all these measures, I felt little security. I hated to see the darkness come rushing and swirling in around us that night.

By nightfall the barometer dropped alarmingly and a high wind moaned across the land, buffeting the roof and nuzzling at the window panes.

We ate supper silently. Afterwards we read and played records. One was a Haydn trumpet concerto. It was curiously comforting to hear the high, pure ring of a trumpet rise above the wind. So proud, so heroic, and unperturbed.

I dreaded the hour of going to bed, but at last it came. I banked the fire and kept up good appearances by chattering buoyantly to Alice. "Let's go south next winter," I said as we mounted the stairs. "One of the Keys. I've always wanted to see the Keys. They say the fishing is spectacular. Let's plan——"

Alice stopped suddenly on the steps and cocked an ear. "What was that?"

"What?"

"That sound. Listen. Just outside."

"It's only wind. Your imagination." I laughed, but I thought for a moment I'd be sick. "I'd love to see the Keys once," I chattered on halfheartedly, as we continued to climb.

We lay in bed that night, neither of us sleeping, just lying there listening to the rain and the wind howling. The hours stretched out, and dawn seemed eons away. At one point I spoke out: "Alice?"

"Yes."

"Are you sleeping?"

"No."

"What are you thinking?"

"About him. Out there."

"Yes. I know."

Our voices sounded strange in the darkness—disembodied—almost like listening to recordings.

"You never really wanted a child, did you, Albert?"

"Why do you bring that up now?"

"Just talking to pass the time." She paused, staring at the ceiling above her. "It's true, isn't it?"

"I don't think that's fair."

"You wanted to be free to travel. Go and come as you pleased. A child would've only gotten in your way."

"It would've made things harder," I said. "But I wouldn't have minded. Anyway, didn't we try time and time again?"

"Yes."

"And you simply couldn't. You know that. The doctor told you." When I said it, I felt a terrible twinge of satisfaction.

"Yes," she said very softly. "I know. But all the same —you were relieved, weren't you?"

I listened to the wind outside.

"Weren't you?"

"Alice—what is the purpose of all this now?"

"Admit it. It's true, isn't it?"

"No." I sighed and turned away. "It's not true at all."

The silence rushed back in upon us. Outside, the wind gnashed its teeth and the bare branches of trees above the roof clicked against each other.

"Where will he go?" said Alice, after a while.

"For all we know, he's found a place already."

"Yes. For all we know—"

"Something better, I hope."

"Yes," she said without too much enthusiasm, and we were silent again.

An hour or so passed, and still we heard nothing. Then, just as I felt myself slipping off, there was the unmistakable sound of a key jiggling a lock at the cellar door. We could hear it quite distinctly, since that door is almost directly beneath our bedroom window.

Alice sat bolt upright in bed. "Albert?"

"Yes. I hear it."

The key continued to jiggle, and I could hear the lock rebuffing it. The noises became rougher and more impatient, full of the sound of frustration and growing anger.

I held my breath, hoping that the new locks wouldn't fail me. I had a sudden, awful notion that I'd put them all on incorrectly. In my mind I saw them yielding or falling out and the doors all opening wide, like unfolding blossoms.

The jiggling went on for some time. It would pause for a while, then resume. I imagined him out there in the wind and the cold, hunched over, the rain streaming in icy rivulets down his face—baffled and furious. The knob rattled and then I heard a sound as of wood straining and creaking against a weight. He was leaning on the door, attempting to force it.

"Albert?" Alice was sitting upright in bed, gaping at the window.

I rose and crossed the chilly floor to the window, parting the curtains and peering down. Each pane was covered with a thin mist. Wiping one of the panes clean, I tried once again to see something.

At first there was nothing but blackness and the swirl of snow flurries coming down dry and hard. They seemed to whisper against the glass. It had become quiet down below. There was no more jiggling of keys in locks or rattling of doorknobs. It was as if he had stepped back from the door and was trying to figure out what had gone wrong. Still I couldn't see him, but I could sense his puzzling it all out just below.

"Albert?" Alice whispered at me from the bed.

I flapped my hand at her to be silent. She was for a while. Then she whispered again. "Has he gone?"

"I'm not sure." I peered down into swirling, impenetrable black and waited a while longer. Then just as I was about to turn from the window, the sound of footsteps crunching over the dry hard snow came drifting up from below. When I looked down I saw a small, black shadow retreating from beneath the window and groping its way toward the woods in the back.

Alice started to get out of bed and come toward the window.

"Go back." I flapped my hand at her again.

She kept coming. "Albert?"

"Go back, I said."

She got back into bed, and shortly after I followed her. We lay there waiting for the jiggling and the rattling to begin again, but it didn't. Then there was nothing but the moaning of wind, and the sound of Alice sobbing quietly into the pillow.

The following morning I was awakened by the squawking of crows and a bright shaft of sunlight falling obliquely across my bed. Alice was not beside me, but I could hear the sound of her spade turning frozen earth below in the garden. I got up and washed, then went down to the kitchen. The sun was shining, the sky was blue, and the earth was covered with a thin sheet of snow. The hills in the distance, sprinkled with a light, white powder, had the appearance of slumbering oxen.

I found the table set and there was the smell of buns baking in the oven and hot cocoa on the stove.

Alice came in, her cheeks glowing, her arms full of freshly picked dahlias. She said good morning to me and started to arrange the huge, brightly colored flowers in a vase.

I watched her puttering for a while, waiting for her to speak.

"What is it, Alice?" I said, finally. "What's bothering you?"

"Nothing, dear," she said blankly and went on with her floral arrangements. "Only—"

"Yes?"

"I wish we'd acted better."

"We're not gods, Alice. We're only human. We did what was best."

"It was freezing last night, and he had no warm clothing."

"I think we've done quite enough for the boy."

"It was cruel to send him out in the cold like that."

"We did what was best," I said again, this time a little abrasively.

"I know. But knowing that doesn't make me feel any better."

"Nor me," I snapped, at the end of my patience. "But I'm sure that what we did was for the best. Now, that's the end of it. He's gone. Let's drop it."

She turned from her dahlias and stared fully at me. I'd never seen such an expression on her face.

Afterward she took her buns from the oven and served them fresh with piping, hot cocoa. We sat at the table eating, and then I said, making idle talk, "It's a beautiful morning."

"Go look at the garden door," she said.

At first I didn't understand, and looked at her blankly.

"Go," she said again.

I went down into the garden and crossed quickly to the small cellar door. Directly in front of it, and leading from it straight across the lawn to the woods in the back, was the trail of a man's shoe prints outlined very clearly in the light fall of snow.

The cellar door had been scratched and splintered in several places as if a large animal had clawed at it. And above the lintel smeared in large red letters was the word GOD, which Richard Atlee had written in the blood he had drawn from lacerating his hands on the cellar door.

Chapter Three

RICHARD Atlee stopped coming after that night. Then strangely enough the weather improved. It went the other way from what everyone expected. In the weeks that followed, Indian summer fell over the land. The sun was warm and the ground that had started to freeze only a few weeks earlier became soft and muddy.

Alice and I fell into our old easy, uneventful routine. Once again she worked in the garden. She pulled up her dahlia tubers and stored them in peat moss for the winter. Together, we seeded all the bare parts of the lawn and then drew the spreader over all the ground fertilizing it for the spring that was to come.

Alice baked pies and buns on the weekends, and on Sundays we would drive over to the small church where we worshipped. After the services Alice would always present a pie or a freshly baked cake to the pastor.

It was a simple church—a white-steepled affair, austere in every way, with a glass clerestory in the tower, where in warmer weather birds swarmed by the thousands.

One Sunday morning, with sunlight streaming through the stained-glass windows we listened to the pastor read the words of Paul from First Corinthians.

> Charity suffereth long and is kind;
> Charity vaunteth not itself.
> Charity never faileth—
> When I was a child I spoke as a child—

And so he went on, midway between chant and talk, and slightly nasal, until he came to the end. "But then shall I know even as also I am known. And now abideth faith, hope, and charity—these three. But the greatest of these"—Alice's glance fell sidewards upon me—"is charity."

I didn't look up. I kept my eyes fixed on my hymnal, and we began to sing.

Even though our lives resumed an outward state of calm and normalcy, inwardly Alice and I had undergone a change. We never spoke of the night I turned Richard Atlee away from our door, but it was clear from our behavior toward each other that neither of us had forgotten it. He existed as an issue between us, and for all intents and purposes, though we had managed to get him out of the crawl, he was still very much present in the house.

For one thing, we talked less to each other. When we met or came together we were, now as ever, civil, but there was something stiff and cool about it. We talked less intimately and more formally. A wall was up between us. Often while we worked together in the garden, or sat at supper, or undressed in the evening, I would suddenly look up and find her staring at me.

It was no anger in her face I saw; there was nothing accusatory or even petulant. It was for the most part questioning. It seemed to say, "What do you want to do now?"

In the few remaining sunny weeks of autumn, Alice and I grew increasingly distant. One night after a dinner eaten in bleak and cheerless silence, I said, "All right. Speak up! What's on your mind?"

"Nothing's on my mind, Albert." She rose and walked to the sideboard, where two cups of pink junket stood, then walked slowly back and placed one at each of our settings.

"Why don't you say what's bothering you?" I said.

"I've forgotten it, Albert."

"I did what was best."

"I know you did, dear."

"Then why don't you let me forget it?"

"I haven't said a word."

I ground my teeth. "It's not what you say. It's the looks. The moping around. The sullen glances."

Her eyes were very steady, and when she spoke her voice was quite calm. "I've forgotten it, Albert."

"You lie. It's that boy. You've never stopped thinking of him."

Flushing with anger, I rose from the table, and as I did a hot pain seared my chest. It was like being pierced with a saber.

I fell back into my chair. In the next moment she was kneeling at my side. "Albert? Are you all right?"

I stared straight ahead, waiting for the pain to subside, for the knot to dissolve.

"Albert— Are you all right?"

Her hand fell over my arm and pressed it. I could see the fear in her eyes. Very carefully I lifted the hand and pushed it away. By then I was able to stand. I did, and in the next moment, I walked quickly out of the room.

Thus our days went—chilly, awkward, hostile.

But one question above all haunted and perplexed me. Why had Richard Atlee written the word GOD above my cellar door. So curious and so incongruous it was to see it there.

I hadn't washed it from where he'd scrawled it above the door. It was almost as if I had a need to go out and see it every day, and confront myself with it. Each day I'd go down to the garden and, standing before the door, ponder Richard Atlee's purpose in putting the word there.

One afternoon late in November a man came to clean the flue. I went down to the cellar with him and showed him the furnace. After he left I remained there in the gloomy half-light of dusk staring around at the place as if I'd never seen it before.

I suddenly remembered the books and mementos Richard Atlee had left in the cupboard and realized I'd completely forgotten to take them out and bring them upstairs. I crossed quickly to the cupboard and found them all exactly where I'd left them. There were the books and the jade paperweight, the white raven and the milk-glass angel smiling secretly into the shadows.

Then something strangely upsetting occurred. I began to tremble. My knees buckled and the tips of my fingers grew icy cold. I had a sensation of falling. Then a sickening vertigo. So intense an experience it was that I had to lean against the furnace.

It passed in a moment, like a wave that crashes over you, then boils on leaving nothing but a series of quiet little eddies in its wake.

For several moments I stood there clinging to the furnace and wondering what it was that had happened to me. I was urgently aware that I wanted to do something—that I had to do something right then. But I didn't know exactly what.

In the next moment I took the flashlight, crossed quickly to the crawl, and hoisted myself in.

It wasn't as dark as I'd recalled it, nor as damp. Curiously the stench of cats seemed to have gone completely. Through a chink in the far wall, a jagged gash of sunlight seeped into the gloom, dappling the ground where it fell. Within that slender thread of light, motes of dust swirled like galaxies. In that strange light I had the curious sensation that I was floating. I was moving past stars and through centuries and eons of time.

Stooping, I worked my way through the crawl. I had no conscious idea of where I was going. Some interior compass seemed to be guiding me. When I reached the place, I turned my light on it. It was all there, just as I'd left it—the straw, the bones, the tin can, toppled and lying on its side, with the cheap, wretched toiletries spilling out of it. A pathetically crude semblance of life lived at an almost prehistoric level.

My foot scraped against something light and brittle in the dry earth. When I turned my light on it, I saw the skeleton of a small rodent at my feet. I imagined it to be a squirrel, or possibly a rat. The flesh had been picked clean with almost clinical perfection. It had been done so meticulously that the entire skeleton had remained intact. There was the small, delicate skull with its tiny vacant eyesockets, and the jaw clenched over tiny razor-teeth, all frozen into a lurid grin.

I swung the light around in a wide circle scanning the rest of the crawl. When the beam fell once more over the straw pallet, something I'd never seen before caught my eye. Just above the pallet, carved into the old timbers and beams, were a number of recently made scratchings. At first they looked like thin white trails gouged deep into the old wood. They were less than an eighth of an inch in width and looked as if they'd been made with a nail or possibly the point of a key. At first they appeared to be nothing more than random lines—curving and criss-crossing and wandering off into nothingness. But the more I studied them, the more they began to take the form of drawings. Rudimentary shapes like circles and squares. And then stick figures. The sort of thing you see in a child's doodling. The drawings had been made recently. I couldn't tell what they were supposed to represent. At one point they looked like children playing; at another, like a hunting scene. For some curious reason they filled me with a deep unaccountable sadness.

In the next moment I sat down on the straw pallet and propped my back against the wall the way I imagined Richard Atlee sat when he had been down there—head tilted backwards, legs drawn up, and eyes closed.

It was an act totally beyond my will or understanding. As I was doing it a shudder of revulsion shot through me. But I was responding to a consciousness much stronger than my own. I sat there, eyes closed, crouching against the walls. I could smell the pipes overhead and hear the pulse of water flush through them like arterial blood. Small beads of water sweated off their casings and dropped periodically down onto my face.

Then slowly, irresistibly, I lay back in the shadows—back until I lay fully flat on the bed of straw, feeling the dampness of the earth seeping into my clothes, through them and into my bones. And the most curious thing of all was that after the initial shudder of revulsion, I felt fine. Almost detached, like a scientist going about some elaborate experiment. Then it suddenly occurred to me that what I wanted was to feel what it was like to sleep on wet straw and have the dank smell of mold and sewage in my nostrils. I tried to imagine myself homeless and penniless. I tried to imagine hunger. For a brief time I tried to become Richard Atlee.

How long I stayed there I don't know, but when I climbed out of the crawl and emerged from the cellar later that day, it was already dusk. My body ached with cramps from the position in which I'd lain. My clothing was damp and smelled faintly of mold.

When I entered the house I could smell supper in the kitchen. It was comforting to be up above again in the lights and warmth, with the sound of Alice moving about in the kitchen.

"That you, Albert?" she called out.

"Yes."

"You about ready for supper?"

"In a moment."

I washed very thoroughly, changed my clothing, and then without a word of greeting to Alice, took my place at table.

In the days that followed, I never mentioned a word to her about my strange experience in the crawl. Frankly, I didn't know what to make of it myself, and to have recounted it to her, precisely as it happened, would've marked me as a lunatic. So I remained silent.

The weather continued unnaturally mild, and one beautiful day toward the end of November we went walking in the forest. The air was bright and clear, and though the trees were completely bare of leaves, they looked precisely as trees look at that time of the spring, just before they're about to bloom.

We walked for several hours along a trail we knew well. To the right of the trail we passed a pond in time to see a covey of geese light on its surface. They hit the water all at once—a single noise and motion for all of them. And where there had been a flat, still surface with trees hanging upside down reflected in it, you could now see a series of watery, concentric rings moving like pulses, skimming over the water, growing larger and larger.

When we crept up close to get a better look at the geese, they suddenly rose in one motion again, and honking, circled the far fringe of the pond. At one point they wheeled so low overhead that the drumming of their wings passed like a wind over us. It was a sound so purely wild, so terrifyingly joyous, that for a moment I thought I would cry.

Alice looked at me uneasily. "Albert? What's come over you?"

"Nothing," I said and watched the line of geese recede in the distance. "Nothing at all."

One day it was like that—the weather warm and clement—and a few days later we were back in winter again. Icy gusts came down from the north. Great schooners of grayish clouds followed, gathering on the horizon like an armada of warships steaming our way.

I put up the storm windows one afternoon and while the wind cuffed me about I replaced all the old shingles on the roof. We had a full supply of fuel, and I stocked the woodbin with choice dried hickory and birch.

That night the barometer fell and a wind started up out of the north. Shortly after, the snow began to fall. It came down in huge, lacy flakes and drifted silently past the windows.

We watched the fire simmer brightly on the hearth, till all that was left of a huge hickory log was a mound of gray, powdery ash and a few smoldering chips.

At last I rose and wound the grandfather clock in the parlor. Then we climbed the stairs and got ready for bed. Alice had taken our eiderdown quilts down from the attic, and when we settled under them for the night, and listened to the snow hissing on the roof, I had a sense of expectation.

For some unaccountable reason, I said prayers that night, my hands clasped under the blanket so that Alice couldn't see me. I hadn't said prayers in bed, before sleep, since I was a child. I'm not sure what I prayed for.

Late in the night and half in sleep I turned, thinking I heard a sound—a low, barely audible whining, like an animal in distress. It came and then it was gone. I pulled the blankets higher around my head and settled deeper into the pillow. The next moment there was a loud banging at the front door. Someone was rapping the knocker and alternately pummeling the door with fists. In all the years that have passed since that moment, I have not been able to get that sound out of my head.

Alice was up in a moment—her head swiveling about —as if she were trying to shake herself awake. It suddenly occurred to me that I had been waiting for that sound for a long time, and now that it had come I felt a fist close over my heart.

I was out of bed and across the room when Alice cried out behind me, "What are you going to do?" She knew as well as I who was at the door.

I turned to look at her cringing behind the quilt, while the pounding echoed up from beneath. The sight of her cowering there gave me a pang of satisfaction. When I turned again and started down the steps, she was still calling out after me. "Let him in," she cried. "Let him in." In the next moment I was standing before the door.

The pounding had increased to a fearful intensity. It came regularly like pulses throbbing through the door. After each concussion I could see the frame of the door shudder and the hasps straining at the hinges. I stood there watching the hinges, and quailing before the noise, with a terrible fascination. Each blow had the force of a clap of thunder. But for me it had the sound of destiny. Richard Atlee had come home.

Chapter Four

IT is curious how Richard Atlee became a member of our family. I'm not sure if we adopted him or he us. It really doesn't matter which. Perhaps it was an act mutually and tacitly agreed upon. He was lonely and so were we. Hence, all was right for the encounter.

The circumstances of his life with us were always strange, but at first they were downright bizarre. In spite of our protestations, he insisted upon living in the crawl-space—like a pet that can't be trusted to come upstairs for fear he'll mess himself and everything around him.

We offered to fix him a spare bedroom on the ground floor, off the parlor, but he would have none of it. He wouldn't come up to eat with us, so we devised a pulley system whereby food was lowered and refuse raised.

He came and went according to his own whims. He continued to spend his days, despite the inclemency of weather, out of doors, leaving the cellar through the garden door and going out into the gray, chill hours of dawn, then returning at night shortly after we had retired. We believed that at night he hovered in the woods around the house, waiting for our bedroom lights to go out, so as to avoid any possibility of having to meet us head-on. As a result, we learned to listen for the squealing hinges of the cellar door as a signal that Richard was home safely and thus we could go to sleep.

It was strange having him there and never actually seeing him. After a while we grew eager for glimpses of him. There were mornings when we rose at dawn and crouched by the windows in the chilly, darkened room just to watch him slip off across the yard swiftly like a young deer and vanish into the deep forest behind the house. He was like a wild creature in that way, solitary and fiercely private. Because of this, when we wished to communicate something to him, we learned never to approach him directly, but rather, obliquely. For instance, since I'd changed all the locks in the house, it was necessary that he be given a new set of keys. I couldn't simply go to him and give him the keys, since it was made abundantly clear to us that he didn't wish to meet us face to face. So instead, I merely made the keys available to him by leaving them in a place where I knew he'd find them—namely, the entrance of the crawl.

In the early days of December, Alice bought yarn and needles and began a wool sweater for him which she hoped to complete by Christmas. This was a tall order for a woman who hadn't knitted in years and had arthritic fingers, yet she went at the task with a passion that was astonishing. Hour after hour, like Penelope at her loom, she would knit away the long mornings after breakfast and the long nights after supper before the fire.

Richard was in all respects an ideal guest. He made himself unobtrusive and at the same time helpful. While each night before a roaring hearth we'd deplete the wood-bin, in the morning we'd find it fully replenished, brimming with fresh-cut wood. On one occasion, when we had snow during the night, we awoke the following morning to find our driveway completely shoveled out. On another occasion, quite by accident, I discovered that he'd cleaned the garage out for me—tossed out the accumulated rubbish of two seasons, stacked neatly in a corner a cord of wood, and put into order a maze and clutterment of crates. I hadn't asked him to do it. I'd been thinking of doing it myself and unconsciously putting it off the way you do with things like that. Yet in some strangely clairvoyant way he knew it was on my mind. He had an uncanny way of divining such things. Alice's reaction to this was pure joy. "Just for that," she'd say on such occasions—clasping her hands—"I'll make him something nice." And off she'd fly to the kitchen.

So he was helpful to us in many different ways and yet, the circumstances of our life together were strange. We never saw him, mind you. Only the effects of his work. He was like the elf in the fairy tale that performs Herculean tasks while everyone else in the house sleeps.

One day after he'd been with us several weeks I was paying bills at my desk when I realized that the jade paperweight was back in its place. I called Alice and showed it to her. Together we rushed to the little curio cabinet where the scrimshaw raven and the milk-glass angel once again sat. The cufflinks, too, were back in my drawer, and my books—all of them—back on the shelves. In a very quiet but real way, we were moved.

Thus whatever wariness I might have felt about Richard Atlee at the beginning of our relationship quickly vanished. Soon we took for granted the peculiar terms of his life with us and then we seldom thought of him with anything other than pleasure and a kind of mellow parental concern.

So at last, Alice and I appeared to be in happy accord about Richard Atlee. But in one respect we were at odds, and that was about the length or duration of his stay.

Of course, we both knew that his visit with us could only be temporary; however, we each had different notions of the extent of *temporary*. Alice felt that no fixed time limit should be placed on the length of Richard's stay, and that when he went, he was to go as a matter of his own choice, and under his own steam. I felt that a definite date of expiration for the visit should be set and under no circumstances exceeded. It wasn't that I was in any way anxious to see him go; it just seemed wiser to operate that way.

Ultimately we came to an agreement. Richard was to remain with us only so long as the time required for him to get a new job. Alice stressed the importance of his getting back into the world and making a place of his own as quickly as possible. I couldn't imagine that it would take very long for him to relocate himself and I agreed quickly to what seemed at that time a fair and perfectly simple solution to our problem. We looked upon Richard then as a wounded bird and considered it our job to give him sanctuary until such time as he was strong enough to fly again on his own.

After we'd reached our agreement, it then became necessary to make our position absolutely clear to Richard, and so accordingly, I determined to go below to the crawl to discuss our decision with him.

It's amusing as I think about it how that first meeting came about. We didn't think it fitting to simply wait for him to come in some night and then go barging down there and pounce upon him with conditions and ultimatums. Instead after much discussion it was decided that I should request an audience. That was done one night by attaching a note to a plate of food that was lowered by pulley into the cellar.

We waited for an answer. But it didn't come immediately. It came several days after in a note scrawled on a napkin in a large rather childish hand and sent back up the pulley on a stack of dirty dishes. It said merely, "To-night." It all seemed very cute to us, and we laughed, enjoying the intrigue of our little game.

So it was that finally, after a period of nearly a month in which he actually lived in our house, I was to have my first face-to-face meeting with Richard Atlee.

Alice refused to go to bed that night at her regular hour. She had to stay up to learn the outcome of our meeting. So we sat up in the parlor and waited together.

It was my habit to dress casually around the house. On a winter's eve at home, my garb usually consisted of a warm flannel shirt, a pair of old corduroy trousers, and warm fleece-lined slippers. But Alice felt that for this oc-casion my dress ought to be somewhat more formal. "It'll make a good impression on the boy," she said. "It shows that you respect him, and what's more, it'll set a good example for him about cleanliness and dress."

So that night I put on a suit and tie, and by midnight I was sitting stiffly in the large Morris chair of my own living room waiting a little nervously for Richard Atlee to come home.

He didn't come at midnight that night, as was his usual custom. Instead, it was about 1 A.M. when I heard the hinges squealing on the door below. Alice, who'd been dozing in her chair, suddenly looked up.

"That's him."

"Yes." I started to rise.

"Don't go down right away. Give him time to settle himself."

I sat back in my chair and fidgeted with the worn edge of one of its arms while the curious animal noises of Richard Atlee rummaging about came wafting up from below.

Finally the noises ceased. Alice and I glanced at each other, and with a sigh I rose and started for the library. As I went I felt her eyes follow me across the room. When I reached the door to the cellar, she cried out:

"Albert."

I turned and looked at her. "Be firm," she said. "But gentle."

I stood there at the door, staring at the floor, listening to her words dying on the air. Then I turned the knob. The door swung open and I prepared to make my descent.

At the head of the stairs leading down into the cellar there's a light switch; this illuminates the stairs and the front of the cellar. Then at the foot of the stairs is another switch, which lights up the rear and more shadowy regions of the place. There's no electricity in the crawl. I threw the first switch and started down the stairs.

The light on the stairway had a strange shimmering quality. Walking through it gave the impression of being under water. My legs were leaden and my breath unnaturally short. I felt more like an alien entering a foreign country than a man entering his own cellar. It was not as if I had called him to come before me, but rather as if he had summoned me to appear before him—a stern and august presence by whom I was to be judged.

I'd been looking forward to seeing him. Now that the time had come, I was in a state of great excitement. But descending the steps something curious happened. I tried recalling his face and found that I had nothing but the most fleeting impression of it. I say "curious" because I'm the sort of person who sees a face and then never forgets it.

At the bottom of the stairs I paused and peered into the shadows. My eyes scanned the cellar, adjusting to the greenish light. All about the cellar was scattered the various garden equipment that had been dragged in for the winter—the lawn mower, the wheelbarrow, the spreader, the seeder; and depending from the ceiling, the long rakes, hoes, shovels, and scythes, all having the look of hanged men.

At the bottom of the stairs I flicked on the second switch, and in the blinding glare of a naked bulb, I looked directly at the entrance to the crawl. In that rather stark, brilliant light, its black square appeared to be floating toward me.

I stood there for some time, fingers still resting on the light switch, almost hypnotized by the illusion of that square. Then I spoke:

"Richard?" I waited for some reply. None came. I tried again:

"Richard."

This time I heard a noise—not a word, but a sound as of someone shifting in the crawl.

"Richard? Are you there?"

"Yes," came the muffled but unmistakable reply.

I waited again, listening to the sound of my breathing and wondering what to do next. Glancing upward over my shoulder I took comfort from the sight of the library door, ajar with the glow of warm orange light pouring through it. I imagined Alice not far from that door.

"Richard. I'm coming in now."

I started slowly toward the square. When I was a yard from it, I stopped again.

"Richard?" This time my voice was a trifle louder. "I'm here." I looked at the square, waiting for some word of greeting to waft out of it. Nothing came.

"Richard. It's me." I waited, then moved a few steps closer. There was a sound like that of the scurrying of small animals. It froze me in my tracks.

"Richard— Are you comfortable?"

"Yes," came the voice finally.

"You have everything you need?"

"Yes."

"Are you warm enough in there? It must be awfully cold."

"It's all right."

"Mrs. Graves worries that it's damp in the crawl. You're welcome to come up and stay in the spare room whenever you'd like."

"I'm comfortable."

"I understand," I said feebly. "But you're welcome, all the same."

It suddenly struck me funny that I'd been talking to a disembodied voice in a black hole, and I laughed.

"Richard—it's a little strange trying to talk this way. Won't you come out of there so I can see you?"

"I'm comfortable this way."

"Oh, come on." I laughed as if it were all a big joke. "Out now." Again his voice floated out of the square. Neither harsh nor defiant—merely final. "I'm comfortable."

I didn't press it further. Instead I changed the subject. "How have you been?"

"Okay."

"Thank you for cleaning the garage. You didn't have to. All the same, it was very thoughtful. You read my mind." I laughed nervously and waited for a reply. None came.

"Do you have enough to eat?" I went on a little desperately.

"Yes."

"You're sure?"

"Yes."

Then silence. I'd gone the gamut of conversational possibilities and run into a dead end with each. The pauses following my questions grew longer and more deadly.

I sensed a growing silence creeping between us and felt that I'd better make the reason for my visit known to him before I lost contact altogether.

"Richard?" I started again but became flustered.

"Richard? Mrs. Graves and I—" That was simpering and apologetic. It wanted more firmness. "Mrs. Graves and I want you to know"—I had the sensation, chatting there affably into that black hole, that I was all alone, talking to myself. It occurred to me I was mad—"that you're welcome in our house. But we want to make one thing absolutely clear—" That was too imperious. I became conciliatory. "That is—Mrs. Graves and I want you to know, that you're free to remain with us until you find some new employment and can stand on your own. There are lots of jobs around here for young men—" I waited, listened for some sound, then barged on. "Clerks, delivery men, dishwashers. I know the gasoline station is looking for a boy to work on the pumps. Nothing spectacular, mind you, but a start. Money in your pocket, and you're your own man once more. Soon you'll go on to something better."

I was pleased with the way I'd presented it, and now I gazed at the square hopefully.

"Richard?"

"Yes."

"Did you hear me?"

"Yes."

"Oh," I said, somewhat at a loss. "Well—I just wanted to make it perfectly clear—" I waited for some reaction, but none came. "Then it's understood," I went on. "You'll remain here with us until you find some work. Then you can set up some place on your own. Which ought to be lots of fun for a young fellow, I should think."

I chattered on blithely, waxing, with each moment, more and more enthusiastic over Richard Atlee's prospects, which I thought were reasonably good. Still he would say nothing to indicate his feelings one way or another.

"I don't think it should take you very long," I said, peering fatuously into that square black void, awaiting some response, some small clue to his feelings.

I waited. No answer came. "Well, then—" I started up again with a burst of tepid cheer. "You're all right?"

"Yes."

"Can I bring you anything? Warm clothes? Books? Can I bring you more books?"

"No, thanks."

"Well, then—This was very pleasant," I babbled on. "Just chatting this way and everything—Let's do it again."

I gazed at the black square, hoping for some small word of encouragement. Nothing came.

"Well, then—I'll say good night."

"Good night," came his reply—perfunctory and final. And that was that.

Then I did something strange. Instead of leaving, I turned and walked directly back to the square. "Richard, I want to ask you something." I held my breath and

waited until my voice grew calm. "Why did you write the
word 'GOD' above the cellar door?" This time I didn't
have to prod him. He answered directly and without pause.

"To remind you."

"To remind me of what?"

"That God loves all things." It was blunt and swift. His
voice boomed out of the square like a clap of thunder.

"I see," I mumbled numbly. "I see."

And in some curious way, I did. Had anyone else said
it—given this time in history, given the essentially mocking spirit of our age—you might have laughed aloud in
his face. Not so here. Mirth was the last thing I felt. It
had all come out of him so earnestly and with such a
naked, childish faith.

"Thank you, Richard," I said feeling curiously baffled
and contrite. "I've always tried to live in that spirit myself. From time to time I've failed, but I trust that I
won't fail you. Thank you," I said again, and I imagine
I said it several more times as well and started to back
out, my eyes riveted to the floor, powerless to raise them
to the level of the square again. In the next instant I
turned and walked quickly back to the stairs. I flicked out
the cellar switch and except for the stairway, still lit by a
shaft of warm, orange light, a mantle of comforting
darkness fell over the cellar.

As I mounted the stairs I felt strangely happy.

Chapter Five

"Do you think he'll like it?" said Alice. She held
up a sweater—a long-sleeved blue affair with white rein-
deers. It was a week before Christmas.

I examined it while lighting my pipe. "The arms are
too long."

"Oh, they're not."

"It's twice his size."

She made a sour face. "You don't even know his size."

"Why bother asking my opinion if you can't accept it when it's given?"

"I accept criticism very well," she said with an expansive tolerance. "But not when it's wrong. If you say this is twice his size, then you simply don't know his size."

"I think I probably know it better than you."

"You do?" She cocked an eyebrow.

"I've spent more time with him, haven't I?"

"That's hardly a yardstick." She half joked and mocked. "You barely know your own size shirt and socks, little less someone else's."

I unfolded my paper with a great flap and started to read.

"Well, how tall is he?" she persisted.

I was growing increasingly irritated. "One moment you completely discount my judgment, and in the next you ask for it again."

"Well, guess. Just make a guess."

I made a great show of trying to visualize him in my mind. "Oh, five-ten, five-eleven, I'd say."

She laughed aloud. "He's nowhere near that. Five-eleven. Oh, Albert. Honestly."

"Well, then. How tall is he? You tell me."

"He's a tiny little fellow," she cooed. "That's what's so endearing about him."

"Endearing? What do you mean, endearing?"

"That he's so small and all that—" She patted the wool sweater tenderly. "I'd be very surprised if he were much more than five-seven."

"You must be mad. I'm five-nine, and he's taller than me." This time she laughed out loud. "You're not five-nine, Albert. I know you've always wanted to be five-nine. I've seen you put it on your driver's license. But all the same, you're not any five-nine, my dear."

I felt my face flush. "I am five-nine."

"Not in your wildest dreams. Not even in your elevated shoes."

"Unless I've shrunk as of my last examination at Dr. Tucker's, I'm five-nine. And that last remark of yours was uncalled-for." With another great flap, I yanked the paper upward again and thrust my face assertively into it.

"I'm sorry, dear—" Her voice now was wheedling and apologetic. "I really shouldn't have—" But she was still laughing.

I plunged myself deeper into the newspaper, and for a while we were silent. She continued to hold the sweater up and admire it—making little cooing sounds to herself. "I can't wait to see it on him," she said.

"I doubt you'll have that pleasure."

"Why?"

"He's not about to come up here and model it for you."

She looked across at the Christmas tree. We'd put it up the week before. It was festooned with tinsel and sparkled with little lights of many colors. Papier-mâché balls, candy canes, and toy soldiers hung from its branches, and at the top a plastic angel with rouged cheeks and vacant eyes gazed benevolently down on the little parlor.

"If I were to put it in a pretty box—" she said. I knew she was plotting something from the way her voice trailed off. "—and set it under the tree on Christmas morning, he might just—"

"Forget it, Alice. Put it out of your mind."

"I worked very hard on this. The least he can do is come up here and show his—"

"Gratitude?" I said.

The word caught her up short. She looked at me ruefully. "I didn't mean exactly—"

"Of course you did. Now that you've given him shelter and cooked for him, and gone so far as to knit a sweater, you expect a return on your investment."

The word mortified her. Her jaw fell open. "That's not true," she protested. But in the next moment, her shoulders sagged and a sigh rose to her lips. "Well—it's not unreasonable to expect—"

"It's unreasonable to expect anything. That's not why we're letting him stay here—" I rose and started off across the parlor. Then I turned and stalked back to where she sat. "Now let's don't start this stuff, Alice. I've told you at least a half-dozen times. Whatever we do for the boy, whatever little is done here, we do without the slightest expectation of recompense or gratitude."

She stared at me for a moment, speechless, then shook her head vehemently. "You're absolutely right, dear. I need never see him wear it. What he does with it is of no importance."

"None whatsoever."

"The only thing that's important is knowing that I made it for him out of a sincere desire to give him something."

"With no strings attached."

"Yes, dear." She bubbled on, happy once again. "And it's sufficient for me just to know that." She sighed contentedly and resumed her knitting. I returned to my chair and paper. After a few moments, she held the sweater up again and laid it flat across her chest, studying it critically. "One of the antlers is bigger than the other."

"I wouldn't worry about it."

She seemed distressed. "What shall I do, Albert?"

"Leave it alone, or you'll wind up botching all you've done."

"Do you think he'll mind?"

"If he does, he's not deserving of it."

She was suddenly quite angry. "Don't say that. He's a good boy and deserving of it in every way." She looked at me as if I were a mortal enemy.

"I didn't say he wasn't, Alice," I replied gently. "Let's go up to bed."

I banked the fire, and as I did so she hurried into the kitchen. It was her custom now to leave out a plate of freshly baked pastries or tarts on the kitchen table. She also left cocoa on the stove so that when Richard came in out of the cold, bitter night all he need do was tiptoe up to the kitchen and turn on the flame beneath the cocoa. This had become a nightly ritual. In the morning we'd find the splashed and spattered residue of those late-hour feasts.

On this night, she came back from the kitchen and waited for me at the foot of the landing while I went around the house locking doors and extinguishing lights. Then slowly we ascended the stairs together.

When we'd both undressed and got into our pajamas, I turned out the light and stood by the window looking out. Alice lay in bed watching me.

"Does it look like more snow?" she asked.

"No. It's quite clear." The moon was out and full, and I could see it glowing over the snowy hills. "It's a beautiful night. Thousands of stars."

"Where do you suppose he is now, Albert? Where do you think he goes?"

I gazed up at the stars for a time. "Job-hunting, I hope." I'd been wondering for the past week or so about his efforts to secure employment. But Alice disregarded my remark.

"Do you think he's warm enough?" she asked.

"I hope so."

"Do you think he thinks of us at all?"

"I don't know. I hope so." I had a sudden picture of him out in the woods someplace, crouching back there in the bogs, trying to duck the icy blasts, the blue frost of a northern night freezing his toes and fingertips. "How he keeps himself alive out there is a mystery to me."

"Why doesn't he just forget about the crawl and come up here and stay with us until he gets some kind of work?"

"Yes," I answered her distantly, not having heard very much of what she said. I was still thinking of him out there in the bog, and of the word GOD still written over my door (although the wind and snow had bleached some of the vivid scarlet out of the letters).

"I wish that, too," I said, looking at the stars shining in the bright northern sky outside our window. "But I know we can't push him about it."

She was silent for a while lying there in bed. "You know what I feel?" she said suddenly, the mattress creaking beneath her.

"What?"

In the next moment she'd slipped noiselessly up beside me. "How uncanny it is."

"What?"

"His coming at this time."

"This time?"

"He's the child I should have had and here he's been given to me at this time."

"What time?"

"Christmas, Albert." Her voice had a sharp edge to it. "Christmas."

I felt a twinge of pain somewhere inside me.

"Well, it's like an omen, isn't it?" she went on.

"Oh, I wouldn't make too much of that."

"Don't deflate me, Albert."

"Deflate you?"

"Just when I start to get happy about something, you cut me down. You've always done that."

"Really? I'm sorry if I have. I didn't realize."

She placed her hand in mine. There was something ineffably tender and childish about the way she did it. Alice is, after all, a woman well on in her fifties. "Well, it is curious his coming to us"—she went on—"this time of year and all. The time of nativity, I mean."

"Yes, Alice," I said hopelessly. I knew what was coming next and wanted to head her off.

"I know it may sound foolish," she continued, "but I can't help thinking of Mary, fallow as she was, and Jesus coming to her in the dead of winter, and his sleeping in that drafty manger with the animals and all—" Suddenly she turned and embraced me in a way she hadn't done in years. "Oh, Albert. I know it sounds foolish—but I feel like a new mother. Like a blessed infant has been given to me."

I took her hand in mine and kissed it, and we stood there in the darkened room in front of the window with the stars in the northern sky shining down upon us.

In the next moment I saw a small gray spot appear at the bottom of the garden. It stood out clearly in the white snow with the moon pouring light down upon it. Alice saw it at the same moment that I did, and as we watched it, I felt her hand tighten around mine and squeeze. Breathlessly we followed the spot as it stole across the garden, moving toward the door beneath the window, our hearts beating madly in our chests.

The following morning I drove the car to town along an icy road. Driving conditions were hazardous. The roads had been slicked over by icy rains the night before. It was like traveling down a narrow strip of glass in roller skates. You could feel no bottom beneath you. There was nothing to hold on to. I had no chains, only snow tires that spun and whined sickeningly as I crept up hills.

Knowing my general condition, I wondered why on earth I was making such a trip. But the answer was quite simple. I had a mission. Alice and I, walking around the house a week or two earlier, had found a wide fissure in the foundation surrounding the crawlspace. It was not new but apparently had been there for several months and gone undetected. It now appeared to be widening. That afternoon we went down to the cellar, and standing at the square we peered into the crawl. I spotted the chink immediately. It was at the far end of the crawl, light pouring through it. A narrow stream of air moving at a high velocity swept through the chink making the sound of a thin, shrill whistle. When I reported this to Alice she was horrified—not because of the danger to the foundation, but rather, the danger to Richard.

My mission on that icy morning was to plaster up the chink so as to spare Richard the discomfort of icy drafts pouring through the crawl at night.

Reaching town, late in the morning, I went quickly to the local hardware store and bought a bag of cement, a mixing basin, and a trowel, which was all carried out of the store by a clerk and loaded into my car.

I wasn't eager to get back on the icy roads, so I delayed it by driving over to my service station to get gas and have the oil checked.

The service station I went to was the one I had suggested Richard apply to for a job. It was the only service station in town and run by a gloomy, taciturn man by the name of Washburn, whom I had grown strangely fond of, chiefly, I suppose, for his frankly antisocial ways. Talking to Washburn was like conversing with a block of ice.

When I drove up that day and gave a light punch to my horn, I could see him through the long windows of the repair shop, stretching his arms upward beneath a car hoisted on a hydraulic lift. For a moment he looked curiously like a man in an attitude of worship.

I punched my horn lightly again. This time he looked at me through the glass windows, then went back to the underparts of the car. He took his time coming out, primarily because I'd punched my horn two times and he simply had to put me in my place.

When he finally came out he was dressed in a mackinaw and a peaked leather cap, with the ear laps of it flapping foolishly about his stormy temples. Coming up to the car, he scarcely nodded at me, although he knew me quite well and had serviced the car on numerous occasions. But that was Washburn. He simply felt he had to put everyone in their place, particularly rude, city-bred types who were always in a rush. He specialized in city-bred types, and he had long ago fixed his sights on me. I rather admired his rudeness. It had a noble honesty about it. He was not the least bit interested in me, and he was not about to expend the effort of my idle chitchat trying to give the impression that he was.

"Good morning, Mr. Washburn," I said, rolling down my window.

"Fill 'er up?" he asked, disregarding my greeting.

"Yes, please."

Through the windshield I watched him crank the pump impassively while a few desultory snowflakes whirled about his leather cap.

"Road coming up from the bog was pretty bad," I said.

"Ayuh," said Washburn. That was his expression of agreement.

"Looks like we'll have a white Christmas—"

"Ayuh—"

I listened to the small bell of the pump, ticking off the gallons.

"You find a boy for that job you had here a few weeks back?" I went on undaunted.

"Nope."

"I sent a boy over to apply for it about two weeks ago. Has he been in yet?"

"Nope."

"I see," I said, suddenly irritated.

"Can't get young folks to work nowadays," said Washburn. "Ain't interested in it."

The pump tolled its final bell and came to a halt. When I paid Mr. Washburn and drove away, I was very angry.

Arriving home, I recounted to Alice my conversation with Washburn. I told it to her over a cup of cocoa and when I was finished, she looked at me reproachfully. "I'm surprised at you, Albert. That's no work for the boy. He's got a brain. He's sensitive. Imagine having to spend every day in the company of that Washburn creature." She made a clucking sound with her tongue. "I'm frankly surprised at you, Albert."

"I assure you I had the boy's interest at heart."

"Interest?" She gave me a scathing, derisive little laugh. "And you threw him on the mercy of Ezra Washburn. Imagine. A gasoline station attendant."

"You find that disgraceful?"

"You don't?"

"No, I don't. Not at all."

"Well, if you don't then I'm sorry for you. I was under the impression you wanted something better for the boy."

"I do, Alice." I spoke through clenched teeth. "But I don't feel he's quite ready for the local bank presidency. Perhaps next week—"

"Don't be sarcastic." She rose and swept my cocoa cup away.

"I'm not finished with that yet." I rose and trailed after her.

"I hope you didn't forget the plaster for that chink," she went right on, not having heard me.

I had a sudden vision of my hair-raising journey over icy roads. In my mind I saw the car skid out of control and plunge down an embankment. It rolled over several times and landed upside down, its tires spinning in the air.

I caught up with her at the sink just as she was about to pour out the remaining cocoa.

"No, Alice. I didn't forget the plaster," I said and snatched my cup back.

There must have been something ominous in my voice, because she was suddenly conciliatory. "Well, dear— You really ought to plaster up that hole before the weather turns, so that he has a warm place for tonight."

I gazed at her for what must have been an unnaturally long time. Then I rose and started from the kitchen. When I reached the door, I turned again and faced her. "I hardly recognize you, Alice. You're like a damned brood hen."

She turned an astonished glance on me.

"You know," I went on. "It's just possible I'm even fonder of him than you are. But I am disappointed that he hasn't at least gone over to see Washburn. I'm not saying Washburn's is the right place for him. I only intended that he stay there a little while until he got on his feet."

She was suddenly quite tender. "He'll get on his feet, Albert. Don't worry. When the right job comes, just watch him snatch it."

I sighed. "I'm sure you're right."

"Of course I am, dear. You'll see. Now just go and patch up that hole down there, while I fix some nice hot soup for tonight's supper. Richard loves split pea."

The rest of the afternoon was spent out of doors, laboring over the chink in the crawl. It was located along the northern exposure of the house, showing clearly through the cement foundation. Here the wind whistled sharply around and rattled the gutters just below the porch roof.

I spent several minutes inspecting the damage. It was a wide fissure with innumerable tiny breaks along its main line, the sort of thing caused by excessive dampness and improperly mixed cement.

I set to work at once mixing cement in a large basin. Not long after, I was applying it with a trowel. I had never cemented before, and of course the workmanship was clumsy. Several times I had to undo what I'd done, chipping away with a mattock at the cement, which hardened quickly in that freezing weather.

All the while I labored there that afternoon, hunched over with the wind whipping at my back, I brooded over Richard's failure to follow up on my suggestion to see Washburn. I had a good sulk for a while and made a few decisions about firmness that I immediately abandoned. Soon I reasoned that although he hadn't bothered to see Washburn, he must undoubtedly be seeing other people about a job and would continue to do so. And I had to admit, there was some truth to what Alice said. As much as I enjoyed Washburn, I knew my fondness for the man amounted to no more than a quaint eccentricity. To have to spend day after day as an employee of Ezra Washburn would be a form of cruel and unnatural punishment. And the work was not terribly challenging or rewarding, either. Richard would have been unhappy at it, and he had the good sense, even if I didn't, to foresee that.

Finally, along about dusk, the chink was filled to my satisfaction, and I went back into the house assuaged by my thoughts.

Darkness came swiftly in that season. One moment you'd be in daylight, and the next moment you'd turn around and darkness had fallen.

When I entered the house I found the parlor lights lit, the Christmas tree aglow, and a cheery fire crackling on the hearth. My back ached from having worked stooped over all afternoon, and my hands and feet were numb from the cold. But there was the savory smell of Alice's pea soup, thick and blistering hot in a pot on the stove. And though I was cold and weary and unsure of how I felt about anything, I was at least pleased with my day's work.

Chapter Six

ONE morning just before Christmas I came down for breakfast and found Alice waiting for me at the bottom of the stairs. "Albert— Come quickly."

I followed her into the kitchen. "What is it?"

"Albert—"

"Yes."

She looked at me. "Can't you smell it?"

"Smell what?" I sniffed, but aside from a variety of cooking odors, I could smell nothing unusual.

"Come over here." She was standing at a corner of the kitchen at a point farthest from the stove. "Smell it now." There was an urgency in her voice.

I pointed my nose upwards and sniffed around in several directions.

"I smell cocoa and bacon."

"Oh, Albert."

"I'm sorry, but that's—" and then it hit me full in the face. She must've seen my expression change.

"It's awful, isn't it?"

"Horrible," I sniffed again. "It's only over here. You can't smell it over by the stove."

"What do you suppose it is?"

I shrugged but offered no answer.

"Smells like a public toilet," she went on. "You think a pipe's burst?"

"Perfectly possible in this kind of weather."

I walked over to the sink and gave the spigots a full twist. The water drained freely. Next I went to the little powder room right off the kitchen and flushed the toilet. There was no back-up. I walked slowly back to Alice.

"Well, it's not the pipes of the septic tank, thank heavens."

She was staring down at the floor, pawing it with her feet. "It's right here."

"What?"

"Right under us."

We looked down at the wide bare planks of the kitchen floor. They were a varnished, wormy chestnut, nailed down with studs and set in with widish spaces between them. It was the original floor and extremely handsome. Just below it, of course, was the crawl.

"Oh, it's just that cat smell down there," I said.

"No. It's not that. I know that smell. This is different—it's awful," she went on. "Isn't it?"

By then I'd put the whole thing together in my mind. I knew exactly what the source of the odor was, but I was determined to minimize it to Alice.

"It's really not too bad."

"Not too bad?" There was a look of disbelief in her face. "It's vile. It's unholy. And it's coming from the crawl, isn't it?"

"Yes, I think so."

Suddenly a look of alarm crossed her face. "You think he's all right?"

"I'm sure he is. I heard him go out this morning."

"Well, if it's a pipe, we have to get a plumber."

"A plumber? Two days before Christmas? You must be joking."

"Well, someone's got to come, Albert. We can't live like this. And I won't permit him to stay down there in that—"

"I'll go down and have a look," I said. I wanted to get her off the subject of plumbers.

"When?"

"After I've had some breakfast."

Her eyes widened and she put her hands on her hips. "You're not really going to eat breakfast with that wafting around you?"

She had a point there. I looked at the area of the kitchen over which the smell had settled like a haze.

"Here," I said, yanking her by the hand. "Let's get out of this. We'll have breakfast in the library."

Later I went down to the basement. The stench was overpowering. I had to cover my nose with a handkerchief and grope my way in. It was fairly obvious that Richard was using part of the crawl as a latrine. Now that I'd sealed up the chink in the crawl, whatever air had ventilated the place before was cut off. The stench in several days' time had simply built up to the point where it was an evil, choking vapor that had swelled and backed out of the crawl until it had filled the whole basement.

There was a dehumidifier down there that we used in the hot, humid months in order to keep the cellar cool and dry. It was also very effective in removing the kind of dank musky odors that are so common to cellars. I didn't know how it would stack up against human excrement, but gasping for breath in that foulness, I tugged the machine out of the corner, plugged it in and flicked it on. When I'd done that and it had been running for a few moments, I dragged it over and started to set it directly in front of the crawl entrance when suddenly a voice boomed out at me from the black square. "What do you want?"

I nearly toppled backwards with fright. It was Richard, of course, but I'd assumed he was out. When I regained my composure, I tried to speak.

"Richard?"

"Yes—"

Gaping at the square speechlessly, I could sense him staring out at me from its other side.

"Didn't you go out this morning? I was sure I heard the door slam."

"I came back. I was cold."

"Why didn't you come and ask me for a heavy coat? I have an extra one upstairs."

"Why'd you come down? What do you want here?" The tone of his voice was nasty. He seemed to be snarling at me. "Are you spying on me?"

"Spying?" I nearly choked on the word. "Spying?"

"What's that thing for?" he demanded.

"What thing?"

"That machine."

I looked at the dehumidifier, which was purring away. "It's a dehumidifier," I blustered. "Mrs. Graves and I—"

"What's it for?"

I felt myself quaking, but I was determined to say what was on my mind. "Well, frankly, Richard, there's this awful smell. I've smelled it down here in the crawl before, and now it's spread up to the kitchen. Mrs. Graves and I—"

There was a full pause while I groped for more words. It was horribly embarrassing. But then he spoke—this time, less defiantly.

"I haven't been able to get out as much as I'd like. The weather—"

"I fully understand, but still there are simple rules of sanitation. What you're doing is extremely dangerous. Not only to you, but to us as well. There's no reason why you shouldn't use the facilities upstairs."

"I don't like to bother anyone."

"I assure you it's no bother. The kind of thing we've had up there this morning is much more of a bother. If you feel awkward about coming up while we're around, why don't you wait till we go off to sleep?"

I waited, watching the square hopefully. There was no answer, and so I spoke again. "That would make Mrs. Graves and me most happy. In the meantime, I'm just going to set this dehumidifier right over here at the entrance to the crawl. I'm sure it will go a long way to improve the situation."

I put the machine directly in front of the square and turned it on to its full power without any further protest from Richard. Then, when I had done that, I was left with nothing else to do. I cast around desperately for something else to say. "Are you feeling all right?"

"Fine."

"Is it any warmer in there now that the chink is caulked?"

"It's fine."

Suddenly a picture of Washburn flashed across my mind,

and before I could stop myself I asked, "Had any luck finding a job?" I regretted it the moment it was out.

"I haven't been out much lately. It's been cold."

"Yes, it has." I heard myself agreeing with him eagerly. Then I was tempted to ask him if he'd been over to see Washburn. I was curious to see what he'd say. But I refrained from that ugly instinct. Instead, I barged off on a tack that even surprised me.

"Richard," I said most gently, "Christmas Eve is tomorrow night. I was just thinking how nice it would be if you'd come up and join us for Christmas supper."

I stared at the square, hopefully.

"Richard?"

"Yes."

"Did you hear me?"

"Yes."

"It'll be very casual," I went on sensing an advantage. "Just the three of us. And I know if you'll come, Mrs. Graves will make something very special."

Still I waited. "We've a pretty tree," I went on. "And some presents. Come. It's really high time you left this hole, if only for a short while." I laughed nervously. "After all, you've been living down here for several weeks now, and we haven't set eyes on you since the last time you came to check our furnace." I laughed again. "Will you come?"

More silence.

"It would make Mrs. Graves and me very happy—" I waited. "Will you, Richard?"

"I can't."

"Why?" I asked, my heart sinking.

"I got nothin' to wear."

His reply was so simply and honestly answered, and as a problem so solvable, that I laughed with relief.

"Don't worry about that. I'll take care of that." I clapped my hands together. "Well, then, it's all settled. You're coming."

There was silence, which I took as a silence of affirmation. "Well, then—" I went on. "I'll be here for you tomorrow night. Say about seven-thirty."

I turned and started for the stairs. Then I turned and marched back to the square. "Richard," I stood there addressing the void. "You don't know how happy this is going to make Mrs. Graves. Thank you, Richard. Thank you."

I hadn't meant to be so grateful. I had no intention, when I went down there, of asking him to dinner. I had meant to simply go down and take care of the delicate business of the smell. And this I did, stating our position and a solution to the problem, all rather tactfully, I thought. But I hadn't meant to leave there like an Oriental—backing out rearwards, with much bowing and wringing of the hands. But I was truly grateful, because all the while I'd been so certain he'd decline.

There was too, now, the business about the job. It was clear that he had not been using the days as I thought, to actively seek employment. Instead, he'd resorted to the subterfuge of slamming the cellar door early in the morning to make it sound as if he'd gone out. Then he'd slip noiselessly back into the crawl and remain there all day hidden from the world.

Had I thought some more about it, I would've been terribly bothered—more than bothered—alarmed. But as it was, I'd already forgotten about it in the midst of all the excitement about his coming for dinner.

By the time I got upstairs where Alice was waiting, I was almost bursting with a new magnanimity for Richard.

Alice and I went to the haberdashers in town that afternoon. We were like doting parents buying a graduation suit for our son. I suppose to the poor clerk—a Mr. Winslow—we must have appeared to be lunatics. First of all, we arrived without the person for whom the suit was being purchased, and then, with wildly different notions of what Richard ought to be dressed in for the occasion.

But Mr. Winslow was a plucky little spirit, not easily daunted. "May I ask," said Mr. Winslow, "on what sort of occasion the suit will be worn?"

"Does that matter?" I asked.

Mr. Winslow smiled patiently. "It would certainly give me a better idea of what we're looking for."

"It's for a small dinner party," said Alice somewhat ambiguously.

"Ah," said Mr. Winslow, lighting up like a billboard. "That's a big help already."

He pulled out racks of suits during the course of the afternoon while Alice and I squabbled back and forth over patterns and sizes. We could give him no tangible guidance as to size. Each time he brought us a new selection, he'd say, "Now, I think this might be just the thing," and then smile cheerily. After we'd veto it for one reason or another, he'd scurry back to the racks just as bravely as ever.

After about an hour of this sort of punishment, beads of sweat began to glisten above his upper lip. "This would be so much easier," he said puffing a little, "if you could just send the boy in to see me." His voice was a little plaintive.

"That's out of the question," said Alice.

Mr. Winslow smothered a look of mild exasperation with his brave little smile. "May I ask for whom you're buying the suit?"

"For our son," said Alice.

"For a friend," I said, at precisely the same moment, our voices colliding.

Mr. Winslow looked at us a little warily.

After about an hour and a half or so of this banter, we made our selection. It was a simple, dark navy suit. To that we added new shirt, tie, several sets of underwear, socks and shoes.

Mr. Winslow stuck bravely with us right to the end. I'm certain by the time we walked out of there he'd come to think of us as harmless lunatics who simply wanted humoring. He promised, however, to have the alterations done on the suit by the following morning.

"You see," he said smiling just a trifle oddly at us, "it's a little difficult altering for somebody who's not around."

"I'm sure you'll do very well, Mr. Winslow," said Alice as we walked out the door. "We have great faith in you."

Once out in the street, Alice wanted to go to the butcher shop.

"I thought you'd already bought a turkey," I said.

"I did. But turkey's so dreary. I want to do something more festive."

"What about goose? Nothing's more Christmasy than goose. Right out of Dickens."

She weighed the idea for a moment. "That's closer to it. But still—" She paused for effect. "What about a roast pig?"

I thought uneasily, for a moment, about the cost of Richard's wardrobe. Add to that the cost of a fair-sized roasting pig with all the fixings and a good bottle of port to boot. But by that time we were in front of the butcher shop, and suddenly I had a vision of the thing stuffed with chestnuts and basil dressing, the skin browned to a succulent crisp, a wreath of roast baby new potatoes all around it, and the apple stuck in its mouth—the whole gorgeous spectacle emerging from the kitchen on a sizzling platter.

"That's perfect, Alice." I was beaming as we marched in.

The butcher looked at us queerly when we'd placed our orders. "I ain't had an order for one of them things in fifteen years," he said. "What about a nice turkey?"

"We don't want turkey," I said. "We want a pig."

"Sorry, I can't help you, pal."

"Do you know where we might get one?" Alice asked, crestfallen.

"Swertfergers," the butcher suggested.

"Swertfergers?" I replied.

"It's a pork farm. 'Bout twenty miles from here."

He gave us directions and we were off the next moment.

It was nine o'clock and dismal and cold when we drove up to our house with the corpse of a dressed pig jammed into the trunk of the car, its snout oozing blood into the newspapers in which it had been bundled.

We were so exhausted from driving forty miles over narrow, icy roads that we could barely eat any supper that night. Still we couldn't rest. The pig needed to be seasoned, the dressing had to be made, several pounds of chestnuts awaited hulling, potatoes wanted peeling, and Alice had to boil several pumpkins for the pie.

It was well past midnight when we climbed wearily up the steps and went to bed.

The following morning I was back on the road early, shortly before nine. The night had been dismal and drizzling, and so I had the same awful business with slick roads I'd had the day before.

Mr. Winslow met me at the door. He appeared to be ecstatic. "I think you're going to be very pleased," he said over and over again, a little breathless as he bustled into the back and vanished behind an arras drawn across an archway.

When he emerged again, he was carrying the suit in both arms as if a body were already in it. He tripped across the floor toward me still saying, "I think you're going to be very pleased." When he finally presented the suit, it was with a flourish.

I wasn't very pleased, but I made every effort to appear so. Such was my gratitude to the man for the enormous efforts he made in our behalf. The mere fact that he completed the alterations a day before Christmas was little short of a miracle.

But if I wasn't very pleased, I was at least moderately satisfied, and Richard had finally a respectable suit of clothes with which he could present himself to prospective employers, as well as come to Christmas supper that night. You see—my motives went a little further than mere philanthropy.

When I left Mr. Winslow's, I had under my arm a large rectangular box swaddled in cheerful red and green paper, with holly sprays splashed all over it. Winslow held the door open as I went out into the blustery noon.

He was smiling and looking very satisfied. "Merry Christmas, Mr. Graves. I do hope your son enjoys the suit."

At first I didn't understand him. Then I did. I smiled and said, "I'm sure he will. Merry Christmas, Mr. Winslow."

I walked down the street, whistling, with the box under my arm and nodding to perfect strangers. Before I left town I purchased the best bottle of port I could find.

I had left Alice at home in her kitchen. When I returned there I found her in a fever of activity, charging back and forth between her oven and her knitting. The good George III silver was out and scattered over a table where she'd been polishing it. She wore a bandanna around her neck, and there were beads of sweat on her forehead.

I kicked the slush off my boots onto the outside mat and stepped into the cozy warmth of the kitchen. There was something already festive about it—the spicy smells, the half-opened packages, the bright gay wrappings of things, the platters all waiting to enter the oven, the look of hectic, purposeful activity.

The moment I entered, Alice looked up. Her eye traveled immediately downwards to the box I carried. Then she gave me an anxious glance.

"Is it all right?"

"I think it's fine. Not Savile Row, but very serviceable."

"Oh?"

The sound of that "Oh?" was enough to cast us both into despair.

"It'll be all right," I said.

She looked at me skeptically. "Go look at the sweater. I fixed the antlers."

"Where is it?"

"Out in the living room." She looked at the gift box again. "What pretty wrapping paper that is."

"Do you want to see the suit?"

"Do you think I ought to?"

I knew wild horses couldn't keep her from it now. "You helped pick it out."

"It was really your choice, dear."

"I couldn't have made it without you."

We looked at each other fatuously. Then a look of alarm crossed her face. "Did he give you the same suit?"

"Of course he did."

"Sometimes they get them mixed up. Particularly this time of the year with the last-minute rush on."

"Well, he gave me the right suit."

"Then I don't have to see it. Anyway, I don't want the wrappings ruined."

I stared around the kitchen. It appeared a whirlwind had been through it. I stood there sniffing the air. "Something smells delicious."

"Pumpkin pie and plum pudding."

"Have you put the pig in yet?"

"It's too early. About two o'clock." She opened a closet door, then came back and flipped a towel at me. "Can you help with the silver?"

She flew past before I could answer, and I was left there watching her with the towel drooping in my hand. She was traveling in the direction of the freezer.

"Alice," I said very softly. She didn't hear me. So I said it again, this time more forcefully, "Alice."

"Yes, dear."

"Alice."

"Yes, dear. I can hear you. I have to make the hard sauce." She dashed past me en route to a cupboard.

"Alice. Will you stop for a moment?"

Something in my voice brought her up. She stopped in her tracks and looked at me.

I started walking toward her. "Alice," I said, "are you happy?"

She looked at me for several moments. There was a blank expression on her face as though she hadn't heard my question. Then suddenly her face flushed and she was smiling. "Can't you tell?"

"Yes," I said, just as I reached her. When I caught hold of her, her eyes were beaming. Then I kissed her. Afterwards, she stood staring blankly up at me. "Maybe I'd better see the suit," she said.

The rest of the day was spent polishing silver and crystal, stuffing the pig, whipping cream, arranging presents under the tree, and doing the thousand and one totally unexpected chores that pop up during the preparation of such a feast.

At about five that afternoon we stood before our dinner table. It was a thing of fragile elegance. On a table cloth of exquisitely wrought Battenberg lace was displayed the very best we had to offer—our fine old George III silver, our Rosenthal, our Waterford crystal goblets, our finest damask napkins. They were beloved things—heirlooms—things we had carefully collected over the years, gathered up in our travels, things purchased at great personal sacrifice, when we didn't have the money for such luxuries.

Above the table hung a 19th-century pewter gasolier Alice and I had found on a trip to England. Its lights cast a warm orange glow over the table; its reflections, trapped in the prisms of the crystal goblets and the silver, transformed the whole thing into something shimmering and magical.

At the head of the room, the Christmas tree, spangled with tinsel, was already glowing with its multitude of colored lights. Our few presents to each other and to Richard were already placed beneath it.

Alice looked at me a little nervously. "What time is it?"

"A quarter past five."

"Do you think you should go down now?"

"Go down?" I asked.

"To the cellar. To give him the suit."

"Oh, my God—I'd almost forgotten." I started for my packages, which were under the tree. "I told him I'd come for him at seven-fifteen."

"But he needs some time to get washed and dressed."

"Of course he does. I hadn't thought of it." I started to gather the boxes from under the tree. There were the shirts and shoes and other sundries I had brought back with me the day before. They were already gift-wrapped. "Do you think he's down there now?" I stood there holding the boxes, utterly confused.

"I haven't heard a sound all day."

"I hope he hasn't forgotten."

"Of course he hasn't forgotten." Alice said, immediately dismissing the possibility.

"I don't think so, either."

"Just take the packages down, dear. If he's there, give them to him. If not, just leave them someplace where he'll find them."

I gathered the boxes and bags and beribboned packages, while we laughed conspiratorially.

I had a giddy feeling as I descended the stairs to the cellar. I was also very nervous. It was the sort of thing I used to feel as a youth when I'd march jauntily up the walk of some young lady's house with a nosegay of posies. It was all so foolish and funny and sad.

With all the packages trembling and rattling in my hands, I slowly crossed the floor to the black square like a votary of some ancient cult bringing offerings to an altar.

A thousand random thoughts came into my head. Was he there now, and if he was, how should I present my gifts? I didn't want to present them in the way of a lord presenting gifts to his chattel. Nor, as I mentioned before, did I care particularly to be there as a votary. I wanted simply to give the gifts in the spirit of the season and for the pure Christian joy of giving.

I stopped before the square, holding all my packages and feeling a little foolish. My two hands were so completely occupied that I hadn't been able to flick on the lights at the bottom of the cellar stairs. So I stood in the gloom and shadows of five o'clock in the afternoon peering into the pitchy darkness of the square.

As always, I waited for some sound acknowledging my presence. None came. I decided to speak:

"Richard?" My voice was high and a little tremulous. "Richard? Are you there?"

Up above me, I could hear Alice's busy, purposeful steps treading between kitchen and dining room. But no sound came from the crawl.

"Do you know what day this is?" I called into empty

space, making an attempt at cheerfulness. "It's Christmas, and—you know what that means."

I waited hopefully. Nothing came. Perhaps, I thought, he's gone out. I suddenly felt idiotic standing there with all my packages—like a man who shows up on the wrong day for a wedding. Perhaps, I thought, he's forgotten; and if he hasn't forgotten, he'll refuse to come. And then it suddenly occurred to me with a shudder of horror, thinking of all the preparations that had gone on upstairs —it occurred to me that he never actually said yes to my invitation. He had in fact answered it with silence, and I had interpreted that silence as an affirmative. Suddenly I felt a kind of panic. "Richard, if you're there, please don't keep me standing here like—" My voice roared back at me through the hollow crawl. It makes me sick to think about it now. Then, once again the silence settled down all around me like dusk filtering through the twilight.

Well, I reasoned, it was entirely possible he'd gone out to do something, some errand, some duty. Possibly he'd even gone to see a prospective employer. All this I tried to tell myself while my heart was sinking. All I could do was what Alice suggested—leave the packages someplace where he could find them.

I started for the crawl, and just as I did, a rock scuffled across the earth from somewhere inside the square. Then someone or something that had been crouching over the entrance to the crawl fell back deeper into it. I heard breathing—the sound of air being gulped, as if someone had been holding their breath under water for a long time.

"Richard? Is that you?"

I was standing right at the mouth of the crawl now, talking into it. The dehumidifier, which had been running twenty-four hours a day for the past several days, had done its job well. There was barely the trace of an odor. Still, when you stood face to face with that square you were aware of something vaguely unpleasant.

"Richard? I know you're there. Why won't you speak to me? I can hear you breathing." I laughed, making a joke of it. "You spoke to me the other day. What have I done to deserve this silence?"

Still no answer.

"Well, tonight's the night," I went on. "I told you I'd be by at seven-thirty to take you up to supper. It's five-thirty now, and I'll be by for you in two hours. Mrs. Graves has gone to a great deal of trouble. I guarantee you won't be disappointed."

I was suddenly aware of all the packages in my arms. "You said you had no clothes? Well, that's all taken care of now." The sound of my voice boomed back at me through the crawl.

I put the packages down on the lower frame of the square and stacked them there neatly. "You'll find a suit and several other things. There are some toiletries in there, too. I imagine you'll want to wash up a bit before you put on your new clothes." I was afraid that might have sounded rude. Nevertheless, I rushed right on. "As soon as I leave here now, Mrs. Graves and I will go directly upstairs and get ready for supper. The downstairs bath is all yours." I peered into the darkness, listening to him breathe. It was a curiously animal-like sound. "Do you still want me to come down and get you at seven-thirty? Or perhaps you'd prefer to come up by yourself?"

My heart sinking, I waited for some response. None came.

"Very well, then. Shall we say you come up at your convenience." I started to turn, then turned back. "I want you to know, Mrs. Graves worked very hard on this Christmas dinner. Seven-thirty is a good time for her. You see, we'd like to finish in time to clean up and go to midnight services. You won't disappoint us, will you?" I suspect by that time I was pleading. There were no answers, no sounds, nothing. When I turned and crossed the basement and mounted the cellar stairs, I was sick to my heart.

I was now absolutely certain he had no intention of coming. Just as the evening before I'd interpreted his silence as an affirmation, I now interpreted that same silence as rejection, an icy rebuff. The whole thing had been a misunderstanding. And not on his part, but on mine. What a fool I'd been. I knew all along, deep down, that he'd never come. He never said he'd come. I merely read it into his silence because it suited me.

When I got back upstairs, I could barely face Alice. Before all this, we had planned a simple, modest supper for the two of us—a roast of some sort and the requisite bottle of good, but not superlative, wine. Now on the basis of some communication I imagined I'd had with Richard Atlee several nights before, we'd purchased about a hundred and fifty dollars' worth of men's clothing and prepared a dinner, something in the style and magnitude approaching a Roman banquet.

When I came up, I went directly to the kitchen. Alice was there, on a chair, wrestling a large roasting pan down from a cabinet. She looked up, her face flushed from exertion and the heat of the kitchen.

"What's wrong, Albert?" she asked, but she didn't have to. She could see it all in my face. She pushed a wisp of hair out of her eyes. "He's not coming, is he?"

"Let's go upstairs," I said very softly. "I'll tell you there."

I took her arm and led her up the steps. She permitted herself to be guided like a child.

"It's all my fault," I said when we'd got upstairs and closed the door. "I simply assumed—"

"But why? Why? Did he give you any reason?"

"He wouldn't even speak to me."

That appeared to confuse her. I went on trying to clarify. But things only got murkier. "The truth of it is, I don't know if he's coming or he isn't."

"What do you mean, you don't know?"

"Just that." I threw my hands up in despair. "He wouldn't talk to me or say one way or another. I know it sounds incredible. I'm trying to think what I did between yesterday and today that offended him."

"Is he there?"

"Of course he's there."

"How do you know, if he didn't talk to you?"

"I could hear him breathing, moving around." I was suddenly furious. "What the devil are we doing with this boy in our basement, anyway? How did we get into this thing?"

She sat down on the bed, her shoulders slumping wearily. "Well, I'm just sick to my heart."

"I'm sorry, Alice. It's all my fault. When I invited him and he said nothing, I simply assumed that by his silence he meant yes. Don't ask me why." I put my hand on her shoulder and she pressed it there with her own. "I'm sorry."

"It's not your fault, dear, any more than it is mine. We both wanted this thing very badly. So we stretched facts a bit."

I sat down on the bed next to her and took her hand, and we were silent together.

After a few moments I spoke: "I did exactly as you suggested. I left the packages where he could get at them easily. Then I restated the invitation to him. I offered him the downstairs bathroom to clean up in if he wanted it."

"Well, then, we've done all we can."

"What shall we do now?" I said.

"Go ahead with our plans just as if nothing had happened." She threw her chin out jauntily. "We'll have our pig and our port and our plum pudding and all the rest. Then we'll go off to services. And when we come back, we'll open our presents and have a glass of mulled cider and go to bed."

"Just the two of us," I said, a little forlornly.

"Just the two of us, dear. Just as it's always been." She said it with so much pluck and good spirits that it made me feel more miserable than ever. I put my arm around her shoulder and hugged her to me.

"Yes, Alice. Just as it's always been."

We bathed and dressed without a word. In anticipation of our guest we'd both planned our wardrobes the night before. I was to wear a rather formal blue serge I'd usually reserved for such occasions of state as marriages, funerals, and the like. Acquired from a Savile Row tailor on a business trip to London, it was easily the best I had.

Alice had a semi-formal gown of fine old peau de soie, I'd bought it for her in Paris only a few years before in a rather fashionable salon for the occasion of our twenty-fifth anniversary. It was by far her favorite.

Now by tacit agreement we were determined, in spite of Richard Atlee, to wear the wardrobes we had planned.

We bathed, dressed, combed and primped, all the while trying to affect an air of nonchalance. But I could tell, as undoubtedly she could, that our hearts were not in it, and that more than anything, we were both listening, hoping against hope for some encouraging sound from below—a door closing, a toilet flushing, the flow of water from a tap, anything. But the silence from below was pitiless.

We were dressed and ready to go down long before the appointed time. But we sat upstairs in the bedroom and waited, hoping—I suppose—for some miracle. Also we had the notion that if by some freakish chance he'd decided to come, and was on his way up just as we were starting down, our too sudden appearance might scare him off.

By six forty-five we could contain ourselves no longer. So together—Alice in flowing peau de soie, wooshing about as she moved, me in stiff blue serge and feeling a trifle ridiculous and forlorn, the smell of moth balls wafting all around us—we started arm in arm down the steps. Just for a moment, one silly, giddy second, while descending, a picture of Alice and me, three decades younger, on a spring Sunday, being wed in the living room of her father's house, flashed before my eyes.

At the bottom of the stair we looked around timorously like strangers arriving at a party too early and fighting the impulse to bolt. I started a fire on the hearth and we sat quietly together on a small love seat before it sipping cream sherry. We made a few miserable little attempts at conversation, at being cheery and casual.

I think the painful faculty of recollection was upon Alice, too, that evening. She kept harking back over the years. We chatted with a lot of bogus nostalgia about

Christmases past and how we spent them. When I was a businessman I always made a point of going on buying trips around Christmas time and taking Alice with me. There'd been Christmases we'd had together in Paris, Zurich, Mexico City, Tokyo, Bombay, Rio de Janeiro, the Bahamas, Nantucket, New York. In the rosy hues of retrospection we attributed to those times wondrous, magical qualities they never really possessed.

Now sitting there that night with the snow falling silently outside we knew in our hearts that all of those past Christmases were as fake and hollow and rotten as the one we were about to celebrate. After a while we abandoned all efforts at lively chatter. Instead, we sat listening to the fire hiss and crackle and sipped our sherry and gave ourselves up to despondency.

There was still no sign of Richard Atlee at seven-thirty and so, the moment the minute hand of the grandfather clock brushed the six, we rose as if by prearranged signal. Alice took my arm, and with all the solemnity and grandeur of a wedding march, together we strode through the parlor and the library to the dining room, where we silently took our places at table.

I'll always remember the first anguished moments of that Christmas supper. I can still hear, over the years, the lonely tinkle of Alice's spoon striking lightly on her melon plate. It's one of the saddest sounds I think I've ever heard. Seeing her in lace seated before all the resplendent finery of that table, I was afraid to look across at her, for fear that if for one moment our eyes met, we would cry. Who would ever have thought we would have taken such a wretched little incident so much to heart?

It wasn't until we had finished our melon and started the soup that we heard the first footstep—and even then we didn't believe what we'd heard. We must have heard it at the same moment, because just as I looked up, Alice did, too. But as I say, we both doubted it. I suppose we were skeptical at that point; or possibly, like the poor, superstitious idiots we are, we hoped that by denying the reality of the footsteps, we could make them come true.

In the next moment another step creaked quite distinctly on the cellar stair. And then another. Alice's face flushed with sudden color. "He's come." It was half whisper, half cry; her eyes beamed. "He's come. I knew he'd come. I knew it."

I recall closing my eyes very tight and clenching my fists, torn somewhere between intense anger and relief, then murmuring inwardly a few words of thanks to Richard Atlee.

At the top of the stairs the footsteps paused and hovered on the other side of the library door. I sat there rigid like something struck in marble, my soup spoon frozen midway between the steaming bowl and my lip. Alice was looking at me and smiling. There was a question in her eyes.

I heard the doorknob turn. Then the hinges of the library door squealed open. Footsteps whispered across the floor. Just outside the dining room there was a moment of total suspension when we no longer heard him. Time seemed to stop. Nothing happened. Our hearts sank. Then he was there.

I have no accurate recollection of that moment or of my first impression of Richard. All I recall is that he stood there in the doorway. Alice and I didn't look up at him. Instead we continued to stare into each other's eyes— Alice still smiling that enigmatic smile, I with my soup spoon still poised in midair.

It was only after he took his place and started his melon that I looked at him and realized that the person I was looking at I'd never seen before. It wasn't the Richard Atlee I recalled from previous visits—that neatly trimmed and pale young man, with the shy, curiously direct eyes and the endearing ungainliness. Then, he wore white frayed shirts and clumsily made ties, his suit cheap and rumpled. Yet, the total impression he gave at that time was conventional. To see him you might have thought he was a bank teller or an insurance salesman.

I say that the person I found sitting beside me was not Richard Atlee because that person was truly unrecognizable to me as the person who had come to service my furnace and had sat at my dinner table. It was Richard Atlee, of course, but the figure seated at my table now bore scarcely any resemblance to that somewhat vague and unremarkable figure. There were still a few vestiges of that person, some lingering shadows of a former presence, but that presence was now almost wholly erased and transformed into a new presence, as far apart from the former as the moth is to the caterpillar when that creature sheds its skin and steps from one stage of existence into the next. The only thing I recognized about him now was the suit and other items of clothing I'd purchased for him several days earlier at Winslow's haberdashery. The rest was all new and strange to me.

Alice and I had both been wrong. The suit was far too small. The person wearing the suit we bought was well over six feet. The suit, at best, could accommodate a person of about five feet ten inches. I've often thought since that time that it was curious that Alice and I recalled a smaller person. We are both fairly accurate and concise people. Yet in this instance we appeared to have shot quite wide of the mark—Alice considerably wider than myself. Consequently, the sleeves and trousers were both too short. The suit had an outgrown look about it as if it had been handed down by an elder brother. But there was nothing comical or even faintly pathetic about the suit or the appearance of the person in it. The single most forceful impression that emerged from all of it was that of dignity, and by that I don't mean for a moment to suggest grandness or stuffiness. I mean *dignity*. Pure inherent grace; the eloquence of simple, unpremeditated gestures; a vast composure. When you looked into his eyes there was no longer a trace of boyish reticence. He no longer kept his eyes down and riveted to his plate. Instead, his eyes were direct, falling very gently upon us—not at all defiant, but rather accepting and beautifully serene.

And yet, I'm sure, there are many who would have looked at him and felt revulsion. There was, of course, the filth. I don't mean to deny it for a moment. It was everywhere to be seen—caked on his hands, encrusted beneath the nails. The hair, which I'd recalled as being rather closely cropped, had now grown out. It spread outwards around his head like a garland and cascaded down his shoulders. The face, once pink and clean-shaven, was now covered with a thick, luxuriant, reddish beard, several shades lighter than the color of his hair. He'd made no attempt to comb his hair or trim the beard. Yet, there was nothing wild or unkempt about him; he appeared as if he had looked precisely that way for centuries. And once seeing him like that, it would've been impossible to imagine him any other way. The person we recalled or thought we recalled was now completely obliterated by this figure. That other figure was in most respects unremarkable. This person, this new Richard Atlee, looked like something out of the Bible. A huge, awesome, prophetic, Old Testament-looking creature—an Isaiah or a Jeremiah. Someone who'd wandered in the wilderness many years, and existed on grubs and berries. Someone who'd lived with himself and within himself and had been conversant only with wild creatures and God.

When he sat down at our table, we didn't speak. He took his place there just as if he'd been doing precisely that for many years. Automatic it was, and natural, like a muscle reflex. Nor was there any conversation when Alice served the dinner. And that curiously enough didn't seem strange, either, but completely natural. It was as if conversation was superfluous. All vain and empty chatter.

But the most curious thing of all was Alice and I. After the initial surprise of seeing him so transformed, we two hopelessly and irretrievably conventional folk simply settled down and accepted this extraordinary stranger without a word of comment. We felt neither awkwardness nor embarrassment nor fear. We felt instead gratitude that he was with us at our table on Christmas Eve.

I carved the pig and we ate quietly—the three of us at our small table, with the fire reflecting in the goblets of port and the snow outside falling silently all around us. There was no strain, such as the kind one ordinarily feels when a stranger eats at your table. But there were no strangers at the table that night. We were a unity. All together and one. I felt an immense gratitude.

There's still one further point about that dinner I want

to make. On the two former occasions that Richard ate at our table, not only did he ravage his food, but the place around his setting and his chair was littered with food. Now, this other person who sat at our table ate with unhurried decorum. He ate, too, as if he hardly tasted the succulent strips of pig and the savory plum pudding. Food to him seemed to be the most unimportant thing, an inconvenience you had to somehow get around, and he ate it with a mild and almost sweet distraction.

The first words uttered during that meal came at its conclusion. Alice turned to our guest and said, "We're going to midnight services now. Would you like to join us?"

He dabbed at his mouth with a napkin and rose slowly. So did we.

We sang "Puer Nobis Nascitur" that night with the organ resounding in our stomachs. The voices of the congregation rose above the cold bare hall, upwards into the clerestory, and hung there, then tumbled downwards over the chilly pews.

"Unto Us a Son Is Born" wafting outwards, out through the doors, across the snowy landscapes, through the forests hushed in the iron silences of winter. How sweet those words seemed that night:

> The king of all creation—
> Came he to a world forlorn—

Our voices mixed and were swallowed up in the voices of the congregation. Richard stood between Alice and me, ungainly and placid, in a suit too new and too small.

All about us was a quiet stir of excitement. His entrance into church that night had caused something of a sensation. People whispered and gaped. They'd never seen anything quite like him. You could sense the smug amusement all around you. It was thick enough to cut.

At first Richard didn't sing. He stood between us, and we moved closer to him, so that all our shoulders finally touched and locked, forming a tight, impregnable unity. It was a purely protective movement on our part. He

sensed it and his reaction was to help. Halfway through
the hymn he suddenly began to sing loudly and with a
voice that had an oddly unpleasant quality—rather like a
harsh croaking—

> Cradled in a stall was he
> With sleeping cows and asses—

The couple standing in front of him, two dour, shriv-
eled souls, turned to gape. It made Alice and me sing all
the harder. Richard was oblivious, lost in the hymn.

> Now may Mary's son who came
> So long ago to love us
> Lead us all with hearts aflame
> Unto the joys above us.

I felt curiously pleased with myself that night. I know
Alice did, too—but we didn't talk about it. Afterwards,
at the conclusion of services, as we made our way out, I
noted that people with whom we used to chat freely now
seemed to hold back—to be strained and unnatural in
their greetings.

On the way out, we waited on line to say good-night to
the pastor and wish him a merry Christmas. Just behind
us were Emil Birge, the town sheriff, and his wife. Birge
was a large, beefy man with a red face, who had a way
of whistling when he breathed. Each of his cheeks was
raked with a spray of fine, purple capillaries. Mrs. Birge,
a small birdlike creature, hovered just behind him. Her
mouth appeared to have sunk into her face, and when
she smiled at you, thin, rubbery lips shrank back over
poorly made dentures. She did a good deal of church
work and on several occasions petitioned for old clothing
to be distributed to worthy charities. Alice sent her several
boxes and not infrequently she would see her own dresses
and coats appear on Mrs. Birge. To the best of my
knowledge, Mrs. Birge had never once thanked Alice or
even acknowledged receipt of the boxes.

Once I went up to the Birges' to deliver one of those boxes for Alice. I didn't find them home, but on the door, hanging from the knocker, was a dead hawk. It had been shot through the heart with a small-caliber rifle. Its eyes were closed, a small, yellowish membrane covering them, and a tiny bubble of blood had dried solid in the corner of the beak. A leather thong noose had been slipped over the bird's head, and it hung from the door-knocker like a talisman, with its broken neck lolling sidewards. I left the box on the porch and hurried away.

Ever since that time, I've had peculiar feelings about Birge.

Ambivalence I would call it, since he's always been very nice to us. The man was obviously a very good person to know. He brought with himself a big, comforting sense of protection. On the other hand there was something beneath the ruddy, good-natured looks that was vaguely disquieting.

Now, as we stood there that Christmas Eve, all queued up waiting to greet the pastor, Birge raised his hat to us. He wished us a merry Christmas, while Mrs. Birge made several pitiful grimaces in an effort to smile. We introduced the Birges to Richard who said "Hello" and was then silent while the rest of us chatted and waited to greet the pastor.

Birge was very friendly that night. "Full of Christmas" I believe was his expression in describing his mood. But all the while we spoke, I couldn't help noticing that he was barely able to drag his eyes off Richard. He gazed wondrously at the long mane of flaxen hair and the great ruddy beard. His eyes traveled from head to foot, and he had the look of a child gazing covetously at a toy in a window.

When we got back that night, we went directly to the parlor, where the ashes from the fire were now gray, smouldering ingots. Alice and I opened presents around the tree with childish excitement while Richard sat silently in his new suit and watched us.

"Exactly what I wanted," I cried and extracted a pair of fur-lined slippers from a mass of rattling tissue paper.

"Try them on, dear. See how they fit. They didn't have nines, so I had to take eights."

I started eagerly into them while Alice chatted on.

"Mr. Winslow said he'd take them back if they didn't fit."

I stood up and shuffled around in them while Alice laughed. "They fit perfectly. Couldn't be better." I kissed her lightly on the cheek.

"See what's in that package over there," I said.

"Which one, dear?"

"The one with the bright yellow paper."

She picked it up and felt the weight of it with her hands. "Oh, I know what's in here."

"Do you?" I winked at Richard and immediately felt foolish when he gazed blankly back at me. He wasn't the sort of person you could easily wink at.

Alice was laughing and tugging at long purple ribbons. Then flinging aside the bright yellow tissue paper, she withdrew a huge Chinese cookbook I'd ordered for her at the local bookshop. She'd wanted it for a long time, but it was the sort of extravagance she would've never permitted herself. Now she hugged it to her breast, trying to look cross. "Oh, Albert."

"Now I expect Peking duck with prune sauce. Just like Singapore."

"If I could reproduce the skin on that duck, we'd open a restaurant. And even if I knew how to do Peking duck, where would we get the ingredients around here?"

"I hadn't thought of that."

She kissed me and laughed. "I love the book. But you're mad. It's such an extravagance."

I suppose I looked dejected about my miscalculation, because she patted my cheek and said, "Don't be unhappy, dear. If we go into the city for vacation next spring, we'll stock up on Chinese vegetables and all sorts of exotic ingredients."

After that there was an exchange of a number of smaller packages—toothbrushes, cologne, socks, what have you.

We were both very happy like children playing there around the tree, all our packages strewn about.

Richard remained silent. He sat in a chair, his legs stretched stiff in front of him, watching us. Several times I stole glimpses at him. It was a curious absorption with which he viewed us, as if we were laboratory animals performing in a maze. I couldn't tell if the spectacle of us playing there with our presents on the floor made him feel pity or contempt. I wondered if he liked us or simply thought of us as two silly, aging fools.

But even as he sat there I could tell he was weighing something in his head. For some reason my mind fastened on violence. I had a fleeting vision of Alice and me on the floor, pools of blood running out of our shattered skulls—blood running in a languid trickle onto the rug, under the Christmas tree, blood blotching the cushions and drapes and spattered over the presents and the brightly colored wrappings. I saw in my mind some lurid tabloid story about a middle-aged couple in a desolate cottage in the bog, cruelly put to death by a young itinerant handyman whom they'd befriended. In a flash I saw it all before me—bright, red, and wet, as if it had happened right there under my nose. That's what I imagined he was weighing that moment—working toward some course of action, some decision that once made would be final, drastic and irrevocable. But I put it all out of my mind, and it was Christmas once again.

In addition to slippers, Alice gave me a fine old meerschaum pipe and a large tin of my favorite tobacco. I filled the pipe immediately and puffed thoughtfully, giving a silly imitation of Sherlock Holmes, saying idiotic things like "Elementary, my dear Watson." It was all very strained and unnatural. Alice's laughter was a bit too strident, and mine much too tense. Clearly we were putting on a show for Richard Atlee. We were demonstrating the warmth and happiness of our household, even though Alice and I knew all that was a lie. That our household —full of beautiful things, to be sure—was no more than a slightly elaborate mausoleum—a dismal, empty place that never knew the laughter or warmth of a real family. We had lived in beautiful cities of the world and collected many rare and exquisite things with which we'd surrounded ourselves. And yet in the final summation, here in the twilight of our days we both knew that our lives added up to zero. And yet, for some unaccountable reason we were acting out some incredible lie for this perfect stranger—this stray cat who had wandered in out of the cold. Why?

"Now I have one last present," I said to Alice. "Wait here." I went upstairs and rummaged through my drawers, finally pulling out a tiny box from beneath a stack of freshly laundered handkerchiefs. I brought it down and presented it to Alice.

"Take it," I said.

She looked clearly puzzled, for this present, unlike the others, she'd clearly not expected. It had been a very well-guarded secret.

"What is it?" she asked.

I waved it under her eyes like a sorcerer. "Take it and find out." She shrank from the tiny package as if it were an insect. "Oh, Albert. What have you done?"

"Now come, Alice. Don't be foolish. Take it." I took her hand and pressed the package into her palm. "Open it and see what you've got."

She undid the ribbons very slowly, then peeled off the paper. Inside was a small black satin box.

"Albert. I'm afraid—"

"Don't be silly."

"I can't."

"Oh, here. I'll do it for you." I flicked open the case and held it out to her. She moved back a step and caught her breath. Looking at her, I laughed. It was one of the only honest moments of that night.

"Do you recall when we were in Bombay—" I said.

"Yes."

"And you saw one of these?"

"Yes."

"Remember how much you wanted it?"

"Yes."

"And I didn't have the money then?"

Her cheeks flamed. "Yes—yes."

"I told you then that one day I'd buy you a star sapphire—" I took her hand, which she offered almost dumbly, and slipped off the simple gold wedding band she had worn for nearly a quarter of a century. I replaced that with the star sapphire.

For a while she held her hand out and gazed at it vacantly, as if she weren't quite sure of what it was or what it was doing on her finger. Several times she made gestures—all futile—as if she were about to take it off, give it back. Then her eyes filled. She became watery and giddy and started to laugh. She held up her hand again and admired the ring, and kept repeating over and over again, "Oh, you dear. You dear dear—"

Then she crossed the room and kissed me warmly. Next she turned and walked quickly to where Richard sat. "This is the happiest Christmas of my life," she said, and she knelt down and kissed him.

We were silent then—all of us. And in some curious way, we were very happy. Richard, as well.

"I bet you think we've forgotten you," Alice blubbered to Richard. After a moment, she rose from her knees, and ran to the tree and got the box in which she'd wrapped the wool reindeer sweater. She brought it back and offered it to him.

That moment might have been amusing if it hadn't been so strange. He gazed from the box to Alice and then back to the box, a look of stony impassivity on his face.

"Take it," she said, very gently. "It's for you."

It took him what seemed ages to open the box and withdraw the sweater. It was a beautiful blue with cable stitching. And there were the two glorious white reindeer knitted across the chest. I'll never forget those reindeer—white, majestic, wild, with a touch of almost the supernatural about them. It was a work of art.

Richard held it in his hands, staring at it blankly. For one awful moment I was sure he was going to reject it, turn it back to her and stalk out. But he didn't. He just sat there and gazed down at the sweater.

"Try it on," Alice coaxed him softly.

"Go ahead, Richard. Let's see what it looks like."

Still he sat there, until she took the sweater and unfolded it. "Stand up," she said, putting some authority into her voice.

He got to his feet and submitted quietly as she pinned the sweater against his chest and studied it critically. "You were right, dear," she said to me over his shoulder. "He is a big boy. I'll have to let the sleeves and the waist out." She seemed dejected.

"But it's beautiful, Alice," I said.

"Do you think so, dear?"

"It's a honey. Don't you think so, Richard?"

At first I thought he hadn't heard me, and I was about to repeat my question. But in the next moment he straightened himself and let the sweater fall from his chest to the floor. It was a perfectly harmless movement but for me it was strangely threatening.

"Do you like the sweater?" I asked again.

"I'm gonna stay here now," he said. Those were his first words to us that night.

"What?" I asked.

"I'm gonna stay up here now," he said.

"If you'd like, Richard," said Alice.

"We wouldn't think of letting you go back down to the cellar," I added.

"There's lots to do round here," he went on, not even hearing us. "The two of you are gettin' on. You need help. I'm gonna help you."

"That would make us very happy," Alice said, her eyes glistening.

"I'm gonna stay here now," he said again. "I'm gonna take care of you."

Chapter Seven

WE were happy in the days that followed. Like new parents. We had a vested interest in the future of our child. We worried about his health and his moods. We still wanted to see him find some form of employment outside of our home. From time to time at supper we'd inquire what progress he'd made toward finding a job.

"Gotta couple things in mind," he'd say. Overjoyed by that we'd decline to pursue the question any further and rush right on to some less delicate topic. We simply couldn't bring ourselves to press him on the subject. But because he appeared to be having difficulty finding a job, we even toyed with the idea of sending him back to school for some further training, although we had no idea of how much schooling he had had. On this subject he was inexplicably wary, and the several times I tried to pump him for information I met with steely eyes and icy rebuffs. Frankly I couldn't see how questioning him about his schooling could offend. Even assuming that he had no schooling at all, such reticence growing out of shame and false pride, if permitted to continue, would get him absolutely nowhere.

"I'm only trying to help you," I said one day in a fit of near despair.

"I can read and I can write," he said and folded his arms with almost imperial finality.

"Yes," I said, still determined to get an answer, "but how much schooling have you had?"

"Enough."

"How much is enough?"

"I got out before they could ruin me," he said and turned abruptly on his heel and left.

And also about his past he remained stolidly private. One day while he was shoveling snow out of the driveway I asked him:

"Richard—where do you come from?"

"Out west."

"Where out west?"

"All over," he said and from the way he said it I knew that our conversation on that score was at an end. There was nothing belligerent about his desire for secrecy. If there had been, we would've become suspicious sooner. It was merely a kind of privacy he wished to maintain, and quite early on in the course of his stay, we came to accept and at last to respect that wish very highly.

From the day he moved out of the crawlspace and up into the house, his living habits as regards personal hygiene, table manners, and simple rules of courtesy underwent an amazing course of transformation. We could see a conscious effort on his part to reform himself in these areas. At supper when he was uncertain of what piece of silver was required for a certain course, he would wait to see what either Alice or I would do, then move accordingly. At such times, you could see his eyes working under his lids, darting right and left to snatch some cue. There was no shame in it. He went about gathering information in a rather cold, ruthless way—like a miser storing up pennies. Once he'd learned something in that fashion he held tight to it. When the same problem of etiquette came up again in a day, or a week, or a month, he'd have it down pat, so that gradually his table manners and general deportment were irreproachable.

He bathed each morning quite early, long before Alice and I got up. When he left the bathroom, it was spotless. He kept his habit of being up very early in the morning and out of the house most of the day. Long before Alice and I were even stirring on our pillows, he'd done enormous amounts of work.

One morning, no more than a week after he'd moved in upstairs, we came down to the kitchen and found coffee, hot and freshly made, and the table in the breakfast nook neatly set. He'd squeezed fresh juice and left a pitcher of it in the refrigerator. He was nowhere in sight, but the woodbox had been stacked with freshly hewn logs and the newly fallen snow in our drive had been shoveled out.

After that time, breakfast and the woodbox were chores he rendered with unfailing regularity. There were other chores, of course, the furnace, the driveway, and later on in the spring and summer, the lawns and gardens and trees.

We bought him several additional outfits of clothing so that he might have a fresh change every day. These he kept in exemplary fashion, laundering and darning them himself as the need occurred.

We made one of the side rooms on the first floor over into a bedroom for him. We bought a new trundle bed and a box spring and mattress. We haunted antique shops and auctions for several weeks and in that way found a chest of drawers, a night table, and an old needlepoint rug, of exceptional quality. Alice insisted upon making him curtains and a bedspread herself.

His room quickly became a source of great pride to him, but when he went out for the day, he always left the door to it closed. One day, however, he walked out and left the door wide open. Alice and I succumbed to the temptation of looking in. We found the bed made, his floor swept bright and clean, and all clothing hung neatly in his closets. After that the door was closed unfailingly each day, but we never again felt the need of invading the sanctity of that place.

Of course, he wanted us to inspect the room—wanted us to check his progress. We'd become not only his sponsors, but his mentors, and he was eager to be judged by us and proved worthy.

Just as before when he lived in the crawl, he made his presence about the house scarcely visible. As I say, he did all of his work, and heavy work it was, in the early morning, before Alice and I were up. Then he'd disappear for the day. Where he went I don't know. Ostensibly to hunt for a job, but more probably to wander in the forest, where he was undoubtedly happiest. The only certainty was that he would return at night to have his supper with us. How we looked forward to those suppers, and what efforts Alice expended to make her menus enticing.

For a while we tried to pretend that Richard spent his days out seeking employment. But of course we were deluding ourselves. Richard Atlee could never have worked for anyone, at least in the sense that people work for people. As in the case of the fuel company, his employment could only be sporadic and short-lived at best. He was by instinct and temperament a transient, and to think of him in terms of long-term employment, a person concerned with pensions, health plans, retirement benefits, was pure self-delusion on our parts. And as I've said before, we didn't press him on the subject, at least in the beginning, because to be perfectly honest, we weren't ready to give him up to a job. We rather liked having him around the house and playing at doting parents. And so, in truth, no job that would've come along then would've been good enough for him anyway. Certainly not the kind of job he could get with Washburn, or Winslow, or the like. It had to be something worthy of him—whatever that was—we told ourselves.

And so Alice and I came to love Richard Atlee with all the blindness and error common to natural parents. We blessed all of his strong points and ignored all his faults. We thought of him as our child and of ourselves as parents jealously guarding that child until such time as he was strong enough and mature enough to fend for himself. Alice said that it was like having a wild creature in the house—an animal—that you'd brought in from the woods and tried to domesticate. And that was in a sense true. Each day watching his growth as a person, and his amazing transformation from that of a wild thing into a civilized being, we congratulated ourselves. We looked on each new achievement, no matter how small, and gloated. We were pleased with ourselves and concluded that we had set an example that Richard Atlee had chosen to follow. He was, in short, the apple of our eye, and a feather in our caps.

I have mentioned all the work that Richard Atlee did about the house. But of all the many jobs that he did that winter, I think of one as especially noteworthy. He built a stone wall at the bottom of the garden where the lawn borders the fringe of the woods leading to the bog.

It was an enormous job, and he did it all by himself, hauling great, frozen boulders in a wheelbarrow that he'd pushed great distances through the forest. It had gone up over the space of two weeks, almost entirely unnoticed until the point where it was just at the brink of completion.

It was a beautiful stone wall such as the kind you see in this part of the country set up to define pasture boundaries. Not an inconsiderable job, I might add, for a single man. The wall was three feet high and ran nearly two hundred feet in length, each boulder of it weighing between fifty and eighty pounds.

When we first saw it, we were delighted. But purely on esthetic grounds. We could see no practical use to it, since the line along which he had built the wall was not a boundary.

That night at supper I asked him why he had built the wall.

"To keep off strangers," he said, and went on spooning his soup.

"You were a stranger when you first came here," Alice said very gently.

"I know," he said. "So I don't want any more comin' in."

We laughed at that, but as we learned later, he hadn't intended it to be funny.

One thing about that wall did disturb us, however. He had never bothered to ask us whether or not we even wanted it.

A small incident occurred during the building of that wall that's worth mentioning.

Emil Birge came up our drive one day in his station wagon with the state police shield plastered over the door. At the time, Alice and I were outside watching Richard working at the bottom of the garden.

At the top of the drive, Birge honked his horn several times in greeting and got out of the car, smiling and waving. He ambled slowly toward us, moving like a big man —shoulders slightly stooped and shuffling immense feet.

When he reached us, he thrust a raw red paw of a hand at me and doffed his trooper's hat to Alice. It all had a ridiculously gallant air about it.

"Howdy. How're you folks?" He put his arm about my shoulder, full of good will. We chatted for a while, and then Alice asked him in for a cup of coffee.

"That's very kind. But no, thank you. Mrs. Birge and I was just wonderin' how you folks was gettin' on through the winter out here. I was in the neighborhood so I thought I'd just mosey out and see if you needed anything."

Just then Richard came thrashing through the woods with his wheelbarrow and halted at the bottom of the garden. Birge's eye traveled slowly down to where Richard, now bent over, was lifting a large boulder from the barrow.

"He building that wall for you?" Birge asked.

"Yes," I said.

"It's mighty pretty," he said.

"Isn't it?" Alice agreed. She seemed very pleased and started to rhapsodize about Richard and all his good works and what a comfort he'd been to us since he'd come.

But Birge wasn't listening. His eyes fastened on the sight of the boy about a hundred yards off, lifting boulders and setting them in place on the wall. He had a distant look, as if he were suddenly deep in thought. After we'd watched Richard working a while, Birge said, "That's a powerful boy you got there."

I laughed. "Powerful and reliable."

"Think he'd like to come work for me?" Birge asked. The question took us by surprise.

"I'm lookin' for an assistant deputy," Birge went on, still staring down at him. "Boy like that'd be just right."

When I looked at Alice, I could tell she wasn't entirely put off by the idea. Although we felt a great deal of conflicting emotion about Richard's going to work, we still wanted to see him get back on his own feet with a job. And a job with Birge was quite a few cuts above working as a service station attendant. There were, too, certain advantages to working in law enforcement: the salary while modest was respectable; there were automatic pay raises as well as the peripheral benefits of insurance, pension, and retirement funds. Most importantly, it was out-of-doors work. He wouldn't be penned up in some airless loft carrying out dreary, mindless little drudgeries. All in all, it sounded good, and I could see Alice was thinking it, too. Still we couldn't bring ourselves to say anything one way or another.

"You'll have to ask him yourself, sheriff," I said.

"The boy makes his own decisions," Alice added.

"Call him up here," Birge said. He appeared suddenly very excited.

Richard had just emptied his wheelbarrow of boulders and was about to thrash off back into the woods when I called:

"Richard— You— Richard."

He turned and gazed back up toward us, shading his eyes from the sun. When I signaled him to come up, he set his barrow down and with hands plunged deeply into his coat pockets, he trudged up to where we stood.

"Richard," I said, when he reached us, "you remember Sheriff Birge."

He nodded and Birge thrust a hand out toward him. Richard's hand fumbled toward it. There was an awkward gap and then Alice said, "The sheriff has something he'd like to say to you, Richard."

Smiling and more expansive than ever, Birge launched into his proposition. He presented it wonderfully, painting a glowing picture of life as a deputy with its challenges and many benefits. All the while he spoke I could sense disaster coming on fast. I could see it coming in the way Richard's body stiffened, in the slight recoil of his body, in the hardening of the jaw line, and the way the lips, whiter than usual, pressed against each other, like thin taut cords.

When Birge finished, his eyes glowed and he was still smiling. "Well, Richard," I said with a lot of bogus enthusiasm. "What about it? Want to go to work for the sheriff?"

The answer was immediate and brutally brusque. "No."
He stared back unflinchingly into Birge's eyes. "I don't
wanna work for him."

The moment that followed was awful, chiefly because
of Birge—the fading smile, the look of disbelief, the color
bleaching from his face, until it seemed that a black
cloud had passed overhead. And then the anger—the pure,
naked anger. Their gazes locked and they glared at each
other, as if there were some ancient unspoken antagonism
between them.

"All right, Richard," I said, my legs trembling a bit.
"Go on back to your work now."

He turned immediately and walked back down to
where his barrow stood at the bottom of the garden. We
watched him lift it, then thrash off through naked branches
and vanish into the forest.

We were left there—the three of us in the driveway,
hanging in a grim gray space. Birge looked awful. As we
walked back to the car with him, Alice stammered a few
hollow-sounding pleasantries, and so did I. Once there,
he said very little, tipped his hat stiffly, got into the car,
and slammed the door. In the next moment, his tires
screeched out of the drive, leaving deep ugly scars in the
gravel.

It was terrible while it lasted, but afterwards, when
Alice and I had calmed down and then discussed the
matter, we both confessed that we were relieved when
Richard turned the job down.

Chapter Eight

WE had no hint of the trouble that was to come
to us until the early spring of the year—those early days
of March when the ground is still hard, when it's warm in
the sun and cold in the shade. Then the buds on the
trees, still closed tight, stand out on the branches like tiny

green jewels, there's a sense of the earth moving beneath your feet, and you can smell things starting to grow.

Those are the days when people begin to think about lawns and gardens and taking down storm windows. And, of course, Alice was thinking along those lines too.

It was our custom to bring Richard Atlee to church with us each Sunday. Mind you, we knew nothing of his religious life. I tend to think he had none, and conversion is the last thing that interests me. But at church, he enjoyed the songs, and in his odd croaking voice, which I always found so curiously touching, it was a great pleasure to watch him singing from the hymnal and looking around at people—the sun streaming down through the clerestory onto his great wreath of hair. For one who was generally tight as a clam, he had the capacity to give himself up completely to song. I think it had some liberating effect on him, and being witness to it was a source of no small pleasure to Alice and me.

Up long before anyone on Sunday mornings, he would bathe and attend rather more scrupulously to his toilet than on weekdays. Next, he would put on a fresh shirt and tie and of course the suit I'd bought him for Christmas. He was ready to go an hour or so before Alice and I were even up. When we'd finally come down, we'd find him sitting all scrubbed and brushed and anxious in the parlor. And while we'd have our breakfast, he'd be outside dusting the car.

I've already mentioned a certain mocking attitude we sensed from our fellow parishioners when we first brought Richard to church. In the weeks that followed, the mocking amusement turned to a chilly remoteness. Then finally, one Sunday, at the conclusion of services, as we were filing out the door, waiting to greet the pastor, instead of shaking my hand he smiled very warmly and stopped me.

"May I have a word with you, Mr. Graves?" His name was Reverend Horn.

"Of course, Reverend," I said and waited there for him to speak.

"No—in my study, if you will—"

"Certainly." I turned to Alice. "You and Richard wait for me in the car. I should be along shortly."

When they left I stood aside and waited for Horn to finish greeting the rest of the parishioners.

Later, following him back to his office through the empty church, our footsteps echoing around the vacant pews, I imagined that he was going to ask me for money for some charity or church function and in my mind I was already computing a figure that I could afford to give without feeling too much of a pinch.

After we'd settled in chairs and exchanged brief amenities, he offered me peppermints from a bag he kept in his desk. "Who is this boy who comes to church with you and Mrs. Graves?" he said quite pleasantly.

"His name is Richard Atlee, Reverend. He lives with us. We've taken him in."

"I know," he said, smiling more pleasantly than ever and twisting in his chair. "Do you know anything about him?"

"Very little. He's not overly communicative." I laughed a little apprehensively.

Horn leaned back in his chair and locked his fingers over an ample paunch. "Isn't that a bit unwise—opening your doors like that to a perfect stranger?"

"He's hardly a stranger, now, Reverend."

"Yes. But he was once. And you say yourself you don't know very much about him."

"Do I have to?" I said, smiling confidently. "We feel in no special danger."

I can still recall the large, well-shaped head nodding as I spoke. When I finished, he shifted in his chair. "I don't want you to be upset by what I tell you now." He spoke in the most earnest and friendly fashion. "But then I'm sure you're aware there's been talk here."

Of course I'd been, but I wasn't going to let on. "Talk?"

"Yes. Talk."

"No. I'm not aware." We were both silent as his eyes fixed me through rimless spectacles. "What sort of talk? Unpleasant talk?"

"Of a sort."

"I can't imagine why. What cause has he given?"

"Oh, it's not so much cause, Mr. Graves—"

"I assure you, the boy's behavior has been exemplary."

"I don't doubt it. But still—"

"Still—" My voice was curt. "What else is there?"

"Now make no mistake. What I tell you now is not the result of a rash decision, but carefully and most painfully considered."

"Yes?" I could barely suppress my impatience.

"The presence of this boy here each Sunday has had a most disturbing influence on several of the members of this congregation."

"Disturbing influence?" I thought I'd laugh. "What could he possibly have done to have any influence whatsoever?"

I suspect at this point that Horn sensed an explosion. His manner became more conciliatory. "It's not so much the adults I worry about, you see, Mr. Graves. But there are children here of an impressionable age."

I was speechless as he rattled on.

"He makes, you will admit, a somewhat unorthodox appearance."

"Well, he doesn't look like everyone else around here, if that's what you mean—"

And it went on that way, back and forth, for twenty minutes while the air heated up and we badgered each other politely. After a while I just sat there like a smouldering rag, while the whole thing took on a kind of horrible unreality. We ceased talking to each other and started talking at each other and when I left, I went with an ultimatum.

"I'm afraid I must ask you not to bring him here any more, Mr. Graves."

"You can't be serious."

"I'm very serious. You and Mrs. Graves are still of course perfectly welcome. But—"

"I understand—"

"You understand my position?"

"Perfectly." I snapped. "All too well."

"Personally, I find what you've done admirable."

"Yes. A bit like the Good Samaritan, say?" I rose to go. "Thank you very much."

"Try to understand." He looked genuinely pained. I think he'd been expecting instant docility and I'd surprised him.

"I understand very well," I said. "You couldn't have made it clearer."

His hand rose in farewell. It was one of those gestures churchmen use when they want to appear benevolent. It looked merely idiotic and as ambiguous and mealy-mouthed as the man who'd made it. "I trust I shall see you next Sunday," he said.

"Very frankly, Reverend, I don't know that you will." I turned to go.

He called after me, "I urge you to find out something about this boy before you go much further with him."

I didn't even pause to acknowledge those last words. I merely closed the door behind me. And so it was.

There was nothing harsh about it. It was all very cordial and civilized, and that made it all the more rancorous to me.

When I got outside in the street Alice and Richard were waiting there in the car. The moment Alice saw me, she could tell something was wrong. I got into the car without saying a word, started the motor instantly, and we drove home. Richard remained wonderfully oblivious to the whole thing. He sat in the back wedged in amidst the grocery bundles we had picked up on the way home. At one point he started to hum "Nearer My God to Thee" while along the road the tight little buds of trees were just beginning to open.

I didn't know what course of action I would take until I got home that day and discussed the entire matter with Alice. Richard had changed from Sunday clothes to his work clothes and disappeared out back. Then, with my voice trembling and my cheeks flamed, I laid the entire business out to her. It didn't take us very long to make up our minds about a course of action. Shortly after, I was able to compose a brief letter to Reverend Horn.

Dear Reverend Horn:

Since I feel closer to the original teaching of the Lord in the presence of our young house guest than I have ever felt in your congregation, I must regretfully tender my resignation from it.

I wish to assure you that my faith in our Lord and His Church remains undiminished. But as to the men whose duty it is to minister to His flocks, I must sadly report that as a result of our discussion today, they have dropped sharply in my esteem.

I shudder to think of the kind of hospitality the infant Jesus and his parents would have been afforded by your parishioners had they shown up here today instead of to that manger in Bethlehem so many years ago.

> Yours very truly,
> A. Graves

So it was. I took that step and took it happily, convinced as I was of the rightness and justice of my decision.

I mark that day as a turning point in our lives. From that time on, we left the fold of our fellow man behind and began to live exclusively for and by ourselves.

Still our lives remained outwardly unchanged. We maintained the same routine we had before our breach with the church. We saw no people socially, but then we seldom, if ever, did. We continued to go to town two times a week to do our marketing. We still exchanged civilities with local merchants and clerks. We nodded to people on the street. The only change that came about was the manner of our weekly worship, and that didn't really change, either, since we continued to worship on Sundays. But instead of going to church, our home became the church, and there on Sundays the three of us said prayers and sang psalms while a benevolent morning sun streamed into our parlor.

If there was indeed any significant change, it wasn't outward. It was rather a change that took place within the three of us. Along with the sense of growing isolation, there sprang up between us a sense of interdependence. We lived by helping and caring for each other. In short, we lived as though we were the last three people on earth, and quite frankly, it didn't seem to bother us at all.

Chapter Nine

ALONG about mid-March we had a visitor.

Alice and I were in the garden turning soil and raking up the debris left by winter—broken twigs and dead leaves, mingled with the desiccated carcasses of birds and small animals that had perished in the icy blasts. It was late afternoon. Richard, as usual, was still off in the woods. I was in the midst of hauling a sack of dead leaves and twigs to a compost heap we have out back. It wasn't a heavy sack, just the sort of mildly strenuous thing the doctors say is very good for a man in my condition.

Just as I reached the heap, a horn blasted in the driveway, and I heard Alice cry out. I turned just in time to see my nephew, Wylie Crane, climbing out of a car and Alice running toward him. When I reached there, he was hugging her and at the same time waving to me.

"Hi, Uncle Albert!"

"For God's sake, Wylie, you might've given us a little warning."

"I didn't know I was coming myself, until about twenty minutes ago. I was on the throughway, saw your exit, and got a yen to see Aunt Alice."

Alice cooed and kissed him again. I made a dour face. "But of course not me?"

"Most of all you, Uncle Albert." He threw his arm around me and we all laughed.

Wylie was attending a polytechnical college in a large city to the north of us. It was his custom to stop off and visit for a few days at least once a year, either going to or coming from school. Generally he'd write or call to warn us. This time, however, he hadn't. But, as always, it was a great pleasure to see him. He was a delightful young man of about nineteen, the image of my sister Blanche, who, of five brothers and sisters, was my great favorite. Now, since her death, whenever I look at Wylie, and particularly when he laughs, I can see Blanche laughing in his eyes. When she died, Wylie grew very close to us, particularly to Alice, who became almost a mother to him.

I reached into the car and grabbed his bag. "You're going to spend a few days, aren't you?"

He looked back and forth at each of us. "Will it be all right? I mean—just barging in and all like this—"

"Frankly it's going to be a great nuisance," I said, throwing my arm around him. "But we'll muddle though."

"Oh, don't pay any attention to your uncle," Alice said. "Have you eaten?" She locked her arm in his and started to drag him toward the house. Wylie saw me lift his bag. "Let me take that, Uncle Albert."

I waved him away. "You have your fishing gear, I hope?"

"In the car."

"Good. We might just as well go up and try the stream tomorrow. I haven't been out yet this season. How's your father?"

When we reached the house, I saw Alice turn and look at the washline just behind the kitchen. Dangling from it was a pair of Richard's overalls dancing in a playful breeze. They had a strangely foreboding look hanging there disembodied and swaying slowly back and forth against the sky. The moment she saw them, a green sickish look crossed her face. "Oh, Albert."

I knew exactly what she was thinking. The room we'd fixed up for Richard was the room Wylie always slept in. Now there was the sticky problem of sleeping accommodations and all that.

Wylie sensed that something was up. "What is it, Aunt Alice?"

"Nothing at all," I said, dismissing it with a wave of the hand. "We have a little surprise for you, Wylie. Don't we, Alice?"

The business of sleeping was straightened out very quickly. We had no intention of displacing Richard during the course of my nephew's visit. We had a cot upstairs in the attic, and that was to be set up in the parlor for Wylie.

Their first meeting took place at supper. Wylie was upstairs having a bath when Richard came in, earlier than usual. He seemed very buoyant, full of good spirits, and unusually talkative for Richard Atlee.

He'd been in the forest all afternoon and later back in the bog. It seemed he'd found a cave there that had gone almost a hundred feet underground. He'd measured its depth by carrying down a full spool of string with him.

"I come across it a couple of days ago," he said, "and brought back string today."

"What'd you see down there?" I asked.

"Nothin' much. Bats and things."

Alice, puttering over the oven, made a sound of revulsion.

"There's a stream down there, too," Richard went on excitedly. "I could hear it right under my feet."

"See any other signs of life?" I asked.

"It was too dark. But there are signs of bear. Probably hole up down there for the winter."

Alice's eyes widened. "And you went down there?"

"They're all out now," he said, and smiled a crooked little smile. Smiling a bit now and then was one of the more recent developments in him.

"I'd love to see it," I said.

His eyes glowed. "Would you?"

"Never mind," said Alice. "Stay out of there, the two of you. For your own good and my piece of mind, as well." She thrust a relish tray at Richard. "Here. Put this on the table."

I'll never forget his face when he saw the fourth setting. I was sitting almost directly opposite him when it dawned on him that there was something different in the design of the table. I hadn't mentioned a word about Wylie to him. Not intentionally, mind you. I'd simply forgotten it in the excitement of the cave story.

At first it was rather funny—that look of puzzlement and disbelief on his face. I was just about to tell him, but it was too late. Suddenly there was Wylie's footstep on the floor above and then the vital sound of boyish steps bounding downstairs. Richard half rose from his chair. In the next moment Wylie turned the corner and peered in. We'd told him as much as we could about Richard, and now, scrubbed and with a flush of good health all about him, he entered the parlor and walked directly to him, smiling with a hand extended. "Hi."

Alice entered with a platter just in time to see Richard's jaw fall and his eyes widen to an awesome size.

"Richard," I said, leaping into the breach, "this is my nephew, Wylie Crane."

But by that time the damage had been done. You could see it all over his face. Resentment rushed in where surprise left off. When we finally sat down to dinner, Richard kept his eyes lowered and looked at everything on the table with suspicion. He was like a man who suspected that his food had been poisoned. He'd been elected to die, and so he sat down now to supper with all of his poisoners.

Supper was a disaster. Several attempts were made at dinner conversation—all abortive. Wylie sensed the need of a special effort and extended himself gallantly.

"You're not from around here?" he asked with the best of intentions.

"Nope," Richard said, scowling into his plate.

"I didn't think so," Wylie said. "You sound Western."

"Uh-huh," Richard said and went on chewing. Then there was silence and all I could hear was the sound of that chewing—quick and angry—while his larynx went bobbing furiously up and down.

"Are you?" Wylie went on undaunted.

Richard stopped eating, his knife and fork poised in midair. "Am I what?"

"Western."

"I said I was."

"Oh," said Wylie, a trifle baffled but still smiling. "I didn't quite get you."

Richard stared at him for a moment and then went on eating. The silence flooded in once more and we all went on eating, buried in our plates while the sound of Richard's furious chewing rang out across the table.

I could see that Alice was miserable, and so I threw myself into the breach. "Any good fishing up your way, Wylie?"

"We were out just last week."

"Any luck?"

"Oh, sure. I got about five. Couple of nice ones, too. Bass, mostly."

"Large-mouth?"

Wylie nodded, chattering on in a lively fashion. When I glanced at Richard, he appeared to be a hundred miles off somewhere.

"I got one eight-pounder. Should've seen him when I brought him up, Uncle Albert. Head twice as big as my fist." It was a joy to be in the presence of all that boyish enthusiasm.

"Get him on a fly rod?" I asked.

"You might've taken him on a fly rod," Wylie laughed. "I was happy enough just to get him on a rod and reel."

"Well," I said eagerly, "tomorrow we'll break out the fly rods."

Alice's gloom deepened. Undoubtedly she felt that Richard had been excluded from the conversation. And in fact he had—by his own choice. She turned to him now, making a valiant effort to smile. "You know, Richard, Albert and Wylie have fished together for years."

"Oh?" said Richard. He fiddled distractedly with some peas on his plate.

She went on hopefully, trying to lure him into conversation. "Albert taught Wylie to fish when he was a little boy." She laughed, but there was a lot of forced merriment to it. "I'll never forget Wylie. He was about ten at the time, and three feet tall. It was about three feet, wasn't it, Albert?"

"Certainly no more."

"Well," Alice went on, laughing in that giddy, desperate way, "you should've seen this poor boy struggle up the dock with a pole three times his size. I tell you it was worth the price of admission. Remember Indian Lake, Wylie?"

"No one ever lets me forget it," Wylie laughed. "All that snagging and the snarled lines. And all the lures I lost for poor Uncle Albert."

I had a sudden vision of a summer's day nearly a decade past. I saw myself ten years younger. Healthy and more vigorous. A sound heart in my chest, and Blanche alive then, with Alice and George Crane, Wylie's father, all watching us from the shadows of a screened porch and howling gales of laughter ringing out over the lake. The moment was alive for me again. Just as vivid as if I were right there. I could hear ice tinkling in a lemonade pitcher from the porch, the rattle of cicada, the barking of an unseen dog across the lake, and the distant buzzing of an outboard motor far out over the water. There was the smell of verbena reaching out across the space of a decade, and the reflection of trees hanging upside down in the water.

"Do you ever fish?" Wylie's voice brought me back from where my memory had just taken me.

"No. I don't like to fish," Richard replied with naked antagonism. He followed that with a few remarks that set my teeth on edge and ended the meal in shambles.

We went out into the parlor and tried to have our coffee there. But the air by that time was so thick with hostility and even poor Wylie's stubborn optimism finally foundered, and we all sat there imprisoned in our chairs, pitched in gloom watching the sparks from the fire snarl and fly up the flue like angry insects.

We went to bed early that night. There seemed to be nothing much else we could do in such a situation.

Richard went off to his room and closed the door with a barely smothered bang. Hardly speaking a word to each other, we made up Wylie's cot in the parlor. When I left my nephew that night, it was with the fixed plan to rise early and spend the morning up at the stream, fishing.

For all the ghoulish ordeal he'd been put through, Wylie appeared to have taken the whole thing with extraordinary good nature. And when Alice and I went up to bed and the door finally closed behind us, I remarked that Blanche would have been very proud of Wylie tonight, for he was growing into the kind of self-possessed, tolerant human being that she herself always admired.

Alice cried that night, very softly into her pillow. Several times I tried to solace her. But it was all futile. She wasn't even angry at Richard. It was herself she blamed for what had happened. She felt, at bottom, that she had failed that night in a very crucial way, and nothing I could say or do was going to dissuade her.

I rose quite early the next morning and shaved and dressed, in what seemed like a matter of moments. We had an excellent morning—the sky brushed red and rose by dazzling sunrise, the air dry and clear. I wanted to get down to the kitchen and make hot coffee and sandwiches before Wylie was up.

But when I got downstairs I found Wylie already dressed and waiting in the parlor. He was sitting deep in the Morris chair, his suitcase packed and parked beside him.

"What are you doing?" I said, sensing something wrong.

"Just waiting for you to get up, Uncle Albert."

He was dressed in a suit with a shirt and tie. His face bore an unaccustomed solemnity.

"Why are you dressed like that?" I said. "Aren't you going fishing?"

"Uncle Albert?"

"What's wrong, Wylie? What's the matter?"

"Uncle Albert, I think I'll go this morning."

"Why? I thought you were going to stay a few days."

"Yes, I know," he said, flushed with embarrassment. "But I really should get back. I have work, and—"

"What is it, Wylie? What's happened?"

I looked across at the door of Richard's room. It was open and empty. "Did he say anything to you?"

"No. Not a word."

He appeared to be absolutely earnest, but even as he looked at me I could tell he sensed my skepticism.

"Honest, Uncle Albert. I swear it."

"I won't let you go off like this."

He wrung his hands futilely. "I want to, Uncle Albert. I think it's best."

I could see that his mind was made up and that there was very little I could say that would change it. I sat down wearily in one of the chairs. "You're going to break your aunt's heart. Aren't you even going to wait for her to get up?"

He looked very pained. "Just tell her I had a lot of work and that I thought it best if I went."

I walked out with him to his car, and after we'd put his bag in and he was settled behind the wheel, we were stuck there with the open window between us wondering how we ought to say goodbye. But I abandoned all that and tried once again to get right down to the heart of it.

"Tell me honestly, Wylie. Did anything happen between you two?"

"Nothing. I swear it."

Wylie was not a natural liar and what he said seemed to be honest. Still, I couldn't believe what he said then, nor do I believe it today. I've seen Wylie several times since. On those occasions we were never quite able to discuss the incident. Once I tried to pin him down and find out what had happened that night between him and Richard Atlee. But he stuck to his story, and so I can only guess.

In the days that followed, I nursed a good deal of resentment against Richard. The more I thought about the precipitate way Wylie left, when I knew very well he wanted to stay, made me furious. I imagined all the kinds of threats and intimidation that were used against him. Alice on the other hand was inclined to be indulgent, and as a result of the incident doubled her attentions toward Richard.

As for Richard, he was sensitive enough to know he'd done something wrong and that he was going to have to make amends. One night he came to me, shortly after supper, meek, flustered, contrite, and stumbling over his words, he invited me to go back into the bog and have a look at his cave. You see, it had already become *his* cave. His presentation was appealing. Even sweet. Perhaps these aren't the right words. At any rate the presentation must have been the right one, because I accepted it right then and there. By next afternoon, trudging through the woods with Richard at my side, I was already in full thaw.

We must've walked for two miles or so under a bright white April sun—through the back woods and out across the bogs, trudging north with squadrons of squawking crows pointing our way. It was a desolate and forlorn place —flat and muddy with a good deal of squat ugly brush all around. Wading through it, we were harried by burrs and sticktights that tore at our clothing. The earth was pitchy black, and as you'd go along, it sucked and gurgled at the soles of your shoes.

Periodically a fat dozy muskrat would amble across our path, be visible for a moment, then slip silently back into the dense undergrowth. Or we'd flush a pheasant. You'd hear it before you'd see it. Then suddenly crashing up through the brakes, it would burst out into the open— ascending heavily on a long low incline, its wings drumming wondrously.

We went on that way for a while. Richard glanced frequently up at the sun until I realized that he'd been finding his direction from it, using a crude mixture of solar and instinctual navigation. Finally, I sensed we were beginning a long, gradual climb out of the bog and into an area of low, squat hills. Curiously I felt no strain to my heart. The walk was exhilarating, and I was glad to be out there.

At last Richard came to an abrupt halt at a place I

reckoned to be the northeastern point of the bog. He looked around and I thought by the way his eyes were darting here and there that he'd lost his bearings. Ordinarily, in such a wild place as this, that might have been cause for some concern. But there was something about Richard Atlee in a wilderness that inspired a great deal of confidence. Much more confidence than you felt with him in civilized and tamer settings.

"Are we all right?" I asked.

"We're here," he said, quite matter-of-factly.

I thought he was joking. I looked around and saw nothing faintly resembling a cave entrance. I'd imagined caves as being in high, rocky, inaccessible places—places more suited to eagles than to men. This was an area of low, almost imperceptibly sloping hills, nearly barren except for sporadic scrub, and covered with a soft, muddy crust of earth.

He stood a few feet off from me and pointed to a small hole in the earth. It looked no larger than a weasel hole.

"You're not serious?" I laughed.

He smiled one of those private little smiles of his, full of mystery and inner satisfaction.

Nearby there was a long, pole-like branch of about ten feet. He picked it up and plunged it directly into the small opening until he was holding the very end of the branch with his fingertips. He looked up at me, smiling, then suddenly let the branch go. It vanished instantly. Then he picked up a flap of earth as if it were a bit of canvas or tarpaulin, and pulled it back, revealing a flat slab of schist rock.

I walked over and stared at it for a while. "What is it?"

In the next moment he lifted the slab and rolled it back. Suddenly I was standing at the edge of a black, yawning hole into which the pole had disappeared only moments before.

Whether it had something to do with the exertion of the walk, or whether it was the sudden vision of a chasm yawning just beneath my feet, I don't know, but I felt a sudden giddiness—a sense of my knees unlocking and letting go. With a small whimpering sound, I slipped softly down on all fours.

The next thing I saw before my eyes was a square black hole floating up at me through space. But it wasn't the entrance to the cave that was wavering in front of me. It was the entrance to the crawl, flashing through my head, and suddenly I was back there again, sick and dizzy, and holding on to the lolly poles for dear life. For a moment I thought I was having another heart attack. But I felt no crushing chest pains. There was none of the awful breathlessness, the terrible lack of air. I thought I was dying, and I said to myself, "So this is it. This is what it's like. Not bad. Not bad at all."

But in the next instant it was all past. The sun flooded back in. A finch hopped in the grass several feet from me. Then the flat, dull croaking voice of Richard Atlee came at me from just above my shoulder.

"You okay?"

"Yes," I said, struggling to my feet, kicking a small avalanche of dirt and stones down the hole, while he held me beneath the arms.

"You okay?" he asked again.

"I'm fine. Fine."

He was peering earnestly into my eyes, which couldn't bear to meet his, for I'd shown such awful weakness.

"We don't have to go down," he said.

"I want to go down. Take me down."

"It's a climb," he said. He knew about my state of health.

"Very steep?"

"No. Not steep. About a hundred feet."

"Gradual?"

"About the way the lawn goes in back of the house."

"I walk that every day," I said. "Let's go down."

"You sure?"

"Of course I'm sure." I laughed. "Just don't tell Alice." I slapped his back and winked conspiratorially.

"Okay," he said. "Take my hand and stay right behind me. It's pretty dark."

His large, wiry hand closed comfortingly over mine,

and like a lost child giving himself up to a kindly adult, I put myself in Richard Atlee's hands and we started our descent.

"Don't be scared," he said, as sunlight faded away behind us and colored pinwheels spun before my eyes. "You'll be okay."

We went down quite a ways following the spool of string that he'd left down there. The deeper we went, the cooler and damper it got. The only illumination we had was a small flashlight that Richard had had the foresight to take with him. He held the light with one hand, and my hand with his other. With my free hand I groped my way along the cold, sweating walls, hearing the high squeaking of bats along the tunnels and the dull roar of a rushing stream from somewhere far below us.

There was a strong musky odor hanging like a mist over the place.

"What's that I smell?"

"Bear."

"You're sure they're not here, now?"

"No. In the winter."

"Oh," I said, quickly relieved. "Surely they don't come through the same entrance we did?"

"No. There's another entrance."

"Where?"

"I don't know. Someplace below, I haven't found it yet."

Our voices boomed as if we were talking inside of kettledrums. We continued to inch our way downward through the tunnel.

We must've gone on for about twenty minutes when the tunnel suddenly ended and we entered a small, chapel-like place. It was a high vaulted room, semicircular in shape. Here we paused.

Richard threw the beam of his light around the room. It was a high, dome-like structure at the apex of which hung a good deal of dripstones. In that feeble light they had the look of sharp, jagged teeth, so that standing on the floor of that room you had the curious sensation that you were in the maw of some huge, primordial creature.

When you looked more closely at the areas between the dripstones, you could see a number of small, black furry shapes clotted on the ceiling. These were the bats.

Richard kept swinging the light, pointing the beam, like an accusatory finger, into every corner of the room. "Typical Indian place," he said suddenly, not so much to me as to the dark spaces around us.

"Indians?" the word caught in my throat. "How do you know?"

He didn't answer, but just kept swinging the light from ceiling to floor.

By that time I was fully aroused. There had been Indians around this part of the country. But they'd vanished centuries ago. Still, there was something wonderfully mysterious about stumbling onto the dwelling place of an ancient people.

At a certain point, while in that place, Richard came abruptly to a halt in one of the far corners of the room. He stood there pointing the beam of his light downward, letting it slide slowly across the sandy floor.

I couldn't imagine what he was doing, but there was something about his absorption at that point that I couldn't bring myself to interrupt.

I watched him for a while until I was suddenly aware that the ground over which he played his light beam wasn't flat like the rest of the room, but consisted of a number of small, raised symmetrical mounds, possibly eighteen inches high and regularly spaced.

"What are those, Richard?"

"Burial places."

My breath caught a little.

"Indians," he nodded. "The ones who died down here through the winters."

"You mean they buried them right where they lived?"

"Couldn't bury 'em outside. The ground was frozen." He turned away from the place, then suddenly knelt down and sat with his back against the wall.

"Let's go down deeper," I said. I could hear water pounding below me. "At least to the stream?"

"No. We're out of string, and it's much steeper down below."

I had the feeling he was making concessions to my health, and it peeved me. "I can do it. Don't worry about me."

"I know you can. Rest now. We'll come back another time."

For a moment I was furious. I knew that if he were there alone, he would've gone much deeper. I toyed with the idea of going on by myself, forcing him to follow me. I knew he would if I'd started. But I'd enjoyed myself too much this far to spoil the rest of the day with an argument. I credited him with having better sense than I did, and inwardly I was touched by his showing that much concern and regard for me.

Richard flicked off the flashlight to conserve the batteries, and then leaning our backs against the clammy walls, we rested on the floor of the chapel.

"How'd you find this place?" I asked after a while.

"I just looked at the ground."

"And you knew it was here?"

"Sure."

I thought about it for a while and laughed. "You like it down here, don't you?"

"Yes."

"A bit like the crawlspace, isn't it?"

He was silent, and I could hear him breathing. "A bit," he said, his voice very soft in the darkness.

"What draws you to places like this?"

For a moment I thought I'd pushed him too far, and that in his typically private way he wouldn't answer.

"It's comfortable," he said.

"More comfortable than my house?"

"Not more comfortable—Safer."

The answer puzzled me. I sat there trying to fathom it. "Aren't you safe in my house?"

"Sure. But safer here."

"What threatens you there that doesn't threaten you here?"

"Things," he said. We were like two blind men sitting

there in total darkness, not seeing each other's faces—just two disembodied voices talking back and forth in the moist pitchy blackness. And the fact that we were no longer people but voices had the effect of opening him up a bit.

"By things," I said, "I take it you mean people?"

"Yes."

"Like Mrs. Graves and me?"

"Yes."

"We threaten you?"

"Yes."

"How do we threaten you?"

He was silent a while, but I could sense him framing his reply. Putting it all together as carefully as he could. "People are that way," he said finally. "One day you think they're one thing and the next day you find out they're something else. There are no people in this cave. Only animals. You know what to expect from animals."

"And you don't know what to expect from us?"

He didn't answer this time. But the silence said enough.

"It works the other way, too," I said. "Doesn't it? We don't know exactly what to expect from you, either—do we?"

"Sure." He said it very matter-of-factly. "One day one of us'll louse it all up. One way or the other."

I was shocked and a little hurt. "Then why stay with us?"

"Because you and Missus are better than most."

"Better?"

"You're kind."

"Kind?"

"Like that thing with the church—"

I hadn't realized he knew anything about our formal break with Reverend Horn and his church. When it had all happened, and he asked us why we stopped going to church, we simply told him that the weather had gotten too bad to drive in each Sunday. When the weather began to improve and he never questioned us about it, we assumed that he'd forgotten the whole thing.

"So you stay with us because you think we're kind?"

"Yes," he said. "Also I gotta try to learn other ways."

"You mean among people?"

"Yes. It's more—" He was groping for a word.

"Natural?" I said.

"Right. That's it. Natural."

"It's more natural," I said, seeing the dilemma. "But more dangerous?"

"Sure. But somehow you gotta take the chance. I've always lived this way." I could feel him beside me looking around the cave, as if he could see things there in the darkness. "And even though it's safer down here," he went on, "it's no good."

"You mean you've always lived wild like this? In caves and woods?"

"Sure," he said, his voice more tense. "Most of the time."

"Have you no people? Family of any kind?"

"Sure. But they're no good. Just people. I come away from them."

"And lived wild?"

"Sure."

"Off the earth?"

"Sure—eat where I can. Sleep where I can."

"And now you want to live with people again?"

"I got to learn."

"And when you went to work for the fuel company, you were trying to learn?"

"Yes." There was such a weary resignation about that last yes. It was so sad and pathetically funny.

"A job means giving up your freedom, Richard," I went on. "It means having to go to the same place every day and working for somebody."

"I hate working." There was a harsh edge to his voice. "Not for myself. But for other people."

His sudden anger made me laugh. "I spent a lifetime working for other people," I said, "and I was well paid for my services. I made other men rich and lost my health doing it. Running around for them. Worrying for them. And now here I am at the end of my life, finally independent with a small pension and a poor lame heart that can quit on me at any time." I laughed bitterly. "That's what I gave up my freedom for—for the dubious dignity of having my own little roof to die under." I could sense him listening to me. "Are you sure you want that, Richard?"

"Sure," he said with that funny, automatic decisiveness of his.

Suddenly I was laughing out loud.

"What's so funny?" he said.

"I'm laughing because it's so sad."

He was silent, and I realized that I'd confused him. "I mean you're wanting to give it all up." I sighed. "It's sad. But, I suppose, it's good too. And if that's what you really want, I'll help you all I can." I groped for his hand in the dark. "Is it a deal?"

"Sure. But I don't wanna work for nobody."

"I understand," I said and pumped his hand in the dark. "There's no reason why you can't be self-employed. Some trade. Some profession where you'll be your own boss. Don't worry. We'll work out a way of life for you. We'll take things a step at a time and have you on your own before you know it."

He leaned back in the darkness and as he did so a long sigh of relief rose from somewhere deep within him. I felt I had helped lift a great burden off him and I was strangely happy.

Sitting there in the moist inky darkness I had a sudden vision of him as he looked in dazzling sunlight, shaggy and beatific. Suddenly a question occurred to me.

"Richard— When we first saw you, your hair was short. Then when you moved in with us you let it grow long. Why?"

"It's always been like this."

"Long?"

"Sure. I just cut it to get the job."

"You mean with Beamish?" I asked, a little stunned.

"Sure."

He said it as if he had done the most natural thing in the world. At first I was appalled, thinking of the deceit and the misrepresentation. But then I realized that trickery was the last thing in Richard Atlee's mind. It had nothing to do with tricks at all. Suddenly I was laughing out loud and slapping his knee in the dark, my hoots roaring back at me through the deepest chambers of the cave. It was all too funny. Too perfectly and marvelously funny. Afterwards we sat there in the dark together, our shoulders brushing lightly, listening to one another's breathing and to the stream pounding below us like an artery. After nearly half a year, we'd at last become friends.

Chapter Ten

ONE day early in April the sun shone, the earth got oozy and we knew that spring had come. Alice and I spent the morning down in the basement counting bulbs and examining dahlia tubers. I oiled the lawn mower and inventoried our stock of seed and fertilizer.

"Let's make a list of what we need, Albert, and then go into town."

"Fine," I said. I looked forward to going into town. There were things I wanted to do. The trout season was well under way, and if I couldn't have a partner in Wylie Crane, I might just possibly have one in Richard Atlee. I didn't even take into consideration the fact that Richard couldn't have cared less about fishing. In fact, on that awful night of a few weeks past, he'd said as much to Wylie. Still, I disregarded all of that. Somewhere down deep inside me I had a desire to relive with Richard those sweet, sad wonderful days when Blanche was alive and we were all together at Indian Lake, when I'd given Wylie his first fishing rod and was teaching him to cast.

So in spite of dire premonitions, I'd secretly determined to buy Richard a rig of his own and teach him fly-casting. That was my chief mission in town that day.

Alice and I were nearly out the front door, about to leave for town, when the phone rang. It was Jennings, my tax attorney from Banbury, a small town about twenty miles due west of here. He'd been working over my returns and had run into a number of questions. Would it be all right if he came over? he wanted to know.

"Is it urgent?" I asked.

"Yes." He felt concerned enough to want to get the matter out of the way, as quickly as possible.

"Well, then, we'd better get it done. Come right over."

When I hung up, Alice, who'd been listening to the discussion, was clearly upset. "Albert, we really should get these supplies in and get started. We're already quite late with the lilacs. They should've been in and limed last month."

I thought about it for a moment. Alice unfortunately wasn't a driver.

"Do you suppose Richard could go into town and pick the stuff up?" I asked.

She pondered a moment. "I don't see why not. It never occurred to me. You suppose he has a license?"

"There's only one way to find out." I was already half out the door.

"Where are you going?"

"To find him."

"Do you know where he is?"

"Possibly."

I went down to the bottom of the garden where the forest comes up on the far edge of the lawn, and where Richard's new wall stood. Beyond that forest lay the bog. If Richard was as far back into the bog as the cave, I knew I couldn't reach him. But if he were merely on the other side of the wood, ambling around in the bog, then I had a good chance.

I stood at the bottom of the garden facing the woods, and cupped my hands over my mouth. "Richard!" My voice echoed through the trees.

I waited and called again. "Richard!" And then once more.

I think it was after the third call. Surely it could've been no more. I heard a noise about a hundred yards or so out in the woods and off somewhere to the left.

Branches cracked. Twigs snapped. Great thudding steps came pounding my way. I thought I was being charged by a large stag, and I had an impulse to run. But I didn't. I stood frozen to the spot.

Suddenly a glimpse of red flashed through the trees. Then Richard broke out into the open, loping through the woods like a wild creature, sweeping toward me, a look of near frenzy on his face.

I'll never forget the look of him when he first saw me. At first I thought it was surprise. Later, when he got closer, I realized it was terror or something very nearly that. Quite a sight it was, too—eyes dilated, nostrils flaring, his chest heaving fitfully.

"Richard— What on earth?"

The moment he saw me, a look of enormous relief spread across his face. Suddenly it was clear what had happened. He'd interpreted my calls as an emergency. He'd thought I was in trouble and had come bounding up. It was immensely touching and something I'd scarcely realized. Richard Atlee was deeply attached to me.

A bit of embarrassment followed when he guessed what I was thinking. I scolded and teased him playfully, as if he were a child who'd acted foolishly but admirably. But even as I made an effort to appear by turns stern and amused, it was perfectly evident to him that I was trying to cover my own feelings, so deeply had he touched me by that simple display of loyalty.

When we'd both recovered our composure I spoke: "Mrs. Graves and I were just on our way into town to pick up some seed and other equipment at the nursery. Something's just come up now and we can't go. Can you take the car into town and get what's needed?"

He looked at me a little skeptically. "The car?"

"Of course. How else would you get there?"

"I can take the car?" he asked again as if he hadn't believed it the first time.

"Of course. Now here's the key, and I want you to take the registration just in case—"

In the library I jotted down a list of items while he went upstairs and changed.

When he came back down to get the list, he was dressed in shirt and tie and had combed back the great flowing locks from his forehead.

Outside in the driveway as we stood beside the car I pressed a fifty-dollar bill into his hand. Just as he slipped in behind the wheel, something that'd been buzzing around in my head suddenly spilled from my lips. "Richard—May I see your license?"

The moment the words were out, I knew I'd made a mistake. I could see it in his eyes. I'd come so far with him in the past few weeks. Overcome so much distrust. And now suddenly to undo it all over something idiotic like this.

"I'm sorry, Richard. But I have to see it. You understand."

But of course he didn't. Something flickered in his eyes and hung there for a moment vaguely. In the next moment he snapped out a cheap, frayed, imitation leather wallet. His fingers flipped through a wad of muddy cellophane envelopes for keeping photographs, papers, and the like. He stopped at one and thrust it out at me. The gesture was not rude in itself. But it carried with it an unmistakable hint of contempt. It made me feel a bit like a traffic cop.

It was a driver's license issued by the state of Wyoming to one Richard Atlee. The most cursory inspection revealed that it was valid and up to date. I had to see no more. But of course I couldn't tear my eyes from the rest of the information given there. I read it, full of self-contempt and feeling all of the bitterness pouring out of him.

Date of Birth: July 22, 1953
Address: 45 Hoover Place
Cody, Wyoming

The rest of it was a description of height, weight, eyes, color of hair, etc. Perfectly innocuous stuff, but my eyes devoured it.

So it was that after a period of six months I'd finally

discovered a few tangible facts in the history of Richard Atlee. None of it told me very much, but having the information gave me a curious sense of satisfaction. As if I'd suddenly had the upper hand on him and if anything went wrong, if he'd stepped out of line, there'd be a way of getting him.

Directly opposite the license, in one of those dirty cellophane envelopes was the face of a young boy. He stood beside an older man in the uniform of a soldier. The man was several inches taller than Richard and stood with his arm around him. The face of the soldier was strong and craggy. He had dark hair and a beaked nose. I imagined him to be foreign. Probably Italian.

The boy in the picture had the face of the young man who had come to service my furnace in October. It was clearly Richard Atlee, only three or four years younger, wearing a sport shirt and jeans—all in all, a very conventional-looking young man. I handed him back the wallet through the window. "The soldier I don't recognize," I said playfully. "But I think I've seen the young man before."

He took the wallet back without a word, and left me smiling dismally all by myself. I wanted to smooth over the rough moment we'd just had. But it was a feeble effort, and it didn't win me back any of the affection I'd felt pouring out of him shortly before when he'd come thundering out of the woods in response to my calls.

"I'm sorry, Richard. I had to see it."

"Sure."

"It would've been against the law to let you drive out of here without it."

"Sure."

"And you can't blame me for wanting to know you better."

He shot me an odd glance.

"Drive carefully, will you?"

"Sure." He turned the ignition and the motor started up instantly. When he was rolling backwards down the drive, I waved to him. "We'll wait supper for you."

That was the first time Richard Atlee went to town as my representative. I felt a great pleasure just standing there watching the car recede into the distance leaving in its wake a languid puff of road dust.

There was a strange inner comfort in the knowledge that he was with us now. Part of us, so to speak. If I were to feel ill or out of sorts or tired and there were errands in town, I wouldn't have to go. Now there was a strong young man, faithful and dependable, whom I could send in my place.

What a comfort that is to a man in my state of health. Some one to lean on, someone to fall back upon in time of an emergency. And also, in the back of my mind—if something should happen to me, Alice wouldn't be alone. Yes, even that crossed my mind. Alice's welfare after my death was a source of great concern to me. Not as regards money, of course. There'd be enough for her to live modestly, if not graciously, for the rest of her life. But Alice is not one to make friends easily.

How very touching, I thought again, that look of sheer relief on his face when he'd crashed through the thickets and saw me standing there.

I spent the afternoon with Jennings sparring about deductions and finally cleared up all the outstanding problems. After he left I gave the rest of the afternoon over to reading. I picked up the Blake that Richard had borrowed and thumbed through. Almost instantly, my eyes fell on the lines:

> The little boy lost in the lonely fen,
> Led by the wandering light,
> Began to cry; but God, ever nigh
> Appeared like his father, in white.

> He kissed the child, and by the hand led,
> And to his mother brought,
> Who in sorrow pale, through the lonely dale,
> Her little boy weeping sought.

It seemed almost fateful, seeing these lines first. And when I at last closed the book I was very happy

Along about dusk a car rumbled up the driveway. I assumed it was Richard and went right on reading my newspaper. After about a quarter of an hour Alice poked her head into the parlor.

"Was that Richard who drove up?"

"Yes, I s'pose."

"He's not in here with you?"

"No."

"Why doesn't he come in?"

"I'm sure I don't know."

She looked at me oddly. "I think he's just sitting out there."

"Oh?"

I put my paper down and walked back to the kitchen. You could see the driveway through the window of the kitchen door. When I peered through it I could see my car, and through the half light of dusk, someone sitting behind the wheel.

"Is it Richard?" Alice asked.

"I think so."

"Well, why is he just sitting there?"

I opened the door and stepped out onto the back porch. Just as I did that, the car door opened and Richard Atlee emerged from behind the wheel.

But still he didn't come. He just hovered there tentatively in the half light by the car door and stared up at the house as if he were unsure about coming in.

"Something's wrong," Alice said and started to push past me. But I stopped her. "I'll go."

He stood in the middle of the living room groping for words while we sat there speechless and quaking, listening to his story:

"I kept waitin' for him to wait on me," he said. "Just kept waitin' and waitin'. And still he didn't pay no attention to me. All these people kept comin' in after me and he'd wait on them first. They just come in and get right in front of me." His cheeks were red and his voice fluttered with emotion. "He'd jus' wait on them and pass me right by."

"Who, Richard?" I said. "Mr. Petrie?"

"I don't know—one of 'em."

"One of the clerks?"

"Yeah—I guess. Some pimply little bastard."

"But who?" I asked again. I was beginning to smoulder.

"Will you stop interrupting the boy, Albert! Let him tell it his own way."

"I kept tryin' to get his attention," Richard went on. "Then he said somethin' under his breath and started shoutin' at me. Said, 'Let's see your money.' Just like that. Over and over again, 'Let's see your money.' So I took out that bill you gave me. He took it and went in the back and stayed there a while. Finally he come out again and started waitin' on other people."

"He didn't come back to you?" I said, growing more furious by the moment.

"No. Just went over to the others. People who come in after me. And started waitin' on 'em. Just like I wasn't there."

"But you asked for your money back?" Alice said.

"I did. And he said I didn't have no money. Said I had nothin' and told me to get out—"

"Did you go?" I asked.

"Sure," he replied, as much surprised at my question as I was by his answer. "Which one was it?" I asked growing more and more livid as the story unfolded.

"I don't know," he said. "This pimply little guy."

"It wouldn't be Petrie," said Alice. "He wouldn't do a thing like that. Not to us. We've given him so much business."

"Richard," I said, "you did mention the fact you were picking these items up for me? You did mention my name?"

He nodded, his head going furiously up and down.

We ate our supper in gloomy silence. Richard scarcely touched his plate. Alice had made him a peach Melba that night. It was one of his favorites, but it remained untouched on his plate.

"Don't let it bother you, Richard," I said. "We'll drive over to Petrie's in the morning and straighten this whole thing out."

Suddenly he stood up. It was a bolting motion that shot him to his feet. It startled Alice so that she dropped a coffee spoon into an empty dessert plate. In the next instant, without a word of parting, he turned and left the table. He went directly to his room.

Alice watched the peach Melba dissolving slowly in Richard's plate. "Poor boy. He feels so bad."

"He feels he's failed us."

Alice turned a troubled face toward me. "I'm worried."

"Worried? About what, for heaven sake? I'll go down there in the morning and straighten it out."

"Do you think so?"

"Of course. Petrie's a good man. He's reasonable. I'm sure there's a perfectly plausible—"

"Albert."

"Yes."

"Do you think he's telling us the truth?" She'd put her finger on exactly what had been troubling me.

"At first, I didn't," I said without any hesitation. "But now I'm convinced of it."

She kissed me and then together we cleared the dishes from the table.

"Mr. Petrie," I said after several routine amenities. It was the following morning and I was standing at one of the counters of the nursery, a handful of people drifting about me. From where I stood I could look out into the greenhouse, cluttered with a multitude of blooms. Sun streaming through the glass transoms was transformed into a soft green diffusion of light. The air was moist and heavy with the dungy smells of fertilizer, peat moss, and verdant growing things. From somewhere in the greenhouse, a canary was singing its heart out.

"What time did you say this was?" asked Petrie after I'd told him Richard's story.

"Around four P.M."

"Yep," he shook his head emphatically. "I was here, all right. But I don't recall no such incident. Leastways I didn't see nothin' like that. Tell me again what the boy looked like."

Again I gave him a fairly detailed description of Richard.

"I'd sure remember somebody who looked like that." He scratched his head.

"Then you don't recall him?"

"Nope. Not offhand."

Petrie was not a good liar. His face flushed when I looked at him closely and he showed the strain of trying to affect a look of earnest concern. He could scarcely meet my eyes.

"Maybe one of the other boys waited on him, Mr. Graves."

"Would you call them please?"

His lashes fluttered like two moths above his eyes. "Ernie," he called. "George."

Two youths converged on us from different directions of the shop.

"This here's Mr. Graves," said Petrie. "He's got some questions to ask you."

The one called Ernie was an oafish, shambling lad whose mouth hung open chronically. The other one, George, was a smirking little character in his early twenties with excessively oily hair and bad skin.

Seeing the two of them there—and with Richard's vague description of a "pimply bastard" to go on, I put my money squarely on George. Even if I'd had no description at all, I'd have put my money on George. There was a slithering, conspiratorial thing about him, from his toes right up to his sleek, little bullet-shaped head.

I related the story once again, this time for the two boys, making sure to present the whole thing in the most innocent light. As if it had been nothing but the most honest sort of misunderstanding.

When I finished I was staring into blank faces. The mouth of the one called Ernie hung open even wider in a look of total incomprehension. Both of them denied having any encounter such as the one I described.

"Now, you're sure," said Petrie, addressing the two of them with a voice full of fraudulent severity, just for my benefit.

They both nodded blankly, while all about them was the look of angelic choir boys.

Petrie shrugged and looked sympathetically at me. "Maybe he went to some other nursery."

"No," I said, "he came here."

"Might've lost the money someplace, somehow, and was too scared to tell you. You know how boys are—" He laughed.

I was about to say something rude, but I checked myself.

"Do you have any other sales help? Part-time people who aren't here every day?"

"These are the only two I got," said Petrie. "Both good boys." George was beaming unctuously at me.

"Wait a moment," I said and marched to the front door. I opened it and called out, "Richard. Would you step in here a moment?"

He'd been sitting outside in the car. It was still quite early in the morning and there were not more than a half-dozen customers in the store. Richard's appearance was such as to pull them all together into a small knot of gaping inquisitive people.

I took him by the arm and guided him to the place where the two boys stood. "Richard, which one of these gentlemen took your money yesterday?"

He pointed instantly to George. "That one."

"He's a God damned liar!" said George, suddenly red in the face. "I never seen him."

Richard stiffened beside me. I now directed my remarks to Petrie, speaking as if George didn't exist at all. "I've known Richard for several months now. I've never known him to lie."

"He's the one," said Richard, once again pointing to George.

"I don't know what he's talkin' about," said George. "I never seen him. I don't have his money. He's crazy."

Richard started to move for George, who quickly ducked behind Ernie. The one called Ernie started to shuffle his feet uncertainly. It was a tense moment when I reached out and checked Richard. A low murmur swept through the store.

"Mr. Petrie," I said, "I won't be able to do any more business with you until my fifty dollars is returned and I have an apology. At that time I'll consider the matter closed and we'll never mention it again. Until that time, I'll take care of all my gardening needs over in Banbury." Petrie was flushed and a little embarrassed about the other people in the store. As he spoke he made a clumsy effort to appear very calm. But his eyes were more guilty than ever. There was a quaver in his voice. "Suit yourself, Mr. Graves, I'll be sorry to lose your business." When he stalked out, George was smiling again more broadly than ever.

Driving home that morning, I sat fuming at the wheel, too furious to talk. Richard was also silent. But at a certain point, more than halfway home, he suddenly stirred and spoke: "I'll get your money back." There wasn't a trace of agitation in his voice. It all had an icy calm to it. I should've heeded those words. I should've paid more attention to the almost nerveless, unfeeling quality with which the line was spoken.

"Don't worry about it," I said, "Petrie's a sensible man. I'm sure we'll find a check in the mail in a few days."

"No, we won't," he said, then clamped his mouth shut as if he never intended to speak again.

I slowed the car down and looked sideways at him. "What did you say?"

But he didn't answer. He just sat there staring straight ahead at the road unfolding slowly before us.

I knew he felt badly—responsible for the loss of the money and thinking that he'd failed us. He'd been gulled by a slick seed salesman and it bothered him. It would've bothered me, too—a sleazy, unctuous petty larcenist like

George. Just recalling that nasty little smirk as we were leaving rankled me. I can imagine what it did to him.

That afternoon I thought it was a good time to unveil my surprise. Shortly after lunch I asked him if he'd like to go fishing with me. To my surprise he said that he would. He seemed almost eager about it. But he said that he had no equipment. Whereupon, I went to the closet and produced a long cylindrical cardboard tube wrapped in gift paper, and handed it to him. I had had it sent out to me from town a few days before.

He was clearly confused. He held the tube in his hand for a while, not knowing quite what to do. I prodded him gently to open it, laughing all the while. Alice came in and watched us. We both teased him until he fumbled with the strings and ties. Finally, standing there with the tube unsheathed and all the wrappings strewn about his feet, he had the look of a man who was defusing a bomb.

He opened the tube and peered down the long black hole. Then slowly he extracted the new fly rod. At the bottom of the tube, he found a small box full of the finest hand-tied German trout flies. The way he held it and looked at it—all red and flustered and making little yipping sounds—was more reward than we'd ever dared to hope for. Alice and I just stood there and had ourselves a jolly good laugh.

"Have you ever used one of these?" I asked.

He shook his head. "No."

"Well, that's yours, then, and I'll show you how to use it."

He appeared to be on the verge of speech, but nothing came. Rather than let him struggle any further for words of gratitude, I picked up his new rod and his box of flies, grasped him firmly under the arm and led him out the kitchen door to the drive, where the car was already waiting.

We spent the afternoon up at a stream far back in the woods. You could drive up a dirt road to within a mile of it. From there on, you had to track out through the woods.

It was a beautiful day. The forest, full of new foliage,

was just beginning to warm up. There was a concert of peepers and crows yawping through the branches and you could smell the earth turning green all over.

Richard walked several paces ahead, carrying most of the equipment. There was something about the way he walked through a track of wilderness. He didn't walk so much as he loped, and he gave the impression that he'd been in those woods all his life and knew every inch of them. Although to the best of my knowledge he'd never been through this particular tract, he seemed to know just where he was, and exactly where we were going. It was very much like the day we walked out to the cave. He was in his own element. He owned the land.

When we reached the stream, I demonstrated for him once the most elementary principles of fly-casting, then turned him loose on his own. At first it was odd and rather amusing watching his arm go up stiffly, and then the awkwardness as he paid out the line. But the awkwardness lasted only a short while. After an hour or so, he held the rod as if he'd been holding it for years. And when he cast, the rod moved as if it were a part of his body.

I was astonished by his facility. "You're sure you've never done this before?"

"Just with a string and hook," he said laconically. "Never with one of these." He looked at the rod worshipfully, still not willing to believe that it was actually his own.

We had a wonderful afternoon. At one point while we stood thigh-high in long rubber boots, a stiff, icy current churning the water white all around us, I shouted to him above the roar, "Who's the man in the photograph?"

He looked up as if he hadn't heard me.

"The photograph in your wallet," I went on.

"What about it?"

"Who is it?"

"My father." He flicked his rod and the line arched out in a graceful curve across the stream.

His answer surprised me. It was hard to think of Richard Atlee as having a father.

"Where is he now?"

"I don't know."

"And your mother?"

"Dead I think."

"You don't know for sure?"

"No."

"Ever try to find out?"

"No."

"You don't care to?"

"No."

All that conversation was conducted at a shout in order to carry our voices above the roar of the flood. But there had been an awful detachment about it, too. Awful, I say, when you consider the nature of the information being divulged. For a moment I thought, "How insensitive." But that wasn't it at all. It wasn't insensitivity. It was something else. Something else completely, and I couldn't put my finger on it.

He caught three superb rainbow trout that afternoon compared to my one scraggly specimen that I begrudgingly put back in. There was in him an almost unerring instinct for laying down a fly precisely where a fish would rise for it. And most pleasing of all was the fact that he was totally unaware of how good he was.

But in spite of his uncanny success, it was clear that he felt only the most tepid kind of enthusiasm for the activity. And that enthusiasm, I'm sure, was simply an attempt to please me.

I can still see that rod of his bending thrillingly beneath the weight of a fish, the red-white bobber skimming frantically along the top of the froth, then going under. The line paying out farther and farther—then suddenly, thirty yards down stream, a sleek, silver knifelike shape breaching water poised in mid-air; then the majestic weight of it, flopping back down with a loud, gorgeous splash—

I was wild with excitement, shouting him instructions he really didn't need. Then when he had it heavy and heaving in his net and had clapped the creel cover over the great whomping weight of it, he seemed to be standing outside of his triumph, aloof and remote. It was as if someone else had caught the fish. I looked at him a little strangely.

When we were ready to go, I asked him what he wanted to do with his trout. He handed them all to me, strung on a line.

"Give them to Missus."

"You caught them. You give them to her."

"I can't."

"Go ahead. Don't be foolish." I thrust them back at him, and in that moment I saw something very close to terror in his eyes. I took back the fish and put them into my creel. "All right, Richard, I'll give them to her. We'll have them for supper tonight."

Chapter Eleven

SEVERAL times in the days that followed, Richard asked me if Petrie had refunded my money. I couldn't report that he had. Then suddenly, I think it was three days after the affair, he wasn't around the house any more. I don't mean that he vanished. He still slept in his room each night, but he was no longer nearby in the daytime, nor did he take his supper with us. He continued to do his chores, working in the early morning long before we woke. Then he was gone for the rest of the day, until quite late at night, when he'd let himself in the front door, after we had gone to sleep.

Alice and I began to feel some concern about his prolonged absences. I suppose that we missed seeing him and were concerned about what he was up to.

One afternoon I sat with Alice in the kitchen and watched her go about the business of making a cake. At one point she looked up from whipping a batter and said, "You don't think he's getting ready to go?"

"Go where?"

"Away. I mean now that the weather is getting warm and everything. You think he's got a job, Albert. Maybe it's a job."

"Maybe," I said. I was tying some trout flies. "I don't think so."

"He acts awfully funny." She paused from her whipping. "Strange."

"Well, he is that," I laughed a little. "I suppose that's why we like him."

"But I mean stranger than average." She went on and started to whip the batter again. "He's very secretive. Have you noticed that?"

"Yes. I suppose I have."

"You don't think he's getting ready to leave us, do you, Albert?"

"I don't know. Hand me those scissors, will you?"

She leaned over and passed me the scissors. When I took them I looked up at her. She was miserably upset.

"Well, he's going to leave us some day, Alice. You might just as well face the fact. It could be today or tomorrow or anytime. He's not tied to us."

She stared into her batter, as if she were reading an augury there. Then after a moment she said, "I think you're wrong, Albert." Her arm swept round the bowl in a circle. "I think he is tied to us. I think he's very attached. I don't think he could bear to leave us any more."

I don't know why, but a curious anger rose within me. "I wish you wouldn't say that, Alice."

"Why?" From the way she said it, I sensed disaster coming. But I was powerless to avert it. I started as reasonably as I could. "Well—for one thing, our whole purpose in this from the start has been to put the boy back on his feet. We agreed to set no time limits, but to let the boy go out under his own power in his own good time."

She was about to protest.

"Didn't we agree to that, Alice?"

She shook her head vehemently, then turned—wheeled, rather—back to the batter.

"You haven't answered me, Alice."

"Answered you what?"

"Didn't we agree to—"

"To what?" she snapped. "Agree to what?"

I felt a rush of heat at the back of my neck and suddenly I could hear my voice, very far outside myself, talking with a quiet fierce emphasis. "To let the boy go at a time when he himself feels he is ready."

"Well, that time is not here, Albert."

"Perhaps it is," I said very softly.

She placed her hands squarely on her hips and faced me directly. "You'd like to see him go now, wouldn't you?"

"I didn't say that."

"You don't have to. It's all over your face. It started with Wylie, didn't it?"

"Wylie has nothing to do with it." My fists clenched. "I was about to suggest that we send him to a good trade school."

"A trade school?" She looked at me skeptically.

"Yes. That's what the boy wants. He wants to be his own man, and I can't say that it's a bad idea to—"

"Trade school?" Her eyes widened enormously behind her glasses. Then suddenly she was laughing mockingly. "Oh, honestly, Albert. You're so transparent. That's just an excuse to get him out of here—

"You've had just about enough of playing father now. You've enjoyed it for a couple of months and now you'd like to go back to those easy days of just going about and pleasing yourself."

"Oh, stop it, Alice."

"Gratifying all your whims. Doing just what you want to do and letting the rest of the world go to hell!"

"We were having a simple conversation about his future," I said, trying to control the quaver in my voice. "Why do you always have to put things on a personal level?"

"Well, it's true, isn't it?"

"What's true?"

"What I said about your wanting to see him go."

"No!" I barely smothered a shout. "I don't want to see him go. But I also realize that you can't tie him down.

I know him a little better than you do. He enjoys his freedom. He needs it."

She laughed scornfully. "You're talking about yourself, Albert. When you talk about freedom, you're confusing him with you. This boy's been starved for a home and a family. Now he's got one——"

"And you'd like to keep him in a state of prolonged infancy——"

"Infancy——" She flung the word back at me, her eyes blazing. "What do you mean, infancy?"

"You know very well what I mean."

"For the life of me, Albert, I think you must be mad." She turned back to the batter and resumed her whipping motion, but the mixing spoon clattered off onto the aluminum counter. "What do you mean, infancy?"

"Cooking for him. Knitting for him. Sewing. Doing laundry. Getting all excited when he's out a bit too late, or when his nose runs."

Her face grew red. She talked across the kitchen to where I sat. "I do very little for him in comparison to what he does for us. And I worry about him because I care for him."

"I care for him, too," I said. "Perhaps more than you do. But I realize that some day he'll have to go. There's a family——"

"Family?" Her jaw dropped. The word seemed to stun her. She grew defensive. "What family?"

"There's a father."

"How do you know?"

"I saw a picture in his wallet."

"And the mother?" She seemed almost to cringe as she said the word.

"The mother's dead. But I'm sure there are other kin."

If she had a spell of fright, it lasted only a moment. In the next instant she folded her arms and was again staring at me as belligerently as ever. "Well, I don't know what kind of kin they are that'd let a boy that age run loose all over the land."

"Well, whether you like it or not," I went on, "those

are the facts. So don't get your hopes too high. I grant the boy does seem fond of us—"

"Fond?" she said and laughed in that irritating way. "Haven't you noticed?"

Something in her voice upset me. "Noticed what?"

"It's much more than fondness. Much, much more."

That afternoon we drove into town to take care of some chores, and while Alice was in doing the marketing, I drove over to Mr. Washburn's to get gas and have the car serviced.

But it wasn't Washburn who came out of the garage when I rolled up to the pumps. To my delight and surprise it was Richard Atlee. It made an incongruous and striking picture, this tall, Biblical-looking creature with his thick tangled beard and his mane of shoulder-length hair, cranking a gasoline pump. He looked a bit like a demented prophet.

At first glance he didn't recognize the car. Then a moment later he was peering at my face through the windshield. Mild surprise fluttered momentarily across his features, then was gone.

"Hello, Richard."

"Hello," he said, and from the cold perfunctory clip to his voice, I realized I was to be treated like any other customer.

"Fill it up, please," I said. "And check the oil and water."

He went about his business without uttering a word. When I paid him, he said, "Thank you." He seemed awkward and unhappy to be caught there—as if he were embarrassed by the job and by having to wear the uniform of a hired public servant.

Just as I was getting ready to drive off, I caught a glimpse of Washburn in the mechanic's shed. It was mild weather and he'd taken off his mackinaw. But he still wore his peaked cap with the ear laps.

He was stooped beneath the hood of a car as I rolled slowly past. For a moment he looked up and gazed at me with all of that majestic contempt with which he regarded

the world around him—particularly people of my ilk. I
confess my affection for the man rose even higher that
day. Of all the people in that little town, with the exception of ourselves, Washburn was the only other person
willing to acknowledge Richard Atlee's existence And
even more than that, to entrust him with a job.

It wasn't terribly difficult to guess why Richard Atlee,
with his marked antipathy for regular employment, suddenly went to work. And our guess was proved out only
one week after he'd started his period of employment.

Alice and I rose one morning at the conclusion of that
week and went down to breakfast. There we found our
freshly squeezed orange juice, fresh biscuits, and a pot of
coffee simmering over a low flame. The table was neatly
set with two place settings, and beside my plate I found
five crisp, new, ten-dollar bills.

Outside, from the garden, came the sound of a spade
turning earth. It was Richard turning topsoil in Alice's
hyacinth and lily beds. We went to the window and
watched him. Now that he'd taken off the green khaki
denims of a garage mechanic and slipped into his old
clothes he seemed more his old self again. His spade rose
and fell, and he worked with enthusiasm. I imagine he was
rather pleased with himself. He'd retired what he thought
of as his debt to me. And having done that, he felt free
to resign his job at Washburn's. He'd got the terrible ordeal over with.

Thus went our lives that spring, and indeed as the
weather grew warmer, we found Richard doing more and
more about the house.

We woke one Sunday morning in April and were
stretching our legs around the property when we noticed
that something about the garage seemed different. During
the winter the structure had taken an awful beating. Pelted
by snow and driving rains, its paint had peeled badly
and its shutters were in a state of disarray. I had bought
paint several weeks earlier and had stashed it in the
garage intending to do the job myself. Like many dis-

tasteful chores I'd put the thing off week after week. Now suddenly the garage rose out of the ground before us, fresh, gleaming, and white, like a wedding cake, with lilacs and white roses sprouting up all around it.

He had painted the outside of the garage, doing his work in the early morning, with such swiftness and efficiency that we never even noticed the transformation that was taking place. It was the stone wall business all over again. He'd never even bothered asking us if he could, or telling us when he had. He'd simply done it in his usual way—while everyone else slept.

The paint job threw Alice into a transport of ecstasy, and that night she baked him a strawberry-rhubarb pie and made a great fuss over him at supper. She was thrilled with the way the garage looked, and so was I. He'd done a superb job, and I was grateful for that, but the manner in which he'd gone about it irked me, and even as she rattled on and cooed over him and genuflected all around, I felt the cold waves of resentment washing over me like a tide.

Several mornings later, along about sun-up, I was awakened by a rhythmic whooshing sound outside my window. I rolled over to see what it was. The bedroom windows face east, and when I turned and opened my eyes I found myself squinting into a shaft of sunlight. While I struggled to adjust my eyes, Richard Atlee's face came slowly into focus—sliding back and forth within the frame of the window. He was on a ladder, painting the wall just beneath the eaves with a halo of sunlight blazing all about his shoulders. He had in fact just started to paint the entire exterior of the house.

I recall the angry haste with which I threw on a bathrobe and jammed my bare feet into cold shoes, and then barging outside, the screen door banging behind me and Alice, struggling into a shift, close at my heels. Then I was standing under the ladder and shouting up at him:

"Look here—nobody asked you to do that."

"It needs it." He made long, rhythmic strokes with the brush, his eyes fixed on the eave beneath the runners.

"Maybe it does," I said, trying to remain calm. "Nevertheless, I would've appreciated your asking me first. Where'd you get the paint for that, anyway?"

"Ordered it."

"You ordered it."

"From the hardware store."

"The hardware—" The word stuck in my throat. "By what right did you?" I roared up at him. "You have no right—"

"Oh?" he said.

"Yes. You have no right to order anything unless I specifically—"

"You like it, don't you?" There was something almost surly in the way he said it.

"I like it fine, but don't you ever do anything like that in the future unless you ask me first."

He kept his eyes fixed stolidly on the dirty, rain-spattered eaves, concentrating intently on the steady rhythmic whooshing of his stroke.

"Did you hear me?" I said now as resolutely as I could.

"Sure," he said, never missing a stroke. He didn't even bother looking up when I stalked off.

We were working out in the garden one morning. Richard had done his chores and was off somewhere. It was a perfect morning—the air cool, the sky a deep blue enamel, and the whole earth full of the smell of new grass. A lot of the birds that had been out of the area for the winter, like the robins and finches, were suddenly back and all around us. We put seed into the feeders and cleaned out the various birdhouses around the property to make ready for them.

When they finally came, they came in profusion—whole chattering, warbling, trilling busy flocks of them—rising and descending, tumbling out of the branches all over the place, with great flashes of color and unspeakably pretty songs.

We went about our work savoring the morning until, quite suddenly, the peace of the moment was spoiled by the high whining sound of a car climbing, in its second gear, the hill running just in front of our property.

When you hear a car in this section of the world you still look up. We did, and saw a station wagon turn into our drive, then bounce and lurch its way up the gravel path and disappear behind the garage.

I dropped my trowel and lumbered to my feet. But before I could get down to the garage, we heard a car door slam and then footsteps on the gravel. In the next moment I saw a tall, square figure turn the corner and move slowly toward us. The first thing I saw was the wide-brimmed hat, and then the boots. Between those two polar points was a long expanse of gray. It was the institutional gray of a civil uniform. Emil Birge was coming toward me.

In the next moment I was staring up into the red, beefy face with the sprays of purple capillaries raked out along each cheek. He was smiling amiably and thrust his hand toward me. I slipped off my gardening glove and took his outstretched hand.

"How are you?" I said while he pumped my hand.

Alice came up behind me and hovered there until he raised his hat to her. " 'Lo, Miz Graves—"

"Hello, sheriff."

"Pretty day."

"Yes, it is," Alice agreed, smiling, a look of apprehension on her face.

His eyes swung easily round the grounds, up past the garage, and on toward the main house. "You folks sure done a lot of pretty work on this property." He was looking at the freshly painted main house. "Quigleys just let the place go to hell. Haven't seen you up to church lately," he went on.

"We haven't been there," I answered somewhat curtly. The subject of the church still rankled in me.

"Missed you," he said. "Ain't had no sickness, have you?"

"No," I said.

"That's good." His tone of voice was full of thoughtful concern.

I had the feeling he was mocking us. Surely he knew

about our banishment from Reverend Horn's congregation. We chatted a bit longer while his eyes continued to swing back and forth over the property, as if he were recording every hill and slope of it for all posterity. For all that smiling and all that affability, there was something unpleasant about the man. Obviously he had something on his mind, and at last I got tired of waiting for him to get to the point. "Is there something I can do for you, sheriff?"

"That boy you got up here—"

My heart skipped a beat. "Richard?"

"Richard. That's it. What's his surname?"

"Atlee," I said.

"Richard Atlee," mumbled Alice right after me.

Birge smiled. "That's it. Richard Atlee." He paused a moment, peering back into the garden. "He still living up here with you?"

"Yes, he is," I said.

"Down in your cellar?" he asked.

"No. He's upstairs with us now," I said.

"We've made up a room for him on the ground floor," Alice added.

Birge's eyes narrowed to a squint. "You folks been awfully good to that boy."

"He's been very good to us," I said. I was beginning to feel a twinge of impatience. I felt I was being toyed with. I could sense him trying to manipulate us by trying to make us guess what was on his mind.

"Where's he at?" he said quite suddenly.

"Just now?" I asked, trying to appear calm.

"That's right," he said.

"He was here this morning," Alice said.

"You don't know where he is now?"

"Probably off in the woods somewhere," I said trying to smile.

"That's what he likes best of all," Alice said.

There was a look of amusement in Birge's eyes. "The woods?"

"That's what I'd guess," I said.

"He been with you regularly?" he asked. "Right along?"

"Since about Christmas, I'd say. Wouldn't you?" I turned to Alice.

"Yes," she said. "It was right about Christmas." She was quite nervous.

Birge nodded his head and kept swiveling his eyes from one area to the other. "You mind if I look around?"

"Help yourself," I said. I couldn't imagine that he could see any more than he'd already seen.

He started to amble off slowly, and we followed him.

"Has he done anything wrong?" Alice asked, her voice full of apprehension.

Birge didn't answer. He just shrugged his shoulders and continued to saunter along at a leisurely pace. We followed him around from the garage to the main house, through the gardens and down to the stone wall at the bottom of the property, Alice and I trotting along at his heel like obedient pack dogs.

"Sure took some strength to build that wall," he said admiringly. Finally I reached the end of my patience.

"You mind telling us what this is all about?" I said.

Birge looked out over the stone wall and into the woods. "Somebody busted into Harlowe Petrie's last night."

"Petrie's?" said Alice again, her eyes widening.

"That's right, Miz Graves."

"Why come to us?" I asked.

"Harlowe said you'd know all about it."

"Know about it?" I snapped. "Does he think the boy robbed his place? He didn't. I'll tell you right now."

"Didn't say nothin' about robbery," Birge said, a look of injury on his face. "Nothing was taken. Someone just got in there last night and made an awful mess."

"A mess?" Alice said, too overwrought to say much else.

"Busted up the place pretty good," Birge added.

I felt my anger mounting. "What's that have to do with Richard?"

"Didn't say it did," the sheriff replied.

"Oh, it's that silly business about the fifty dollars," Alice said.

"What business is that, Miz Graves?"

"I'm sure Petrie didn't tell you about that," I said, feeling vindicated and scornful.

"He didn't tell me nothin'. Only that you'd know somethin' about what happened to his place."

I told him the story about Richard's encounter with the sales clerk at Petrie's and about the fifty dollars.

"You got that sales clerk pretty well pegged, don't you?" said Birge, when I'd finished.

"You wouldn't have to be Sherlock Holmes to know it," I said with growing anger. "You just speak to him."

Birge lifted his hat and scratched his head. He pawed the earth with his foot, pointing the toe down like a ballet dancer. "Where was he last night?"

"Right here!" I snapped.

"All night?"

"That's right."

"You know that for sure?"

I didn't know, and for a moment I ransacked my brain for some clever reply. "He had supper with us. At nine o'clock he got a book and went to his room. At ten I saw the light go out under his door. It was about ten, wasn't it, Alice?"

She nodded to Birge. "He always goes to bed at ten."

"We went to bed around eleven," I added. "He was still there."

"How do you know?" Birge asked.

The question pulled me up short. Of course I didn't know. "Well, where else would he be?"

Birge smiled as if my blustering had told him all he needed to know.

"Would you be surprised if I told you he was seen over in town about midnight?"

"Last night?" Alice asked, looking very skeptical.

"That's right."

"And when did this Petrie business take place?" I asked.

" 'Bout two A.M."

I caught a glimpse of Alice's eyes—full of hurt and disbelief.

"Oh—I don't believe it," she said.

I must admit very frankly that I half did. But I wasn't going to say that. For some reason we'd simply assumed that having a room upstairs and a place to eat regularly had put an end to Richard's nocturnal ramblings. For the life of me now I can't imagine what reason there was to justify such a wild assumption.

"Well, he's not a prisoner here," I said. "He's always been free to go and come as he pleases."

Birge looked at me, "Oh?" he said, his voice full of portentousness.

"Is that bad?" I said, already a little terrified that I'd made some huge blunder and inadvertently turned the key in the cell that would encage Richard Atlee forever.

"Nope," said Birge. "Ain't bad at all." His eyes swung out again across the patch of wood and settled fixedly on the stone wall. "He sure done a pretty job on that wall for you, Albert, ain't he?"

It always irritated me the way Birge would slip into first names after he'd been calling you by your surname for the past half-hour. "Look here," I said finally, at the end of my patience, "are you charging him formally?"

"Not charging anyone."

"Then I'm not going to answer any more questions. And if you want my opinion of Petrie, he's a son of a bitch. He knows as well as I do that oily worm of a clerk he's got working for him stole fifty dollars from the boy!"

Birge gazed at me silently, his greenish-yellow eyes narrowing again until they were thin gashes in his head. "How would you like to come over to Petrie's with me and have a look around?"

"For what purpose?" I shouted.

"Don't get yourself all het up," said Birge.

"I will not go down there!" I added emphatically. By this time small pinwheels were spinning before my eyes.

"Why should he have to go?" Alice said.

"No one sayin' he has to. But I think it's something he oughta see. Somethin' the two of you oughta see. I tell you, it'd be an education."

It wasn't the words, but the way he said it. The effect of it was to change the whole gist of our thinking.

"Very well," said Alice, after we'd exchanged a brief glance, "we'll go right away."

It was a grim spectacle we saw there that morning, the glass walls and roof of the greenhouse punched out; jagged shards of glass still hinged to the window frames, like broken teeth in a shattered mouth; the splintered glass counters; the big fifty-pound bags of seed and humus, gouged and slashed, their innards seeping slowly outwards onto the floor; the floor strewn with glass and peat; dozens of pots of plants and flowers, overturned, uprooted, or hurled against the walls with such violence as to fracture and perforate the plaster in many spots. And the machinery—the harvesters and tractors, the spreaders and power mowers, all horribly hacked and smashed. And above that, hanging like a haze, the nauseating choking stink of dung fertilizers.

But it wasn't the mere spectacle of destruction that shook me so deeply—as total and final as that was. What stunned me was the force of violence in the act. As I stood there I tried to compute in my head the amount of sheer hate a single person, acting alone, had to generate in order to wreak that much devastation. When I thought about it, it made me feel a little giddy and weak in the knees as we stood there in the doorway with the waves of fertilizer dust pushing outwards against us.

"Surely you don't think one person could have done all this?" I said.

Birge walked slowly to a corner of the nursery, the sound of grinding glass beneath his heels. His back was to us when he reached a point and stooped over. When he stood up again and started back toward us he was carry-ing a long-handled lumberman's ax. He carried it head down and dangling at his knee. "It was done with this."

"Just that?" I asked.

"That's all we found." He watched me closely as he spoke. "Didn't even bother tryin' to conceal it, either. Just chucked it off there in the corner when he was finished."

"Are there any fingerprints?" I asked.

"Sure," Birge said, with a smile that was a little patroniziig. "Hundreds of 'em. Thousands. This thing's been settin' around this placc for years. Probably find the fingerprints of the whole damn town on it, includin' yours and mine as well."

"But there must be fresh prints," I said.

Birge sighed. "I doubt it."

"Why?"

"Person who did this," Birge said, his eyes scanning the ceiling and the floors, "was a pro. Had to be in order to get as much done as he did. A pro don't have no prints around. He's very clean. Wears gloves." He held the ax up for me to inspect. "We'll check it for prints," he said. "But we ain't gonna find none."

Alice stared at the ax, a sickly expression on her face. "You mean to tell me that nobody heard all this going on last night?"

"This is a pretty far piece from town, Miz Graves. No houses or people 'round. Nobody to bother a man if he's bent on trouble."

Just then a small bell jingled and Petrie appeared from somewhere in back of the store. Standing behind him was a drab, wispy-looking creature with small, frightened eyes. I took this to be his wife. Petrie himself appeared to be among the living dead. His clothing was rumpled, his eyes dazed and ringed with red. His tousled hair appeared to have gone full gray overnight.

When he saw us, he stiffened. Then he made a move toward me and stumbled, but the tiny creature at his side caught his sleeve and held him fast. Just then Birge grabbed him.

Suddenly Petrie, with both feet set unsteadily on the floor, swaying a bit like a harbor buoy, raised a long, hairy arm and thrust an accusatory finger in my direction. "You know who did this!" The voice came out a hoarse, raspy whisper. "You Goddamn well know who did this—"

"Harlowe," sobbed the little birdlike thing still clutching his sleeve. He snatched his arm from her as if he were about to fling her off. She fled backwards more from fright than the violence of the motion.

"You Goddamn well know who!" Petrie thundered. "And you're gonna pay. Hear me? You're gonna Goddamn well pay."

When Birge half-guided, half-pushed us out the front door, Petrie was still thundering, his face the color of ashes, and wagging a finger at me like a specter. Standing outside by the car I was terribly rattled. I could still hear the man ranting inside the nursery.

When we got into the car, I rolled the window down and Birge stood there stooping and chatting with us quietly, sweating under his trooper's hat.

"He's wiped out," Birge said. "Under-insured."

"I'm sorry about that," I said curtly. "That's awfully short-sighted. Having a business and not having proper coverage."

He made a sound halfway between a word and a grunt. "Well, like I say, I wanted you to see it."

"Well, now I've seen it," I replied, my eyes fixed straight ahead. "And it proves nothing."

"That's right," said Birge. "Seeing as how the boy was home with you all night."

"He may very well have been," I said, bristling at the sarcasm. "It's my word against the word of this person who saw him in town."

"That's right," said Birge. "That's right." He said it as if he were pacifying an hysterical child. "Tell me—you know anything about this boy you got up there with you?" he said.

I glared at him stonily. "I know everything I have to know about him."

We drove back in silence, the sky blue and splashed with long white feathery clouds, the earth green and the air heavy with new foliage. And in my mind, sharply and indelibly etched a picture—sun slanting through jagged shards of glass, and the bags of seed, slumped over and oozing their contents out onto the floor. I tried over and over again to relate the picture to Richard Atlee.

There was a part of me that wanted to see him wielding the ax, see the blade flashing in wide whooshing arcs, impacting with a sickening thud on the stuffed bags and shattering the glass. I could see a body in shadows, nearly faceless, caught up in that fury like a windmill run amuck. But I couldn't attach that sweet, shy, almost saintlike face to the body. None of it was plausible.

Halfway to the house, Alice, her eyes fixed straight ahead and riveted to the road, suddenly said: "He was out last night."

The car swerved a bit. "Oh?" I said. That was all I could manage to say, and then I drove on quietly, conscious of a long sigh coming from me.

"I heard him come in about four o'clock," she went on.

"You did?"

"Through the cellar door."

"I see."

"What does it mean? After all, it doesn't actually mean—"

"For God's sake, Alice—"

"I know," she moaned softly. I thought she was going to cry.

"The cellar door?" I said it over and over again as if the act of repetition could obliterate the fact. "He hasn't come in that way for months. He uses the front door now, doesn't he? At least that's what I thought."

"I know," she said very softly. "I know you thought that."

I looked at her cringing now in her seat. "Doesn't he?" I asked again with a terrible sense of foreboding.

This time she didn't answer, but merely kept her eyes riveted to the road.

"Has he been going out nights again?" I asked. "Regularly, I mean?"

I feared the answer, knowing it full well before it came.

"Pretty much." She whispered the words almost under her breath.

I drove a bit further through the spring morning, watching a lofty mushroom of a cloud, fixed and unmoving in the distance as if it were etched on the sky. "For God's sake, Alice. Why didn't you say anything?"

I felt her turn and stare at me while I watched the faded white line running down the center of the road.

"Say what?" she gasped. "Say he was out last night? Are you mad?"

"Well, I didn't mean——"

"Put him right in the hands of Birge. He'd just love that. Say something, indeed. Would you have?"

She has a way of putting things right on the line, Alice does. It's a kind of bluntness that's made me blanch in the past. Her question had gone right to the heart of the matter, and my response to it was immediate.

"No," I said, a little shocked at my own reply, "I wouldn't have."

We made a right turn off the main highway and started up the Bog Road.

After a while I said, "He wouldn't have much of a chance with these people here."

"None," she said flatly, her voice a peculiar mixture of defiance and fright.

"Well don't worry. We're not going to let them railroad the boy."

"They'd love to," she said. "Oh, wouldn't they just love to!"

"Yes," I said. "But I won't let them."

Those were bold words coming from the likes of me. Even as I said them, hearing my voice a little tinny and tremulous, coming at me over great distances, I could barely get my poor trembling hands to steer the car safely over the gutted, crumbling road to home.

"What are you going to do?" she asked after a while.

"For God's sake, Alice——"

"Well, tell me. I want to know."

"Did you see that mess there?"

"Tell me, Albert."

"Oh, for God's sake. How should I know?" I said and drove on.

Just before we reached the house she put her hand

gently on my wrist. "Listen, Albert— That thing I said to you the other night—"

"What thing?" My mind was a total blank.

"About you wanting to get rid of him."

"Yes."

"I'm sorry."

"Oh, forget it."

When we got home, there was still no sign of Richard. We ate our lunch and speculated over the possibility that he might have left—got frightened by the realization of what he'd done and run off. Halfway through lunch we tiptoed like thieves across the parlor to the closed door we'd vowed we'd never open again, and opened it.

Spotless and immaculate it was, like the billet of a first year cadet—everything sparkling and in order, everything in place, nothing gone. We finished our lunch with a great cloud of worry hovering above us.

In the early afternoon we decided to take a walk through the woods—far back to the geese pond where we hadn't been since the late autumn. It was beautiful— full of new birds and the signs of wild life, chattering squirrels and chipmunks, fresh deer droppings all about the pine spills. But even as we strolled there amidst that peaceable kingdom, there was between Alice and me a clammy apprehension. The scene at Petrie's that day had scared the life out of us and now we had a kind of unspoken dread of seeing him that night or, for that matter, ever again.

I mark that moment as a turning point in our feelings about Richard Atlee. There was nothing dramatic about it, mind you. It wasn't that we were now so decidedly against him, so much as we weren't any longer so decidedly for him. But at that time, we were scarcely conscious of any of that ourselves.

It was late afternoon when we started back. Somewhere along the way Alice said, "Maybe it wasn't him. Maybe we've jumped to conclusions."

"Maybe," I said, lunging at the possibility. But even as I said it, I didn't believe it. Not for a moment. Still, I was very eager to entertain the thought. And so was Alice.

"After all," I went on heatedly, "no one saw him. And the mere fact that he was out late last night—"

"Of course," said Alice, brightening noticeably. "And what Birge said—"

"You mean about his being seen in town?"

"Yes."

"I wouldn't pay too much attention to that. After all, Richard is a nocturnal creature by habit."

"That's right, dear. That's right."

"And if he'd been out nights breaking into places in the area, we'd certainly have heard about it long before this."

"Of course we would've," Alice breathlessly agreed. "Birge would've been up after him a long time ago—"

We walked back feeling our spirits lighten a bit and our wavering courage return. But when the chimneytops of the house came into view soaring above the trees, we were suddenly back in the trough of despond, with all the old doubts and anxieties roaring back at us with a vengeance.

It was nearly dusk when we tramped up on the back porch. To our great surprise we could see lights burning in the kitchen and the living room.

"He's home," Alice whispered almost grimly.

"Yes," I said, a fist closing over my heart.

We turned the knob and entered.

It would be hard to adequately describe the curious scene that followed. I'm sure I don't recall it all. Only a long, stuttering series of fragments—the lights all on, the Haydn trumpet concerto blaring on the phonograph, the table in the dining room set with the best china and silver, the damask napkins curled and set out in the old brass napkin rings, a lively fire crackling on the hearth, all of it reminiscent of our Christmas feast. There was a large centerpiece of freshly picked lilacs in the middle of the table and out of the kitchen wafted savory scents. It wasn't what we'd expected at all.

Picture next Richard Atlee appearing like an apparition from the kitchen, dressed in his work clothes with one of Alice's aprons tied on over that, the lumpish, mud-streaked overalls showing beneath the frilly borders of the apron, and his hair flowing wildly over his shoulders. For a moment I wanted to laugh. It was all so ludicrous. But instead I stood there speechless, my jaw slung open and drooping idiotically.

Alice moved behind me. "Richard?" she murmured. "Are you all right?"

He smiled and looked a trifle surprised. "Sure."

"What's going on here?" I said, trying to be heard above the trumpet concerto.

"I made supper." He spoke with a sweet, almost angelic emphasis.

"Oh," was all I could say. Then I stood there looking at Alice.

"How sweet, Richard," she said. "The table is beautiful." She had that sickly frozen smile on her face. I could see her struggling for words. She glanced at the phonograph. "May I lower that?"

"Sure," he said, rather in the way a father grants a child a second piece of candy.

Alice crossed the room and lowered the volume of the phonograph. "Now," she said, "we can all hear ourselves think."

"I made supper," Richard volunteered again, giving it the same sweet emphasis he had before.

"How thoughtful," said Alice.

"What a wonderful surprise!" I said, and we stood there shifting from foot to foot, gawking at everything until Richard bade us enter and we stumbled forward into the dimly lit parlor and took our seats before the fire while he served us each a sherry and then disappeared into the kitchen. Imagine—serving sherry and smiling like an angel after a night of nearly apocalyptic violence.

When he'd gone, Alice and I exchanged plaintive glances and sipped our sherry. Sitting there it suddenly occurred to me that I now felt a curious strangeness about the parlor—that parlor, always so familiar to me that I knew every object and detail of it by heart—the white mantel with the French ormolu clock, the old brass andirons in the fire with their proud lions of St. Mark atop great brass balls, the hand-hammered Victorian tongs, the shovel and whiskbroom leaning against the white brick, the two bergeres in which we sat, the long needlepoint footstool before the brass fender of the fireplace, and the small Kirman throw rugs scattered round with the wide-plank chestnut floors showing between them—all of that so familiar to me that I could catalog it for you—was suddenly all strange and unrecognizable. The very chair I sat in, always so perfectly suited to the curvature of my back, was suddenly all new and stiff to me. It was nightmarish—just as if you'd stepped out of your life for a moment and couldn't get back into it. I was in my parlor, but I was a total stranger there. And so was Alice. But Richard, on the contrary, seemed more than ever to belong there. The place would have been inconceivable without him. You see, Alice and I were no longer the hosts of Richard. We'd become his guests in our own house.

When Richard reappeared it was to summon us to the dinner table, where supper was already on. There in the center was a platter with fresh steamed brook trout in a lemon and butter sauce. He'd also found baby asparagus, a favorite of mine, and put together a bright fresh garden salad. It would be hard to imagine a more tasteful or appealing table.

We sat down precisely as he directed us and then gazed, speechless, as he deboned the trout with surgical skill and served.

He watched us as we took our first bites. Alice responded at once. "Exquisite, Richard."

"Outstanding," I added. "Where'd you get the trout?"

"Up the stream. Wanted to get some more practice in on my new rod," he said, a look of great satisfaction on his face. I was certain that the business about the rod was meant to soften me.

Several times during the course of the meal I found my eyes fastened on the lineaments of that face, trying to relate it to all of the grisly violence that had boiled over the night before in Petrie's nursery. The more I studied the face, the less sense the thing made.

After we'd finished he cleared our plates. Alice attempted to help him but he insisted she sit in her place while he looked after dessert. By that time we were eating out of his hand, anxious to comply with his every wish.

When he returned, he had several porringers of fresh raspberries and new whipped cream. There was also a pot of hot mint tea. It was all so lovely, you see, so terribly insidious.

We made no mention during supper of the Petrie business. Actually, by this time, under Richard's wizard-like spell, we'd already forgotten it. But with the end of supper, the table nearly cleaned except for the scooped-out dessert plates, the old anxiety came gnawing back at me again, and I determined to speak.

"Richard," I said, with a sternness that must have sounded ridiculous. "Will you join me in the library?" It had all the portentousness I could muster.

We settled in there with a great rattling of chairs and clearing of throats. I made a few limp attempts at idle chatter. Richard wasn't very good at idle chatter. It didn't ruffle him to sit there and utter nothing but monosyllables at me. At last I decided to simply wade in.

"Richard—Do you know who was here this morning?"

"Nope."

"Emil Birge."

I watched his face for a sign of something significant. Not as much as a twitch did it betray. Instead, I was staring into an impenetrable calm. For a moment I thought he hadn't heard me.

"I say, Emil Birge dropped in today."

"Oh?"

"Harlowe Petrie's place was destroyed last night by an intruder—or several intruders," I added, hoping he'd take the bait and run with it. But he didn't. Whatever I was saying or insinuating was to him a matter of stunning indifference.

I was groping for a way of saying what I wanted to say. But what I really wanted was for him to lie to me in as bald and shameful a fashion as conceivable. I wanted him to give me some reason to despise him.

"You weren't out last night, were you, Richard?"

"Yes. I was out."

"Oh." I paused, then stumbled on. "You don't know anything about this Petrie business, do you?"

"I did it," he said. Just like that, unfalteringly, without batting an eyelash. And all the while he was confessing his guilt, he was beaming, radiant, angelic.

"It was justice," he went on gently. "He did you an injustice and I paid him back."

"Paid him back—"

"Sure," he said sympathetically, as if I were an obtuse child who couldn't get his lessons straight, "it was justice."

"That sort of justice is against the law."

"What law?"

"The common law. The civil law. The law of the land, if you like." The back of my neck began to sweat, and I wiped it with a handkerchief.

He was smiling indulgently at me. "If someone hits me, I hit back."

"There are all sorts of ways of hitting back," I snapped.

"Oh, you mean the courts and all that? I don't have no faith in that."

"You don't?"

"It only works if you're somebody rich or important." He shrugged. "It never worked for me." There was no bitterness to it.

"That's true, Richard. The law's not equal and never has been. It does tend to work a lot more equably if you can afford an expensive attorney. Now, you're not of a privileged group. Nor can you afford an expensive attorney." My eyes fixed him as I spoke. I had his attention now, and he was listening to me. "That's why someone like you has to be particularly careful about breaking the law. What you did last night is of the gravest seriousness. These people here would like nothing better than to ride you into jail and throw away the key. And believe me, in your case they'll do it on the slightest provocation they can find."

He was nodding his head, but it appeared to me that

what I was saying wasn't making the slightest dent in that surface of impassivity.

"The law here," I went on, "the judicial system is not exactly attuned to the kind of simple code of justice you seem to be talking about."

"That pimply bastard stole your fifty."

"I know he did," I pleaded weakly. "But what you did last night was despicable."

"You did nothin' about it. So I had to. Matter of pride."

The remark was shattering, the logic inexorable. He'd not put it in the form of a charge or an accusation. He'd merely stated it as a matter of fact. And since he had done so in that fashion, there was very little I could say by way of defense. I couldn't even enjoy the satisfaction of disliking him for saying it.

It went on like that for a while—back and forth—all empty words and futility, and in the end I yielded. "You realize, Richard, that Mrs. Graves and I have badly compromised ourselves already? But I assure you, if something like this happens again, you're on your own."

He didn't appear the least bit troubled by my words. As a matter of fact, in his own peculiar way he appeared pleased and eager to cooperate.

"Now if the sheriff should question you," I said, standing at the door of the library and wagging a finger, "you just say you were home all last night. He'll say you were seen in town last night, but Mrs. Graves and I will back you up." I patted him on the back and added sternly, "But remember, just this once."

When Richard had finished the dishes and gone to bed, Alice and I sat in the parlor and watched the final sparks of the fire simmer and crackle on the grate.

I went over in my mind the whole story of that day at Petrie's as he had related it to us. I recalled that I'd been a bit surprised that he hadn't made more of a fuss after having been gulled by George. I put it down then as a kind of timidity, or possibly shyness about causing a scene in a public place. I couldn't have been more wrong.

For now I realized that it wasn't Richard Atlee's style to make loud protests or grand fusses about indignities, real or imagined, that he had suffered. He was far too secret and oblique a person for that. Instead, I knew now that if you did him a wrong, he would probably just walk away. But that wouldn't be the end of it. Hardly. For he would carry that wrong around with him for a good while, brooding over it, outwardly calm but inwardly smouldering, calculating an advantage, plotting his vengeance, and waiting for the right moment to pounce.

I couldn't really say that my talk with him that night had done much to reduce my uneasiness. On the contrary. It occurred to me I was more frightened than ever. And precisely what did he mean when he said the courts had never worked for him? How many courts had he been involved with, how many crimes had he been sentenced for?

It was amazing, the rapidity with which Birge appeared to drop the whole business. I couldn't quite believe it. It was so unlike the man. All the following week I kept waiting for him, expecting him at any time to come rattling up the drive waving a subpoena, full of irrefutable evidence and eyewitness accounts of that awful night. But nothing of the sort occurred, so that soon I began to breathe freely and imagine that the whole affair—ugly as it was—had finally blown over.

But, of course, that wasn't the case. Nearly three weeks after the incident, I learned through Washburn, of all people, that Birge had come around asking questions about Richard's period of employment there.

"What sort of questions, Mr. Washburn?" I asked, a slight quaver in my voice.

" 'Bout the boy, mostly. Who he was. Where he came from. Know nothin', I says." Washburn ran on full of indignation, "And that's zactly what I told him."

I drove back home down the Bog Road, a little troubled and moist in the palms. Then shortly after I got into the house I concocted an excuse to call Beamish, the oil supplier.

When I got him on the phone he was full of noisy amicability and bursting with good will. I don't recall how I got him off the subject of boilers and fuel prices, but in the next instant we were chatting about his erstwhile employee Richard Atlee. He appeared to have no reticence about discussing that subject, either, and sure enough, in the next moment he was babbling on about a visit he'd had from Birge just a few days before.

It was very much the same sort of thing I'd had from Washburn, but Beamish went him one better:

"They sent some fingerprints off to Washington." His voice was almost musical as he said it.

"Oh, did they?"

"Said they got 'em off one of them busted display cases up to Petrie's. Yes, sir. Sent 'em down to the capital to see if they couldn't tell 'em somethin' there."

So Birge was on the prowl. But of course, as I saw, I expected it. I wasn't terribly disturbed about the fingerprint business, either. After all, Richard had gone to Petrie's during a normal work day. Finding his fingerprints on a piece of shattered glass there would not be a very startling disclosure.

Well, so it was. Birge was not going to be content to let sleeping dogs lie. On the contrary. His blood was up now. He was on the trail of something, and even if police records failed to tell him what he wanted to know, I could be certain that in the matter of Richard Atlee he was now going to be increasingly vigilant.

But life still went on in precisely the uneventful way it had before the Petrie incident, expect that Richard had so enjoyed the experience of making our supper that he now insisted upon doing it several times a week. And he was not merely a good cook. He was an artist. He had a way particularly with fish and poultry that really made you sit up and take notice. And he possessed an almost religious feeling about vegetables. When he prepared them, they were memorable.

So on alternate days Alice would be banished from her kitchen, which at first she seemed more than eager and

pleased to be. But Alice Graves is a woman who enjoys
her kitchen, and though she made a great show of loving
the banishment, of savoring her new freedom, I had more
than a sneaking suspicion that the uniqueness of the experience of being cooked for and then served on expensive service would begin to wear thin. I was right in this,
for later on she began to resent her banishment and
showed it in a million small ways. I could see it, for instance, when Richard brought her food to her—something
about the way her eyes arched, or a certain strident crack
through the sweetness of her voice, when she would ask,
"And what's this one, Richard?"

"Stewed leeks."

"Oh," she would say, and in that single monosyllable
you could tell all.

The weather grew warmer and the days longer. We
spent more time out of doors. We planned things.

As a result of Richard's demonic energy our little house
on Bog Road underwent a magical transformation. The
exteriors he completely painted until they sparkled like
a bright new penny. He made major repairs on the vital
organs of the house, modernizing the heating system and
rewiring the house, putting in heavier wire so that we
could have an air conditioner—something I dearly wanted.
It was a job that local electrical contractors said would
cost a fortune. Richard was able to do it at very nom-
inal expense.

Nor did he for a moment ignore the grounds. The lawn
was mowed weekly and watered each night. The bushes
and shrubs around the house, which we had permitted
to grow shaggy and unkempt, he pruned and sculpted
impeccably. As for flowers, everything he'd put into the
garden came gloriously into full cry. The dying catalpa in
the back of the house he pruned and fed and sprayed and
tended so assiduously that in the space of a few weeks
there was a visible splash of new growth at the top and a
luster to the leaves I would've thought was impossible.
There was nothing he couldn't do. No task, no matter
how onerous, that he resented or shirked. Whatever he

put his hand to, he achieved. He was a wizard of all things.

But there was a price to be paid for all this, too, for very shortly Alice and I had nothing to do. We'd wake up in the morning and face each other across our breakfast, which Richard had already prepared. And after we had finished breakfast we would sit and stare into the dregs of our coffee cups while the bees buzzed at the screens and the long summer's day spread out pitilessly before us.

"What would you like to do today, dear?" Alice would say.

"Well, I thought I'd like to clear out the cellar and make room for my new workshop."

"He did that Tuesday."

"Oh, did he?"

"You seem surprised."

"Surprised?" I laughed. "Nothing about him surprises me."

She looked at me and we both laughed aloud. But it was the quick, guarded laughter of careworn people. When we stood up, she leaned over to me and whispered in my ear, "Do you suppose he'd permit us to do the dishes?"

"We might just sneak them into the sink right now and do them while he's out."

"I'd love to do some dishes," she said a little wistfully.

"What he doesn't know will never harm him." I winked at her, and so we did the dishes.

Between the two of us, we had recently taken to referring to Richard as "he," or "him."

Not only did Richard Atlee attend to our physical needs, but apparently he felt it was his duty to minister to our spiritual requirements, as well. Though he never said it, I knew he felt a deep responsibility about what had happened between me and Reverend Horn. It bothered him that we were now without a place of worship, and so on Sundays he would wake us, somewhat earlier than usual. We would wash and put on our Sunday clothes and stumble down to the living room, where we would hold services among ourselves, reading from the Bible and singing from the Hymnal. On these occasions I would preside. During the singing, Richard's voice could be heard above anyone else's. With its pathetic croaking and grating nasalities it would fill the room and, so it seemed later on, the whole house.

So the days came and went, moving slowly and uneventfully but bringing with their virtually unbroken tedium a highly encouraging note. We heard nothing from Birge about a police record on Richard, and apparently all efforts to locate such a record had not panned out. Also, to the best of my knowledge, Birge had stopped asking questions of people around town. He had still not come to ask any additional questions of me.

However, there was an ominous note to all this calm. On several occasions, once in the front yard, once in the driveway, and once peering out the library windows, I saw Birge's station wagon out on the road, cruising slowly past the front of the house. And from the way he went past, I had the distinct impression it wasn't merely a chance passing. It was perfectly clear, he wanted us to see him.

I never mentioned this to either Alice or Richard, even though it troubled me. But still, from the way things looked, I commenced to believe that the matter was being slowly forgotten. It seems I was wrong. It had not been forgotten. And from an incident that occurred one afternoon, the point was made abundantly clear to me.

For several days, Alice was going through a spell of high fever and sore throat. I had Dr. Tucker out to see her. He confined her to bed and wrote a prescription for antibiotics. Someone had to get the prescription filled.

Because of the high fever, I didn't want to leave Alice alone by herself in the house. Nor did I want to leave her with Richard and go myself. Ever since the Petrie incident, I had sensed in Alice a growing although still unspoken fear of Richard Atlee, and quite frankly I didn't want her to wake from her fever and suddenly find herself alone in the house with him. So there was no one else to send except Richard. I'd made a point of not letting him go into town since the Petrie business. By this time I was fully aware of the hostility some of the people in the town felt toward him. We'd had a rash of nasty, anonymous phone calls, and I dearly wanted to avoid another unpleasant incident.

The situation was clear. I couldn't leave Alice, and the pharmacy wouldn't make a delivery that far out of town. So I had virtually no choice but to send Richard to town in the car.

When I presented the problem to him he was eager to go and as flattered this time that I'd trust him with the car as he was the first time I sent him. He seemed oblivious to the fact that the task held certain dangers. He was like a young boy entrusted with the keys to his father's car.

When he emerged from his room prior to departure, I noted that he'd washed, changed into his suit, and combed back from his forehead the great long flowing locks.

Standing out in the driveway I handed him the keys and registration, as well as money to pay for the drugs.

"Now, Richard, don't spend a minute more in town than you have to. Just get the prescription filled and come right home. Mrs. Graves needs those pills as soon as possible."

He nodded his head, and from the way he looked at me I could tell that he knew my concern went a good deal deeper than Mrs. Graves's needs.

We waited anxiously for him to return, and after two hours had passed, I sensed trouble. I called the pharmacist at the drugstore and was informed that Richard had left with the medicine an hour before. The drive out from town was approximately forty minutes—a half-hour if you sped. Twenty minutes overdue was nothing to be alarmed about. So I went back up to the bedroom, where Alice had dozed off, and sat in a chair beside her bed in the gathering dusk of afternoon. In another half-hour a car pulled into the driveway. Alice was still dozing when I rose and tiptoed from the room.

The first glimpse I got of him was in the kitchen. I imagine I moved toward him smiling, feeling all kinds of gratitude and relief. At first I didn't even notice the blood. Most of it had clotted and faded into the wild entanglement of his beard. As I say, it was dusk and the light was poor. But then suddenly I was up close beside him and peering into a barely recognizable battered face—blood oozing from the nose and a cut on his lip. He had a nasty bruise over the eye which had started to swell and turn a yellowish violet. The worst of it was the bleeding and the clotted gore which he kept wiping away with the sleeve of his jacket.

"What in God's name—"

"It's okay," he said and thrust the vial of tablets toward me. "How's Missus?"

Later, when I'd washed him and dressed his cuts, he was still unwilling to talk about it. But gradually I was able to extract from him the major details of the story.

Richard had got to town and had the prescription filled without incident. When he got back to the car, he found an automobile parked directly behind ours. In it were three of the young local toughs. If you've ever spent any time in a small town, you know the type very well. Teenagers or in their early twenties—shiftless and surly. Most of the time you find them squatting on the steps of the Post Office or the drugstore, ogling girls, spitting on the pavement, and drinking from quart bottles of beer which, for some curious reason, they keep in paper bags.

At any rate, three of these fellows followed Richard out of town in their car. When he finally got out on the Bog Road, which is a nearly always deserted ten mile strip of badly chewed-up tar, they forced him to the side of the road, dragged him from the car, and proceeded to beat him. They also took whatever change he had left from the money I gave him for the drugs. It was an insignificant sum of three or four dollars.

"Don't worry," said Richard when he'd finished his story. "I'll pay you back."

"Don't bother. It's not important. The important thing is that you're all right."

"I'm fine," he said. "But they won't be when I get finished."

The remark made in that flat, dull emotionless way of his made my blood run cold. It was precisely the kind of thing he had said after his encounter with Petrie's clerks.

"Now, Richard, I don't want you to do a thing about this. I'll take care of it in my way."

He looked at me oddly. There was nothing mocking or impudent about it. It was more like a skepticism that I saw in his glance—a distrust born, no doubt, of the meek manner in which I accepted the Petrie business. The skepticism and distrust goaded me.

"I promise you, Richard," I said more forcefully than ever. "Now I want you to promise me that you won't go off and do something foolish—"

For a moment I thought I saw the trace of a smirk on his lips.

"Like taking the law into your own hands again," I went on.

He looked at me, oddly surprised for a moment, then shrugged.

"Sure." He said it with a kind of carefree indifference that made me feel foolish. As if he were saying, "If it means so much to you—"

"Good," I said, full of false satisfaction, not certain whether or not we'd reached any kind of an understanding.

Something flickered in his eye again, lasting for only a moment. Then it was gone and he seemed more himself. "Missus feeling any better now?"

"Fever's gone and she's resting comfortably."

"Can I go up and see her?"

I looked at the mauled, purple thing that was his face. "Let's wait till she's a bit stronger."

He accepted that easily and smiled his wry, twisted little smile. "I'll go make her some soup now," he said. And then he was gone.

The following morning at the stroke of nine I was at Birge's office in the county courthouse. He was already there at his desk in his shirt sleeves having a doughnut and a cup of coffee from a paper container. When I arrived, he cleaned off the desk top, leaned back in his swivel chair, and threw his booted feet up on the desk.

"Have a seat, Albert," he said with all that bogus amiability of his.

It was the first time I'd come to see Birge in a professional capacity. I confess I was rattled. I told him the story with emotion and a great deal of unevenness. There were gaps in the narrative, and after I'd told it once, he made me go over it again and fill in for continuity.

"Is the boy all right?" Birge asked when I'd finished.

"He's pretty badly banged up. His face—"

"Any broken bones? Anything requiring the attention of a doctor?" He'd taken out a pad and started scribbling on it.

"No," I said and our eyes locked for the first time. "What do you propose to do?"

He leaned back in his chair and clasped his raw, red paws behind his head. "What do you propose I do?"

"Find those boys."

"I don't have to. I know who they are."

"Then you've heard about this thing already?"

"Heard somethin'."

"And you haven't done anything about it?"

"Been intendin' to," he said, and studied his fingernails.

"Well, I want to press charges."

"Charges?"

I had the feeling he was laughing at me. "I want those boys brought in. I'm going to press charges of assault and battery."

Slowly he uncrossed his legs and lifted them from the desk top. "Oh, you don't wanna do that."

"I most certainly do."

"Only make things worse."

"Things?" I said, growing a little furious. "What things?"

"The situation, Mr. Graves."

I'd started off as Albert, and now we were back to Mr. Graves again. "You know," he went on in his cajoling way, "people 'round here are fond of you and Miz Graves. And you're as welcome as ever. But—I must say —this boy you got stayin' up there with you—Why, only the other night Darlene was saying—" I assumed Darlene was Mrs. Birge. It was hard to think of her as having a first name, and Darlene, at that.

"We've had some ugly experiences here with drifters and hoboes," Birge went droning on. "I don't mind tellin' you—we don't countenance 'em. Ordinarily, we run 'em out soon as they come in."

"The boy's no drifter or hobo. He worked for the fuel company before he came to me. He's worked for Washburn. No one's had a bad word to say about him. Go talk to Washburn." Birge seemed scarcely to be listening. "He's proved to be an invaluable help to me," I went on doggedly.

"Oughtn't to be in your house."

"Whom I choose to take into my house is my business."

"You don't know nothin' about him—"

"I know everything I have to know!" I snapped. "Now I want those boys brought in."

"You don't wanna press charges," Birge drawled and crossed his legs again.

"I certainly do. I fully intend to press charges."

Just then someone stepped into the outer office and waved at Birge through the open door.

"Mawnin', Darrel." Birge waved back, and they chatted there for a moment while I slumped in my chair and fumed.

"I have every intention of pressing charges," I said again when the person had left.

The grin that had been on his face during the brief exchange of a moment before still lingered there. Now it seemed that my words were coming slowly through to him.

"These boys," he said, "are just a pack of young

fools and hotheads. But if you was to press charges against them, there's some round here who'd take it poorly."

"I don't care how they take it!" I was on my feet and thumping his desk. "I want those boys prosecuted. I want justice."

"Now don't get yourself all lathered, Albert." He made a quieting gesture with his hand. "I intend to see you get justice."

I stood there hunched above him, glowering, my knuckles white and mashed down on the rim of the desk. "How?" I said, full of skepticism.

He lit a vile little stump of a cigar and tossed the match into the paper coffee container. "We don't wanna go through the business of formal charges, do we?" I watched him as he sucked on the cigar, generating enormous quantities of smoke around himself. "Lemme take these boys aside and put the fear of God in 'em." He spoke out of the side of his mouth, giving the illusion that he was talking to me in the strictest confidence.

"The fear of God?" I said eagerly. There was something in me that wanted to succumb to him.

"How will you put the fear of God in them?"

Birge puffed deeply on the cigar. "I have my ways."

"Your ways?"

Birge nodded.

"What ways?" I asked, beginning to yield.

"Never you mind. Just leave this to me."

And so we left it.

Later, when I'd left Birge and was standing in the street outside his office, I knew that very little would be done to redress the wrongs. But then, I wanted so much to wash my hands of the whole unpleasant business. I started to think about my health and worried about what excitement could do to it. I told myself that I believed Birge even when I knew I didn't. And my greatest concern that morning was whether or not I could get Richard to believe Birge. And even if Birge were telling the truth, I wasn't certain that Richard's acute sense of justice would consider a tepid reprimand from a conniving small-town law official fair exchange for the gratuitous beating he'd taken on the Bog Road the day before.

Early on, I said that you would get to loathe me. It was just this sort of flabbiness of character that I had in mind.

Chapter Twelve

THERE'S a month of the year I hold most bitter and most sweet, and that month is April. I claim no great originality here. At least a dozen poets and sensitive types in general have noted the peculiar melancholy of that month. By that time the birds are all back from wherever they've gone, and the old brown earth has turned full green again. There's not a bare branch around, and the heady scent of lilac and honeysuckle hangs heavy over the dreamy, lengthening days. It's a time of renewal, and yet the bitter taste of winter and death lingers on in our heads.

It's time made doubly melancholy for me because the anniversary of my father's death falls in that month, and since that day in April nearly forty years ago, I've celebrated the anniversary of his death by his graveside.

It's a peculiar and barbarous custom, I know, and yet I yield to it annually, almost unwillingly, like a reflex action you have no control over.

When you think about it, it's almost comical. You go forth to confront old ghosts and commune with old guilts. You hope to exorcise old griefs and leave some awful burden there, like a bundle of dirty laundry, beside a mouldering stone.

But nothing like that ever really happens. You simply place a small nosegay of flowers by an old stone, mumble a few silly endearing words, or a formal incantation (which is even sillier), and shuffle off through the neat little aisles of stones and ghastly funeral statuary.

Afterwards you go to some restaurant and eat a bad meal. But by then the thing is safely out of your head for another year. I've long since given up trying to understand the whole silly business. It's grist for the mills of psychologists and anthropologists who've been enterprising enough to turn that sort of thing into a thriving industry.

My father is buried in a large city due north of here, about a day's drive on one of the great, ugly turnpikes of the nation.

Alice and I have always celebrated the day in precisely the way I've described it. Only, now that we were living in a rural region, we took the opportunity of turning the trip of grief into a small spree. Like bumpkins, we'd fly to the city wide-eyed and innocent, with some extra money in our pockets, and as soon as the period of lamentations was safely out of the way, we'd doff our sackcloth and ashes and dash off to the shopping districts. Antique shops and clothing boutiques were our chief targets. At night there'd be a play or a good foreign film. Then supper at a French restaurant. I suppose the pattern is common enough to most suburban couples who've transplanted themselves from large cities. Most of us are even able to be a little humorous and self-mocking about it.

At any rate, the anniversary I've spoken about came upon us in this year as a complete surprise. I suppose our forgetting the date had something to do with the presence of Richard Atlee in our house. But lo, the date was upon us before we knew it, and it was late afternoon before we realized the oversight. I fumed about it for a while and carried on. But I reasoned if we were to drive all night, there'd be time enough to reach our destination early in the morning, go directly to the gravesite, have our day in the city, our night in town, sleep in a hotel, and leave early the following morning in time to reach home late that afternoon.

Such a situation before would've presented no great problem, but now there was Richard, and what troubled us was the fact that he was away from the house for the day and couldn't be found in any of the usual places in order to tell him we were leaving. It occurred to me that he was at the cave, where I was certain he'd been spending increasing amounts of time. If that was the case, then I was sure I couldn't locate him, because I could never have found that cave without him, although I knew in which direction it lay and the general vicinity of it.

It wasn't our intention to take him with us. We simply wanted to tell him we were going and when he could expect us back. There were also a few elementary instructions about the running of the house in our absence—dreary little matters about the hot water heater and the oven, and some instructions Alice wanted to convey about the watering of the lawn—all things, knowing Richard, which he would have taken care of automatically anyway.

At any rate, we finally settled on writing a small list of instructions, told him where we were going, where we could be reached in the event of emergency, and when we'd be back. We urged him to take full advantage of the house and the larder and gave him our best. Then we were off.

We had our day in the big city and did everything we ordinarily do when we go on such junkets. We had supper at a French restaurant. It was neither memorable nor gracious, but it was good just being there—in the din and clatter of that hot little place—watching the waiters and the people in all that happy turmoil of activity. Afterwards we saw a comedy at the theater and laughed a lot and suddenly realized how long it'd been since we'd had a good laugh. We even managed to buy a full complement of Chinese vegetables and condiments, and a wonderful cast-iron wok, just as Alice had said we would on Christmas Eve when I gave her the Chinese cookbook.

It all seemed perfectly harmless and we laughed most of the way back, with the packages of food and vegetables and the large, improbable wok, all rattling in their wrappings on the back seat. It was a good trip, highly therapeutic, and driving home that day we were very pleased with ourselves.

It was only a matter of two nights that we were away —slightly more than forty-eight hours in all, but driving up the gravel path, the place already had a foreboding look about it. I shouldn't say that. There was really nothing terribly untoward about the way the house looked. It was rather more something in the mind of a person given to sinister premonitions. I knew something was wrong even as we were coming up the drive. Maybe it had something to do with the way the light of late afternoon fell over the place.

The air was sultry, and there was an imminence of rain. A curiously unnatural quiet hovered over the grounds —a hush born of the absence of customary bird chatter and insect buzzing. The place too had a vaguely unpleasant air about it—the way a house looks when someone has died in it under violent and rather shadowy circumstances. There was a kind of sullenness about it now—a jarring and uncharacteristic inhospitality. And the way the sun's rays slanted on the windows, its brilliant orange light imprisoned in the leaded panes, gave the casements a vacant look, like the eyeless sockets of a skull.

What we found inside was not that immediately remarkable. What I most recall, going from room to room, was the uneasy stillness of everything, and the thick, oppressive mustiness, as if the place had been shut up for years. At every corner I turned I expected to find something grisly or horrible. But everything in the house appeared to be just as we'd left it.

I was about to laugh at myself and scoff at my suspicious nature, when Alice, who'd wandered up ahead, called me from the kitchen. I went there immediately and found her staring at the floor. What her eyes had fastened on I didn't see immediately. But then, suddenly, I was staring at the jagged shard of a shattered coffee cup just beside the sink. Then it seemed dozens of other pieces from the same cup, strewn all about in different corners of the room, came slowly into view.

On the far side of the kitchen, still clinging to the wall, where the cup had undoubtedly been flung, were the remains of the coffee that had been violently dashed at the wall. The hundreds of tiny grounds that had been flung there inscribed a large, graceful curve like a piece of calligraphy. You might have thought it was the signature of an artist appended to an enormous canvas. There was the great pride and defiance in the work.

In terms of money or value there was no great loss. Just a bit of cheap crockery. All quite replaceable. But in terms of our feelings about Richard, and our own peace of mind, something had changed drastically inside us that afternoon.

There was no sign of him. We looked in his room. It remained neat and spotlessly perfect, but absolutely vacant of its occupant. When Alice, somewhat later, checked the refrigerator, she found the thing we'd left him—cold chicken, meat loaf, salad fixings, and a quart of ice cream —all untouched.

We walked back into the kitchen and examined the large coffee stain on the wall. For some reason I'd been reluctant to wipe it off, I suppose because I wanted to confront him with it when he came back. It would be something with which to glare at him across the kitchen, when he opened the door.

What we saw on the wall and strewn across the floor was appalling. In its meanness, in its willfulness, and in its careful deliberation, it was a threat, bald and naked, and not to be countenanced. You could read there on the wall in the large, graceful arc of spattered coffee grounds all the rage behind the act. It had all the earmarks of the kind of fury that was vented on Petrie's place. In fact, it was Petrie all over again on a midget scale. At the point on the wall where the cup had impacted against it, the wallpaper was torn open, and a nearly perfect crescent of plaster had been gouged out behind it.

We walked around the kitchen for a while, weaving our way through the shards of crockery, trying to avoid each other's eyes.

"Now what the hell do you suppose this is all about?" I said, finally at the end of my patience.

She sat there merely shaking her head, unable to speak.

"Well, I'm not going to stand for it this time," I went on.

"Albert," she said trying to hush me, as if she were afraid he might walk in any moment.

"He promised me, Alice. I made it very clear. He promised there was to be no repetition. He promised—"

She stood up and walked wearily to the sink, where she found a damp sponge on the drain and started to saturate it with liquid detergent. Then she turned on one of the taps. A tepid stream of water leaked out onto the sponge, and she stood there for a time leaning against the sink with the sound of water splashing on the porcelain just below her. When she'd finished, she turned off the taps and with the sponge in hand started for the stained wall.

I headed her off. "No. I don't want you to do that. I want him to." When I snatched the sponge from her she tried to take it back from me.

"No, Alice. He's going to clean it up. He's got to learn—"

All the while we'd wrestled for the sponge, she'd been rigid and wild-eyed. Now suddenly she sighed and collapsed wearily into one of the kitchen chairs.

"What's going to happen?" she said.

"Nothing—absolutely nothing. He's going to clean the wall. That's all."

Suddenly she grabbed my hand and pressed the back of it to her burning cheek. Hot, tired tears rolled down that cheek onto my hand.

"Alice, dear. Don't."

"I'm sorry. I am so sorry."

I stroked her head desperately, as if I were trying to console a small child.

"What's going to happen, Albert?" She was weeping freely. "I'm tired of him, and I shouldn't be. I'm tired of his waiting on me. I'm tired of his fussing in my garden and all around my house. I know he means well, but dear God forgive me, I can't stand him around me any more. The sight of him makes me sick, and I hate myself for it."

It had all come out of her like pus from a suppurating wound.

"It's all my fault, too, isn't it?" she went on.

"No. Of course not."

"You would've never taken him in if I hadn't goaded you."

"No. No, Alice. That's not true. I wanted this just as much as you did." Suddenly I saw myself lying flat on my back in the crawlspace, on that mound of damp, mouldering hay. "Maybe more." I said, "Maybe even more."

"It's my fault, Albert. It's my fault."

"No, dear. We did it together."

She turned her face and buried it against my thigh and wept bitterly.

"We wanted to do something," I went on. "Something worthwhile— It just didn't work out. That's all." After a while I took her shoulder firmly and forced her to look up at me.

"What do you want me to do, Alice? Tell me what you want me to do and I'll do it."

"I don't know. I don't know." She shook her head despairingly back and forth.

"Do you want me to send him away?"

"Oh, no." She half-rose, a look of horror on her face.

I forced her gently back down into the chair. "Tell me what you want me to do."

"I'm so frightened. Something about him frightens me so."

"Frightens you?"

"I'd be afraid to send him away now. He'd never go." Her body was convulsed with sobs. "God knows what he'd do now if you tried to send him away."

I'd been kneeling by her side. Suddenly I stood up. "Well, that settles that—"

"Oh, Albert—" She half-rose again as if to head me off.

"He goes."

"Oh, I don't know—"

"Nonsense, Alice! We can't live this way."

"He has no one. He's so alone and so attached to us."

"You just said you were terrified."

"Yes, I am. But he's tried so hard to please."

"And at the same time made us outcasts in a community where we were once welcome."

I could see she was relenting now. "He's a good boy, Albert."

"He is a good boy. But there's an aspect of him that's so unpredictable, and we can't afford to take any more chances."

So we went on like that, back and forth, alternately reproaching and absolving ourselves of any guilt.

Finally I said, "I'm sorry, Alice. My mind's made up."

"Well, all right, dear. If you think it's for the best."

She gave in like that—Alice, who's as stubborn a woman as ever lived. I'd said exactly what she'd wanted me to say for weeks. And when I made my decision, she looked at me with a grief-stricken face. But I knew that inwardly she was grateful and relieved.

It's amusing, as I think about it now. It's more than amusing; it's hilarious. Just think of it—all that decisiveness and finality, all of that moral rectitude and puffing of the chest in the face of a few coffee streaks and a handful of broken crockery, when we'd been perfectly willing to forgive and forget the holocaust that had been visited on Harlowe Petrie. Oh, yes, in the case of Petrie, we were perfectly willing to be magnanimous.

I don't know what possessed me next, or what supernatural hand guided me, but before I knew it I had a flashlight in hand and was descending the stairs into the basement.

Outside the sun was just beginning to set, and I stood for a moment at the bottom of the stairs peering into the green shimmering light of the cellar. The rakes and hoes and shovels all hanging from beam hooks and sharply silhouetted looked like a forest at dusk. It gave the illusion of standing at the bottom of a murky pond with sunlight filtering down upon you through the muddy depths.

I looked directly across the cluttered space to the black square which seemed once more to be floating in mid-air. Like a sleep-walker, as if in a dream, I started toward it. Outside a bird was chirping on the lawn above.

At one point it passed directly between the setting sun and the basement window, casting a huge, terrifying shadow of itself on the cellar wall.

I've never thought of myself as clairvoyant or prescient. I tend to scoff at such things. But I knew even as I stood there, just as I'd known upstairs when I reached for the flashlight, what I would find in the crawl.

It was all there, of course—the mound of hay, the tin can and cardboard containers recently opened and strewn about, the can of crude toiletries—and amid all the trash, lying on a newspaper dated two days earlier—the fresh carcasses of two small birds (I think they were doves). The bones were picked clean. Feathers still floated eerily around in the dim narrow space. And above it all, the sickening, choking, miasmal stench of human waste. In our absence, he'd gone back to live in the crawl.

He came that night at his usual hour and went directly to the kitchen to start supper. Hearing the dull clomp of his steps on the back porch, I looked up from my newspaper. Alice was already staring in the direction of the kitchen.

"I'll go," I said. I rose and tossed aside my paper. Alice made a motion to come with me, but I waved her back.

"No—I prefer to do this myself."

She dropped back into her chair obediently and watched me leave the room.

When I entered the kitchen he was already on his knees picking up the shattered bits of crockery. He didn't look up at me, but stared at the floor as he spoke.

"I thought you run off," he said before I could utter a word. His voice was a curious mixture of apology and defiance.

"Now, you know very well we'd never do that. Where would we run, for heaven's sake?"

"I come in and you and Missus was gone."

"I left you a note."

"You forgot about me. You just run off and left me. You can't do that."

"Can't?" I said, trying to suppress the tremor in my voice. "Why can't I?"

"You got responsibilities."

"Responsibilities?" It was like GOD scrawled above my cellar door.

"You got 'em to me just like I got 'em to you. We're a—" he paused, his eyes defiant and shy, searching for a word—"family." He'd almost choked on it, but when he found the word, he held on to it for dear life. "We're a family. And you forgot—"

His chest heaved and he was fearfully overwrought. "I waited for you. I waited all night. And still you didn't come."

"But Richard, I left a note." I gave up completely the attempt to control my voice. "You knew we were coming back."

"Don't matter," he said woefully. "Notes don't matter to me. Had plenty of 'em in my time, and what they say ain't true."

"What made you go back down to the crawl?"

He looked like a cornered rat. For a moment I felt certain he was going to lie.

"Why'd you go back down there?" I said again.

"I thought you left!" he shouted. "So I left you!" His voice reached a fearful pitch, and he was on the brink of tears. "Don't leave me like that again!" he shrieked. "Don't you ever—"

There was something tyrannical and abusive about those last words. They were full of threat. Meant to be a warning. Take heed, they said.

Yet I wasn't offended. On the contrary, I found myself oddly touched. He looked suddenly like a child. Worried and desperately frightened. And all because he thought he'd lost us. He thought we'd deserted him, and he'd been nearly out of his mind with fright. Even a note that spelled out clearly our intention of returning couldn't allay the panic of a suspicious and distrustful mind. He made me feel guilty. As if I'd betrayed him. I was angry and at the same time horribly sad for him. My eyes began to fill foolishly, and in the next instant I turned and started for the door.

"You better not try that again," he cried after me. I turned and glared back at him. His eyes were immense and ringed with red, as if he'd been up worrying the whole night. "Promise!" he cried at me across the shadows, his voice a long pathetic whine.

"I'm sorry, Richard," I said, the words strangling in my throat. "I promise it won't happen again."

By the time I left the kitchen, he'd already picked up all the shattered crockery and was just beginning to sponge off the wall.

Chapter Thirteen

WE entered now a curious period of transition. To a stranger first entering that house there would have been no perceptible signs of friction among the occupants. Things went on very much as they had. Meals were served at regular hours. People retired at regular hours. Work around the house continued as usual. A stiff civility obtained between us all. But there was a new tension, a kind of tacit hostility born of mutual mistrust. Richard believed we had betrayed him. Alice believed I had betrayed her. And I believed that Richard had betrayed me. We were watching him, and he was watching us. There was a friction now between Alice and me. I had promised her I'd turn him out and I hadn't. And for this, though she said nothing, she judged me harshly.

As a result of our little tiff you might have expected that Richard Atlee's passion to serve us would have been somewhat impaired. On the contrary, it was heightened, and often to ridiculous and embarrassing extremes. He became assiduous in his duties. For instance, he took to shining my shoes. He would do this unfailingly, each night, whether they needed it or not. In the mornings I'd find them spotless and shining outside my bedroom door. At first I protested. But he scarcely heard me. A short time later, I found my trousers freshly pressed and hanging in the closet. And this too was to be done on a daily basis.

He would collect the laundry at least two nights a week from the upstairs and downstairs baths, and those nights he would spend washing and ironing.

Alice had very specific ideas about laundry, and early on, the laundry business was a source of continual and growing friction.

"Richard," I heard her say one evening, a strained sweetness in her manner. "This is not the way Mr. Graves wants his shirts folded." It was a curious remark, because I never had any special opinions about the way my shirts ought to be folded.

I watched Richard stand there nodding while she explained systematically how I liked my shirts folded. He nodded and appeared to understand. But I'm sure he didn't hear a word she said. He had his own notions of how shirts should be folded.

"Really, Richard," Alice went on a little apologetically, "I appreciate all of your help, but I do think you should leave the laundry to me." She laughed nervously and he appeared to understand and even agree. But two nights later, long before she herself could get to the hampers, he had emptied them of dirty laundry and taken them down to the machine in the basement. Once again, it occasioned a terrible row between Alice and Richard and ended with her sweeping imperiously out of the kitchen. Later, I found her crying in the upstairs bath. A short time after, she went quietly to the kitchen and baked raspberry tarts for him.

It was not an easy thing to live with, but so we lived.

One night toward the end of May I stirred in my bed. Through my sleep I imagined I heard cries in the night, shouting on the road. I raised my head from the pillow and through sleep-drugged eyes saw the headlights of a car sweep the circle of our room. Then it was gone. I thought I'd dreamed it. But the following morning at breakfast, Alice said: "Did you hear anything last night?"

I looked up from my paper. "Did I what?"

"Did you hear anything last night?"

"Did I hear anything?"

"Yes."

"Like what?" You see, I'd forgotten it already.

She placed a piece of French toast on my plate. "Noises. Shouting."

I thought about it for a while with the memory of it slowly awakening in me. Now I recalled hearing something, but I was uncertain of what I'd actually heard, and even if it was the night before I'd heard it.

"I did hear something," I said, a little vaguely. "But for the life of me I couldn't tell you what it was. I'm not even sure it wasn't a dream."

"Was it last night?"

"I'm not sure."

"Shouting? Was it shouting?"

"Oh, I don't know." I picked up my paper again. "Probably the raccoons fighting."

Two nights later Alice woke me at about 1 A.M. "Albert. There are people out there."

"People?"

"Listen," she whispered. "Cars."

I listened for a moment and heard nothing. Then I heard voices wafting upwards in the night air through our opened windows. When I got up and went to the window, I could see lights bending around the corner of the garage. They appeared to be coming from the road that passes in front of our house.

I went downstairs to the front parlor, where I could look out toward the road. Down below I could see a car parked about a hundred yards off at the foot of our driveway. Its headlights were on, its doors were open, and it was blaring music.

I went to the front door, opened it, and looked at the car. Then I could hear laughter and occasional shouting above the music. There were young boys in the car, and they were undoubtedly drinking.

I'm not the kind of person to go out and face that sort of thing myself. My first instinct was to call the police. When I turned to go back into the living room, I walked straight into Richard. He was standing in the darkness in his pajamas watching me. I could see clearly the whites of his eyes.

"Richard?"

"Yes."

"They wake you, too?"

"Yes. Been goin' on almost an hour."

"That long?"

"Yes."

"Why didn't you wake me?"

"Didn't see much need. They usually go on 'bout an hour."

"Usually? Have they been here before?"

"Couple of times." He yawned and scratched his ear. "They park out there and shout. Bust a couple of beer bottles. Then they go off."

"How long has this been going on?"

"Couple of weeks. I just clean up the mess every morning."

"For God's sake. Why didn't you say something?"

"Saw no need," he shrugged. "Just a pack of fools."

"You know who they are?"

"Sure." His voice was faintly mocking. "Don't you?"

"Should I?"

He looked at me skeptically and shrugged again.

"Who are they?"

"The fellas I run up against in town."

"Are you sure?"

"Sure. I seen 'em. They come right up here to the door one night. It's them three and a few others."

I started for the phone. Just then Alice called down. "Is everything all right, Albert?"

"Everything's fine, dear. Go back to bed."

"Are you sure?"

"Yes. I'm coming right up."

When I reached the phone he was standing right behind me. "What are you gonna do?"

"I'm going to get Birge out here."

He smiled at me. It was the first expression of pure cynicism I'd ever seen on his face.

I felt myself blushing red. "What do you mean by that?"

He looked away to spare me any embarrassment. "Oh. You know." He shrugged and started slowly back to his room.

Of course, I was the offending party. Again I'd promised him justice through Birge, the established instrument of justice. And now the very people whom Birge promised to put the fear of God into were out there scot-free and taunting him again.

I tried to reach Birge that night. Of course he couldn't be reached. But I spoke to a deputy who promised to send a patrol car out immediately.

Shortly after my phone call I heard the motor of the car at the foot of the drive being gunned. Then a couple of wild Indian-like shrieks tore through the darkness, followed by the sound of shattering glass, and the car roaring off into the night.

We went back to bed. If a patrol car ever did come, I can't say. I tend to doubt it, however.

The following morning I went down to the foot of the drive to see what I could find there. What I found was about a half-dozen smashed beer bottles and a few obscenities scrawled across the face of my picket fence. There was also a crude drawing of a skull smeared on with what appeared to be a black, tar-like substance.

When I turned, I found Richard standing behind me. He was staring quietly at the skull on the fence, a pail of warm, soapy water dangled from his hand. In the next moment, without so much as a word, he fell to his knees and began to scrub the vile words and the ugly little skull from the fence.

Later that morning I stood in Birge's office, panting above his desk, telling my story. He pretended to be deeply concerned.

"You promised you'd talk to these boys—"

"I did, but in all fairness, Mr. Graves, we don't know if this is the same bunch—"

"I told you it was. He saw them from the window."

"Oh, he did?" Birge said and made a little sneering expression with his mouth.

"How many did you say they were?" he asked.

"A carful. Four, at least. But I'd guess from the racket they made, more likely six."

He nodded. "And they just sat out there drinkin' beer and smearin' up your fence?"

"That's right."

A mean little smile crossed his face. "Why'n't you go out there and run 'em off?"

"That's not my job."

" 'Course 'tisn't." He laughed. "This sounds to me more like that bunch come over here regular from Batson."

Batson was a small hamlet about twelve miles north.

"What cause would they have?" I snapped. "They don't even know us."

Birge leaned back in his chair and swung his feet up on the desk. "Oh, I wouldn't be too sure. You folks are pretty famous 'round these parts."

He looked at me and saw I was clearly upset. It pleased him, and that made me dislike him all the more. He must have sensed what I was feeling, because suddenly he was once more all care and professional concern for our safety.

"Well, that's out-and-out vandalism, Albert, and I won't tolerate nothin' like that in my county. If a man can't lay his head down on his pillow at night without fear for himself and his family, a place ain't fit to live in. I come down special hard on vagrants and vandals. I got a reputation for it. And that kind of trash knows enough to give this county a wide berth."

He said all that with a straight face. I could've laughed out loud. Instead, I nodded mutely while he walked me to the door, his huge bear arm around my shoulder.

When I left I muttered some tepid threat about calling the governor if I had no satisfaction. He nodded his big head and gave me his assurances that the next time we were bothered by that "Batson trash," all we had to do was call and he'd have someone out there in a patrol car within a half-hour.

Nothing happened that night or the night after. Undoubtedly because we sat there waiting for something to happen. I don't mean with the lights on fully clothed and ready to evacuate; I mean we just lay in bed listening to the crickets and the bullfrogs and each other breathing, straining our ears to hear some suspicious sound in the night. All the groanings and creakings of the house were magnified a hundred times by our anxiety. We didn't sleep.

The third night we relaxed a bit, and that's when they came—two carloads full. This time they didn't bother parking down at the foot of the drive. Instead, they pulled right into the driveway and roared up to the kitchen door, where they turned their lights out and then sat.

Alice heard them first—the brakes squealing to a halt, then catcalls and ugly laughter.

"Albert," she whispered. "They're here again."

I was up in a moment and struggling into a robe.

Alice followed me out of bed in a kind of frenzy. "Don't go down there."

But I was already at the door, leaning into the darkness of the hallway. "Call Birge's office," I called over my shoulder. "Tell them they're back and to send someone out immediately."

Groping downstairs in the darkness, I kept thinking something dreadful was going to happen. Perhaps I'd be killed, or I'd have another seizure or some such thing. But oddly enough those thoughts didn't stop me for a moment.

Richard was already at the foot of the landing when I reached there. At the bottom step we nearly collided.

"They're here," I said.

He muttered some inaudible reply.

"Don't be frightened," I went on trying to assume an attitude of complete command. It was a superfluous remark. He appeared totally collected—almost detached. And yet he was fully aware that the object of these repeated and ugly nocturnal visits was himself. The potential danger to himself—to all of us—seemed scarcely to faze him.

Suddenly there was a loud, jeering sound from outside —then something resembling an Indian war whoop. After that came a loud crash of shattering glass from the kitchen.

We made our way through the darkened living room to the kitchen, where the first thing I saw was the large picture window over the sink with a sliver of moon gleaming palely through the jagged spikes of glass, hanging like icicles in the demolished window frame.

I crossed the kitchen and started for the door with Richard right behind me, a little surprised that my first instinct was to march directly out there and confront them. I had nothing with which to defend myself, however, and it was for that reason that I paused. There was in the broom closet, I recalled, for I'd put it there, a heavy garden rake with steel tines. Several of those tines had broken off in the course of years of heavy use, and I'd put the rake in the broom closet, where I intended to keep it until I could get it to a hardware shop for repair.

It was that rake I now groped for in the dark. Having found it, I armed myself and made my way back to the kitchen door. The catcalls and jeering had increased in ugliness and intensity.

"You wait here," I whispered to Richard over my shoulder. The next moment I flung the door open and stepped out into the night.

It was a disquieting sight that lay before me. First of all, there was the darkness with the driveway cut through it like a long strip of silver in the quarter-moonlight. Some fifty paces off I could see the squat, hunched silhouettes of two automobiles—their headlights out now, and the orange tips of cigarettes glowing from within.

Appearing the way I had, with unexpected suddenness, had a salutary effect. I imagine I looked slightly demented in my bathrobe, brandishing a rake—a bit like something rising out of the grave—a vengeful spirit come back to earth to right old wrongs. It threw them off balance. The catcalls and war whoops suddenly died, and once again the silence and the crickets and the scent of lilac floated in.

Feeling the advantage was now mine, I made my next move—a bold ten strides or so out into the center of the driveway. Imagine it. This timorous and aging man, with two coronaries already under his belt and all the scar tissue to show for it, surging into battle with a broken rake, jaunty as all get-out.

I still don't know what demons possessed me that night, because in past emergencies I'd always acted like a craven beast. But that night with my broken rake and my tattered robe I felt I had a touch of true and divine madness in me. Perhaps it had something to do with my need to show Richard that I wasn't completely spineless.

I wasn't alone, I should add. Richard had disregarded my warning at the kitchen door and followed me out. Now, barefoot and dressed in pajamas, he armed himself with two large rocks and shambled along behind me.

So we stood out there in the dim moonlight, in the darkness of the driveway, staring down our tormentors, a thin space of taut, eerie quiet between us, while we took the measure of each other.

I waited, considering the next move, while Richard strained like a leashed dog behind me.

"Go back in," I said to him over my shoulder. "Go back in."

His voice came back at me through the darkness, calm and firm and strangely comforting. "I'm fine."

"All right, then," I said, "follow me." And I surged out further into the drive with Richard at my heels, the two of us marching inexorably toward the cars.

The moment I reached the first, its headlights went on. I stood there momentarily stunned by the glare, pinned like a deer in the beam. Then the horns started—jeering at me—first those in the lead car and then taken up by the rear car, which had also put its lights on. Suddenly the driveway was flooded with noise and light. The effect was total havoc.

I don't know how it happened, but in the next moment I'd rushed the lead car and before I'd realized it, the rake was over my head and starting down. I must've looked like the wrath of God.

The first blow struck the hood full on with a loud, rattling crash. I could feel the metal shiver and buckle beneath the rake. I raised it again and brought it down. This time I bashed out one of the front headlights.

The sound of Alice screaming above the blare of horns tore across the night. Suddenly Richard shuttled past me —a shadow and a puff of air hurtling through the dark. I caught a glimpse of long hair flowing out behind him. All the while he was moving, a hoarse bellowing boomed from his throat, and he was flinging rocks at the rear car; I heard at least two find their target and rumble like thunder over its hood.

Again I raised my rake and surged forward toward the lead car. But this time a fearful commotion was going on within it. Apparently its occupants had had a change of heart. I heard the ignition whine and an engine turn over. Then the lead car started slowly backing off down the driveway, teetering a bit in blind retreat with moths diving madly into the beam of its single headlight.

In his haste to get out from under my rake, the lead man backed into the second man. Flustered and panicked, he gunned the motor instead of braking and the two cars smashed bumpers. Still they didn't stop, but continued to lurch back down the driveway, intermittently banging bumpers as they went, under a hail of blows from my rake and Richard's stones.

At the end of it we stood at the bottom of the drive panting and watched the red taillights of two fleeing cars streak off down the road until they vanished in the night.

When we got back into the kitchen the lights were all burning and Alice was waiting there—ghostly white. She looked from Richard to me and back again, not quite believing we were actually there. Several times she started to say something, but each time she failed. Instead, she cried.

"It's all right, dear," I said, and put my arm around her. She huddled against me. "They've gone now. Haven't they, Richard?" I looked over my shoulder at him. He was in a pair of oddly incongruous pajamas—palm trees and coconuts—that sort of thing. It struck me suddenly very funny, and I started to laugh. At first my laughter confused him. Then apparently he understood, for then he was looking at me in my tattered robe, still clutching my broken rake—more broken than ever as a result of this night's work. Then suddenly, standing there in the wreckage and debris of the kitchen, we were all laughing.

But that ended quickly. Alice was gaping at the floor near Richard, a look of horror on her face.

"Your feet!" she said to him.

We looked down at once. He had come out in bare feet, crossed the kitchen floor, strewn as it was with shattered glass, and cut his feet to pieces. He was bleeding profusely on the kitchen floor.

In a matter of moments Alice had boiled a kettle of water. I sponged the crusty gore from his feet and started the bleeding freely again. Then with tweezers and a magnifier that Alice held for me, Richard's leg propped up on my knee, I extracted all of the glass, and dressed and bandaged his feet.

When I'd finished, she suddenly turned to me. "Albert —are you all right?"

"I'm fine."

She looked at me skeptically. "Are you sure?"

"Of course I'm sure," I laughed. "Never felt better." And, in some curious way, that was the truth.

Alice was still horribly frightened, and while making hot milk at the stove for us, she sobbed softly to herself. A short time later, with Richard hobbling on bandaged feet and leaning against me, I helped him back to his bed. It was nearly dawn when we all got back to sleep, tired and exhausted, but curiously pleased.

Of that night I need mention only one additional point. Birge's deputy, whom Alice had reached, and who assured her that he was at that very moment starting out for the Bog Road, never arrived.

The following morning was a Sunday. Despite our exhaustion from the night before, we rose early and went down to the living room to conduct our services. We prayed and sang and gave thanks to the Lord for delivering us from the dangers of the night. After that we had our breakfast. Then I called the glazier and asked him to come out and repair the window.

It was clear to me now—abundantly clear—that I could expect no help from Birge or any of the four other men who comprised his force. As of the night I just described, I realized that any plea for assistance I might make would fall on deaf ears. Birge was part and parcel of the system that deprived me of my right to worship at church. Why, then, should he bother to extend me the simple courtesy of protecting me and my family from vandals and hoodlums?

The next morning Richard and I set out for town. We arrived there by careful design shortly before lunch hour, when working people are setting out for the noon meal and housewives are flooding the small shopping area.

I made a special point of taking Richard with me, knowing his appearance in town would cause a mild sensation. For some curious reason, he seemed taller to me that day. Perhaps he carried himself more erect than usual, as if to flaunt his own sturdy durability right in the heart of the enemy camp. His hair was thicker and longer. Since his stay with us he had fleshed out, though he was still lean and knotty with muscles. And from constant work in the out-of-doors, his skin had been burnished a rich coppery bronze.

Our path took us, also by design, directly past Birge's office in the Town Hall and down the Main Street where people peered at us out of car and shop windows, and turned to gape after us in the streets.

It was a proud and foolish march we made that morning. By it we wished to advertise the fact that we'd survived the night and intended to continue surviving whether they liked it or not.

Our path came to an end at the local hardware store where we entered and strode assertively up to the gun racks. I know something about guns, having served as an infantry officer in the Second World War. At the completion of that war I gave up guns and swore never to touch one again. Up until that day I had kept my oath and could never bring myself to respect people who found guns indispensable to their existence, for whatever reason.

Now, with Richard standing beside me, I felt the weight and balance of a number of rifles, and worked the bolts of several rather convincingly, putting on a show such as I'd never thought I was capable of.

Richard, too, hefted several of the guns while the salesman, a small, nervous individual by the name of Fletcher, regarded us anxiously.

Richard's facility with the guns was frankly astounding. In his hands the ugly things took on a quality of grace, and he could make them behave as if they were adjuncts of his body. His hands flashing over the bolts gave him the look of an extremely adroit magician doing marvels. Several people in the store paused in spite of themselves to watch him and gaze in frank admiration.

"Which one do you think we want, Richard?" I asked, after a moment. He paused, silently regarding each, checking their sights and peering down their barrels. At last he held one of the guns out toward me. "This is the one."

He chose a 30/30 with an automatic load of six cartridges. I chose for myself a Smith-Wesson .45 pistol. When we left there that morning we had our weapons and a full supply of ammunition.

That afternoon Richard and I went down to the bottom of the garden. We set up a row of empty tin cans and commenced our educations. That education lasted for a period of nearly three days, during which time we worked steadily at perfecting our use of each weapon, both of us alternating between rifle and pistol.

Nothing of any particular importance happened within those three days to interrupt our training, either, except that within that period, on four separate occasions, Emil Birge's green station wagon cruised slowly past the front of our house. Never once did he stop to chat or say hello or even to continue his pretense of being a dedicated civil servant concerned with our safety. His appearance was more in the manner of a military reconnaissance

—an intelligence-gathering mission upon which future activities would undoubtedly be determined.

Richard and I with rifle and pistol gave him, no doubt, sufficient to think about.

Chapter Fourteen

I HAVE always been a believer in law and order. I have always believed, or tried to believe, that justice serves man and that the good are protected from the evil by the forces of justice. I know now that I've been naive.

It's sad to reach somewhere beyond mid-life and discover that you've lived your life in a kind of mindless, undiscerning daze, rather like an infant in a nursery of your own creation. Think of me—a man of peace and good will, certainly not an impetuous man, but a wary and prudent man with all of the ailments and complaints of the aged—suddenly reverting to the rule of guns. I who had observed the law all of my life, eschewed violence, and believed childishly that justice was done in the courts.

And I hasten to point out that it was never my intention to use my guns immorally; that is, to prey on the weak or slaughter God's creatures. My only purpose in having guns was as a means of survival. And I must say that guns brought me the peace that Sheriff Birge declined to bring me. At least for a while. Then, as so often is the case with guns—you buy them to insure and protect your own peace and suddenly you find your guns have commenced to breed more guns and lo, you are at war.

From the very first day they came into the house, Alice hated the guns. She hated their noise, she hated the sight of them, and she hated to see me handle them. Right from the start she was accusing Richard of talking me into buying the guns and saying that by doing so I'd unwittingly escalated the tension that already existed around us.

One day she endured a particularly grueling afternoon of target practice, and it set her teeth on edge. That night, when Richard was out of the house, she suddenly put down her knitting and said, "I want the guns out of the house."

I looked at her for a moment, then continued reading my paper.

"Albert—did you hear me?"

"Yes."

"I want the guns out of the house."

"And the hoodlums in your house, I s'pose."

"Better the hoodlums in the house than the guns. Let them do to us what they will."

"You talk very bravely in their absence." I kept my face in my paper as I spoke.

"We've never had to live with guns in our house before," she went on, undaunted. "I don't see why we have to now."

"You don't!" I folded my paper and slammed it shut on my lap. "What do you propose to do when that bunch of lovelies comes back here some night? Call for Birge?"

Her gaze faltered and dropped. She looked as if I'd struck her. I went on: "You don't suppose they're finished with us, do you?"

"They would be," she said, her cheeks flamed, "if only—"

"If only I'd send him away."

"Well, why not?" she said, half rising. A ball of yellow yarn tumbled from her lap and rolled ridiculously by me. I stuck a foot out and trapped it under my heel. When I got it, I flung it back at her, much harder than I'd intended. She tried to catch it, but she couldn't. Instead, the ball of yarn struck her high on the head and bounced off somewhere behind the sofa. She was on her feet the next moment and shouting, "You said you were going to send him away. You promised—"

"I promised no such thing—"

"You lie."

"Don't say that, Alice."

"It's true, nevertheless."

"If I ever said such a thing," I spoke through gnashing teeth, "it was before all this business. You wouldn't put him out now."

"Why not?" she said. "Why not?"

"Why not?" I was a little stunned and speechless. She went on:

"His presence here is a threat to our lives. I should think you'd care enough—"

Suddenly I was laughing out loud. It was a scornful, withering laugh and it took her aback.

"When I think of all those fancy speeches!" I said.

"What speeches?"

"Those lovely little things about awakening motherhood. I was the one who never wanted a child. Remember? I was the one who got tired of playing father. Remember? I was the one who wanted him out of the house. Remember?"

She appeared to stumble and then sag under that hail of blows. All the starch was out of her. She had a stricken, pathetic look. But she went on feebly:

"Yes, but—"

"Yes, but—" I said in a whiny imitation of her. "Now when the chips are down, you're tired of playing mother and you're ready to toss your pup to the wolves outside."

"Yes," she said hotly, looking a little like a cornered animal.

"You really want me to knuckle under to that filth out there?"

"Yes."

"And to Birge and Horn and that pious, priggish band of little freaks that call themselves a Christian congregation?"

"Yes."

"And to that pack of thugs who come here at night like vigilantes?"

"Yes. Yes." She'd recovered all her starch and a little more to boot. "Yes, I do!" she said, and the next moment she was back on her feet, her eyes blazing, and stomping

up the parlor toward me. When she reached me she
planted herself squarely before me, the ball of yarn
clutched in her fist. "To save our necks!" she screamed.
"If you don't care enough about that, at least I do. I want
the guns out. And I want him out!"

As she said it, she flung the yarn wildly back at me.
It struck harmlessly above my eye and glanced off. She
was still shouting as she whirled to go. But her voice
trailed off like a dying phonograph and suddenly she was
staring at the parlor door, a look of sick surprise on her
face—staring at the door where Richard Atlee stood, where
he had been standing for the past few moments, erect
and rigid, filling the frame of it, and regarding her quietly.

Still, if we didn't have domestic peace, we at least had
peace from the nocturnal visitations of strangers in unlit
cars. We breathed easier and our life took on, once again,
a semblance of normalcy.

I say "a semblance of normalcy." Still—there were very
troublesome aspects to our days. One of these was
that the freedom of movement we so enjoyed in past years
was simply no more. In our little village, where for the
past several years we'd done our banking and all our
marketing, we were suddenly pariahs. Not that people
refused to sell us goods or to transact with us; I would've
preferred that; it would've been more honest. Instead,
while perfectly willing to take our money, they were at
the same time cold and rude. Nor were these isolated
cases; it was general and throughout—the kind of tacit
mealy-mouthed conspiracy that small-town folk appear to
excel in.

This was true of all the merchants and bankers in the
village with the single exception of Chester Washburn at
the service station. On the several occasions during this
period that we went into the village and bought gasoline,
he appeared to make a conscious effort to extend himself.
By this, I don't mean to imply that he slapped our backs
and invited us in for coffee and cake, but as he filled our
tank and checked the oil he would now make a few
conversational thrusts, and instead of gazing stonily off into

space, he now deigned to look at us. For Washburn that was no mean accomplishment.

That summer was unnaturally hot. Day after day the temperature soared well above the 90s. From about 11 A.M. on, you couldn't go out in the sun. The days were sultry, the nights balmy and insufferable. There was no respite from the heat and humidity in the day, and no sleep at night. You wrung out your clothes at dusk and suffocated in your sheets at night.

On top of all this a terrible drought had struck that part of the country. There was no rain, and no hope of it. The grasses and foliage all quickly withered and turned brown. Very shortly the countryside looked as if it had been put to the torch. We tried watering our lawns and shrubberies, but because the water levels were so precariously low, there were very severe restrictions on how much water might be used for this purpose. The amount was not enough to save our grass and plantings, and the sun, like a ball of white fire, bore down remorselessly, day after day.

Between the barely veiled hostility of our neighbors and the inclemency of the weather, we frankly wanted out. At least for a few months until things cooled down all around. Quite unexpectedly one day, Alice and I decided that we'd like to go up north to the mountains. Only two hundred and fifty or three hundred miles north of where we were the radio was reporting superb weather—cool dry days and chilly, sleepful nights.

It sounded like a perfect remedy for our ills, and so simple. But, of course, there was the matter of Richard. We couldn't just go off and leave him. In fact, we couldn't even discuss the matter with him. The mere mention of our going off anywhere by ourselves pitched him headlong into attacks of the greatest anxiety. He'd become sullen and moody and would watch our every movement like a cat.

Nor would we consider going off and leaving him there by himself. Alice, if urged, might've been prevailed upon to leave him behind. As for myself, the thought of Birge and night vigilantes, the memory of strewn crockery and coffee splashed across the kitchen walls, of Harlowe Petrie's greenhouse, was still too fresh in my mind. Leaving him there was out of the question. Taking him with us, however, was not.

I confess I approached the whole thing full of misgivings. I wasn't looking forward to transporting Richard two or three hundred miles northward. It wasn't as if he were any other normal human being. We'd have to go to restaurants and hotels. There'd be the stir upon our arrival, the usual looks of shock and amusement. I'm not a superman. I've never pretended to be. I'm a very private sort of man, full of ungainly self-consciousness in crowds. I deplore public scenes, and the thought of being the object of one is enough to produce a line of cold sweat up and down the length of my spine. Even to be witness to such a scene is enough to make me wish to be invisible.

As for Alice, I knew that such a trip, under such circumstances could only be unpleasant and trying for her. Yet, she was willing to undertake it, thinking just like me, that the best solution for us all was to leave the heat, the town, and the problem.

I asked Richard that very night, thinking he'd jump at the chance. His answer, while it shocked me, was typical:

"Why?" he said, cocking an eyebrow at me.

"Why?" I said. "I should think that'd be obvious. The weather's miserable. Things around here are miserable—" I was cross and my voice had a nasty edge to it.

"Oh, look, Richard," I said, suddenly apologetic. "Things around here are pretty unpleasant now. Mrs. Graves and I would frankly like to get off for a while. Up north they say it's very cool. And up there nobody knows or gives a damn about this whole bloody business."

He kept watching me warily as if he were trying to find something insidious in my suggestion. He had the look of a deer just catching the scent of wolves. I went on:

"It's beautiful up there. High mountains. Deep, cold

lakes. So cold you can barely get into them. Takes your breath away. Fisherman's paradise. They've got some streams that have never been fished. I've caught brownies up there—" I indicated the size with my hands. "It's a fisherman's dream, Richard." By that time I was glowing with excitement. And when I finished my little spiel I was ready to pack my bags and leave that very moment. I stared at him idiotically, looking for some sign of consent, pleading with my entire being for some small crumb of enthusiasm from him. But all I got for my trouble was a cold, belligerent glare.

"Richard—?"

"I ain't goin'."

I started toward him. He turned away. "I ain't leavin' here."

"For God's sake, why?"

"I ain't goin'."

"Why?"

"You know why. You know damned well why."

"You think we're gonna run out on you up there? Ditch you by the side of the road or something? Is that it?"

"Yeah!" he shouted. The noise of it brought Alice flying in from the kitchen. He snapped his head in her direction. "She would. She would—She'd just love to—"

The three of us stood there, glaring at each other, a strange trinity, frozen into a nightmare.

"You know, Richard," I said, with a kind of whispered portentousness. "If we'd really wanted to do that, we could simply drive off any night while you're sleeping—"

Suddenly his eyes were blazing. His whole frame seemed in the midst of upheaval. His arms and legs went off in all different directions like a puppet driven by a mad puppeteer. "Try it!" he said venomously. "You just go ahead and try it! You'd be awful sorry if you did."

"What's that supposed to mean?" I said, nearly purple with anger. But he didn't answer. Instead he stalked out, slamming the door so hard behind him that the frame shuddered. Several flakes of plaster wafted slowly down onto the kitchen floor.

Now it was clear. Any possibility of Richard Atlee's

leaving was out of the question. His intention was simply to remain with us forever. We were locked to each other, inextricably. All of us. Like three creatures trapped under a bell jar, peering at the sun shining in and the world outside—the world we'd lost and didn't know how to get back into.

Suffice it to say, we didn't go north. Richard was unbudgeable, and without him we couldn't move. There was no further quarreling on the subject. We capitulated, and the only thing that was left was a kind of smouldering resentment that hovered above us like smoke after a battle.

Richard stopped going out. He wouldn't leave the house during either the day or night. He'd still do his chores around the house, but he wouldn't leave the grounds, for fear we'd run off without him. Most of the time he remained in his bedroom, coming out only for meals. He refused to permit Alice and me to go marketing by ourselves. Whenever we went to town, he'd come along and sit sullenly in the back of the car, waiting for us to get done and anxious to get back home. But all this was as nothing compared to the days immediately following when we faced with Richard the greatest crisis in our mutual relationship.

There came a day when Richard was not around the house. Not in his room, not around the grounds, not anywhere to be seen. When we discovered it, Alice and I had the same idea at the same time, and that was to get away from the house. Not to flee, not to escape, but merely to get into the car, just the two of us by ourselves and slip off for a few hours, like the old times.

Leaving the house that afternoon, we were almost stealthy, sneaking out the back door and scurrying down the drive to where the car sat. We were desperate to get off before he'd come back and ruin things.

I'll never forget the dead, dry, choking sound when I turned the key in the ignition, and then Alice's pale face like a mask painted on the windshield, peering at me forlornly while I fumbled beneath the hood. When I came back and stood beside the car and looked at her through the open window she seemed to know everything. "What's he done?" she asked pitifully.

"Taken the distributor."

"The distributor?"

"It's a part," I said, strangely calm. "The car can't go without it."

She looked so utterly defeated. In the next moment, she opened the car door and started out.

"Where are you going?" I said.

She shrugged and smiled pathetically. "I guess I'm going back into the house."

"I bet I know where he's put it."

"In the crawl, I s'pose."

I nodded. "Go back in and wait for me. I'll get it."

Alice waited upstairs while I went down. I think she sat at the breakfast table having a cup of coffee and possibly one of Richard's freshly made corn muffins. I imagined her sitting there resignedly, sipping the coffee, nibbling half-heartedly at the muffin, and not believing for a moment that I'd find the part, or if I'd find it, that I could put it back in, or if I put it back in, that he wouldn't suddenly appear and stop us in some other way.

Standing down there in the shadows, facing the black square of the crawl, I had a sudden sensation that I was in a dream and that I'd dreamed the dream many times before I saw myself entering the square—entering that cold, wet, dark place with the awful smell of sewage and human waste, the dry, hard ground crumbling, sinking beneath my feet, the straw pallet mouldering in the darkness. I saw myself moving directly to the spot where I'd found the cigar box before with the Iron Cross and the cheap bric-a-brac, and the little desiccated bones of birds and rodents. I could see myself reaching for the cigar box and opening it, and finding there precisely what I'd come for.

In the next moment, I was standing directly outside the crawl and peering in against a wall of blackness. I flicked on my flashlight and prepared to enter.

The reality wasn't quite like the dream. The place had a vacant look, like a dwelling that had been unoccupied for a long time. There was something else unusual about it. It was cleaner and more orderly than I'd ever recalled it. The pallet and all the anonymous debris that had accumulated there over the years were gone. The cobwebs, the dust, the cakings of dirt and mud were all gone. There wasn't the trace of an odor.

Evidently, he'd cleaned it all out. I imagine the crawl was for him a bad memory and the act of cleaning it out was his act of self-purification. As if he wished to violently expunge the whole wretched period from his mind.

Everything I'd imagined only moments before was wrong with one exception. I found the cigar box in precisely the same spot where I'd found it the first time, many months before. And now as before there'd been absolutely no effort to conceal the box; it simply lay there inclined at a tilt on a small mound of earth.

I opened the box. The Iron Cross and the other trinkets he'd taken from the house were no longer there. In their place I found what appeared to be old talismans—bits of stone, chiseled and cut into the shape of amulets and scarabs, small dolls cut from small branches, leather thongs from which hung bits of bone cut into different shapes, rather like charms cut into the shape of different animals, an owl, a deer, a beaver, and so forth. But no distributor. It all had a pathetic kind of childishness about it, like the hiding place of a small boy where marbles, skate keys, and rabbits' feet are secreted. But there was something ghastly, too, about these toylike figures fashioned out of the bones of innumerable devoured animals.

I stood there looking at it all, debating what I should do next, when suddenly I heard a small scratching sound behind me.

"This what you looking for?"

I whirled in the direction of the voice, causing the beam of my light to swing in a wide arc around the crawl. At first I saw nothing and spun round again and again like one of those small shooting gallery targets that pivot stiffly around when you hit them.

It was the third time—just as my light splashed across the wall opposite the place where the chimney comes down into the crawl—that I saw him. Not him—of course—at least, not all at once. It was just the boot, at first—muddied and disembodied in the dark. Then my light traveled up the leg.

He was sitting there. But not really sitting. Just squatting on his haunches, leaning slightly rearward against the wall.

A strange, choking sound rose from my throat and clogged there. I stood there coughing and clearing it, like a man with a fishbone stuck in his gullet. In my fright I nearly dropped the light. Recovering instantly, I aimed the beam directly on his face and held it there as if I could pin him to the wall with it. And so we remained for an interminable second—frozen into immobility, in all that darkness, two figures in a frieze—not speaking, the two of us at two ends of a beam of light, regarding each other.

I can't imagine what I looked like, but as for him, his face showed not the slightest trace of an expression—not surprise, not fear or anger, not even amusement of the malicious sort he might have indulged in at that moment—just that terrifying blankness I'd come to know so well.

"You lookin' for this?" he said, holding up the distributor so that my light beam bounced off it and back into my eyes, blinding me momentarily. His voice was nearly as blank as his facial expression.

"Yes," I said.

He looked at it, dully, as if it were something he barely recognized. "I took it this mornin'."

"I know you did. You had no right to."

Suddenly the distributor hit the earth beside his boot with a dull thud. He didn't drop it or throw it. He merely let it slip to the earth from a limp, open hand.

I picked it up instantly, wheeled around, and started out. As I did, I nearly struck my head on one of the low joists just above me. In the process the light fell and I stooped for it. In that moment Richard rose and started toward me.

I'll never be certain if he was coming for me or to retrieve the distributor, whether the movement was a gesture of threat or one of assistance. It was that ambiguous. I scrambled for the light and, reaching it first, held the beam directly on him as if I could hold him back with that. He stopped dead in his tracks.

"I didn't want you to go nowhere," he said.

"You don't have any right to stop me. And no right to touch my car. That's not your property."

I started to turn.

"I ain't never leavin'!" he screamed at my back.

I hadn't asked him to leave. I hadn't even mentioned it. I didn't have the stomach for it. But now that it was out, now that he'd given me the opening, I charged right in.

"Richard," I started quite reasonably, trying to suppress the tremor in my voice, "I've been thinking. You said you wouldn't mind working for yourself. What about a little business of your own? A store—or a little repair shop of some sort. Actually I think you'd be terrific in that. What if I set you up in something? Somewhere far away from here where people don't know anything about—I'd be more than happy to advance the cash—"

I can't begin to describe the look of contempt on his face. He knew full well that he was being bought off, given a sum of cash on the condition that he quickly and forever disappear. Suddenly it was all clear to me. Clear in a way that it hadn't been since the very beginning.

"All right then," I said in a voice that was now quiet and remarkably controlled. "I'm going to give you a week. By that time if you haven't found a job and a new place to live, I'm going to ask you to leave. And if you don't go, I'm going to have to have you put out."

I watched his face for a moment, fascinated by it in the beam of my light. At first the only emotion it revealed was a minor fluttering at a corner of the mouth. Suddenly, something animated the rest of the features, as if some powerful creature chained beneath that mask of impassivity was thrashing around struggling to get out. Then, suddenly, it was loose and charging.

I lunged for the gray square of light just outside the entrance to the crawl. He came after me, and as he did I turned and struck him across the head with my light. The blow caught him high up near the temple. But it was a feckless little thing and hadn't fazed him a bit.

He made a funny face—an expression I couldn't quite associate with him. Rather like pity for a man who could strike such a pathetic little blow. Of course, he didn't believe that I would hit him, and up until that moment I would never have believed it myself. But in that queasy instant of metal impacting on flesh and bone, a strange look came over his features. It went quite beyond pity or contempt. It was simply a face I'd never seen before.

Following that, I knew it was all over. Whatever moments of friendship and trust, however brief and tenuous, we'd shared, were now at an end. The cord was severed. There was something unmistakably final in the sound of that dull thud on the head, and even as we gazed at each other I could feel the walls growing up between us.

We stood looking at each other across a small space, both of us a little breathless and crouching beneath the joists. He tried to speak, but only a hoarse, gurgling sound spilled from his throat. Then for the first time I looked into Richard Atlee's eyes and saw pure hate.

He was only inches from me when he raised his arm as if to strike. The strength in those arms I knew to be formidable. I'd seen them chop wood and lift rocks. I knew what they could do. And as that arm went up, I'd already begun to recoil under the force of it.

But incredibly it went up, reached its high point, and never came down. It was as if something stayed the arm trembling above me as if he were Indian-wrestling some invisible other hand above us.

When I scrambled through the square and out into the cellar he shouted after me—crouched just inside the entrance—his face framed in black.

"I ain't goin'. You hear? I ain't never goin'. Never! You hear? Never!"

When I reached the foot of the stairs his voice was still roaring from the crawl, but somewhat muted now and muffled by distance, like sound filtering through plaster.

I looked up and saw Alice at the top of the stairs, a look of horror in her eyes. She'd heard the shouting and was starting down. I waved her back. Then, clattering up the stairs, I turned to look again at the black square, which appeared blacker at that moment than I could ever recall it.

His face was gone now, and suddenly there was no further sound from the crawl. It had stopped as if at a signal, and all I could hear was the terrible flutter of my heart, banging away at my ribs.

When we got back to the parlor Alice led me to a chair and I collapsed heavily into it.

Her face was white as raw mushrooms. "What in God's name—"

"He was down there—"

"I heard voices. I couldn't imagine what—"

"I asked him to go."

"You did?" she said, looking at the filthy distributor, poised in my lap. "You asked him?"

"I gave him a week—"

"A week?" She was holding her flamed cheeks between the palms of her hands. "A week—?"

"Yes," I said. "Yes."

"You dare live with him for another week?"

"Yes," I said. "We owe it to him. It's all our fault. We misled him."

She stood there speechless, still holding her cheeks.

"One more week," I went on, panting like a winded dog. "Seven more days and then, job or no job—out."

She studied my face for a moment, a small anxious smile flickering across her mouth. "You feel better now?" she said. "Now that it's over?"

"Yes," I said, a little surprised by her quick change of mood.

"But nothing's done yet, Alice. This won't be easy."

Suddenly I remembered something. "Alice," I said pointing to the closet right off the parlor, "go get me the guns now and all the ammunition."

Somewhat later that day I had dizzy spells and I took to bed with pains in the chest. Alice wanted to call in Dr. Tucker, but I made light of those distinctly ominous symptoms and assured her I'd be up and on my feet again soon. In a short time the dizziness and pain subsided, and by supper time I felt well enough to take a cup of soup.

Of course, Richard Atlee didn't appear at supper that night, but surprisingly, Alice set his usual place for him at table. I tell you—it amazed me. Even now over the space of time, I can still see that cold bare plate with the pieces of silver and the napkin set beside it, looking so vacant and forlorn, rather like the crib of a child who's just died.

I made it all sound so melancholy. And mind you, it was. In one sense we were bereft. We couldn't have been more bereft if he'd been our own child. I couldn't bear to look at Alice. Nor she at me. No talk passed between us. The only sound was the sad tinkle of our spoons scraping along the bottoms of our bowls. We pretended that his setting wasn't there, but I rather suspect that Alice, just like me, was waiting for him to come up from the crawl. We were both waiting to hear a footstep on the cellar stair—part of us wanting to hear something, and another part dreading to. Nothing came, however, and it was all—yes—so melancholy.

By the time we were ready to go to bed that night, we'd still heard nothing from Richard. We weren't even certain whether he was in or out of the house.

Just before turning out the lights, I put the unloaded rifle in our bedroom closet with all the cartridges. I loaded the Smith-Wesson and placed it under my pillow. I did the latter in such a way that Alice might not see, but her quick, sharp eyes caught my fumbling movements, and she made a small whimpering sound and turned away.

Shortly after the lights went out, we had our answer about Richard's whereabouts, for we heard the cellar door to the garden squeal open and footsteps climbing out from beneath the house into the night. It was, of course, Richard, and he was leaving—going out through his old point of egress, as he hadn't done for many months.

"He's going," Alice said in one of those clipped, breathless whispers.

"Yes," I said.

"Maybe for good."

"Let's hope."

"Yes," she said. And we both lay there quietly listening to his steps, neither hurried nor furtive, recede down to the bottom of the garden to the stone wall, the wall that he'd built to keep intruders out, and then beyond that to the woods, where, after a while, we heard it no more.

"Let's hope," we'd both said. But even as we lay there and said it, we knew it was a vain hope, and that the real crisis was only just beginning.

That night was a trying one. For sleeplessness and morbid thoughts it took the cake. I kept recalling the incidents of the day—Richard and myself in the crawl; the expression on his face when I asked him to leave; and that moment of sheer despicable pleasure when I snatched the distributor up and told him the car was not his property, that it was my property, implying as much that nothing in our house was his property, or indeed ever had been.

And in the moment that I told him he would have to leave, that was the moment that I felt the most exquisite sense of relief, as if a painful boil had been finally lanced and the heat of infection and the poisonous fluids were all boiling off.

I dropped off into fitful sleep and when I did, I dreamed of him. I saw him towering, giantlike, above me, his face swollen and horrible, the saint's eyes red and blazing like ingots, his arm cocked above his head to strike, like some remorseless, retributive angel. When I woke I was in a cold sweat with dizziness and the chest pains of the day returning.

I have never paid much attention to my mortality, being content in the past to trust to God on that score. I suppose that in some naive and childish way I believed I was going to live forever and that death is an accident that only happens to someone else. But of course we all think that way.

On this night I lay in bed listening to the beat of my heart, which had been slamming away at the mattress beneath me. Suddenly it appeared to flutter and then stop. I could hear it no longer. Silence such as I'd never heard or ever believed was possible on this earth of birds and insects and machines—that was the silence that swarmed in upon me. And in that moment I believed I'd died or that I had reached the moment directly preceding death —the transitional moment where a person stands on the threshold of two worlds, not quite in either.

It was a moment of sheer panic. My instinct was to cry out and leap up, to somehow claw my way back into the world of the living. But I was petrified of moving, for fear that the slightest motion on my part would drive me over the precipice.

I can't recall how long it was I lay that way—eyes open, staring into the darkness of the room, feeling a creeping iciness at my fingertips and toes, and wondering how long the body lives after the heart ceases to beat. "So this is the way it is," I thought. "It will be like this."

I must've laid there like that for hours, too petrified to move, until I realized that Alice was sitting up in bed beside me.

"Did you hear that?"

I'll never forget the sound of her voice, shattering the awful silence, and the sudden rush of affection I felt for her.

"Did you hear it, Albert?" she said it again, just like that, a kind of whisper it was.

I sat up feeling the reassuring rush of blood flowing back into me. "Hear what?"

"Outside. Just now."

I listened for a moment. "I don't hear anything." Then, suddenly, just as I'd said that, the garden door squealed open again, and then closed softly.

"It's him, isn't it?" Alice said.

I looked at the luminous dials on the clock. It said three.

"Yes," I said. "It's Richard. He's come back."

Chapter Fifteen

THAT week, the one meant to be his last week, he came back again and again. He went out each night at a set time and returned at a set time, just as he'd done months before, when he'd been living in the crawl. Now he'd gone back to that dark, murky place once more.

In the morning when we rose and went down to breakfast, no longer did we find the table set in the breakfast nook, with the vase of freshly picked flowers, and the kitchen warm and full of the comforting smell of biscuits and perking coffee.

We'd eat our breakfast in silence and go out to work in the garden in silence. The garden, too, was a mess, for no longer did Richard go out there each day to look to the picking and weeding and pruning. Everything was tangled and overgrown, and in some curious way Alice and I had forgotten how to cope.

From meal to meal we waited for him to return, waiting for the sound of the footsteps on the stair. But it never came. Instead, we'd hear him coming and going in darkness, like the sounds of faceless transients you hear at night in shabby little hotels moving along the corridors outside your door.

Though he was nowhere to be seen, he was never out of my mind. In the daytime I imagined him squatting on his haunches against a wall in the half shadows of the crawl, just as I'd found him the day I'd gone down to retrieve the distributor. It would be just as he had sat with me in the cave a few months before, stolid and squatting, something a little atavistic about it, as if he had sat the way men sat eons before in the icy twilight of Pre-Cambrian caves.

I imagined now that he had gone back to those grisly little feasts of his—the small wild birds and the field rodents, tearing the fur and feathers from them and eating them raw. I wondered if he thought back wistfully of Alice Graves's table, of the pink and white bone china and the savory scents, and of friends and easy chatter about a warm, lighted table.

One night early in that week we sat at supper, not eating, not seeing each other, just waiting for time and the week to pass. Steam rising from bowls of soup curled listlessly up between us. Suddenly, a pair of heavy steps thudded on the bottom cellar stair—like the sound of stones dropping. Alice's gaze locked in mine as we listened to the steps, unhurried and relentless, mount the stair, then pause at the top just outside the library door.

I recall watching my hand reach for a fork, my grip closing down hard on the handle, and the five sharp tines gleaming in the gasolier. I could hear him breathing in the moist, mouldy, cellar darkness just beyond the library door, imagining his hand reaching for the knob and then the door swinging open. My fist closed tighter on the fork handle and, my eyes still locked in Alice's, I half rose expecting him to suddenly appear before me. But the door never opened. Instead, the steps started back down, still unhurried and relentless, like a tide receding.

There was something calculating and nasty about it. As if he wanted us to hear him—wanted to tease and taunt us. Give us a fright and turn away sniggering. As much as to say, "Not this time. Maybe next time."

And there was a next time. Several next times. But he never came in. Just paused and waited outside the library door breathing so we could hear him.

Hate isn't an emotion that comes easily to me. But I tell you that now I commenced to hate him. Not merely because I feared him. I did fear him. Now much more than even at the very beginning. The unpredictability, the violence—it was all so terrifying. But quite beyond that normal fear, I began to have some deep and horrible loathing for him.

One day, shortly before that week was up, I nailed a heavy plank of wood against the library door, and once again I changed all the locks in the house—except the one on the cellar door.

Alice said, "Why? Why not that one, too?"

Yes—why not the cellar door with the bleached and runny letters GOD nearly all faded now about the lintel? Why not? Why not?

But I couldn't say "Why not?" then. I could now. But why go into it?

Then Alice said to me around the fifth day of that week, "If you won't put him out, call Birge. Birge'll do it."

"I know Birge will do it. He'd love to do it."

"Then call him," she persisted. "If you won't, I will." Her face had a nastiness I'd scarcely ever seen there before. There was something petty and vengeful about it. Imagine that! That from Alice. Alice, the gentle and mild; the friend of the poor and defenseless; the protector of lame birds and stray animals; Alice, who had made the Christmas feast and sung hymns in church beside a strange young man she thought of as her own son, attaching to his appearance proof of a divine will. Even succeeded in making me believe he was somehow my son, as well.

Now she was quite ready, eager in fact, to turn that son over to Birge. And, of course, she was right. If I had no stomach for the business, I could easily call Birge. Birge had stomach enough for everybody. Men like Birge exist for just such things—to carry out the will of the squeamish majority. People just like me—mouthing pieties, regurgitating all kinds of rosy, idealistic twaddle, and not for a moment wanting such things to come to pass.

So I left the garden door open. And I didn't call Birge. I didn't have to. He called me.

It was strange the way that call came. Almost as if he were thinking of us at the same moment we were thinking of him. Only he'd reached for the phone first, and all I recall, hearing that voice, was the enormous sense of relief

I had—the way the appearance of an approaching ocean liner must affect a man stranded on a sinking raft.

"Albert," came that low, familiar drawl, "I was passing by the other day and almost stopped in. But I didn't. The place looks a little strange. How are you and the Mrs.?" His voice was oddly compassionate.

For a moment I almost believed he was serious and genuine. I had an urge to fall on my knees before him and weep with relief. But then the old voice came, wheedling and unctuous, confident of its great, persuasive powers. "You're a good fellow, Albert. A gentleman. No one would question the decency of your motives. But I feel you're into something way over your head. Some kind of trouble?"

"Trouble?"

"With that boy."

"No trouble with the boy," I blustered. "Only with the people who come around here bothering us."

He paused, letting me hear something like the scratching of a pen on a pad coming from his side.

"I don't like this boy," he said.

"I'm sure of that."

"I've got bad feelings about him. My feelings don't often mislead me."

"You wanted to hire him once. Make him a deputy."

"I only wanted to help you out of an awkward spot. This boy's a drifter. What we used to call a box-car rat." He paused again, as if he were weighing the effect of his words. "What would you do," he went on, "if a rat got into your house? You'd smoke him out, wouldn't you? Or call for the exterminator?" he added with a small laugh. "Well, I'm the exterminator."

That's when the anger came over me, just as I imagined him thinking he had me right in the palm of his hand, panting to be saved.

"Tell me, Albert. Has this boy threatened you? Are you afraid to say something? Because if you are, you don't have to be. I'll run him off. Just say the word. And you don't have to worry about his coming back. Once I run 'em off, they don't come back. I promise you that."

When, at the end of it all, I said, to my own amazement, and sick to my stomach, "No," and hung up the phone, there was Alice, standing there, where she'd undoubtedly stood for the greater part of that conversation. She had the look of one betrayed, full of bewilderment and hurt and growing rage.

So we lived that way for several days beyond the week's time limit I'd set for Richard to vacate the crawl, not knowing what to do next, and barely suspecting even what I wanted to do. Until, that is, the smell came again.

It's curious the way that started—first faint, barely perceptible, seeming to hover over a small corner of the kitchen. Then, suddenly, it was swift and everywhere, like a plague sweeping across a blighted land. Rising up from one story of the house to the next. That same harsh, fecal odor, like raw sewage. We opened the kitchen windows, and when it spread to other parts of the house, we opened more windows.

Alice cried now every day and prayed every night before going to sleep. Then she'd sit on the edge of the bed watching me check the rifle and the pistol. Now when I stuffed the pistol under the pillow I didn't even bother to conceal it from her.

"He's punishing me, isn't he?" she said one night.

"Only you?" I said with bitter irony.

"Yes. He's always liked you. It's me he's never been able to accept."

"Oh, Alice." I rolled over so that my back was to her.

"He's punishing me," she persisted.

"What for? What have you ever done to him but shown him kindness?"

"He's never seen it as that," she pleaded, and turning over with a pathetic whimper, she cried herself to sleep.

The next morning, shortly after she rose, she told me that she was going to call Birge.

"No," I said emphatically. "You will not."

"Why— Why, in the name of God? Will you tell me why?"

Her voice rose and I hushed her, for he was undoubtedly below in the crawl straining to hear everything we said. She started again. This time more softly: "Tell me why?"

It was an answer I felt I owed her, and so I set out to make my case. "In the first place, I will not put that boy into Birge's hands, because he means to kill him—"

She started to protest, but I waved her to silence. "Don't ask me how I know that or even dare to think it. But I know just as surely as I'm talking to you this moment that if I turn that boy over to Birge, it'd only be a matter of days until we'd hear that he was dead. Quite accidentally, mind you. Terrible tragedy, and all that, but the boy brought it on himself. That sort of thing."

She stared at me a little queerly, half believing what I'd said.

"In the second place, if we turn the boy over to Birge, and it turns out I'm wrong—that Birge doesn't kill him but merely chases him out of the county—where do you think that leaves us?"

"Leaves us," she murmured, confused by thoughts moving too fast for her.

"Yes," I said, a little cruelly. "Where do you s'pose that leaves us?"

She saw where the line of thought was going, but refused to pursue it. I pursued it for her.

"Suppose Birge runs him out of the county. Knowing Richard and what he is, how long do you think he'd stay out? And if he were to come back here some dark night —show up on your doorstep, or even better, get back into your cellar—how do you think things would go for us then, my dear? How much charity do you think he'd be prepared to show his old benefactors who'd crossed him? About as much as he showed Petrie when they crossed him."

"You don't think he'd—"

"Kill us?" I said almost charmingly. "I most certainly do."

I had to laugh a little at the neatness of the dilemma I'd just posed. But Alice didn't laugh. She just stared at me, a kind of sick, idiotic expression on her face. I was about to turn and leave, but she caught my arm. "Then let's go ourselves."

She whispered it at me with a kind of hissing desperation. "Yes. Why not? Why not just drive off ourselves?" Her eyes implored me. "At least for a while."

"You won't find a house here when you get back."

"I'm willing to take the loss. At least then he'd be gone."

There was a kind of bold, if not desperate, logic about it. And I must confess the idea was not totally unappealing. Perhaps it was an easy way out, but it seemed so drastic a step. Like burning down a house to get rid of a rat.

"He can't keep it up much longer," I said, finally. "Soon he'll go himself. Of his own accord."

"Of his own accord?" She said the words over again, as if she hadn't quite understood them the first time. "Is that what we're waiting around here for?"

She didn't wait for my answer. She gave a short, mocking little laugh. "Poor Albert." She laughed again. "Poor. Poor. Sweet. Simple Albert." Gales of laughter were suddenly pealing from her.

"Don't talk to me that way."

"What way?"

"In that tone of voice. As if you pitied me."

"I do pity you, Albert," she said, her eyes all wet, and red in the face from laughing. "I pity us. You and I for what we are."

"And what are we?" I shouted.

"Ssh," she whispered and winking, pointed with her finger to the kitchen floor.

"What are we?" I shouted again.

"The meek of the earth," she whispered and then she was gone.

The following morning the stench was unbearable. We opened all the windows wide and got out of the house as early as we could. We stayed out all morning and came back at noon only to get a bit of food and carry it back outside to eat it. In the afternoon we went walking in the woods. I don't know how long we stayed out there. It was already September and the days were beginning to grow cool and shorter.

We argued back and forth. It's useless to recount the nasty scenes and the bitchy sentiments of that afternoon, but at the end of our walk in the woods, we had come to a decision. We would go ourselves. Not permanently, to be sure. Just a short trip of an indefinite length, without any fixed destination, so as to make it very difficult for us to be followed. Perhaps we would be gone two months, maybe three—at the end of which time, he would surely be gone, and we would move back in. Assuming, that is, that we still had a house to move into.

That night was the first night of the phone calls. They were ugly things. We've all had them from time to time —the phone ringing later than it should, and nothing but heavy breathing on the other end. We had one of those the first night; two or three the second. Then nearly a dozen the night after.

Then the calls began to come earlier—usually just about the time we'd finish supper—and then continued right up until about bedtime. They were always the same thing —no words and a lot of heavy breathing.

At first we tried to pay no attention, but after the calls continued for several nights, it began to grow unbearable. At first I thought it was the bunch that had come out to the house that night several weeks back. It occurred to me that by these calls they were watching our movements, staking us out, as it were, for yet another nocturnal assault.

But after that I began to think that it was Richard Atlee (at this point we never knew if he was in the house or not), and for some unaccountable reason I found this second possibility more plausible than the first. It suddenly occurred to me that what he was doing was trying to make us believe that the calls, by their frequency and number, were the work of the same vile bunch that had visited us before. By doing this he meant to frighten us, to drive us out, leaving him behind as the heir apparent to all our possessions. Right then and there I decided, come hell or high water, I would not leave the house, with all our possessions and everything we'd accumulated over the years, to Richard Atlee. Not to him and not to any pack of roving vandals whose only purpose was to loot and mutilate.

One night we thought we heard someone prowling around outside in the dark, near the house. It might have simply been imagination or a case of badly frayed nerves. By that time we were pretty rattled. Also the phone calls that night had grown so frequent and jarring that, much against my better instincts, I called Birge's office.

The phone was answered by a deputy or some assistant. I told this person who I was and asked to speak with Birge. He promptly informed me that Birge was out and very politely asked if he could be of any assistance. I explained our situation—told him about the calls and the noises about the house. I started to tell him about our prowlers of several weeks earlier, but "Of course," he said, he'd heard all about it already. I asked him when Birge was expected back, and he said not that night, and even as he was saying it I heard Birge's soft, mocking laughter in the background.

The deputy assured me that he would send a patrol car out to the house immediately, and with a sinking heart I hung up the phone.

Alice did a curious thing that night. Just prior to going to bed, she went into Richard's room, which had remained shut for several weeks. She put on the lights, poked her head in the door, and gazed quickly around. She stood there a moment, then crossed quickly to the bed, sat down and fingered the edge of the blanket thoughtfully. Then she rose, flicked off the lights, and closed the door of the room behind her. It all must have taken no more than a minute or two, but it left a very strong impression—almost as if she were certain, poor woman, that if she'd only open the door and look, she'd find the sweet, lambish infant she'd lost somewhere, curled safely in its bed.

After that we locked all the doors, turned out the lights, and went upstairs to get ready for bed.

I undressed swiftly and got into pajamas. All the while that we were undressing the phone kept ringing, but now we didn't even bother answering it. In the next moment, Alice slipped despairingly into bed.

But I didn't get into bed. I went to the closet and took out the rifle along with several boxes of cartridges. Alice watched me with an expression of tired resignation on her face. She knew now I would never leave the house until the situation was resolved one way or another.

"What are you going to do with that?" she asked, looking blankly at the gun.

"Don't worry."

I flicked out the lights, then walked to the window and opened it as softly as I could. Next I drew up a chair and placed the rifle with the safety catch on across my lap.

There was no moon, but there were innumerable stars such as there are in early autumn. Outside the window I could see nothing but an inky curtain of blackness. I sat there listening to the night sounds, letting them flow in upon me—the cicadas, and the late peepers, an owl hooting in the branches of the witch hazel, and a chorus of bullfrogs intoning down along the bog. It was the sort of night that ought to bring peace and deep, healing rest to any man. Only a year ago, I could've felt that such a night was a sure sign of God and His infinite benevolence. Now the very lushness of that night, heavy with the scent of pine and twice-bloomed sweet pea, only seemed like evidence of some universal treachery. The night cast a protective shawl over the furtive movements of the intruder. The night was the friend of the thief and the murderer.

Alice called me softly from the bed. "Albert."

"Go to bed."

"Albert."

"Go to bed now. I just want to sit here a while and see if I can see anything."

"Do you think they'll send someone out to help us?"

"Didn't you just hear Birge's man say they were sending someone out? Go to bed. I'll be along soon."

I wasn't very convincing, nor did I try to be. By this time, she knew as well as I did just precisely what could be expected of Birge and his deputies.

"No, they won't," she said softly. "They won't send anyone at all."

The phone rang again—a jarring rattle beside the bed. We listened to it ring insistently for nearly a quarter of an hour; then suddenly and ominously it stopped altogether.

Once again I peered out into the darkness and thought about all the hours that lay between us and dawn—like a weary, shipwrecked man swimming doggedly along, thinking of all the dark, cold water between himself and shore.

"Albert."

"Go to bed, dear. I'll take the phone off the hook."

"No—Come here."

"I will. In a few minutes. Go to bed now."

"Albert. Please."

Sighing, I leaned the rifle against the window sash, stood up, and made my way across to her in the dark.

When I reached her she thrust her hand out from beneath the blanket and snatched mine. So suddenly old and withered that hand felt to me in the dark.

"Now, now, now." I patted her hand reassuringly.

She looked up at me through the darkness. "We never really wanted him, did we, dear?"

"Not quite so deeply as he wanted us."

"We led him on, didn't we?"

"Yes. I think that too, now."

"It wasn't really his fault—any of it."

"It wasn't anyone's fault," I said, still patting her hand.

"And all the good work he's done for us," she went on. "The stone fence and the painting, and the electrical wiring, and all the other little attentions. The suppers and the laundry."

"He was trying so hard to please."

I could sense her studying me in the dark. "It is," she went on, "a kind of love. Isn't it?" She had to hesitate and swallow before she could bring herself to say the word.

"You mean all this clawing and clinging? The refusal to go?"

"Yes," she said. "Even the smell. That, too."

"Yes," I said, suddenly feeling sorry for her. Sorry that she had not had more love in her life. And sorry that she had not had an opportunity to give more love, for surely no one had a greater capacity to give love than Alice. And my fault, I suppose, had always been a kind of unresponsiveness to that. While loving her in my fashion, I'd always kept her somewhat at a distance. And wasn't it sad, I thought, that now, at this late period in her life, when this boy, this lonely and graspingly possessive creature hungering for affection, comes along to her, isn't it sad that he should turn out to be like Richard Atlee— a creature who could not take or give love with any moderation or balance? Only with insane excesses? And just as sad for Richard Atlee. Just as sad for him, given his ungovernable hunger to be loved, that he had to stumble into a household where demonstrations of affection, when on those rare occasions they occurred, could only be described, at best, as restrained.

"I'm only sorry it didn't work out," I said.

She started to cry softly to herself. I took her in my arms and held her there, rocking her back and forth as if she were an infant.

"Will we be lonely, again?" she asked.

"A little perhaps, at first."

"We weren't lonely while he was here, were we?"

"No," I said wearily. "Not in the way we were. But in a different way."

"In a different way?" she asked, peering up at me. "I don't understand that."

"Neither do I," I said and laughed. And for a brief moment we were like that, holding each other and laughing softly together in the dark.

While I held her thus, the silence of the night was suddenly broken by the sound of the cellar door squealing open.

Alice suddenly clung to me.

"Yes," I said, still patting her hand. "He's on his way out again."

Shortly after, we were asleep. I dreamed about my father, who'd been dead nearly fifty years. He appeared to me as a young man—in the full glow of health and vigor, a shock of splendid black hair atop his head, and the brown, gentle eyes I recall so well. We were sitting in a canoe far out on a lake, fishing and laughing, and eating sandwiches, the way we had so often, so many years ago. It was a sad, strange dream.

But the dream didn't last very long, and I was awake an hour or so after I'd retired—awakened by the sound of a car rattling up the drive.

I lay there listening to it, imagining it was Birge or his man, come to check on the noises I'd reported. Then, as I lay there, it occurred to me that I heard another car, although I doubted my senses. Birge certainly wouldn't have expended two patrol cars on me. I was quite astounded that he'd bothered even sending one.

Still I lay there, wondering if I oughtn't to get up and look, and that's when I heard what I thought was yet another car. And only then did I decide to get up.

Alice was already awake, sitting up in bed, staring at the window. "What is it?"

"Probably Birge," I said, pretending to be casual.

Just as I said it we heard another car come rattling up the driveway. That was number four. It was then I got out of bed. "Wait here," I said.

"Albert—"

"Wait. I'll be right back."

From the bedroom window I looked out into pitchy blackness. In the next moment I heard another car and then voices, muffled and somewhat muted by distance, come drifting round the corner of the house and up into the bedroom.

I turned and went back to Alice.

"What is it?" she asked.

"They're back," I said, and feeling myself grow icy, I started for the rifle.

"Don't go down there." She got up and tried to block me, but I grabbed the gun and pushed easily past her. "You stay here. Don't move."

"Albert!" she cried out after me, but I was already descending the stairs.

From the kitchen it was possible to see more. There were fewer trees, and the night from there wasn't quite so impenetrable as it was around the back of the house. Here there were large gray spaces in the black, and as I stood by the kitchen door I could make out shapes huddled in the darkness.

There wasn't too much I could see at first. However, there was no mistaking the fact that the driveway was lined with cars, their headlights out, and people sitting in them. I guessed there were five or six cars, because they appeared to extend the entire length of the driveway.

The front car was nearly just outside the kitchen door, its low, humped silhouette appearing like a large bug dreaming. I could hear voices floating out of the open windows and see the orange tips of cigarettes inscribing glowing arcs within.

Suddenly the doors of the lead car opened and several people got out. Then I could hear doors opening a little further down the line and slamming, and then the crunch of footsteps on the gravel.

In a moment there were small clusters of figures all over the driveway and out near the garage—small huddled masses. I could hear talk and then laughter—ugly laughter, sniggering and muted—the sound of shabby little men grown bold on cheap wine and beer. Just the sound of it made the flesh on the front of my scalp crawl. There were nearly two dozen out there.

I called Birge's office again from the downstairs phone, keeping my voice low so as not to arouse Alice any more than she was already.

This time I reached Birge directly, feeling once again grateful at the sound of that unctuous, wheedling voice on the other side. Even as I was spewing the story out to him I realized it must have sounded wildly incoherent.

When he answered me, his voice had that irritatingly soothing quality as if he were talking to an hysterical child.

"You've got to come," I kept saying over and over again.

"Now, just relax. I told you I'm sending a car right out there."

"Never mind a car. You come. You come—"

"He'll be out there very soon."

"I don't believe you."

"Ain't nothin' to worry about, I told you. You're just a little overwrought."

"Don't tell me I'm overwrought. I must've called you a half-dozen times. You never sent anyone out here. And I don't believe you're going to send anyone out here now."

"Now you're wrong there, Mr. Graves."

I was "Mr. Graves" again.

"You're wrong there," he went on. If you could've heard the smirk in that voice it would've made you sick.

"And I'll tell you something else," I went on heatedly. "You sent these boys out here. And don't tell me you didn't."

"Course I did," he said, and started to laugh. "I swear I don't know where you get your ideas, Albert. I been lookin' out for you right along. If I hadn't, you'd been dead long ago." He laughed some more; then there was a click on the phone, and then silence.

Once again, the night closed in and we were all alone. I went back upstairs. Alice was still sitting up in bed. She gaped at me. "Who were you talking to?"

"No one," I said and took her by the hand. "I want you to get up now and put your bathrobe on."

"Albert—"

"Please don't argue with me. Just do as I say."

The tone of my voice made her suddenly docile, and she got quickly to her feet and stood beside me shivering in the dark. I led her across the room to a closet and took out a bathrobe. I think it was mine.

"Put this on," I said and helped her into it. Suddenly she appeared very tiny and helpless to me, like a small child, and in the next moment I was full of pity for her.

"Now, come with me," I said and led her to the bathroom. When we reached there, I pushed her gently in. She was about to put on the light, but I stayed her hand.

"Keep the light out."

Suddenly a pane of glass shattered somewhere down below us.

"Albert—"

"Now, lock the door and don't come out until I tell you to." I went to my bed and got the Smith-Wesson from under the pillow, then went back and handed it in to her. I could see her staring at it, the ugly metal barrel glowing in the dark.

"Take it!" I said, impatiently. She shrank backwards into the bathroom, away from it, and I had to follow her in. When I reached her, I took her palm and planted the pearl handle firmly in it. She was about to protest but in the next instant I slammed the door between us.

Another window pane shattered somewhere in the house. "Lock the door!" I shouted through the partition. I could hear her breathing on the other side. I stood there waiting to hear the bolt click, but I heard nothing.

"Lock it!" I shouted again. "Lock it!" Then the sound came—a small, high, metallic click. I turned and started for the rifle.

It was only a matter of moments before the whole house was under a hailstorm of rocks and flying debris. Large boulders struck the roof, then clattered and bumped their way down the length of the gables, making a fearful racket as they went. From time to time, several boulders would land on the roof at one time, and the sound of them bumping and rolling down the eaves was amplified into booming claps that echoed horribly in the empty attic.

The rocks landing against the side of the house would

strike the clapboards with a loud crack. When I first heard them, I thought they were rifle shots.

I ran from window to window trying to get a glimpse of my assailants. But each window was being systematically punched out. Glass was shattering all around me, and rocks ricocheted off the walls inside the house. After a while I just huddled in a corner with my rifle, wondering what to do next.

They'd ringed the house by this time, and the darkness was completely on their side. I could hear them outside thrashing all around the house, hooting and shrieking like Indians, and trampling through the bushes and the garden. It was horrible.

But curiously enough, after I'd bundled Alice up and taken her to the bathroom and locked her in, I ceased to be frightened. The fear just melted off me like an old reptile skin, and what was left in its place was a hate the depth of which I never knew existed in me.

I've often thought of that in past years, that sloughing off of fear. That's not to say I haven't feared things since. A fearful man is a fearful man. But that night, for as long as the horror lasted, I ceased to be frightened of it. I can't say exactly why. Perhaps I was too numb to fear or to comprehend danger. But more and more I'm convinced it had something to do with my need to take care of Alice.

The torrential downpour of rocks increased at such a rate that at one point it sounded as if the house were in the crushing embrace of some huge, mindless creature who'd made a plaything of it. The walls and floors and joints creaked and shuddered. It was as if the poor place, somewhere down deep in its foundations, was groaning with pain.

Then suddenly, as if by some preordained signal, it was silent. The rocks stopped, the hooting ceased, the thrashing movement came to a halt, and once again the night flowed in upon me with all of its beautifully disarming sounds—the crickets and the cicada, the hoot owls and the frogs. It was a kind of mockery.

But even more disarming was the fact that I'd now lost track of them. Before, when they were howling and screeching like banshees, and rocks were flying off the house, I knew where they were and what they were up to. There was a curious comfort to be taken from that. Now, suddenly, I could see and hear nothing.

I went back upstairs to check on Alice. I heard her weeping behind the bathroom door. I went quickly to it and spoke to her with the door still closed between us. "Are you all right?"

"Yes," came her muffled voice. "Are you?"

"I'm fine. I'm going back downstairs to look around. You stay right where you are. Don't move."

With the rifle in my hands, I hurried quickly back downstairs, for the fear I had was that this silence indicated that they would now try to enter the house.

I was amazed at the speed and deliberation with which I moved. It seemed so purposeful. So much to the point. I appeared hardly the invalid I knew I was. Civilized man simply doesn't know, or has forgotten, the amazing resources of his body—the vast reserves of endurance that can be called up even by a flabby, diseased body.

When I reached the lower floor, I found the place a shambles. Even in total darkness I could see how much destruction had been done, windows punched out, curtains torn down and hanging from the rods, bric-a-brac, lamps, crystal, smashed—all beautiful, irreplaceable things Alice and I had accumulated over a space of thirty years of marriage. And the floor, strewn with jagged shards of glass and rocks that had been tossed in from the outside, so that you had to tread your way very carefully.

As far as I could determine, no one had yet entered the house, although the kitchen door, which had sustained an awful beating, now hung on its hinges, like a loose tooth just waiting to be plucked out. Inside the kitchen, midway between the table and the door, lay an enormous boulder that had undoubtedly been tossed against the door by several of them, with the purpose of stoving it in. The device, while barbarous, had worked admirably.

It was to this door that I went, still holding the rifle, a little coyly, like a man holding a dead rat by the tail.

The safety catch was still on and the weapon, pointed downwards, dangled clumsily in my hands.

When I reached the door, I swung the rifle barrel against the few jagged spikes of glass still remaining in the door frame. They flew out and landed on the brick step outside with a high, almost musical sound. Then, peering out through the empty frame I saw something that turned my bones to jelly.

At different points in a rough perimeter of sixty yards or so, I could see fiery pinwheels twirling in the dark, all around the house. Undoubtedly, they were rags, soaked with gasoline and then ignited. There were nearly ten I counted, twirling around out there. It was almost pretty, I thought, those orange-yellow circles spinning against the black night, disembodied and scorching the night air, like some fantastic fireworks. The pleasant smell of them came acrid and pungent to my nose, faintly reminiscent of burning punk on Halloween.

Suddenly there was a long, blood-curdling shriek, and one of the pinwheels with an unseen person at the end of it started to streak toward the house, moving in a line directly toward me, where I stood in the open doorway.

I don't know what I thought. I don't suppose you ever do in moments like that. The mind goes a total blank, and you see the thing—this ball of whirling fire streaking toward you like a meteor—with someone at the other end of it shrieking out there in the darkness.

In the next instant I jerked the rifle clumsily up with the intention of shooting high over the runner's head, hoping that the sound of a rifle report would be enough to turn him off. I hoisted the barrel skywards and squeezed the trigger. The only sound that followed was a sickening click. I'd forgotten to release the safety.

Some twenty paces off and to the right, a face illumined by a torch light suddenly burst out of the darkness. It was the face of a young boy. Not an unpleasant face. The kind of face you see at high school football games or at a dance. And to my horror, I suddenly realized that I recognized the face. It was the young boy who for the past several years had been waiting on me at the tobacconist's shop in town. His parents often sat next to us in church, and I had frequently chatted amiably with the boy himself.

But now those boyish features were twisted into an ugly snarl. He stopped dead in his tracks about ten paces from where I stood and shouted an obscenity. Then he raised the flaming torch.

I watched the orange wheel above the boy's head grow larger and begin to whirl faster and faster. I gazed at it in a rapt detachment—like a spectator at an accident—wondering almost impassively when he would let it fly from his hand. I had forgotten the gun or abandoned the notion of even using it—one or the other.

In the next moment he screamed and once again started streaking toward me, the flaming rag spinning madly above his head. He seemed to grow larger and larger until he no longer seemed like a boy, like a living creature, but rather like a thing—a piece of machinery gone haywire—a runaway locomotive that nobody could stop.

Then he was so close I could hear him breathing. For a moment our eyes locked and we contemplated each other in a shower of sparks.

Just then a mass of black shuttled across my line of vision. That's all I saw at first—a black blur between the boy and me. The figure twirling the firebrand tumbled heavily on the earth a few feet from where I stood. It was as if he'd been lifted bodily off both feet and flung down; the torch fell harmlessly aside. The two figures rolled over it, sending out a great upward shower of sparks, and then rolled past into the shadows. There was a scramble and then some grunting, and then a dull sickening thud.

I knew it all before I got there. I didn't need the little bit of light still flickering in the trampled torch to tell me what had happened.

When I scrambled down the steps and stood there, the unfired rifle still dangling at my side, what I saw was like a little vignette you come upon in stained glass in some old church: some grisly Old Testament tale of pride or lust or murder—Cain and Abel, I suppose, or Absalom and David—telling an ancient parable of violence.

That's the way Richard Atlee looked at that moment, panting there like a winded animal and crouching over the limp carcass of the boy. In his fist, the heavy boulder with which he'd bludgeoned him was still swinging from the momentum in his arm.

Richard stared up at me. I could see his face clearly in the orange shadows of other burning rags. They were still all around us, ringing us, but now they'd moved closer and their pinwheels were strangely still. At a certain point they all halted, not twenty feet off, and silently watched the little scene being played before the kitchen door. There was no sound other than the hissing of the burning rags and the sound of crackling sparks flying upwards.

I stooped over the boy, trying to see what had been done to him. At first he seemed to be sleeping, strangely childlike, his hands folded across his chest in an attitude of beatific repose. Then when I knelt down I could see that the front of his skull was caved in. A large flap of flesh had been gouged out by Richard's rock and hung loosely from the front of the boy's head. From beneath that, small bubbles of grayish matter were seeping out at the edges. The eyes were still open, but the pupils had rolled upwards, only their bottoms still showing from beneath the upper lid, like thin, black crescents.

I looked back up at Richard crouched above me, panting. For the first time since I'd known him he appeared to be frightened. It had finally gotten through to him what he'd done, and now he was looking at me beseechingly, as if for guidance.

In the brief time that we stood there it was clearly evident to everyone that something quite awful had happened, and now in that strange glow of burning rags, many of them shuffled silently forward to see. They stopped in a ring about twenty feet from us and stared at the scene.

I imagine I stood up then and looked around at them. Richard dropped behind me, falling back into the shadows. They were all boys, just like the one lying crumpled there on the ground, most of them no more than seventeen or eighteen years old. They'd been drinking. You could see it in the wild flush of their faces. But now they were all suddenly sober and frightened.

"Get out," I shouted at them at the top of my lungs. "Get the hell out of here."

I started toward those faces swinging the rifle at them from the barrel end in wide whooshing arcs, looking, I suppose, like a madman. They fell back before me. The ring of them broke open and they started streaming for the cars. Doors slammed. Lights went on. Motors turned over. They were all suddenly scurrying out of the driveway like so many frightened roaches, leaving the burning rags to die in small smouldering heaps all around the grounds.

After they'd gone, there was nothing left but Richard and me confronting each other over that poor smashed form sprawled on the ground, the little gray bubbles oozing from beneath the torn flap in its skull. I reached for the boy's wrist. It was still warm and it dangled limply while I felt for a pulse. But there was no pulse.

I'll never forget the expression on Richard's face. It was an appeal. "Help me!" it said, but he never spoke those words. He kept looking over his shoulder, as if some instinct were telling him to run and he was trying desperately to fight that instinct. His eyes flashed wide, however, and he already had the look of a fugitive.

If he was looking to me for advice, he was wasting his time. Though my mind was numb, it seemed to be going a mile a minute. But I couldn't put a plausible thought together in his behalf. Birge would be out there momentarily. As soon as those boys hit town or a nearby phone, Birge would know. I knew that'd be what they'd do first, and then Birge would be out to see me, in an official capacity. Not to help me, mind you. And certainly not to help patch together what was left of my house—and certainly not to apprehend the people who'd torn it apart; not even to give solace or comfort in that hour of loss. (The patrol car he'd promised to send had never come, of course.) No. He'd be out there seeking justice for the apple-cheeked boy whose wrecked body lay crumpled on the ground in the dying light of a few smouldering rags.

But most of all, Birge would be out there seeking Richard Atlee. And the full implication of that had only just now, for the first time, registered on Richard. Gone was the impassivity, the almost god-like absence of human emotion that was so characteristic of his features. Now, for the first time, he seemed aware that he was in danger. He was genuinely frightened, and I must confess it pleased me.

He stood there breathing heavily and waiting for me to tell him what to do. Still, I couldn't get myself to speak, nor did I even want to. For if he wanted me to help him to escape, I wasn't about to. My instincts at that moment were all for self-preservation. I had a dread of seeing Richard fall into Birge's hands, but I wasn't about to compromise myself any further by helping him get away. I could see the possibility of Birge's linking me to him as an accomplice. At first it sounded absurd. But I wouldn't put it past Birge. For him, it would've been two birds with one stone. He would've liked nothing better than to charge me with harboring a dangerous criminal. Richard kept staring at me, waiting for me to speak. I half believe he'd read my thoughts, that he could see me plotting my own salvation at the expense of his. Suddenly there was a look of betrayal on his face. He gazed down at the crumpled figure at his feet and appeared to be saying, "I did this for you. And now see how you repay me." That's what he appeared to be saying to me.

Suddenly he whirled, spun around, till his back was facing me. Then he whirled again, a small yipping sound like that of a frightened puppy squeezed from his lips. Then he was running, but not moving—just standing in one place—a flurry of agitation at his feet and small puffs of dirt and gravel rising all around him. Then he was streaking full speed up the drive. I thought for a moment he was heading toward the bog, and I was already congratulating him for having enough brains to save his skin, as well as sparing me a great deal of difficulty.

But just as he was passing the back porch, he veered

sharply and ducked into the kitchen door, still hanging open on one hinge. I started to call out his name, but nothing came except a half-strangled cry. I stood there goggle-eyed and unbelieving. He'd gone back into the house.

I found an old tarpaulin in the barn and with it covered the body of the boy, then went quickly in after Richard.

The first thing I did was to release Alice. I took the pistol from her and led her back into the bedroom and sat her down on the edge of the bed. She appeared to be in a state of shock.

"Wait here, I've got to make a call."

She nodded as much as to show me she understood. I left her there and went back down and called Birge's office. A man answered. I didn't even ask to speak with Birge. I told the man who I was and that a dead body was lying out in my drive. Then I told him to tell Birge to come and fetch it.

This time there was no smirk in the voice I was speaking to. The person on the other end sounded startled and a little frightened. Clearly at a loss for words, he kept calling me "Sir."

"Send Birge to collect the body," I said again. "It's on his head. Not mine."

When I hung up the phone, there was Alice standing there, ankle deep in wreckage, her face gone a sickly white.

"Is the poor child out there?" she whispered.

"Yes. Spattered all over the driveway."

"Oh God, no—Richard."

I tried to lead her off, but she held back, clutching my hand.

"Where is he?" she asked, her eyes staring terribly.

"Richard? In the crawlspace."

"What's that you said about the driveway?"

"The driveway?"

"You said Richard was spattered on the driveway."

I suddenly realized she didn't know anything about the dead boy on our driveway. She thought I'd been talking about Richard.

"No," I said, "I was wrong. I misunderstood you. Richard is fine." I moved to her. When I reached her I put my arm around her. She seemed so pathetically small. "Come," I said, "I'll take you upstairs."

She seemed to accept that, and only then did she permit me to lead her back upstairs. "Poor child," she kept mumbling all the way. And even when I put her to bed, half in shock and half in a daze from two powerful sedative tablets, she was still mumbling those words: "Poor child. My poor, poor child."

"Get him out," I thought to myself clattering back down the steps. "Get him out?" But not for one moment did I believe that he had any way of getting out, even, that is, assuming he were willing to go—an assumption that struck me as highly improbable.

Undoubtedly Birge, by this time, was well aware of what had happened. He was most certainly already on his way out. I'd called his office about fifteen or twenty minutes back, and there was no answer. The trip was about forty minutes. It was only a matter of moments before he'd be here pounding on the door, or what was left of it, demanding blood for blood.

"Richard." I stood outside the crawl entrance calling softly into it. I couldn't see him, but I could hear breathing somewhere back deep in the hole—a hoarse, rasping ugly sound.

"Richard." I called again into the darkness and heard him scurry and dig further back into the shadows.

"Richard. The sheriff is going to be out here any minute. You've got to get away from here."

I waited, staring into darkness. "I can't guarantee your safety if you should fall into his hands."

Still no answer.

"I have two hundred dollars in cash in the house," I went on. "I'll give it to you. I'll give you the car. Take it and run. As far as you can."

Silence roared back at me from out of the hole.

"Richard, I can't help you any more." My voice was a mixture of pleading and exasperation. "I can't save you this time. You're in great peril, and you've got to try and save yourself."

The only sound I could hear was the sound of my pulse throbbing at my temples. "For God's sake, what do you want?" There was another scurrying movement, this time toward me. And then he spoke:

"I ain't goin'."

"Birge'll be here any minute."

"I ain't leavin'."

"Birge'll be here any minute."

"I ain't leavin'."

"The boy out there is dead. You killed him. Do you understand that?"

"I ain't leavin' here."

"These people here—if they get their hands on you—"

"Never leavin'—"

"Richard. Believe me. I'm not trying to get rid of you. But it will be very bad if you stay."

"Never, never leavin'."

He went on like that. Not sentences. Mindless, detached little mutterings. Things I couldn't hear and didn't want to. Past all reason.

But of course I'd known it all along—just how he'd react. I knew he couldn't get himself to go. He'd wandered and searched for nineteen years just to find us; now that he had, he wasn't going to let a little matter such as the safety of his own neck endanger anything he'd won over the past few months.

I stood there a while longer wringing my hands and gaping at the hole. Then I turned and walked slowly up the stairs.

When I got back up, it was close to 2 A.M. Birge was already out in the driveway with several other men. He'd got there only moments before. There were two cars parked out in front of the kitchen—one a patrol car and the other, Birge's station wagon with a tower light swiveling round and round on the roof, thrusting a blood red shaft of light far out into the night.

From where I stood on the back porch I could see Birge crouching over the body on the ground. He had pulled back the tarpaulin and was groping for a pulse. Several times he prodded the body with his finger. It was the same sort of motion you see women use to select meat in a supermarket. After a while he pressed his thumbs on the lids of those ghastly upturned eyes. Then dragged the tarpaulin back over the body.

He looked up and saw me walking toward him. "Bobbie Winton," he said when I reached him. "Nice boy."

"Delightful," I replied. "He tried to burn my house down tonight." Young Winton's arsonist tendencies didn't appear to faze Birge. Still crouched over the tarpaulin, he looked up at me. "You got yourself some trouble here."

It angered me, the way he said it. Smug and satisfied it was, as if he were saying, "Now I gotcha."

"You got yourself a pack of trouble now," he went on.

"You've got some trouble, too," I shot right back. "If you'd sent someone out here when I called—"

"I did send someone out. They looked around. Found nothin'. And come right back."

He said all that with a straight face and a voice full of touching sincerity.

"Ain't that so, Brody?" He turned and spoke to one of the men hovering just behind him. "Mister Graves here looks a little dubious, Brody. Tell him what you seen."

A great hulking creature with a beer belly and the smell of stable leather all about him shuffled out of the shadows. He wore one of those wide-brimmed trooper hats, and when he spoke the red beam from Birge's tower light kept swinging across his bloated purplish features.

"That's right," he said in a voice almost comically high for a man his size. "Jes' like the sheriff says—I come out here 'bout eleven-thirty or so and looked around. I seen nothin!"

"That's a lie!" I fumed. "That's a damn lie! If you were anywhere near here at eleven-thirty, you would've seen this driveway choked with cars and those boys swarming all over the place."

"I come right in here," he went right on as if I hadn't said a word. It was as if he'd memorized it all by rote and was afraid to stop for a second for fear he'd forget his lines. "I walked round the barn and the back of the house and all round the grounds. I seen nothin'."

Birge shot me a look of glowing satisfaction.

"He's lying," I said. "Can't you see he's lying?" I grabbed a flashlight from the trooper who'd just spoken and threw a beam from it up over the house, so that it fell on the windows and the kitchen door, with all of its glass punched out and hanging on a hinge.

"You think that's a figment of my imagination?" I snapped at Birge.

"Didn't say it was. Just said my man wasn't out here when it happened."

"Well, he damned well should've been. I've called your office at least a half-dozen times in the past month with prowlers and intruders and God knows what out here, and you deliberately—"

I could see his face turning as I spoke. It was like watching a bowl of milk curdle. But I couldn't stop myself now. I rolled right on.

"Don't think this is the end of this thing for me, either, sheriff. I've only just started. And there'll be reports and investigations—right on up to the governor—"

Up until that moment he'd spoken civilly to me. Or at least there was a pretense of speaking civilly. In the next moment something harsh and ugly crept into his voice. "Where's that animal you keep down your cellar?"

At first I didn't know what he was talking about. "If you mean the boy, he's not here."

"I got twenty witnesses or so, say they seen him beat the livin' hell out of the Winton boy tonight."

"What're you going to do about those twenty witnesses?" I asked. "You think they were just out here sightseeing tonight?"

"You leave them boys to me."

"I left them to you once before, and they beat up my boy."

"Your boy?" Birge shot me an amused glance. Thinking back to it, it was a peculiar thing for me to say at that moment.

"Where is your boy?" he said with all the sniggering malice he could muster. "You better tell me now."

"He's not here," I said.

"Then I don't s'pose you'll mind my taking a little look around."

"You don't suppose he'd be fool enough to sit around here and wait for you."

"I frankly don't know what a freak like that'd do." He laughed and looked around at the others. They all laughed along with him as if on cue. Birge was clearly pleased with himself. "I'll just take me a little look around."

My mind was going at a feverish pace. "Not if you don't have a search warrant."

I knew he didn't. It pulled him up short, and there was a look of surprise on his face. Frankly I was surprised, too, at my own audacity.

"You sayin' I can't go through here without a warrant?"

"Exactly."

"Now I know you don't mean that, Albert."

"I assure you I do. And to you, it's Mr. Graves." I enunciated my name in a very brisk, clipped manner. He was still incredulous.

"You mean to say I got to have a warrant?"

"I don't say it, sheriff. The law says it. And you above all ought to know enough to respect that."

He stood there for a while a little puzzled, his hands on his hips, his high black boots spread wide, and shaking his head. He knew I had him, at least for the moment.

"Okay, Mr. Graves. I'll get you your fucking warrant."

"Thank you, sheriff."

He looked at me for a long while just oozing hate. Then he addressed Brody over his shoulder while still staring at me.

"Go on back to town and wake Judge Harrington. Tell him what happened out here tonight, and you tell him Mr. Graves says I got to have a warrant to search his place. You tell him I want that warrant quick. Now."

"You gonna stay out here?" Brody asked him.

"Gonna sit right out front in my car. Make sure no one leaves here."

My heart sank then, thinking about Richard below in the crawl.

"Not on this property," I said. "If you care to wait you can go out on the road. But you can't wait on this property."

Birge crossed his arms and stared at me. There was now a look of exasperated amusement on his face. I got the feeling he even admired me a little.

"Okay, Mr. Graves." He flicked the wide brim of his hat so that it made a snapping sound. "I'll be glad to wait out on the road."

He and the others started for their cars. When Birge reached his, he took the floodlight on his side window and played it up across the face of the house where he could see all the pits and scars of recent battle.

"Kind of reminds you a bit of Harlowe Petrie's place, don't it?" he said, and they roared out of the drive laughing and leaving deep tire scars in the gravel.

Chapter Sixteen

IT WAS getting on to 3 A.M. when Birge and his men backed out of the driveway. I could still see them out on the road huddled in conference. Then one of the cars made a sharp U turn and sped back in the direction of town. Birge's station wagon remained there pulled up on the side of the road with the red tower light swiveling slowly round and round, like a dragon's eye in the dark.

There was very little time left before Birge's men would be back with the warrant. I calculated an hour and a half at best. If Richard was to get away he'd have to move quickly in order to put some distance between himself and Birge. There was no hope now of his leaving by car, for that would mean having to drive off in front of Birge. No. The way out now was through the back. Out the cellar door and across the bog.

When I got back into the house I found Alice in the darkened kitchen, seated at the table amid the wreckage and debris.

"Albert," she said very gently.

"I thought you were asleep."

"I was."

"Did they wake you?"

"Yes."

"I'm sorry."

"Can you put the light on?"

"I'd prefer not to. He's sitting out there watching our every step." I looked at her a little anxiously. "Did you hear?"

"Everything. I was standing right at the door. He's still here, isn't he?"

There was nothing accusatory or harsh when she said it. It was just sad.

"I'm going to get him out right now," I said, bolting for the library door. "Birge'll be back with a warrant very soon. What a mess. What a Godawful mess!"

"Albert," she called out from behind me. "Why didn't you just let them come in and take him?"

"I don't know why," I snapped angrily. "How the hell should I know why?" I lunged for the door.

"I'm going down there with you." She started after me.

"You stay right here and watch Birge out there. If he moves out of that car, you call down and let me know."

She started toward me again. "Albert, tell them. Just tell them and let them take him away."

"Let's not discuss it any more."

"Albert—I'm begging you—"

"Never mind!" I snapped and started down the cellar stairs. "What a mess," I muttered as I went. "What a Godawful mess!"

"Richard!" I shouted into the dark. "They've sent a man to town for a search warrant. He'll be here in less than an hour. Birge is sitting out front in a car. You've got to go now."

Of course no answer came. I didn't really expect one.

But I could hear the breathing—harsh and rapid—that horrible trapped animal sound.

"All right—it's your funeral. Once these people get their hands on you, just forget about justice or any kind of fair play. It's no holds barred."

I started out in a huff as if I were leaving. But it was only an act, and he knew it. I took about ten steps, then turned, barged right back to the hole and started shouting again, "I'm coming in."

The moment half my torso was through the hole, I felt him spring toward me in the dark and land in such a way that he was right beside me, coiled above the hole. For a moment I was sure he was going to strike me, and I was already flinching, awaiting the blow. It never came, and after I huddled there a bit, my neck retracted turtle-like into my shoulders, I dared to look up. He was still there beside me, poised like a serpent, waiting. Finally, I dragged the rest of my body through the hole.

The transition was too abrupt, moving out of a warm dry cellar into the moldy chill of the crawl. And of course there was the smell. It was like death. Like something had died in there. At first I lay there on the cold earth floored by it—all the sensibilities outraged. Then I just lay back and succumbed to it—the way a man struggling against a tide finally consents to go with it.

I lay there on the ground, slightly winded, my face inches from his boot, ransacking my brain for the right words with which to get through to him. But then suddenly, amazingly, he was speaking. "I'm sorry. I'm sorry. I never meant to hurt him. Never meant to hurt no one. Sorry. I was only thinkin' of you and Missus, I'm sorry. Sorry. Sorry."

It came out a long, grievous lament which he kept repeating over and over again. "Sorry. Sorry. Sorry." All the while he said it there was a dull, hard, thudding sound directly above me. At first I couldn't imagine what it was. Then I realized—it was his head. He was banging it violently against one of the wooden joists.

"I seen him start to whirl that fire," he said. "And I

went crazy. I seen that fire and all them rocks and dirt they was flingin' and all I could think was that new coat of white paint, and you and Missus inside. That's all I kept thinkin'. Sorry. Sorry."

"You don't kill a man for throwing rocks at your house any more than you wreck his store because he cheated you out of a few dollars." The venom in my voice appeared to stun him, and that awful chanting of his came suddenly to a halt.

"You've got to go now," I snapped.

"Never leavin'. Can't. Can't." The awful thudding resumed once more overhead.

"We don't want you here any more!" I shouted at last, at the limit of my patience. "It's been nothing but trouble since you've come. You've messed up our lives. Our house is a shambles along with all of our possessions. We're wiped out. We don't have a single friend left in town. It's enough now. Enough. We don't want any more. We want you to go. Do you understand, Richard? We don't want you here any more."

It had all come out of me in wave upon wave. Like steam escaping from a valve under great pressure—with a long, sibilant hiss.

But having said it, after so long, it brought no relief. Only a kind of curious aching from somewhere deep inside me. At the end of that tirade I lay back against the wall, spent and overcome. An immense weariness had overtaken me. I was full of a sense of terrible defeat and trying to muster enough strength to crawl back out of there when the sound started.

At first it was a long, low wailing from somewhere in the crawl. It was like nothing I'd ever heard before. Once it commenced, it didn't stop. It didn't rise; it didn't fall. It merely persisted on a single tone and filled the place. It was an inhuman sound. The kind of thing one associates with mourners in wild strange lands. Primitive and aboriginal. It wasn't weeping, either. It was a deep, inconsolable grieving of a most profound and heart-rending sort.

What I did next, I barely recall. Only in a general way I recall squirming through the hole, struggling back toward the light in the cellar, and then running. But I wasn't running from him. I was running from the sound. When I reached the top of the stairs I could still hear it behind me. Then I slammed the library door shut on it.

I slumped for a moment against the door, looking at Alice across the parlor in the kitchen sweeping up glass and debris. Suddenly she looked up and saw me. She didn't say a word. She could see it all in my face.

She crossed the parlor, coming toward me, still holding the broom. "Did you hear it?" I said when she'd reached me. "Did you hear it?" I was about to ask her again when we heard the click from downstairs. When I looked at Alice I saw that she heard it, too. We stood there holding each other, listening to the squeal of the garden door, faint but unmistakable, and after that the dull thud of it closing.

It was Richard Atlee. He had left the house. "He's going," I said. Hopefully, I told myself, forever. I hoped that he would start running now and not stop until he'd placed a continent between us. There's a part of me that thinks like that, that has a kind of childish faith in all things turning out well. But there's another part of me harsher, more fatalistic—and that part told me that Richard had only vacated the crawl temporarily. He was heading out across the bog, probably to the cave, and would lie low there for a while, like a wounded creature. But, sooner or later, he'd be coming back to us.

All this I thought as Alice and I went back to the kitchen and once again resumed the job of cleaning up the awful mess.

Shortly after, we heard Birge's steps coming up the drive and halting just outside the kitchen door. He stood there peering in at us, his large red face framed in shattered glass, smiling mockingly and dangling a sheet of official-looking paper through the gaping hole.

"I got that warrant for you now, Mr. Graves."

I continued sweeping, not even bothering to look up. "Fine," I said. "Go search to your heart's content."

The only place he looked was the crawl. He went directly down to the basement followed by several other men. They stayed down there for nearly half an hour. We heard them rummaging around, their muffled voices seeping up through the floor boards.

Then they came back up.

"Where is he?" asked Birge.

"I told you I don't know," I said. "I hope he's a thousand miles from here right now."

"You know that if you helped him, you're an accomplice. That's punishable by law."

"I didn't help him," I said, suppressing a desire to laugh. "I tried to, but he wouldn't let me."

He looked at me coldly for a moment, clearly stumped.

"But if he'd asked me to," I went on, "I would've. Without a moment's hesitation."

"He ain't no thousand miles away," he said. "I got the feelin' that if I just look under a few rocks in the general vicinity here he'll come squirming out."

"I wish you luck," I said.

He nodded and smiled, then flicked his trooper's hat to Alice. It was done with an idiotic flourish which I'm sure he thought of as very dashing.

"I'll be back," he said, and started out. When he reached the door he turned. By then I'd resumed my sweeping, and just as I looked up he was standing there smirking at me.

"What the hell you s'pose he's been doin' in your crawl?" he said. "Smells like a Goddamned zoo down there."

We didn't go back to bed at all. It was nearly dawn, so we stayed up trying to clean up as much of the mess as we could.

Sometime, shortly after Birge left, a large black car came out from town and picked up the body in our driveway.

After the sun had been up at least an hour I called the glazier in town and told him to come up. Then I called an exterminator and told him that some kind of an animal had died in my crawl and that I wanted to have it fumigated.

Then Alice and I went back to work, picking up the debris, trying to salvage things and mend those other things that had not been completely destroyed.

We spoke very little but worked on with a grim, almost obsessive, determination. I knew she was thinking about Richard just as I was—wondering if he was out in the bog or in the cave, or if he'd been smart enough to clear out of the territory completely. Of those three alternatives I fixed on the second, then preoccupied myself with the awful question of how long he would stay in the cave before he'd try to get back into the house. Then, too, there was the question of Birge. What would he do next? But there was really no question there. I knew exactly what he'd do next.

Shortly after, we heard a car pull up in the driveway. I imagined it was the glazier or the exterminator and simply went on with my work. The doorbell rang, but when I looked up, I saw neither a glazier nor an exterminator. Instead I saw Ezra Washburn at the kitchen door. He was standing there stony and awkward in his mackinaw, his funny hat with the ear laps folded up and his face partially thrust through the bar broken frame of the door, waiting to be acknowledged.

I opened the door and let him in. He stepped over the threshold stiffly, yanked off his cap, and peered around. He seemed to understand at a glance what had happened the night before.

"I come to tell you to get the boy out of here," he said.

"He's gone."

"You sure? Not just hangin' around the woods someplace, is he?"

I shook my head, playing dumb, not certain how candid I could be with him.

"If he's just hidin' out back someplace," he went on, "they're gonna get him. And if they do, they'll kill him."

A short, quiet moan escaped from Alice. Washburn looked at her and then at me. "A bunch of them is over to the jailhouse with Birge right now. Deputies he calls 'em. Drug'm all out of the tavern early this mornin'." He made a face of pure contempt. "He's issuin' rifles. They don't like nothin' better than rifles, that bunch. Killed three young fellers here a couple a years back for break-in' into the hardware store. Never was a trial or inquiry. Nothin'. Not a question asked."

I was on the verge of telling him all. He sensed it and before I could, he headed me off.

"Don't tell me nuthin'," he waved his hand at me. "I don't wanna hear it. Just get him out of here. As far away as you can. They're comin' out here now. If they find him, they'll kill him and ask questions later."

He reached for the door, and it fell off in his hands. He struggled with it for a moment doing a little dance with the teetering door while Alice and I flowed toward him. Then finally he leaned the thing back up against the corner of the jamb and clapped his hands as if he were cleaning them off. When he had done that, he turned back to us. "I liked the boy. He was a good boy."

Then he was gone.

The first cars arrived about ten-thirty, gathering at the foot of the driveway and alongside the road. Almost immediately there was an awful excitement—brakes screeching, doors slamming, dogs barking. In fifteen minutes there were nearly fifty men out there with nearly as many dogs howling and straining on leashes. All the men had rifles and wore troopers' hats, although none of them were actual troopers—just a lot of scum and unemployed riff-raff coming out for the fireworks.

Alice and I kept on working and tried very hard not to notice them. But it was almost impossible to blot them out. At one point I simply went to the kitchen door and looked down at all the noise and confusion at the foot of the drive. There was almost a festive air to it—jesting and merriment—a lot of *gentlemen* come together for a fox hunt.

Birge's car was the last to arrive. I could see the roof

of the station wagon glide slowly through the milling throng and come to a halt. When the car door opened, the top of his hat suddenly appeared above the mob of converging men. I learned a little later that road blocks and checkpoints had been set up all along the Bog Road.

They huddled there and conversed for nearly half an hour, Birge's immense figure soaring like a totem pole above all the others—giving directions, coordinating movements and final instructions to lieutenants. Then, quite suddenly, as if at a signal, they all fanned out in a wide skirmish line, and with the dogs barking and straining at their leashes, the men shouting and waving to each other, they entered the field alongside the property and started down toward the woods.

We watched them from the window until the woods swallowed the last of them up. But even hours later we could hear the barking of the dogs many miles off.

I don't recall what Alice and I did during that time. I suppose we continued working—or pretending we were working. Actually, we were waiting—almost rigid with fright—and coiled to flinch at the first crack of a rifle shot. But there were no shots.

Late in the afternoon they were back again, streaming out of the woods behind the house, scrambling over the stone wall and moving down to the cars in small, weary knots of two and three. The dogs, free and off the leashes, nosed along the turf in front of them. All the straining, noisy enthusiasm of the morning was gone, and in its place was weariness and surly dissatisfaction.

Alice and I looked at each other. She gave a long sigh which I took to be relief. But at the same time, there was a look of sickish apprehension in her eyes. I suppose that same look was in mine. Evidently Richard Atlee had managed to elude his hunters, for which I was profoundly grateful. But at the same time we had to face the disquieting fact that he was still alive.

They gathered down by the road again, and from the window we watched Birge give new instructions. Gradually, one by one, we heard engines turning over and we could see cars starting to drive off. This continued until only one car with several of Birge's fake deputies was left. This car remained behind.

Both the glazier and the exterminator came. They arrived together—a look of bug-eyed disbelief on the glazier's face as he stared around at the place. It was his second trip out there in a little over a week. They did their work quietly, and as it struck me then, a little nervously, anxious to finish and be gone, as if they were afraid to be caught collaborating with the enemy.

By dusk the door was back on its hinges and glass back in its frame. Most of the windows, too, had been repaired, and the glazier promised somewhat ruefully to be back the following day to finish the job.

Sometime shortly after supper the cars returned. At first Alice thought it was the bunch who'd tried to burn the house down. But it wasn't. It was Birge's men. They'd had their dinner and a couple of cans of beer and were rested. Now they were back again with the dogs and torches, their troopers' hats set at jaunty angles, and thrashing back into the woods.

That night Alice and I lay in bed, sleepless and scarcely breathing, waiting for the sound of a rifle shot.

At one point she said, staring at the ceiling above her, "He's in that cave, isn't he?"

"Yes. I suppose so."

"They'll never find him, will they?"

"I'd be very much surprised if they did."

She was silent a moment. "You know where it is?" she asked.

"The cave?"

"Yes."

"In a general way," I said after a pause.

"Where is it?"

"Why?"

"Shouldn't I know?"

"It's not important."

"Why won't you tell me?"

"It's not important," I said again and rolled over, turning my back to her. She was quiet then, but she knew perfectly well why I wouldn't tell her.

We heard no shot that night.

They were back the next morning quite early. And that night they came back again. On the third day the dissatisfaction of the men deepened into an all-pervasive gloom. You could see it in the weary slump of their shoulders, in the way those once cocked rifles, carried smartly at the port, now dangled limply at their sides, and in the way their boots scuffled and dragged along the dry hard earth. Even the dogs ambled along now with a kind of sleepy disinterest, perking up only at the scent of a raccoon or a flushed partridge.

But down there amid all those drooping spirits, I could see the figure of Birge soaring high above all the rest, ramrod erect and barking orders, his arms cocking here and there like a piston.

I was standing out in the yard watching them file out of the woods and trekking up through the back. This time they took the liberty of crossing our property. At one point Birge passed within five feet of me. He saw me but looked right past me and then trampled deliberately through a bed of prize hybrid tea roses, leaving in his wake a trail of smashed flowers with snapped and lolling necks.

They came for three days and two nights after that, always leaving one car behind when they'd depart. But the third night they left no car. And they didn't come back.

That afternoon as dusk gathered around us we seemed very much alone. Alice had been quiet all the while Birge's search had gone on. Now that it was over and they were all gone, she suddenly grew moody and restive.

"He's going to come back now," she said.

"Maybe not. Maybe he's gone."

"You mean away? Far away?"

"Yes."

For a moment I thought she was going to cry. "You don't believe that."

I tried to read my paper, but she went right on. "Now that they've stopped looking, he's going to come back and move right in and we'll start all over again. Only this time it'll be worse."

I rose wearily and started up the stairs.

"Is that all you can do?" she shouted after me. When I turned and looked at her, her eyes were all watery.

"What do you want me to do?"

"Do something. Anything!"

"You were hoping they'd kill him, weren't you?" When I said it, it was just as if I'd slapped her. She seemed to shrink back into the shadows. But in the next moment she was composed again.

"Well, what if I was?" she said very softly. "Weren't you?"

Of course I couldn't begin to face that question. Even now with several years behind me, I've barely been able to look it squarely in the face.

I came back down the steps and put my arm around her shoulder. "Let's wait and see," I said. "Maybe he really has gone."

We waited for a week, and when there was still no sign of his coming back, we started to breathe a bit easier. But the next night at dusk, I finally saw him.

Strange, the way he appeared. Like a deer suddenly wandering out of the forest. He came out by the stone wall and clambered up onto it, standing motionless there in full view staring up at the house. From that distance, if you didn't know any better, you might have thought it was a piece of garden statuary.

I watched him from the bedroom window while Alice, totally unaware, worked a jigsaw puzzle behind me. I could feel my fingertips growing cold, but I said nothing, merely stared out at him while he stared back at me. Although he couldn't see me from that distance, I'm absolutely certain he was aware that some one was watching him. It all had a streak of perversity. An act of almost suicidal defiance. He wanted to be seen. No matter what the risks. Then, as suddenly as he'd appeared, he turned and disappeared back into the woods.

He came a second night and a third—always at the same time, dusk, and in the same place on the stone wall. I watched him each time—fascinated and repelled—while Alice still remained unaware of his incredible proximity. He appeared to be taunting me, defying me. It was as if he were saying, "It's only a matter of time. Then I'm coming back in and there's nothing you can do about it."

Then the fourth night, Alice finally saw him.

"What are you going to do now?" she said, her face all white and the shrillness edging back into her voice.

"I'm going out to that cave tomorrow."

She started to protest. I knew what she was going to say, too. She was going to say she had no faith in my word any more or in my ability to correct anything. I knew all that, and I didn't blame her. I hadn't been exactly a tower of strength.

But before she could charge me with all this I waved her to silence. "Don't worry, I promise you he'll never set foot back in this house."

The next morning while Alice lay in bed, tense and watchful, I dressed and got ready to set out across the bog.

I said very little to her, only that I expected to be back sometime in the early afternoon. Just as I was about to leave, she said, "Will you please tell me where the cave is?"

"Why?"

"In case anything should happen."

I looked at her a long moment, knowing exactly what she had in mind.

"Nothing will happen," I said. "And don't try to call Birge."

It was one of those bitter moments that are never forgiven or forgotten no matter how much time passes or how many sweet words or deeds follow.

She reached under my pillow and came up with the pistol. "At least take this."

"I don't want that," I said quite firmly and snatched it from her. I started to put it in the closet, but in the next moment I had a change of heart. I stuffed it in my belt and stormed out.

It was just sun-up when I started out across the woods, full of misgivings about my ability to find the cave. Great rags of mist still clung to the treetops, and the fat black crows that lived in the wood were squawking interminably. It was now late September, and the first leaves of autumn had already drifted down over the spongy sodden earth.

The mist was even thicker in the bog when I finally broke out of the woods. Great gobs of it swirled like gauze all around me, making the job of setting an accurate course even more difficult.

I had at best only a general idea of where the cave was. I knew it was in the northeastern corner of the bog, just where the flats appear to rise into the scraggly pine-spattered foot-hills. I navigated that morning by the seat of my pants, as they say, turning and twisting by sheer instinct through the high canebrakes and the deep mullein grass tunnels made by the deer moving through there at high speeds.

I was haunted by the fear that Birge or one of his men was following me. Every snapping twig and rustle of grass became magnified in my mind, until I conjured up a swamp filled with Birge's bogus deputies crouched and leering all around me.

A curious thing about my heart in those desperate days; considering the stress and strains, it was better rather than worse. When I think of it all now——the long treks across the bog, the climbing in and out of the crawl, the endless scurrying up and down the cellar stairs, I realize just how foolhardy I was. But necessity appeared to have improved me. I felt none of the old ominous symptoms——no chest pains, no dizziness, no noticeable shortness of breath. The organ appeared to be serving me nobly, and the effect of that was to make me more foolhardy. I began to develop a sense of indestructibility. I seemed to be doing more each day, pushing myself harder, challenging the organ, and ever testing my faith in its ability to sustain life no matter what the emergency.

After about an hour I reached a place that I calculated was the northeastern corner of the bog. But when I looked around, my heart sank. None of it looked the least bit familiar.

Of course, this was a different season from when I'd first been out there. Landscape has a way of changing when the foliage goes.

I started up a shallow slope looking for the slab of schist rock that marked the entrance to the cave. When I found I was climbing and getting nowhere, I went back down and started off in a different direction.

I made three or four different attempts —all to no avail. Then I thought of calling his name out loud, but the possibility of Birge's people lurking about kept me hushed.

I was wearing a hat—a soiled and battered thing for which I still have a lingering affection. It was chilly that morning, but the sweat band was already thoroughly drenched. I recall yanking it off and drawing the sleeve of my jacket slowly across my brow. It was at the completion of that movement, just as my hand moved past my eye, that I saw what I thought was a short chaparral pine. It was about twenty feet off, all shrouded in mist. In the next moment the pine moved about a yard to the left. Then I saw him. He was the pine.

I took about five steps forward and stopped dead in my tracks. He was just standing out there in full view regarding me quietly across a narrow ribbon of land. I could see only the top of his body. The lower half of the torso was shrouded in curling mist.

"For God's sake," I said in one of those whispered shouts. "Don't just stand there!"

He scarcely moved. I waded toward him through a clump of hip-high bushes like a bather walking through surf, the marshy earth sucking at my shoes, burrs and nettles tearing at my trousers.

"Don't just stand there," I pleaded when I reached him. "Birge's men might've followed me. Get in the cave!"

I tried to tug him, but of course I didn't even know where the cave was. And he was unbudgeable.

"At least get down," I said. He let me push him to the ground until we were both crouched in concealment below the level of the bushes.

Suddenly I saw him as he really looked. His hair, dirty and unkempt, had grown out even further. The beard, several shades lighter than his hair, was mangy and wild. Little bits of unsavory things clung there, tangled in it. His clothing was torn and covered with burrs; they were lice-ridden from sleeping on the dank earth underground. He had the look of one of those medieval hermits who've wandered in the woods for forty years or so, subsisting on grubs and locusts.

"Richard, I want you to forget about what I said the other day," I blurted out. "It was stupid and cruel. And moreover, it was a lie. Mrs. Graves and I have been very fond of you, but what you did was wrong."

He was sitting now in a small cavity in the ground, his knees drawn up hard against his chest and his arms locked over his knees so that he appeared to be hugging himself for warmth. There was a small muddy puddle of water all around him. He was sitting directly in it, oblivious of the fact, with his face, stony and impassive, set westward toward a low range of mountains in the distance.

"You're going to have to face the legal authorities," I went on. "But this is not the place to do it. We'll go someplace where you'll get a better chance—"

He continued to gaze off into the distant west as if I weren't even there.

I rushed on now a little desperately. "It's not a crime to protect yourself from arsonists and vandals. What these people were doing was an act of violence against not only Mrs. Graves and me, but you, as well, since you live in that house. What you did was in self-defense. It won't be very hard to prove that, and no jury will ever convict."

He didn't speak. His face was still set firmly westward

in the direction of the low hills. He sat erect and rigid, his shoulders thrown back as if he were in a deep trance.

In the next moment I withdrew from my pocket the thick brown envelope containing two hundred dollars in cash.

I thrust the envelope at him. "Take this."

He didn't stir, and the envelope fell with a thud between us. I picked it up again. "Take it and get out of here. As far as you can go. When you get where you're going, write me. By that time I'll have a lawyer. We'll arrange for a trial. Somewhere far from here, where there's not so much feeling against you. Take it!" I poked the envelope at him, going a little red in the face. "Take it. It's your only chance."

Just looking at him, I felt something sink inside me. The tension in his spine appeared to stiffen even more. The shoulders flung back even farther, like a bird about to take flight. Then, without even looking at me, and still gazing off at the hills, he spoke. "I'm comin' home tonight."

"We'll talk about coming home when this is all over. Right now, you've got to get out of here."

"I'm comin' home tonight," he said blankly, unemotionally. It was stated as a firm, incontestable fact, like the date of the Battle of Hastings or the discovery of America.

"After this is all over," I said, trying to blot out his words—to shout over his voice—"we'll go up north to the place I told you about. You and Alice and I. All together again. Just like it used to be."

I tried to make it sound as rosy as I could, the way I knew he'd like it. But even as I was saying it, I could hear it all coming out empty and heartless

"We'll buy a camper," I went on, caught up in my own momentum. "I've always wanted—"

"I'm comin' home tonight," he said again.

Something snapped inside me, and the next thing I knew I'd flung the envelope at him. He took it right across the face like a slap, barely flinching. I struggled to my feet while it floated down between us. The pistol handle was icy to the grip, and as I waved it at him, my hand trembled wildly.

"Go!'"

He didn't budge.

I picked the envelope up again and tried to stuff it into his hands. But it simply floated right back down to earth.

"Pick it up!" I said. "And go!"

Still he didn't budge. In the next moment I was pressing the cold barrel to his temple, my finger curling around the trigger. "Go!"

"I'm comin' home tonight."

"Go!" I said it again, and by that time I was shouting so loud I could hear my voice floating far out across the bog. But his voice was even softer than it had been before. "I'm comin' home tonight."

That's when I first consciously wished him dead. I closed my eyes and tried to pull the trigger. But in the next instant I could see the pistol, silver and glinting, arching high in mid-air over the brakes and scrub. I never saw where it landed, only heard a dull, squishy thud about fifteen yards off. And then I felt the awful shooting ache in my arm from having flung the thing so hard.

"You can't come home tonight!" I shouted. "You can't ever come home!"

Then I was wading out through the hip-high bushes, the nettles and thorns ripping at my trousers, my eyes filling idiotically. I turned around and shook my fist at him and shouted through the mists to where he was now standing, looking once again like a solitary pine.

"Don't come back. I warn you!"

I got back home just as I'd predicted, shortly after noon. The skies had lowered, and great black blotches of rain clouds scudded swiftly overhead.

Alice was waiting for me at the door. She just looked at me—then led me in without a word. My appearance told all. My pants leg had a great gaping hole at the knee, and every part of me from head to toe was studded with small, prickly burrs. Alice said later that I looked "sick-ish" and "white in the face."

"Go upstairs to bed," she said instantly.

"No." My answer was emphatic, but that's where I dearly wanted to go.

"Lie down. You look as if you're going to drop."

"I'll sit right here." I sagged into a chair and sat there panting and crumpled like a lot of old rags.

She watched me eying the telephone. There was a look of pure hate on her face.

"Yes—I am going to call, Albert."

"I know you are. The moment I lie down somewhere and close my eyes."

"Well, you won't. You won't do what has to be done. He's coming back here, isn't he?"

"Tonight, he says."

"Then I'm calling Birge, now." She started for the phone.

"Don't!" I shouted after her. Something in my voice brought her up short.

She looked at me uncomprehendingly, a look of pro-found hurt in her eye, like a child who's been punished for something she doesn't understand. "Albert—Please—"

"Just let me think a while."

She looked at me pityingly while I sat there, crumpled in the chair with my chin slumped down on to my chest.

She left me alone for about an hour. When she came back I was still slumped in that chair, precisely as she'd left me, and there was no more pity left in her eyes.

"Call him!" she said. She was standing framed in the parlor door, her arms crossed and her eyes the color of dry ice.

I sat there with my moist hands folded in my lap, knead-ing them together until the bones groaned and cold white crescents glinted on the knuckles.

"Call him!" This time it was a hoarse shout that filled the room, filled the house, and spilled out all over the earth around us.

I stood up a little shakily and started out across the

parlor. I didn't stop when I reached her. I simply pushed past her toward the kitchen door while her body fell easily aside.

"Where are you going?" she shouted when I'd reached for the knob.

"I don't know," I said, and slammed the door behind me.

It was true. When I got in the car I hadn't the slightest idea where I was going or what I was up to. When I got out of the car I was in town and on my way into a drugstore.

It was strange—the effect my appearance had on the people there. I was still in the clothes I'd worn into the bog. I was covered with burrs and a great white patch of bare knees showed through my trousers where they'd been torn. But by strange I don't mean mysterious. I mean funny—the way they all stopped and looked up, the people at the drug counter, the clerks, the pharmacist with his chaste, rimless glasses and his rat-like frightened eyes, the people at the fountain with their spoons of ice cream and their sugar doughnuts and cups of coffee—all paused midway between the counter and their lips—all frozen still and mute in time.

I recall eyes following me to the phone booth and then yanking the folding glass doors aside and entering that musty, coffin-like cabinet. I can still see the cheap, black leatherette seat with its gaping puncture and the dirty cotton wadding bubbling out through it. And the gum and candy wrappers strewn on the floor. And the catalog of obscenities and phallic scribbling etched into the walls of the booth by means of keys and penknives.

The came Birge's voice strong, calm, and self-assured through the receiver, followed by the timorous peeping of my own. I didn't even bother identifying myself, and when I finished, I slithered out of that coffin feeling wormy as the grave.

Chapter Seventeen

THERE was nothing left to do except wait. And when I got home that's what we did, waited from late afternoon until shortly after eight o'clock. That's when Birge and all the cars came back with the men and the dogs and the fiery torches, all gathering at the foot of the drive, funneling into that point like a confluence of streams, moving and shifting about—a turbulent eddy—in a fierce glow of light.

Then suddenly the skirmish line was moving again, looking like a fiery bracelet spread out across the dark line of woods, and the hoarse bark of the dogs echoed far out across the chill, clear, moon-filled night.

We waited until shortly past midnight. That's when we heard the first shots booming up out of the bog. There were four of them in rapid order. Then four more. Then it was silent.

A short time later we climbed the stairs and went to bed. We didn't speak. We just lay there in the dark, the moon streaming through the casements, a naked branch scratching along beneath the eaves, and listening to each other breathe.

I tried to think of him as he'd looked that day, that wraith-like figure swaddled in mist. But I couldn't reconstruct his face—not a feature of it—not even those icy blue eyes staring determinedly westward.

At a certain point I heard Alice sob. It was brief and over in a moment. She turned and stifled the rest of it into her pillow. Then there was nothing but the trembling of the mattress beneath her.

I don't know how many hours were spent that way, and though we never spoke or touched each other, we were curiously together that night—more together than we'd been in a long time. Together with our guilt and our self-

disgust, with our hate for each other, and with our
pity.

What came next is hard to say. Alice has her version.
I have mine. We both agree that it started with the sound
of footsteps. You could hear them coming at a run from
the direction of the woods and churning heavily up through
the garden in the back. Then they were outside the door,
and the next thing we heard was the well-known jiggle
of the key and click of the bolts in the cellar door, the
hinges squealing open, and then the dull thud of the door
closing.

Alice was sitting bolt upright in bed, the whites of her
eyes glowing in the dark. I recall lying there, wanting to
say, "He's dead. He's dead. Don't worry. He's dead," but
finding no voice with which to say it. Instead, a sour little
puff of air rose from my throat, and I just lay there
panting and winded on the pillow.

Then, next, the footsteps pounding up the cellar stairs,
and the impact of a body crashing against the library
door, still locked with a board nailed across it.

It's curious the way the mind, in such dire moments,
calculates almost coolly the chances of survival. I remember lying quite still and thinking about the library door
and the lock and the bar of heavy wood I'd nailed across
it. How long could it last? I wondered.

Then I heard the noises—loud, shattering cracks, one
following the other—heavy and rhythmic, like strokes of
fate, and Alice moaning softly beside me. Then the sound
of wood seaming and splitting open, being gouged out and
hacked aside as if by some single-minded, ungovernable
machine. Then, finally, the hinges screaming as they were
ripped out of the timber, and the wrecked door smashing
down on the floor of the library, like the crack of doom.

Something got me up then—up by the scruff of the
neck and out across the floor to the closet. To this day,
I don't know what it was. Given my state of mind, my
physical condition, and the abuse it had already taken in
the course of that day, I don't know what tiny residue
of will—what small hard nut of self-preservation there still

remained to have gotten me up and across the room—but I moved through the darkness as if I were floating.

I was standing over by the closet clutching the smooth, cold stock of the thing and I recall thinking, "My God, what am I doing with this thing now?" Alice had shrunk back against the headboard of the bed, still under her sheets, digging deep down into the bed like a small burrowing creature, as if she were digging a hole, encapsulating herself in a warm, dark cocoon. The moon fell directly across her sheet-swaddled form, and a small moan rose from somewhere far down within it.

Downstairs, the heavy footfall of Richard Atlee could be heard clattering swiftly across the parlor toward the stairs. Then I could hear him breathing as he started up the steps, taking them two at a time.

It seemed a lifetime before he reached the top of the landing. While waiting for Richard to reach that point, I recall thinking of my father, curiously enough, and seeing him quite distinctly at several stages of his life.

Richard appeared to pause at the top of the landing for a moment, as if he were gathering all his strength for the final push.

Then it came with a heavy thud. It was the bottom of his boot against the door. The door burst open, slammed hard up against the wall, and started to bounce back. But he stopped it with his fist.

At first I saw nothing. Nothing at all. Then Alice screamed. I saw an immense black shadow pass like an eclipse across a shaft of moonlight between the window and me, and move on toward the bed, where it finally came to a halt just at the place where Alice's sheeted figure cowered against the headboard.

I watched with a peculiar fascination the arm rise high above her and pause. It was like the gesture of a priest in benediction. At the very top of that arm, something glinted and flashed in the moonlight. It glowed eerily for the briefest moment and in the next instant started down.

Then there was the thunder and the jagged blue-white

flash of the gun as it leapt out of the end of the barrel reaching like a fiery finger across the room.

Then I was moving—dropping down somewhere, with two walls of blackness converging on either side of me. I was being swept swiftly backwards through a long dark tunnel while a bead of light ahead of me grew smaller and more distant. That's all I recall.

I was rushed to the hospital, where the admitting physician pronounced me dead on arrival. Another doctor verified his findings. They took me to the hospital morgue, where I was laid out on a slab in preparation for the morticians who were to come early in the morning.

I'm told I lay there for nearly four hours—no heart beat, no pulse, no blood pressure, and that the night man —a kind of night watchman who checks the morgue several times a night—discovered that I was alive.

I never met the man. Several months later I tried to find him and thank him, but by that time he was gone. He was, they tell me, a simple uneducated soul, a Central American—part-Indian, part-Spanish—who could barely speak a word of English. He had tried to live in this part of the world because he had heard of the great opportunities. But he found none and he went home.

When he was making his routine check of the morgue, I was lying there on a slab. He said that when he saw me, it seemed to him that he could hear breath—faint and feeble, but nevertheless breath. He pressed a small glass under my lips, as he'd been told by an old Indian cacique that this was the only sure test of death. When he'd done this, instantly he saw small beads of mist clouding the glass, and then he ran and fetched the night doctor.

I lay in a coma between life and death for five days. I have no recollection of any of it. Except that during that time I had a dream, or at least it seemed a dream, only more so. Perhaps "experience" is a better word, since what I saw was more vivid than any dream—more actual. Perhaps it wasn't a dream at all.

With my first recollection of consciousness I discovered that I was still in my body but that my body and I were now separate. I know that sounds confusing, but I beg you to bear with me.

Because of this separation within me I was able, for the first time, to look at myself—look at my own body. I could see all the wonders of my anatomy, tissue for tissue, and I could see my own soul carefully interwoven into that dead body.

I assumed I was dead. I was completely calm and at peace. "I've died," I said, "as men term death, and yet I'm as much myself as ever. I'm about to get out of my body."

I watched the whole process by which my soul separated itself from my body. By some power not my own, the soul was rocked, to and fro, sideways, like a cradle is rocked. That gentle rocking motion was the method by which the soul was gradually disconnected from the tissues of the body. After a short time, the lateral motion ceased, and along the soles of my feet, beginning at the toes, passing rapidly to the heels, I felt and heard the snapping of innumerable small cords. When this had finished I began to feel myself retreating from some point within myself. I was moving upwards, as if I were on an elevator, moving from the feet toward the head. Like the way a rubber band shortens after tension is taken off it. I remember reaching my hips, and saying to myself, "Now there's no life below the hips."

I have no memory of passing through the stomach and the chest, but I recall perfectly when my whole self appeared to have been funneled into the head and was contained there. Then I thought to myself, "I'm all up in my head now, and soon I'll be free."

I moved all around the brain as if I were hollow. I compressed it and its membranes gently toward the center and peeped out between the sutures of my skull until I could see myself emerging, being oozed out like the flattened edges of a bag of membranes. I recall how I appeared to myself, something like a jellyfish in color, texture, and form. As I emerged, I saw two ladies sitting at my head, two men at my feet; another man, a shadowy figure, stood in the corner of the room. I stood up before them and then I realized that they couldn't see me because I was no longer mortal, I was something else.

When I was fully out of the head, I floated up and down and laterally like a soap bubble attached to the bowl of a pipe until I finally broke loose from the body and fell lightly to the floor where I slowly rose and expanded into the full stature of a man.

I seemed to be translucent—of a bluish cast. I moved toward the door past the men and the women grouped around the bed. I turned and faced them. As I did so, my left arm grazed the elbow of one of the men. To my amazement my arm passed right through his without any resistance. He gave no sign of having felt the slightest contact. He just stood there gazing at the bed I'd just left. Then, when I looked in the direction in which he was gazing, I saw my own dead body. It was lying just as I'd left it, flat on my back, my feet close together, and my hands clasped across my breast. I was a little shocked at the paleness of my face. I hadn't looked in a mirror for some time and hadn't realized how ghastly pale and sickly looking I was.

Now I could see clearly the people sitting and standing around the body and noticed again the two women. One was Alice. She was kneeling by my left side. Her eyes were red, as if she'd been crying a good deal. Another was the nurse, a Mrs. Plesdish. Dr. Tucker was there and another doctor whom I didn't recognize, but he was the one with whom my arm collided. I was now standing beside the figure in the shadows and it was my nephew, Wiley Crane.

I tried to get their attention with the object of comforting them—to tell them there was no reason for grief. I ran back and forth from one to the other trying to shake or jostle them. But I made no impression on them. Then the situation struck me as uproarious and I laughed aloud. They must have heard that, I thought, but no one lifted their eyes from my body. They can't see me, I thought. They're looking at me but they can't see me. They keep looking at that body. That's not me. This is me, and I'm as much alive as ever.

Then I was walking out an open door and descending some steps, walking down a corridor, down some more steps and into the street. I stopped and looked around me. It was the Main Street of the town, but I'd never seen anything like it before. I could see the grayness of the pavements and the redness of the soil in such a light and intensity that I thought it would blind me. I could see millions—billions of ants and worms alive and dwelling in it; I saw the dazzling greens of trees and grasses, the most brilliant blue sky I'd ever seen, and the fantastic washes the rain had made.

Then I discovered to my delight that I'd become taller than I was in life. I was just the height I'd always wanted to be. "How well I feel," I thought. "Only a few moments ago I was sick and miserable. Then came that change called death which I'd always dreaded. It's past now, and here I am, still a man, alive and thinking, thinking as clearly as ever, and how well I feel! I'll never be sick again. I don't have to die any more."

Then I lost consciousness again. When I awoke I found myself on the bottom of a narrow roadway that was inclined upward at an angle of about forty-five degrees. I looked up and saw sky and clouds above me. I looked down and saw the tops of green trees. I seemed to be facing directly north. I was very high up, and yet I had no fear of falling. In life I'd always been terrified of heights. I kept climbing upward, and though the road was steep I felt absolutely no fatigue. My feet seemed light and my step was buoyant as the step of childhood.

As I walked I thought again of my illness, and the last sickly years of my life, and now I rejoiced in my perfect health and strength. I kept climbing and surveying the scenery. It was glorious. I'd never felt such perfect peace. To the east, mountains as far as the eye could see. The forest below me extended to the mountains, reaching up their sides and on up to their craggy summits. Beneath me lay a forest and a valley through which ran a beautiful river full of shoals and rippling eddies and white spray. It reminded me of the Saco River, where I swam when I was a boy.

Still I saw no one. I thought surely someone from the other world would be here to meet me. But oddly enough, there wasn't one person whom I wanted to see. Then I started to think of such things as heaven and hell and divine retribution, in which I'd never really believed, and suddenly I was frightened.

Then something happened which is very hard to describe. At different points about me in space I was aware of the expressed thought: "Fear not. You are safe." I heard no voice. I saw no person, yet I was perfectly aware that at different points, at varying distances from me, someone was thinking that thought for my benefit. How I was made aware of it, I can't say, but from that moment I ceased to fear anything.

Suddenly I saw up ahead of me three huge rocks blocking the road. I knew I couldn't get past them, and as I stood there wondering what to do, the same extraordinary thought came filtering down on me: "This is the road to the eternal world." There was no voice and no person visible, just the thought filling everything up around me. "Yonder rocks are the boundary between the two worlds and the two lives. Once you pass these rocks, you can no more return into the body."

Suddenly I was filled with an overwhelming conviction that Richard Atlee was standing just on the other side of the rocks. I could see no sign of him, and I don't know where the notion came from, but there was such a strong, unmistakable aura of him all about the place. And then, most curious of all, for the merest moment, on the center rock and graven just beneath the pinnacle of it, I thought I saw the word GOD written in scarlet letters, just as it had once been smeared above my cellar door. But it was gone the next instant.

I tried to peer past the rocks. The atmosphere was green. Everything seemed cool and quiet and unspeakably beautiful. I made ready to cross. By that time I was determined to get past those rocks. But just as I tried to go forward a voiceless thought came to me again. "You can't cross here," it said. The world beyond those rocks seemed more beautiful than ever. I started to go toward the rock, but I found myself struggling. "Richard," I cried, "please let me in. I want to be with you. Richard— Please, Richard—Richard—Richard—" I felt the power to move or think leaving me. My hands dropped powerless to my side; my shoulders and head dropped forward; the cloud touched my face, and I recall no more.

Suddenly my eyes were open and I was looking at my hands and once again I could feel my body. Then I was looking into the kind, drab features of Mrs. Plesdish, and the first thing I said was, "Where's Richard? Is he all right?"

"You're fine," she said. "You're going to be all right."

I recall my heart sinking when she said it, and all I could say was, "Must I die again?"

I lived for several weeks in the intensive care unit of the hospital. I was kept in an oxygen tent in a perpetual gray twilight of semi-consciousness. Unfamiliar figures drifted back and forth like fish in water just beyond the plastic sheets of the tent. From time to time I would see Alice—distant, yet unmistakable—seated in a rocking chair beside my bed. I recall her knitting and rocking gently back and forth in the chair. Whenever I stirred, her head would bob up quickly.

I was kept under heavy sedation. The doctors claimed that it was a miracle that I was still alive, considering the amount of heart damage I'd sustained from previous seizures coupled with the kind of massive cardiac arrest I suffered this time.

All the while I lay in the tent, I kept thinking of Richard. I had no way of knowing if he was alive or dead, if my bullet had hit or missed. I kept hoping that I'd missed and that he was alive in prison somewhere, awaiting sentence. For if that were the case, I planned, lying there in the oxygen tent, to hire lawyers and seek an immediate appeal. If that was the case I'd consider myself lucky, I told myself. But down deep, I knew that wasn't the case.

All the while I was in the hospital, I never actually

learned what Richard's fate had been that night. In one respect I was too weak to ask and—in another—not well enough to be told. But then Alice and I had reached an agreement. We had reached it by mutual and tacit consent and neither of us sought to violate it.

I knew that at a given moment which she would deem both appropriate and safe, I would be told everything, and against that time we would keep our lips sealed.

The day I left the hospital was a gray, dismal time in early November. Small flurries of snow swirled meanly around, then disappeared while the sun lay flat against the sky like a great, white disk.

As we stepped out of the hospital doors, a car drew up at the entrance. I thought it had come to drive us home but when we got in I saw our suitcases strapped on a luggage rack in the back, and I knew we were leaving there forever.

Once in the car and out on the road with the meadows and the low hills sliding past us and small hard flakes of snow whispering on the windshield, Alice told me that she had sold the house. The news neither surprised nor displeased me. I felt a twinge of sadness and then a long sweet breath of relief.

Alice had conducted the entire sale herself with the assistance of brokers and our lawyer. In all that time she had returned to the house only once, to supervise our packing. The rest of the time she stayed in a small hotel in town within walking distance of the hospital.

Doctor Tucker recommended a warm climate for the winter, and so Alice, recalling my wish to visit there, rented a small house on one of the more remote Keys. The car in which we now drove was taking us to an airport.

Once on the plane and underway I felt an urgent need to have my unanswered question about Richard Atlee put finally to rest. Alice sensed this great agitation, and after we'd been aloft for an hour, she handed me a crumpled envelope. It was addressed to me at the hospital, and its postmark was dated several weeks earlier. It was from Mr. Washburn. It was rather a touching letter full of illegible and misspelled words in which the poor man blamed himself for not having done more to avert a tragedy that he knew was inevitable.

Then Alice told me how Birge broke into the house that night and found us—she upstairs in the bedroom in a dead faint, and Richard sprawled on the floor face down beside the bed—a small hand-made hatchet beside him, and shot through the heart. But I was nowhere around. She told me how they searched the house from room to room and finally found me below, in the crawlspace. I don't know what I was doing there, or even how I got there, but Dr. Tucker claims that that's where the coronary struck me and it was a massive one.

Alice told me how in the days that followed Birge tried to make himself helpful. Several times he had come to see her at the hotel, shamefaced and contrite, putting himself at her disposal, offering all kinds of assistance. But she would have none of it.

When we reached the Keys, even before we settled into our new home, I drafted a letter to the governor and the attorney general's office of the state we'd just left, detailing all the facts leading up to Richard's death, and pinpointing clearly the role I believe Birge played in it.

We never had an answer. Not even a form letter by way of small acknowledgment. But of course you know how these things go. They're sticky business, politically, and once a touchy matter disappears beneath a cloud, no one appears too anxious to go and dig it up again.

I was told by several people, acquaintances in high positions, that if I could substantiate any of the story—the nocturnal attacks on our house, the daily harassments, Birge's refusal to come to our aid—that I should give the story to one of the state newspapers. I tried that with several papers, none of which would consent to investigate the story, regardless of how much of it I could substantiate. I've applied to Washburn to tell what he knows to high state authorities. But he hasn't done so. He didn't say he wouldn't. He simply hasn't done it.

There is something about injustice. Once it starts, it spreads like contagion. First, you have one small injustice;

then a whole conspiracy of subsequent injustices are required to support and sustain the initial injustice. And so very quickly the whole atmosphere of a place is irreversibly polluted.

Chapter Eighteen

OUR life in the Keys is very quiet. It has to be for my sake. I spent most of the first few months on my back sunning myself in a beach chair beside the ocean, which is in our front yard. We went virtually nowhere, sought no friends or lively diversions. All of that was now apparently forbidden to me. Instead, Alice and I stayed alone with ourselves, locked in our silence and grief, trying to find our way back to each other.

Our house here is built up on the dunes. The land around us is desolate and sandy. Alice couldn't bear to see so much space without vegetation, and very soon her horticultural passion drove her to resume gardening. In no time at all we had sweet peas, hibiscus, and mariposas blooming all around the house. And in a curious way, when her garden started to bloom out of that dry, sandy earth, she herself started to come back to life.

Gradually I was encouraged by an engaging young cardiologist in that area to start on a regimen of short but daily exercise of a mild sort. Much to my great delight he recommended swimming. Each morning and each afternoon I was permitted for short periods of time to bathe in the warm, clear waters of the ocean.

Eventually I grew stronger, and as I did my taste for sporting activity increased. Soon I was fishing the lagoons and shoals near our house for bonito, yellow jack, and bonefish.

So our lives went for several months—routine, uneventful, and not at all unpleasant. But still the thought of Richard Atlee persisted in my mind, lingering like a bad taste in the mouth, that cannot be scrubbed away. I have a strange need to return to it over and over again in my mind. I relive our Christmas feast with him and all those Sunday mornings singing hymns beside him in the sun-filled parlor. Sometimes I even think I can smell his coffee and buns cooking on the stove. Over and over again I go back to that last day in the bog with him. I play the whole scene back, hearing it ring clearly in my ears as if it were on a tape recorder. I dredge up out of my memory everything I said that morning. And then what he said. Sometimes I try to change the words to make things come out differently—better. But when I do, the scene blurs; the clarity of my memory fades, and I'm left alone. So I go back to the scene, exactly as it was, examining and re-examining my words for every possibility and nuance, as if in doing that I may discover some clue to the mystery of Richard Atlee. He knew that by coming back to the house that night he would die—not necessarily by Birge's hand (that was obvious), but by mine. He seemed to have known that I was going to be the one who would kill him. He seemed to have wanted that; indeed, to have set things up in such a way that I would have to be the one to kill him. Why? I keep wondering, and sometimes I think I almost know. But not really. There's so little we can ever hope to know about things like that.

I keep telling myself that what I offered him that morning was a real alternative. And not merely courageous, when you consider Birge's vengefulness, but even quite generous, when you consider what he had done to our lives. After all, expert legal counsel is not inexpensive. But the money was the last thing in my mind. And then to offer him the thing he wanted most of all—another home—well, I call that downright handsome.

I did not want him to die, I tell myself over and over again. I wanted him to live, and if he'd listened to me at the start, and got away from there as far as possible, and laid low for just a little while, he'd still be alive today. And he knew that, mind you. He knew it. So what made him choose the other, knowing full well how the other would end, as if what I'd offered him was so absolutely worthless?

How I regret what I said to him in the crawl that awful day about our not wanting him any more. Possibly those words cut too deep, tore too much of a breach, and left unhealable scars.

Sometimes I think that when I made my offer to him that last day, he heard something in my voice that I myself wasn't even aware of. And that was undoubtedly insincerity. Yes, I'm sure of that now. And what I ask myself is "How is it that he knew it, and I never did?" All the time I was saying it, painting rosy pictures of our future together, I believed—or I think I believed—every word of it, and yet he seemed to know it was so transparently—so pathetically—a lie.

One afternoon I was drowsing in a beach chair in the yard when Alice gently nudged me. I looked up at her through squinting eyes and she told me I had a visitor. She ushered in a tall, swarthy man with ramrod posture. He was lean, and all of him sinewy muscle. He wore a plaid sport shirt open at the collar, a pair of chino slacks, and light sandals over bare feet. The impression he gave was that of a man who had spent all of his life out of doors, working close to the soil. He had, too, that likable shyness and awkwardness you find in big, physical men.

Then as he started to speak I had the curious feeling that I had seen him before.

His name was Jimmy Graycloud, he said, and then he added, "I come to thank you for takin' care of my kid."

At first I didn't know what he meant. I looked at him blankly while he studied me. I had the feeling he knew everything about me in the first ten seconds or so.

"Your kid?"

"Richie."

Then suddenly it was all there—Richard's wallet, and the photograph of the man Richard called his father.

"Graycloud?" I said, with the inflection of a question in my voice.

"His mother's name was Atlee," he said.

I must have sat there blank and stunned for a while, staring at him. I could see Richard's expression now in the cut of Graycloud's eyes. They had that same stony impassivity, as if they were gazing far off into the distance. The face, too, had that flat, slightly brutal quality you associate with primitive people.

"He wrote me all about you once," said Graycloud. "Said you was good to him. I'm grateful to you."

He said it just like that, without batting an eye. Not a tinge of emotion about it. Just as you or I might remark about the weather.

And so I met Richard Atlee's father, or Richard Graycloud, or whatever. And this is the story he told me.

Jimmy Graycloud had been in the army for twenty-five years. He was at the time I met him just retiring on full pension, having achieved the rank of master sergeant. He was a full-blooded Cheyenne Indian who had grown up on a Cheyenne reservation in Wyoming.

At the age of twenty, while in the army, he met Emily Atlee, a woman ten years his senior who was employed as a barmaid in one of those sleazy little saloons that proliferate around military posts.

Graycloud met and married her all on a weekend pass. The marriage, of course, was a disaster from its inception. They lived together for a month, and then sporadically for two months after. Their relationship centered around drinking and the act of love, in which time he took to periodically beating her. She, in turn, would call the police and they would come over and jail him for the night, then release him to the military authorities.

After three months their marriage was dissolved by mutual consent. But at that time she was already pregnant, and Graycloud eagerly volunteered to give Emily half his monthly salary as contribution toward the support of her and the child.

The child was born prematurely four months later and christened Richard Graycloud. "He used her name, though," Graycloud said. "He was ashamed of being part Indian. By that time I was in Asia and after that Europe.

I didn't set eyes on him once till he was five or six. But all that time I kept sendin' money for her and gifts for him. Then I got transferred back to the States and one day I decided I wanna go see my kid.

"I drove up to Cheyenne to see Emily so's I can see my kid. I find her livin' in a trailer camp outside an army post. The place was filthy. It stunk. Beer cans and unmade beds. You could see a lotta men been there."

When he said it he had to lower his eyes as if he were overcome by the shame of it.

"I went up to the post," he went on, "and found her workin' at the PX. I asked her where my kid was. She told me she give him over to the Indian Reservation outside of Cheyenne. When I left, she never even asked me once where I been or what I been doin'.

"I drove over to the reservation right then and there. When I got there, I asked the people for Richie Graycloud. They told me he wasn't there just then. Told me he run off someplace, but not to worry, that he'd done it at least a dozen times before. At first, when his mother gave him to the reservation he kept slippin' off at night and runnin' back to her. To get back to that trailer camp it meant crossin' thirteen miles of hills and deep woods at night. How he did it I don't know. He was only five or six, and that's a lot of miles for a kid that age—and the woods at night are pretty scary and all that. But anyway, he'd do it. And when she'd wake up in the mornin' she'd find him sittin' out there on the step of the trailer waitin' for her. So she'd give him breakfast and drive him right back out to the reservation. He'd do it over and over again. And no sooner would he show up than she'd pile him right back into the car and run him back out to the reservation. Until he finally got the idea she just didn't want him.

"So he grew up on the reservation. He hated it. Didn't consider himself no Indian and wouldn't mix with Indian kids. I guess he got that from Emily, who kept tellin' him his old man was a no-good drunken Indian.

"Anyway, they give him over to a Cheyenne family on the reservation. They couldn't do nuthin' with him at home. They couldn't do nuthin' with him at the school. So they just let him run wild. He lived out in the woods by himself for weeks—months—at a time. They used to call him—" (then he muttered a name like "Kayseehotame" or some such thing like that). "In Cheyenne," he went on, "it means 'Running Cat.'"

Alice had been standing in the doorway while Graycloud was speaking. Now she came out on the small veranda and stood behind him, listening to his story.

"I was lucky," Graycloud continued. "I hung around out there a couple of days, and sure enough, one afternoon that kid just come right down outta the hills. It was the first time I seen him. What a sight. A small, mangy-lookin' kid with big eyes. He was all skin and bones and looked like he been sleepin' with the animals out there.

"I told him I was his father. His face screwed up and he kinda looked at me skeptical. He didn't believe me, he said, and then he spit and called me a 'God damned Indian.'" Graycloud laughed. "Anyway, I brought him some swords and flags and things I picked up abroad—"

"A German Iron Cross?" I asked.

He looked at me oddly for a moment. "Yeah—I think so." Then continued right on. "And I took him out with me to a restaurant and a couple of movies and bowlin' and pretty soon we were fast friends.

"But in a couple of days my leave was up and I hadda go. When I told him, he said he wanted to come with me. But I told him I couldn't take him. I told him I was being sent far away, and when I told him that he cried. I told him I'd write him regular, and that now that I knew where he was, I'd come back and see him whenever I could. He didn't believe me, though. His face just screwed up again and he looked at me skeptical."

The sun was now directly overhead burning brilliantly down upon us. Graycloud paused for a moment to watch the gulls wheeling over the blue-green water.

"I kept my word, though," he continued. "I sent him money whenever I could and come up to see him every chance I got. He stayed on the reservation till he was about sixteen. Then he went into Cody to some trade school there. Wanted to learn to become a mechanic. Said he wanted a skill, a trade, 'cause he didn't wanna live like no Goddamn Indian. He got through that school pretty good, though. Then he was on his own.

"We kept in touch alright, and from time to time I'd get cards from him all over the States. That's how I heard he was livin' with you. And I was glad for him. Grateful. 'Cause he never had no home like that."

Graycloud appeared to be finished. Now he looked once again at me, considering me, not at all sure if he approved or disapproved.

"How did you find us?" I asked.

"Your wife wrote and told me what happened."

I looked at Alice still standing behind Graycloud. She was staring at me, her eyes rimmed with red.

"When it happened," she said, "they asked me if there was a next-of-kin to notify. I recalled some talk about a father and a picture in Richard's wallet. They found the wallet on the body and the picture with an address on the back of it." She looked at me apologetically. "I'm sorry, dear. I didn't tell you because you weren't in any condition to hear."

I asked him if he was bitter about the manner in which Richard died. "No," he said almost coldly. "If it hadn't been up there, it would've been someplace else. He was a queer kind of kid, and folks don't tolerate too much queerness."

It seemed scarcely to grieve him. Or if it did, he had his own special way of grieving, which I imagine was something he'd do in a very private, solitary sort of way.

Then I asked him if he had any bitterness toward me. His eyebrow rose and cocked high. "Should I?"

Suddenly I felt a need to tell everything. To unburden myself. "When things got very bad—"

"Albert!" Alice started toward me, but I waved her back.

"When things got very bad," I started again, "we got very frightened and I asked him to leave. I ordered him out—"

"He killed someone," said Graycloud. His voice was like stone.

"He killed someone defending us, and I abandoned him," I said.

"I don't blame you," said Graycloud. He was watching the gulls again. "What you did, you hadda do."

"I could have had the decency to die with him."

Graycloud's eyes narrowed exactly the way I'd seen Richard's do so many times.

"That's what an Indian would've done," he said. "White men are something else." There was no accusation in it. He had simply stated a matter of fact as he saw it.

Graycloud stayed a while longer. He drank a glass of lemonade and when we tried to persuade him to remain with us for supper, he said he couldn't. He said there was someone waiting for him at a nearby motel. I got the feeling that it was a woman.

And that was the last we saw of Graycloud. But since that time, each Christmas we get a card from him. It's written in a large rather clumsy handwriting, and its message is usually the same thing. It wishes us a merry Christmas in the season of the Prince of Peace.

That's all a long time ago. But Alice and I, though we never mention him, still think of Richard Atlee. The reason I know this is because several years after Graycloud's visit, I woke up late one night and found Alice sitting up in bed crying. When I asked her why she was crying, she told me she was crying for Richard Atlee. She'd had a dream about him. She said he'd been in her mind almost constantly. I told her that that had also been the case with me, and then I told her, for the first time, about that strangely lifelike dream I had in the hospital and that because of that dream in which I'd been rebuffed and turned away by him, I had no hope of ever again feeling the quiet ease of a soul at peace with itself.

What is one supposed to do for one's fellow men? What is one supposed to be? I confess I know no more now than I did before.

We bought the place on the beach and have now settled in there more or less permanently. I don't think we will ever move again. It's curious to think of buying a house in which you know you will someday undoubtedly die. To have come at last to your final address in life, far from being disturbing, is a curiously comforting thought.

One day, a stray cat wandered into our yard and decided to stay. For three days he crouched under a tree at a distance of twenty-five feet or so, just watching us come and go about our business. Then one day he accepted food and entered our house.

Since that time he's become a great comfort to me. At night I lie in bed with Alice sleeping at my side and feel the cat, in bed, too, warm and heavy against my leg. Outside the wind whines over the sand gnashing its teeth against the branches of the plum tree just beside the window. If you listen, you can hear the low, ceaseless rolling of the ocean tumbling gently down on the shore.

These I count the best hours. It's oddly comforting to feel the cat warm and heavy against my leg and Alice, far, far away, sleeping deeply at my side. Sometimes I can feel the cat's heartbeat through the mattress, or feel him purring in his dreams. It's a peaceful sound, and from it I gather that he takes as much comfort from the warmth and nearness of my body as I take from his. On those long, sleepless nights it's nice to know as you lie there waiting for dawn that you're not the last living creature on earth; that you're united with the other sleepers and dreamers and those who are simply waiting.

I think that is really all there is here—just a handful of creatures huddling together on a wild plain in the chill, dark hours before the morning, taking succor from one another while waiting for a dawn that scarcely even promises to come.